Praise for the R[...] [...]

'Lin Anderson is one of Scotland's national treasures . . . her writing is unique, bringing warmth and depth to even the seediest parts of Glasgow. Rhona MacLeod is a complex and compelling heroine who just gets better with every outing'
Stuart MacBride

'From Glasgow's real underbelly, Lin Anderson will have you biting your nails and wondering why you ever bought a telly. Inventive, compelling, genuinely scary and beautifully written, as always'
Denzil Meyrick

'Hugely imaginative and exciting'
James Grieve (Emeritus Professor of Forensic Pathology)

'Vivid and atmospheric . . . enthralling'
Guardian

'Shades of *The Wicker Man*, with a touch of Agatha Christie. Superb'
Daily Mail

'The bleak landscape is beautifully described, giving this popular series a new lease of life'
Sunday Times

'Greenock-born Anderson's work is sharper than a pathologist's scalpel. One of the best Scottish crime series since Rebus'
Daily Record

'Guaranteed to grip the reader's imagination. Lin Anderson writes at a cracking pace . . . Very readable. Every last word'
Sunday Herald

The Special Dead

Lin Anderson is a Scottish author and screenwriter known for her bestselling crime series featuring forensic scientist Dr Rhona MacLeod. Four of her novels have been longlisted for the Scottish Crime Book of the Year, with *Follow the Dead* being a 2018 finalist. Her short film *River Child* won both a Scottish BAFTA for Best Fiction and the Celtic Film Festival's Best Drama award and has now been viewed more than one million times on YouTube. Lin is also the co-founder of the international crime writing festival Bloody Scotland, which takes place annually in Stirling.

The Special Dead

LIN ANDERSON

PAN BOOKS

First published 2015 by Macmillan

This edition published 2019 by Pan Books
an imprint of Pan Macmillan
20 New Wharf Road, London N1 9RR
Associated companies throughout the world
www.panmacmillan.com

ISBN 978-1-5290-0068-9

3 5 7 9 8 6 4 2

A CIP catalogue record for this book is available from the British Library.

Typeset by Palimpsest Book Production Limited, Falkirk, Stirlingshire
Printed and bound by CPI Group (UK) Ltd, Croydon, CR0 4YY

For Detective Inspector Bill Mitchell

If you are reading this then I am dead.

To know a person's name is to conjure with it.

1

The green eyes were regarding him candidly. Mark suspected she was weighing him up and wasn't sure she liked what she saw. Jeff, on the other hand, was having an easier time with the girl's friend. *Trust Jeff to strike it lucky, the bastard.*

Mark took another slug of his pint. If the girls came as a pair, then the fact that green eyes didn't fancy him might mean Jeff got the brush-off too, which would bring Mark no end of grief. As though reading his mind, Jeff threw him a look that urged him to try harder.

When Jeff had suggested he come through to Glasgow for a Friday night on the town together, Mark had jumped at the chance. True, he'd had to cover his tracks a bit with Emilie and make out he was playing five-a-side football with Jeff and his mates. She'd been a bit suspicious about that, until Mark had suggested she could come with him and watch if she liked. That had done the trick. Plus he'd promised to be back to take her out for lunch in Edinburgh on Saturday. A promise he meant to keep.

They'd been in four pubs before this one and Mark had lost count of the variety of drinks he'd consumed. None of the previous pubs had produced the possibilities of this one and he owed it to Jeff to play it out. Mark marshalled himself for one more go, but he didn't get the chance.

'So,' she said suddenly. 'Want to come back to my place?'

To say he nearly fell off the chair was putting it mildly. He shut his mouth, realizing it had dropped open, and tried to look nonchalant.

'Sure thing.'

She immediately stood up. Mark expected the pal to get up too, but she didn't. The two girls exchanged some unspoken message and the pal laughed. Jeff, equally surprised by the way things were going, looked askance and not a little jealously at Mark, who grinned in triumph, then followed green eyes to the door.

Outside, he offered to wave down a taxi.

'No need. It's just round the corner.'

Mark felt himself stir in anticipation. It looked as though Jeff wasn't the lucky one after all.

She ushered him inside and shut the door firmly behind him. A black cat appeared from nowhere to rub itself against her ankle. When she lifted it, the purring grew louder. The cat fastened its eyes on Mark and he was struck by their similarity to the girl's eyes. Through the alcoholic haze, sharpened by the coke he'd snorted in the last pub toilet, the scene took on a bright hallucinatory hue.

The long hallway was dimly lit and painted blood red. He identified a series of doors that shifted and merged until he closed one eye.

'In here,' she said, throwing open a door on his right. She gave him a slight push and he stumbled inside what was definitely a bedroom. The cat, discarded from her arms, mewed in annoyance and darted off, tail stiffly upright.

'Take off your clothes,' she ordered. 'And lie down on the bed.'

Mark had experienced a variety of sexual encounters

under the influence of alcohol and coke before, but he'd never been bossed about. He found he rather liked the experience.

'Are you for real?' he grinned.

'Just do it.'

Her expression suggested if he didn't do what was asked, he would be out the door. Something he definitely didn't want.

Mark pulled off his shirt, then his jeans and stood in his boxers.

'What's your name?' he said, suddenly feeling he should know what to call the girl he was about to have sex with.

'You're not here to ask questions.' She ran the green eyes over him from top to toe. 'Now the boxers.'

In a show of bravado, Mark exposed himself.

She studied him intently, then licked her lips. The result of which was a shot of an aphrodisiac he didn't require.

'Okay. Now lie down.'

Relieved that he had passed muster, Mark did as ordered.

The few clothes she wore were removed in seconds, then she stood before him in all her glory. Mark drank in the smooth white skin, the pink pointed nipples, the neat brush of auburn hair highlighted between the long smooth legs.

Who was the lucky one now?

When the cat suddenly jumped on the bed to spoil his view, Mark tried to sweep it aside.

'Leave it,' she said sharply.

Before he could protest, the cat had settled on his face, its silky warm body acting like a suffocating blindfold. The purring rose to a crescendo as its open claws kneaded his shoulder. Mark's surprised cry was smothered in hot fur.

He could no longer see the girl, but he felt her climb

aboard and firmly straddle him. As she lowered herself, pain and pleasure met and exploded in his head.

His stomach heaved, bringing him back to consciousness. Mark rolled onto his side and vomited a pool of warm stale beer on the carpet.

Where the hell was he?

He shivered suddenly in his nakedness. Flashes of memory began bombarding his brain. The girl staring down at him. The smothering action of the cat. The crazy coupling. He turned to check the other side of the bed but there was no one there. The luminous dial on his watch told him it was five o'clock in the morning.

Sitting up, he swung his feet out of bed, trying to avoid the wet patch caused by his vomit, but not entirely succeeding. He contemplated his next move, which should be to get dressed and leave as quickly as possible. Rising a little shakily, he located the pile that was his clothes. As he dressed, a pair of green eyes appeared suddenly in the semi-darkness.

He recalled the cat settling on his face and the girl ordering him to leave it there. The memory brought a rush of pleasure. For a moment he was back there, wanting more of the same, then the whiff of his vomit reminded him it was wiser to leave. Now.

Dressed, he checked the corridor, found it empty and stepped out of the room to be presented with four doors leading off the hall, all of them closed. Mark stood for a moment, trying to recall last night and which door might be the exit point. Finally accepting that he had no idea, he chose one and attempted to open it as quietly as possible.

Immediately the cat tried to squeeze past his ankles,

mewing loudly. Mark swore under his breath, attempted to stop it with his foot and tripped over it instead. The cat sprang into the room, tail bristling, with Mark stumbling headlong into the darkness in its wake.

He eventually righted himself and stood very still, praying the room, whatever its purpose, was unoccupied. Moments later, he decided it was, although something had definitely spooked the cat. Its mewing had changed into a high-pitched keening sound that reverberated through his brain and would eventually rouse anyone else who might be in the flat.

Which meant he should get out of here, and quickly.

Mark swung round, desperate now to make his exit, and immediately walked into a small hanging object. As spooked as the keening cat, he tried to sweep it aside only to have it swing back at him, and poke him in the eye.

Swearing under his breath, he caught the offending item in his hand.

In the faint light from the hall, he now saw it was a doll.

Naked, long-legged, with pert breasts and flowing silver blonde hair, it hung from the ceiling via a length of cord wound tightly round its neck.

Jesus. Last night had been weird, but this was even weirder.

Mark released the doll in distaste and it swung away from him, only to immediately collide with something else, setting off a series of eerie clicks and clacks accompanied by the creak of moving objects.

What the hell was that?

Mark stood stock-still, knowing he shouldn't turn, but aware he would anyway.

When he did, he found that the doll wasn't alone.

There were at least twenty of them, swinging in the light

filtering through from the hall. Blondes, brunettes, redheads, naked, eyes glinting. All were suspended from the ceiling by a string tied round their necks, all set in perpetual motion by his action.

The swaying scene was grotesque, but not as terrible as what Mark now discerned beyond the hanging dolls, and the true reason for the cat's distress.

2

Rhona stared up at the ceiling. Beside her, the soft sounds of Sean's breathing only emphasized how awake she was herself.

This is one of the reasons I prefer sleeping alone.

She threw back the covers, knowing leaving the bed wouldn't wake Sean from his slumbers. Grabbing a dressing gown against the night air, she went through to the kitchen. The wall clock said 3.25 a.m., which meant she'd had about three hours sleep. Not enough to face a day's work, but judging by her busy brain, she was unlikely to get any more.

She spooned some coffee into the filter and filled the water reservoir. If she was determined to be awake, there was no point in avoiding caffeine. She took up her favourite stance at the window as the coffee machine hummed into action. Three storeys down, and bathed in a soft spotlight, the statue of the Virgin Mary stood resolute against the surrounding darkness. Soon the lights of its neighbouring convent would spring on, heralding the nuns' early start to the day.

In that respect, at least, I would make a good nun, Rhona mused as she poured herself a mug of coffee. She carried the coffee through the hall to the living room, pausing for a moment to glance in at the sleeping Sean. He had moved onto his back, losing the duvet in the process. Naked, his body seemed to gleam like marble in the moonlight that shone in through the open curtains.

If she chose to go back in there now and stroke him into wakefulness, they would carry on where they'd left off. Rhona contemplated the prospect, albeit briefly, before entering the sitting room and closing the door behind her.

Settling herself at the desk, she opened her laptop and logged on. As though on cue, Tom arrived to take up his place on her lap. She was never sure if the cat sought company or her warmth, or simply liked the comforting electronic hum to accompany his own soft purring.

Beyond the window, dawn was beginning to break over the great sleeping mammoth that was Glasgow. Unlike New York or London, Glasgow did at least appear to slumber, usually between three and five in the morning. Or it seemed that way from her vantage point, high above the green expanse of Kelvingrove Park.

Dispensing with this thought, Rhona turned her attention to the screen.

The case she was in the process of writing up hadn't proved forensically challenging. A middle-aged man had visited a gay bar where he'd picked up a teenage foreign national and taken him home, only to be stabbed to death.

The perpetrator had dumped the knife in a nearby bin along with his backpack. Later, apprehended by the police, he'd confessed to the killing, stating that his victim had launched an attack on him during sex, and that he had retaliated.

As far as Rhona was concerned, the crime-scene forensics matched the perpetrator's story. Deposits of both men's semen and blood had been identified at the scene. The victim's fingerprints had been retrieved from the perpetrator's neck, suggesting he'd been throttled, perhaps during the sex act.

The knife cuts on the perpetrator's scrotum had definitely been inflicted by a left-handed person, i.e. the victim. Furthermore, the stab wounds in the victim's chest had been made by the same knife, wielded by a right-handed person, which the perpetrator was. The toxicology report suggested both men had been high on crystal meth at the time. The sexual game, perhaps begun by mutual consent, had ended in death.

Tragic, horrifying and almost inevitable, if the sad saga of abuse that had been the perpetrator's life was true. It seemed that the victim had been seen by the young man who'd killed him as just one more abuser, against whom he had finally retaliated.

One life lost, another ruined, the path that had led to murder seemingly unavoidable. The darkest corner of her mind believed that, yet the 'if only' aspect still prevailed. What if the victim had treated the young man differently? What if he hadn't tried to control him? Abuse and threaten him? What if they had shown respect for one another?

Both might be alive, and no one a murderer.

But that 'what if' was of no use now. The deed was done, recorded forensically to be shown in court.

Two hours later, her report complete, Rhona shut the laptop, just as a still-naked Sean appeared in the doorway.

'Was I snoring?' He looked apologetic.

'No, I had a report to write.'

'And you've finished?'

'Yes.'

'I'll make us some breakfast.'

9

'No, thanks. I've had coffee already.'

He regarded her with a smile. 'So you still don't eat breakfast?'

Rhona gave him a pointed look in return. 'And you still make coffee looking like that?'

Sean glanced down, as though only just registering his nudity. 'I'll go and get dressed.'

Rhona rose, picking up her laptop. 'Don't bother. I'm on my way out, anyway.'

Sean looked a little nonplussed by that. 'Will you be at the jazz club later?'

'Not sure,' Rhona said, determinedly non-committal.

A small smile played at the corner of Sean's mouth. 'Fine,' he said and was gone.

Rhona heard the tap running, then the spurting sound of the coffee machine, accompanied by Sean's distinctive whistling of a well-known Irish tune.

He hasn't changed and neither have I. If it didn't work the first time, why should it work now?

She and Sean Maguire had history. Lots of it. The Irish musician had walked into her life at the fiftieth birthday party of DI Bill Wilson, her friend and mentor, held in the jazz club which Sean part-owned. Sean's dark hair and blue eyes, coupled with his Irish charm and musical skill on the saxophone, had been difficult to resist. In fact, Rhona hadn't really tried. Sean had approached her with a bottle of wine when he came off stage and asked if he might be allowed to join her. She'd said yes. When he'd walked her home, Rhona had asked him up without hesitation.

Last night I did the exact same thing. Talk about history repeating itself.

As Rhona set about packing up her laptop, her mobile

rang. A glance at the screen indicated it was not a caller she particularly wanted to speak to. Nevertheless . . .

'DS McNab?' she said.

'Dr MacLeod. Top of the morning to you.'

The jibe, aimed no doubt at the reappearance of her Irish lover, only served to irritate Rhona, which is what McNab intended.

'What do you want?' Rhona said, keeping her voice even.

'I'd like you to take a look at a suspicious death.'

'Why me?'

'DI Wilson suggested it should be you.'

Rhona bit off a further retort. If Bill wanted her there, then she would go. Of course McNab knew that, which is why he said it. Whether it was true or not was another matter.

'I'll send a car for you,' he said before she could ask for further details.

'Tell them to buzz when they get here.'

Rhona rang off before McNab could indulge in any more comments on her love life.

She quickly showered, then dressed in the bathroom, keen to avoid encountering Sean again, naked or otherwise. Maybe he had the same plan, because he didn't reappear, although she heard the notes of his saxophone from the spare room.

The familiarity of that sound in the flat disturbed her, but she reminded herself that the instrument was only there because they'd come straight from Sean's gig at the jazz club the previous night. Its presence in no way signified that Sean had become a permanent fixture.

She contemplated asking when he was leaving, but the buzzer sounded before she could bring herself to, so she made a swift exit with a shout of goodbye. Hopefully when she returned, Sean would no longer be there. Rhona was pretty sure he had got that message, although Sean had a habit of interpreting her responses in a way more suited to himself.

Now, outside the main door, Rhona realized the car McNab had 'sent' was in fact his own. It was a neat trick. He was well aware that had he indicated he would be the driver, she would have definitely declined. As it was, she now had little choice.

Rhona slid into the passenger seat without comment.

'Chrissy's on her way,' McNab offered by way of an olive branch.

'Good.'

He headed for town.

Travelling with McNab was never uneventful. He always drove as though he had a blue light flashing even when he didn't. The one-way system didn't serve as any deterrent. Glasgow city centre was as busy on a Saturday as during the weekday rush hour, which made the experience even more hair-raising than usual. Rhona was aware he was trying to provoke her into remonstrating with him, so she chose not to. In a show of determination, she didn't even grip the seat.

He finally took a sharp right into a back lane, just off Hope Street, where a police van was already parked.

'Okay?' he said.

'Never better.'

Short looks and few words were all they exchanged these days. The secret that they both shared lay uneasily between them. McNab had offered her the chance to 'spill the beans' to Detective Inspector Bill Wilson. Rhona hadn't as yet, knowing that it might end McNab's already shaky career. She'd told herself that was the reason, but was unsure if it was, and the longer she kept quiet, the more difficult it had become.

McNab gestured to an open door. 'First floor.'

Rhona got out and began kitting up. The lack of conversation in the car meant she had no idea what she was about to walk in on, which could be an advantage. Forensically, the first image of a crime scene was a powerful and informative one. From her experience, the questions that immediately sprang to mind were often the most important ones. There was, of course, a routine to be followed, a structure to every investigation, to ensure nothing was forgotten in the emotional impact of the moment, but first impressions mattered. A lot.

The steps of the stairwell were well worn, the walls patterned with glazed green tiles. When she reached the first landing, she found the single door there standing open, an officer on duty.

Recognizing her, he stood aside to allow Rhona entry.

She tucked her hair under the hood and pulled up her mask, then stepped over the threshold onto one of the metal treads already laid out on the floor to avoid contamination, indicating that McNab was treating this suspicious death seriously.

The hall was painted red and poorly lit. There were four inner doors, three of which stood open. A swift look established that one led to a bedroom, another a kitchen, and the third a toilet and shower room. A crime-scene photographer was already busy in the bedroom. When he spotted her, he indicated the closed door was the one she sought. Rhona nodded her thanks and approached it. Then she heard a terrible sound, which made the hairs on the back of her neck stand up. High pitched, almost a scream, she recognized it as a cat in distress.

'It's in there with the body,' the photographer told her. 'We haven't been able to catch it yet. They've contacted the SSPCA.'

As Rhona cautiously opened the door, the suffocating scent of death escaped, her mask barely weakening it. She stepped inside and quickly shut the door.

The image that presented itself in the blazing light from two arc lamps shocked even her. Rhona had prepared herself for a body, and a mourning cat, but not for the curtain of naked Barbie-type dolls that hung from the ceiling.

The draught generated by her entry had set them in motion, the noise of their hard plastic limbs clicking off one another as disquieting as the sight of them. What was even more disturbing was what she glimpsed beyond the curtain of dolls.

The young woman was naked, her body suspended from a large hook in the back wall via a red cord wound round her neck. Her green eyes were wide open and staring, the tongue protruding between swollen lips. At her feet stood a large black cat, hair bristling, tail upright, the tip swishing back and forth in a warning.

Rhona met its green glare and knew that it meant business, and with the cat there, she had no chance of examining its owner. She didn't even attempt the *Here kitty* routine. Her best chance, she decided, was to let it come at her, which it surely would, then do her best to catch it.

As she got closer to the body, the cat arched its back and hissed. Rhona braced herself, conscious that the flying claws might pierce her forensic suit. But it had given her too much warning and she was ready for it. With a practised hand she grabbed it by the scruff of the neck and held it away from her body, the paws and tail thrashing thin air.

Rhona made for the bathroom. The shower cubicle seemed the ideal place to corral it. She dropped it in and swiftly shut the door. The cat, further infuriated by its enclosure, clawed and spat at her through the glass.

Retreating, Rhona shut the door behind her, before warning the photographer of the menacing presence in the bathroom.

'I've never seen a cat so mad before,' he said.

'Neither have I,' Rhona agreed. 'Let me know when the SSPCA arrive.'

Free of the enraged feline, Rhona re-entered the room and was struck again by the image of the dolls and the body.

Hanging was a fairly common method of suicide. Accidental hangings were less common, and homicidal hangings rare. True, murderers sometimes tried to cover strangulation by stringing up their victim afterwards, not realizing that the signs of each method of death were easily distinguished.

Most suicides, if determined to succeed, stepped off a raised object, such as a chair or a ladder. No such object existed in the room. In fact, the room was bare apart from the victim and the spooky dolls.

The body hung four inches above the floor. On closer inspection, the cord proved to be a knotted plait of a red silky material. Looped round what resembled a large meat hook, it was finally tied together at the right-hand side of the neck to fashion the noose.

The body appeared unmarked apart from two tattoos, consisting of a small Celtic cross in the middle of the forehead and a pentagram about two inches in diameter in the region of the heart. The hair was dark auburn, cut short, the body slight, the breasts small. There were no piercings apart from the earlobes, where the small silver earrings were the same design as the forehead tattoo.

The face was very pale; the green eyes had dilated pupils, their whites marbled red by tiny burst blood vessels. The protruding tongue was cyanosed – coloured blue by deoxygenated blood. All features of hanging.

In cases of suicide, the ligature mark generally followed the line of the lower jaw, before going upwards behind the ear, depending on whether a fixed or running noose was used.

The mark from the plaited cord was incomplete and above that normally seen in strangulation by ligature. The forearms, hands, legs below the knees, and feet showed evidence of lividity, which suggested the body had been suspended for at least three to four hours after death.

It had all the hallmarks of a suicide, but the question remained. How had the victim got herself onto the hook?

The door opened and Rhona turned to find Chrissy, her forensic assistant, eyes wide above her mask as she registered the dolls.

'I used to have one of those,' she said. 'Two if you count Ken.'

Chrissy began zigzagging her way through the curtain of dolls, sending them into a paroxysm of stilted movements, their outstretched arms and legs glancing off one another like maracas. Finally she emerged to confront Rhona and the body on the back wall.

Chrissy ran a practised eye over the victim.

'If it had been a man I would have taken a guess at

auto-erotic strangulation, especially with the field of naked female dolls on view.'

A thought already contemplated by Rhona.

'So what do you think?' Chrissy said.

'I think it's a suspicious death.' That's all Rhona would commit herself to.

Chrissy looked about, obviously checking for the missing step.

'There wasn't one,' Rhona said.

'So she managed to hang herself without her feet touching the ground? *Very* suspicious, I would say.' Chrissy wasn't one to mince her words.

Rhona set Chrissy to work on the surrounding area while she concentrated on the body.

A little over an hour later, Chrissy had completed her forensic search of the room and Rhona had almost completed her sampling of the front portion of the body. A presumptive test for semen had indicated the likelihood that the victim had had sex prior to her death. Rhona had swabbed all orifices and taped the skin, locating two white fibres from the roof of the mouth.

The fingernails had also proved fruitful. This time the fibres were fine and red and may have come from the ligature, something she would check in the laboratory under the microscope. A presumptive test for blood under the nails had proved negative, so it didn't look as though she had fended off an attacker. Neither did Rhona find evidence of obvious bruising anywhere on the body.

Although women were less likely than men to indulge in erotic asphyxiation, there was an outside chance this could be the reason for the hanging. If so, the victim would have needed help to suspend herself and someone on hand to rescue her after climax had been achieved.

If that had been the case, the sexual partner may have panicked and left when things went wrong, thinking it better to make it look like suicide than be blamed for her death.

Rhona set about recording the scene for herself. She wouldn't remove the cord prior to the post-mortem, for fear of damaging evidence. Only when it was taken off could they be sure that there were no other marks on the neck indicating injury before the hanging.

By now the heat and the smell in the room were becoming overpowering, and Rhona could feel the trickle of perspiration constantly running down her body inside the suit. Thinking about a shower reminded her of the cat and she wondered if it had been removed by the SSPCA yet. She hoped not.

Emerging into the hall, she was rewarded by a cool draught from the open front door and the sight of an SSPCA officer heading into the bathroom. Rhona followed him.

The cat stood in the cubicle, hair bristling, defying anyone to approach.

'Sorry, we're a bit overstretched,' he said, explaining the time lapse since they'd been contacted. He eyed the cat's angry glare. 'Well done in isolating it.'

'It was standing guard over its mistress's body.'

'Unusual for a cat.'

'Are you going to sedate it?'

'It might be necessary. It's pretty distressed.'

Rhona explained her thoughts on how the animal might provide evidence, if she could take some samples.

'Okay, give me five minutes and ignore any screams from me or the cat in the interim.'

Rhona moved into the hall and shut the door, silently wishing him good luck.

Laid out now on the bathroom mat, the cat bore little resemblance to the furious creature she'd first encountered. Rhona focused on the front claws, where a presumptive test indicated the presence of blood. Under a magnifying glass, she also located skin particles. She had managed to avoid its claws, but it seemed it had succeeded in attacking someone, and recently.

Once the cat was safely on its way, Rhona checked with the photographer, who told her the cat had been in the room when he'd arrived.

'Do you know who discovered the body?'

'DS McNab said it was the postman. He found the front door lying open, heard the squealing cat, knew something was wrong and called the police.'

'Did the postman or McNab enter the room?'

He didn't know for certain. 'You'll have to ask the DS.'

Rhona had only glimpsed the bedroom in passing. Now she studied it in all its glory. Painted a midnight blue, the drawn curtains were similar in colour, patterned by silver stars and crescent moons. The room was dotted with candles and night lights, particularly round a mirror shaped like a five-pointed star. To add to the reflective possibilities, the wall behind the bed was occupied by a large ornate mirror, as was the ceiling above it and the opposite wall. The room smelt of vomit and sex, barely masked by the scented wax of the candles.

'The bed's covered in cat hairs,' Chrissy informed her. 'There's evidence of blood in small quantities on the pillow and semen on the undersheet. And, of course, the watery vomit on the carpet next to the bed. Beer, I would say, but thankfully no diced carrots. Plenty of fingerprints. I retrieved a decent man-size bare footprint from the carpet, probably from inadvertently standing in the vomit.'

'So more than just the victim in the room recently?'

'I would say so.'

Rhona nodded, pleased at Chrissy's thoroughness.

The body, released from the hook, now lay on the floor, the crooked stiffness of its limbs mirroring those of the surrounding dolls.

As the photographer captured this on camera, Rhona checked the victim's back to find no obvious signs of cuts or bruising. She counted nine knots tied in the cord, including one at each end, probably to prevent fraying. The remaining seven were distributed evenly along its length. She would need to wait until the cord was cut free of the neck to study the noose knot in detail.

Whatever had taken place here, the red silk cord looked significant to the proceedings. If it was a suicide, then the victim had knotted the cord round her own neck. Easy enough to do that, then step off a ladder or a chair, but . . .

'You nearly done?' McNab's voice came from the doorway. He was kitted up to match Rhona, only the blue eyes showing above the mask. 'The mortuary van's here.'

Rhona nodded. 'I've left the rope in place until the PM.'

'So you don't think it's a straightforward suicide?'

'Do you?'

McNab looked up at the hook. 'How the hell did she get herself up there? That's what I'd like to know.'

'Me too.' They could agree on this at least.

'Fancy a coffee when you've finished? I'd like to discuss

this further,' he added, as though to make things perfectly clear.

Rhona still brushed him off. 'Let's wait for the post-mortem, then we might have something to discuss.'

McNab's eyes flashed back at her. He looked as though he might argue, then wisely chose not to.

'I'll leave you to it,' he said curtly, then turned on his heel.

Rhona heard further murmured words and laughter and realized he'd moved on to Chrissy. Her forensic assistant held McNab in high regard and had reason to. He had saved her unborn son by taking a bullet in his own back. McNab was a hero in Chrissy's eyes.

The memory of that night and McNab's near-death experience didn't make Rhona any more comfortable with the situation that currently lay between them.

Damn blast the man, for putting her in this position.

Taking down the dolls for transport to the laboratory was more time-consuming than moving the body. There were twenty-seven of them and, on closer inspection, they proved to have patterns drawn on them similar to the victim's tattoos. Each one was attached to the roof with a large tack, via a length of standard household string wound round the doll's neck.

They had worked out a method of getting them down which consisted of Rhona standing on a chair taken from the kitchen and Chrissy bagging each doll as she took possession of it.

'My brothers used to pinch my Barbie and torture it,' Chrissy informed Rhona as they worked.

This latest revelation about the male members of Chrissy's

family came as no surprise to Rhona. Chrissy had three brothers, only one of whom, Patrick, Chrissy had any time for. The other two were carbon copies of her father. Mean, spiteful, drunken, brutish pigs.

'It used to reappear with a leg missing or an eye put out,' she elaborated. 'But I always got my own back.'

Rhona had to ask how.

'Various ways. Mostly involving their prize possessions.'

'Which were?'

'Their pricks, of course.' Chrissy grinned up at her. 'Remember itching powder?'

She took a flame-haired doll from Rhona and slipped it into an evidence bag. 'I always wondered why it was okay to give the female doll tits, but the male equivalent, Ken, had no dick.'

Rhona decided there was no answer to that.

Once the room was bare of body and dolls, Rhona settled down to write up her notes while everything was fresh in her mind. Now that the smell of death had been removed, other scents resurfaced, the predominant one being damp.

There was only one window in the room. Grimy with the dirt of the inner city, it looked out over the back lane in which she'd been deposited abruptly by McNab some hours before. Looking out, she suddenly registered exactly where she was. The block directly in front of her was the north side of the Lion Chambers, an art nouveau building, eight storeys tall, listed, but in critical need of repair. Originally designed and built as artists' studios, it was an early example of reinforced concrete construction, waiting, she suspected, to be knocked down. Yet its countenance was still regal, even though the lion carvings were encased in wire netting.

Looking down into the lane, she noted that there was only one car there now, Chrissy having hitched a ride back to the lab with the dolls via the forensic van. The car, she suspected, was McNab's. She pictured him sitting there, waiting for her to emerge, with an offer of a lift back, either to the lab or home.

Rhona exited the flat and the officer on duty closed the door behind her. She stepped out of the forensic suit, conscious of the stink of perspiration, chemicals and death about her person. Catching the tube or a taxi smelling like this was out of the question. She would accept a lift from McNab, regardless.

He was sitting in the driver's seat, deep in thought. Rhona stood for a moment in the doorway, watching him, before he sensed her presence and turned. For a moment he smiled, that dazzling smile that had melted a few hearts before her own. Then the dark clouds were back.

Settled into the passenger seat, Rhona responded to his questioning look.

'Home,' she said quietly, then added, 'please.'

The *please* slackened McNab's taut jawline. He visibly relaxed and the return journey was considerably less fraught. He even slowed on approaching traffic lights as though hoping they would change before he got there. Still they didn't speak until Rhona finally asked if he or the postman had fought off the cat.

'The postman claims he didn't go into the flat. The open door and the noise from the cat was enough to make him call us. He said the girl, Leila Hardy, treated the cat like a person.

'I took a look in the room,' he went on. 'It was obvious

23

she was dead, so I backed out to avoid the cat. No point contaminating the locus. Then I called you.'

'You said you spoke to Bill first,' Rhona said accusingly.

'I knew you would agree if you thought the boss wanted it.'

When Rhona didn't respond to his honesty, he said, 'Why did you ask about the cat?'

'I retrieved blood and skin from under its claws.'

McNab waved his unmarked hands briefly in the air. 'Not guilty.'

The words *not guilty* escaped his mouth to hang between them like a bad smell.

McNab, sensing this, covered his dismay by suddenly upping speed, only to have to brake suddenly as a bus pulled out in front of them.

Rhona almost felt sorry for him in that moment.

Perhaps sensing this, McNab turned and said, 'So, when do we go to the boss and tell him what happened that night in the stone circle?'

It was the question Rhona didn't want to answer.

3

McNab watched the door swing shut behind Rhona. He'd broached the subject for the third time and still received no answer. She'd just observed him with those eyes, examining what churchgoers might call his soul. McNab thought of it more as his Mr Hyde, although he wasn't at all sure that his outer persona had ever reached the standards of Hyde's better half, Dr Jekyll.

They had to eventually talk this through. He knew that. She knew that. The unspoken secret just kept getting bigger.

One option would be for him to go to DI Wilson alone and confess. After all, it was his actions that had created the problem. But, he acknowledged, Rhona's inaction in not immediately revealing what had happened put her in the frame too. Which was, of course, his fault. He had gone against her wishes that terrible night barely two months ago in the stone circle. He'd let a killer die while she'd been trying to keep him alive. *Let him die or made him die?* Had he been Hyde that night or Dr Jekyll?

The circular nature of these thoughts frustrated him further and brought to mind a saying of his late mother.

When in doubt, do nothing.

It had been her way of encouraging him to think before he acted. Acting on the spur of the moment had proved his downfall on a number of occasions. She had been well aware of that and had often sought to persuade him to go more cautiously.

Well, he'd definitely been cautious on this occasion, and it had only made matters worse.

McNab turned the car round and headed back to the police station.

Shannon Jones was twenty-four years old, petite, blonde and very frightened. She'd arrived at the dead girl's flat late Saturday afternoon, worried by the fact that her friend wasn't answering her mobile. When she'd discovered the police presence, she'd had a nervous breakdown on the doorstep, which only got worse on hearing that her friend was dead.

McNab had asked DS Janice Clark to talk to her before he did. He couldn't order Janice to do anything, since he was no longer her superior officer. In fact, this was the first time he'd had to engage with Janice since his demotion.

When he was first a DS, she was a DC. When he was promoted to DI, she was promoted to DS. In that particular game of snakes and ladders, he'd found himself quickly sliding down the snake, and was now on the same level as his former right-hand woman.

It wasn't a comfortable place to be, but Janice, as always, strove to make it so. McNab hadn't encountered any animosity or glee at his demotion from that quarter, although there were others, particularly Superintendent Sutherland, who obviously relished it. He continually wore the *I told you so* expression. Sutherland didn't like officers who wouldn't play the game as dictated by him, even if they got results. The search for Stonewarrior had been a case in point. McNab going AWOL had got a result. Two results in fact. They had caught the perpetrator and McNab had lost his promotion.

McNab thought that a fair exchange. Sutherland regarded it as a personal triumph. Fortunately, their paths rarely crossed now that McNab was lower down the ranks again, which suited both of them very well.

Shannon brought the cup of coffee shakily to her lips. The movement reminded McNab of when he'd been drinking heavily and his hand had trembled just like that.

Not any more.

'Tell me about Leila,' he said gently.

They were seated in a side room which housed a coffee machine, a few easy chairs and a table. Used to give bad tidings, it wore the scent of absorbed despair.

'She was funny and clever.' Shannon wobbled a little on the past tense, a common reaction when the idea of someone being dead hadn't quite registered. 'She liked a laugh.'

'And you were out having a laugh last night?' McNab said.

'We went out for something to eat and a drink after work.'

'Where did Leila work?'

'With me, at Glasgow University library.'

'Tell me about last night.'

She cleared her throat as though about to make a speech. It sounded guilty but probably wasn't. She was blinking a lot, but contrary to popular opinion that didn't mean she was about to lie, just that she was stressed. Then again, people get stressed when they're lying.

'We ate pizza in the Italian in Sauchiehall Street near the Buchanan Galleries, then went for a drink at The Pot Still in Hope Street.'

McNab knew the place, mainly because of its extensive

collection of malt whiskies. Many of which he'd enjoyed, probably too much. He nodded at her to continue.

'Two guys started chatting us up. At first Leila didn't look interested, but I knew she was playing him along, making him worry. Then she suddenly stood up, gave me a knowing look and off they went together back to her place.' She halted, fear crossing her face. 'He looked okay. He'd had a drink, but he wasn't really drunk.' She rushed on. 'If I'd thought he would hurt Leila . . .'

McNab interrupted her. 'We don't know that he did.'

Shannon looked from McNab to Janice and back again.

'I don't understand. You said Leila was dead. How did she die if he didn't kill her?'

'She was found hanged.'

The shock of his words hit her face like a punch, draining it of blood. 'Hanged?' she repeated in disbelief.

'We have yet to establish whether it was suicide.'

'No way.' She shook her head vehemently. 'Leila would *never* commit suicide.'

If McNab had a tenner for every time he'd heard the friends and family of suicide victims say exactly that . . . He waited a few moments before continuing. 'We won't know for certain until after the post-mortem.'

The girl wasn't really listening to him. 'Leila took him home for sex,' she said firmly. 'That's what she wanted last night. That's what she did. For fun. No strings attached. That's the way she liked it.'

McNab sat back in the chair and contemplated the young woman before him. He believed her when she said that's what Leila did, but he wasn't sure that was the whole story.

'And what about you? Was that your intention too?'

Blood flooded back into her face, reddening her cheeks in embarrassment. 'Maybe, but it didn't work out like that.'

'Why?'

'After they left, the other guy went to the toilet and never came back.'

McNab looked at the girl before him, pretty and probably willing with a little wooing, and wondered why her suitor had given up so easily.

'Why do you think your one bailed?'

It was a harsh question, indicated by Janice's frown, but you couldn't always be nice in this job.

Shannon said outright, 'I wondered that myself. We were getting on well, better than Leila and his mate. He looked really pissed off when they left.' She paused. 'I think they had a bet on who would score first. And when it wasn't him, he lost interest.'

'Do you remember their names?'

'It was noisy in the pub. I think mine said George.'

'And the other one?'

She shook her head. 'No idea.'

'And you didn't exchange numbers?'

'We hadn't got that far.'

'Is there any chance he followed Leila and his mate?'

She looked startled by the suggestion, then took a moment to think about it.

'Time-wise it's a possibility. But why would he do that?'

McNab could think of a number of reasons. None of them pleasant. If there had been two of them, getting the victim onto the hook would have been easy. His imagination working overtime, he did a rerun of the previous night's events. Leila taking guy number one back to her flat. Guy number two joining them there.

'She definitely didn't hang herself,' Shannon said again. 'Leila wasn't suicidal. She had . . . beliefs.'

McNab's ears pricked up. 'What sort of beliefs?'

Shannon shifted a little in her seat. 'New Age stuff. That life is precious. That we're one with the universe. That sort of thing.'

'What about bondage and sadomasochism?' McNab said.

'What?' Her eyes widened.

'Could Leila have hanged herself during sex?'

The face paled again. 'No way.'

'What about the room with the hanging dolls?'

There was a moment's silence while she digested his words and tried to make sense of them. 'I don't know what you're talking about.'

'There were nearly thirty Barbie-type dolls hanging from the roof in the room where we found her.'

Shannon was definitely freaked by that. 'No way. I never saw that room.'

McNab changed the subject. 'Have you given Detective Sergeant Clark a description of the two men?'

Shannon looked a bit worried by this. 'I did, but I was pissed to be honest, and it's a bit of a blur.'

'We need to contact Leila's family. Do you have a phone number or address?'

'She has a brother who lives in Glasgow. His name's Daniel. He's a musician. Plays in a band called the Spikes. They're on Facebook if you want to contact him. I don't have an address.' She looked grief-stricken at the thought of him being told about his sister.

McNab gave her a moment to collect herself, then thanked her and told her she could go.

'When will you know what happened to Leila?'

'In a couple of days,' he said, hoping it was true.

Janice was the one to show Shannon out, while McNab took advantage of the coffee machine. Strong coffee had replaced whisky as his stimulant of choice. The buzz wasn't as good, but then again there was no hangover. He chose a double espresso, drank it in one go, then pressed the button for another.

When Janice came back he asked if she wanted one. She asked for a latte and he did the honours. He realized he felt easier in Janice's company since his demotion. In fact, he felt better because they were now equals. He couldn't boss her and she couldn't boss him.

'Well,' he said. 'What do you think?'

'That she's telling the truth. They had a drink and met two guys. Leila took hers home. What happened next, I don't know. When's the post-mortem?'

'Scheduled for Monday morning, first thing. D'you want to come along?'

She nodded.

They sat in easy silence for a moment. McNab pondered this strange turn of events. That he and DS Clark should be comfortable in one another's company. He stole a sideways look at her as she sipped her latte. Her expression said she was also pondering something. There was a small crease in her forehead and a faraway look in her eyes. She wore no make-up. She wasn't pretty, but she was certainly arresting to look at. He thought of a younger Annie Lennox or Tilda Swinton.

When they'd first met he'd hit on her. She'd turned him down, which had irked at the time. So he'd put it about that she must be gay. DI Wilson had ordered him into his office and torn strips off him. McNab still flinched at the memory.

He'd retreated after that. Janice hadn't held a grudge. In fact, if it hadn't been for her support in the last case, he might have lost his life, rather than just his promotion. He contemplated whether he should offer to buy her a drink as a belated thanks, then remembered he was on the wagon.

'What's the plan, then?' Janice said.

'How do you feel about contacting the brother?'

It was by far the hardest of the jobs and she knew it.

'Okay,' she said.

'I'll speak to The Pot Still contingent.'

Janice raised an eyebrow, which suggested that word had got out about him being off the booze.

'We can swop if you like,' McNab offered.

'No need.'

What she was really saying was that she trusted him, although in view of the *Stonewarrior* case, she had little reason to.

McNab felt a surge of respect for Detective Sergeant Janice Clark. When Janice climbed the ladder to detective inspector, she wouldn't slide back down the snake, as he had done.

4

The delicious smell of cooking met Rhona as she approached her front door. Her plan had been to order in food, for despite being in the presence of death most of the day, she was starving. But the aroma suggested that Sean, rather than leave, had stayed to cook for her.

She paused before putting the key in the lock, trying to decide how to deal with this. If she appeared welcoming, that might suggest she was glad Sean had stayed on. If she was annoyed, that might give the impression she didn't want him there at all.

Neither way was how she felt.

On entry, the cat came bounding towards her. Tom was no longer the small furry ball Sean had bought after her first cat, Chance, had been killed, murdered by a psychopath as a warning to her. She'd been annoyed with Sean for making the decision about a new cat without consulting her, but had gradually warmed to Tom's presence. Yet the cat, appearing now, simply reminded her of the psychological games her former live-in lover was wont to play.

Rather than seeking Sean out, Rhona dropped her forensic bag, removed her jacket and headed straight for the shower. Fifteen minutes later, smelling a good deal better, she entered the kitchen to find it empty.

The table was set for one, with a note on the waiting plate.

Food in the slow cooker. Should be ready by six,
but won't spoil. White wine in the fridge. Enjoy. Sean x

The wrath Rhona had nursed under the heat of the shower dissipated and she felt foolish, and then a little annoyed.

Why? Because he'd done what she'd wanted and left?

Rhona retrieved the wine and poured herself a glass. The slow cooker, bought by Sean when they'd lived together and which she'd buried in a cupboard when she'd told him to leave, was back in pride of place on the work surface and emitting the delicious aroma she'd encountered on the stairs.

Rhona decided not to ponder Sean's motives or how she should interpret them, but rather just eat the food he'd prepared for her. The contents of the cooker turned out to be chicken casserole. That and the wine were definitely up to Sean's usual standards and, she had to admit, better than the meals she generally phoned out for.

Hunger assuaged, she took her wine through to the sitting room and settled on the couch with her laptop. There was a message from Chrissy to say she'd logged the samples taken from the flat, including the creepy dolls, then gone home. As Rhona read this, another email pinged in, this time from McNab.

Rhona regarded it for a moment. The title 'Monday morning' immediately made her think he'd decided to confess to Bill Wilson. She hesitated, then opened it, and found it was simply alerting her to the post-mortem on the possible suicide.

Her relief at this irritated her. She wasn't usually prone to indecision, but this case wasn't usual. If McNab would just lay off the subject, she would make up her own mind what to do. Even as she thought this, she was aware that this line of reasoning was just a way of blaming McNab for her indecision.

Well, he'd put her in this position.

To take her mind off McNab, she fired up the photographs from the crime scene. Scrolling through them, she decided the images of the dolls were almost as disturbing as those of the victim.

Now, observing the dolls en masse, Rhona realized they were arranged in three rows of nine, and that each row was divided into three, by hair colour, making nine blondes, nine brunettes and nine redheads in total. Since the cord used in the hanging was also knotted nine times, it did seem that the number nine was significant in some way or other to the victim.

She decided to do a little online numerology research.

When she entered 'the significance of nine' into the search box, Wikipedia popped up first. The detailed and substantial entry provided a great deal of information on the place of nine in mathematics, including the simple fact that when you multiply any number by nine, then add the resulting digits and reduce them to a single digit, it always becomes a nine. Intrigued by this, Rhona tried a few herself just to make sure. It seemed, said the entry, 'that from a numerological perspective, the 9 simply takes over, like the infamous body snatchers'.

There was also a mention of nine in Chinese lore and in Tolkien's *Lord of the Rings*, with the nine companions of the ring and the nine Ringwraiths, matching good and evil. She learned quite a bit from her study of the number nine, but none of it offered an insight into the pattern of nine in the hanging dolls or the use of nine knots in the plaited cord.

Of course, should the post-mortem conclusion be that it wasn't suicide, then the cord might have been the property of the perpetrator, rather than the victim. Which led Rhona to wonder if the presence of the dolls could also be the work of the perpetrator.

Her first thought when she heard the door buzzer was that it might be Sean returning, but she dismissed that as unlikely. At ten o'clock he would just be starting his set at the jazz club.

When she answered the intercom, there was a moment's silence as though her visitor might have rung the wrong flat. Rhona was about to put the receiver down when McNab finally spoke.

'Can I come up?'

'No.'

'Please? We need to talk.'

Rhona wanted to tell him to go away, but found herself unable to. Maybe he was right. Maybe they did need to clear the air.

Rhona released the door and let him in.

Michael Joseph McNab looked better than he had done for some time. Gone were the shadowed eyes. He'd shaved, and he definitely hadn't been drinking. When she'd offered him a whisky, he'd turned it down and asked for coffee instead.

'Make it strong,' he requested.

Rhona did as asked then poured herself another glass of wine.

McNab sniffed the air. 'Been cooking?'

'I don't cook. You know that.'

He smiled. 'Smells good whoever made it.'

Rhona sipped her wine in silence. McNab swallowed the coffee and held the cup out to be replenished.

Eventually he spoke. 'I'm in a better place now. Off the booze, for a start.' When Rhona didn't respond, he went on. 'That night at the stone circle, I'd had God knows how many drugs pumped into me. I was high and mad and when I saw that bastard on top of you, I . . .' He halted.

His words had conjured for Rhona a memory as vivid as when it had happened. Suddenly she could smell him again, feel his weight bearing down on her. She stood up and walked to the window and looked down on the tranquil scene below, trying to dispel that other image.

'I've written it all down,' McNab said. 'Everything I can remember. You can read it if you want, before I hand it to the boss.'

Rhona didn't turn from the window.

'We were both debriefed. Neither of us told the full truth then,' she said.

'I'm going to tell it now,' McNab said.

'If you do, then I'll be the liar. By omission.'

'Not the way I've told it.'

'Then it's not the truth,' Rhona said.

She turned and their eyes met and held for the first time since that fateful night in the dark, in the middle of the stone circle.

'I have to fix this,' he pleaded.

Rhona slowly shook her head. 'It's unfixable.'

McNab was trying to read her expression. 'You want to let it go?' he said, surprised.

In that moment, Rhona made her decision. 'Yes.'

A flurry of emotions crossed his face, relief and hope among them. Rhona felt a little of both herself. McNab had offered on numerous occasions to reveal the last moments of the serial killer they had come to know as Stonewarrior, yet she had refused to discuss it with him.

Now that she had made a decision, it was as though the weight of the killer's body had been lifted from her.

'Can we change the subject now?' she said.

'Gladly.'

'I've been studying the photographs from the suspicious death,' Rhona said.

'And?'

'Did you notice the presence of the number nine?'

'Not particularly,' he said cautiously. 'Unless you mean that twenty-seven dolls constitutes three times nine.'

Rhona beckoned him to follow her through to the sitting room and fired up the laptop again. She showed him the photographs she'd taken of the dolls. McNab's recoil at that image reflected her own.

'There are nine of each hair colour,' she said. 'Each row is made up of nine dolls, divided into threes.' Rhona pulled up an image of the red cord still encircling the victim's neck. 'You'll have to take my word for it until the PM, but there are nine evenly spaced knots in the ligature used to hang her.'

'So what's special about nine?'

'Lots of things.'

She brought up the Wikipedia page and watched as McNab's eyes glazed over.

'For fuck's sake. Don't make it maths or we'll have to bring in the nutty professor again,' he said, alluding to Professor

Magnus Pirie, criminal psychologist and McNab's very own bête noire.

Rhona ignored the dig at Magnus. 'I don't think it's anything to do with the maths properties, but it's significant in some way.'

'Her pal said Leila was a New Age believer, if that helps,' McNab offered.

'It might.'

Rhona tried a search on 'nine' and 'New Age'. What appeared was anything but enlightening, unless you believed that the Masonic Lodge was behind the Twin Towers attack and that both the Bible and the devil used the number nine in their scriptures.

Rhona closed the laptop.

'I didn't think you would give up so easily,' McNab said.

'I haven't.' She looked pointedly at her watch.

McNab took the hint. 'Okay. I'd better head for the pub, before it's closing time.'

'What?' Rhona said.

He smiled at her reaction. 'To talk to the barman on duty last night when Leila met her man.'

She didn't return the smile, irritated at him for setting her up, but then again, that was the real McNab. She walked him to the door.

Rhona didn't want him to bring up their earlier discussion and was keen for him to leave. Sensing this perhaps, he exited, but as she made to close the door behind him, he stopped her.

'We *are* okay, Dr MacLeod?' he said.

Rhona wasn't willing to go quite that far.

'Let's wait and see,' was all she could manage.

He appeared to accept this, because he nodded, then headed downstairs.

Rhona stood for a moment, listening to his echoing footsteps, hearing the main door slam shut behind him.

What the hell had she done? Whatever way you looked at it, she had bound herself to McNab by keeping the secret.

And secrets, she knew, had a habit of coming back to bite you.

5

Mark checked his watch for the umpteenth time.

They must have found her by now.

He felt his heart quicken at the thought. Funny how he'd never noticed the speed of his heart before, not even when he was playing football. Now he heard every beat resounding in his head.

What the hell had he done?

The trouble was he had no idea. He remembered fucking her, the weird cat digging its claws into his shoulder, then nothing until he was sick. *What happened in between? How had she got in that room and onto that hook? And the dolls. Those freaking dolls.*

He suddenly registered Emilie calling to him from the bedroom.

'Coming,' he shouted back.

He observed himself in the mirror, then splashed his face with cold water. He needed to stay calm and focused. Emilie didn't suspect a thing. He'd turned up at her flat as promised to take her to lunch. She hadn't seemed interested in knowing about the football, but had regaled him with her own story of a meal out with friends.

After lunch they had come back to her place.

Emilie had been up for sex and he'd obliged, but only after he'd snorted a line to blot out last night's lingering image. She'd spotted the cat's claw marks on his shoulder, but appeared to buy the story of a fall during the football game.

Re-entering the bedroom, he gave an audible groan and even managed to limp a bit. Emilie was sitting up in bed, arms stretched above her head, her breasts eyeing him in the hope of a second round.

Something Mark didn't think he could manage.

He groaned again.

'What's up?' Emilie said.

'My shoulder where I fell. Think it's stiffening up.'

She eyed his penis, which definitely wasn't.

He gave her a plaintive look. 'Would you mind if I went home for a kip?'

This time suspicion did lurk in those baby-blue eyes.

Mark leaned over and kissed her. 'I could come back later?'

Somewhat mollified, she stroked his hair. For some reason, that got a response where the pointed breasts had not. Noting this, she slid her hand downwards to massage his growing erection.

Mark blanked all thoughts of last night and got on with it.

He left Emilie at nine o'clock. After round two, she'd phoned out for pizza. Mark had eaten his quickly, after which he'd indicated just how tired he was by a series of yawns, and had eventually been permitted to leave.

Outside now, he took a deep breath of cool night air, then pulled out his mobile, which he'd kept switched off all day. There were three messages from Jeff, all brief, asking in a variety of ways how he'd got on last night. The final one had come in around eight o'clock.

Mark decided to look at that positively. Jeff obviously hadn't heard about the body of a female being discovered in a flat near the pub, or he would surely have mentioned it.

He knew he should text back. Jeff would expect that. But what to say?

I had sex with her, then found her hanging in the next room.

The half-digested pizza flipped in his stomach, making him feel nauseous.

Let's face it, I'm fucked whatever I do.

He set off towards the Grassmarket, deciding a pint would help him think.

The night was fine and pleasantly warm. Being Saturday, the tables outside the string of pubs that called the Grassmarket home were full.

Mark gave up on an outside seat and, choosing the bar emitting the least noise, went inside. It took him a good five minutes to order a drink, but he did manage to find a small corner table next to the toilets, where he could sit in relative peace.

Free now of Emilie and her keen observance, he ran over last night's proceedings. At least, what he could remember of them. He could recall how everything had been sharpened by the coke. Colours, sounds, touch, all enhanced by that snap pack of white powder. He had a sudden memory of laughing when she'd ordered him to strip. God, that had been a turn-on. He realized with a start that had she wanted to whip him, he would have readily agreed to that as well.

Which stirred a sudden memory. *The knotted cord.*

After she'd ordered the cat off his face, she'd made him

sit up and, his penis still inside her, had bound them together round the waist with a red knotted cord, pulling it tighter as he'd reached climax.

Mark's heart was racing now, as though he'd taken another line of coke. He brushed away a drop of perspiration that ran down the side of his face, realizing if she hadn't been dead, he would have gone back for more.

A thought struck him.

What if she wasn't dead? What if he'd been hallucinating with the mix of coke and alcohol? What if it had all been a bad dream?

Then he remembered the smell.

When he'd opened the door and the cat had pushed its way in, there had been a bad smell. Like piss or shit. Then the cat had wailed and he'd seen her, the red cord round her neck, those eyes staring at him.

That's what he'd smelt in that room. Death.

His hand trembling a little, Mark drank down the remainder of his pint and ordered another, then set about scouring the news on his mobile, looking for some mention of a dead girl found last night in Glasgow.

Twenty minutes later, he had nothing, which either meant she hadn't been found or that the police hadn't released details yet. But she would be found eventually and, he decided, probably by the friend.

The friend who had watched him leave with her, which would make him a suspect. And he'd watched enough cop dramas to know he was all over her, the bedroom *and* the red cord. Still, DNA was no use without a suspect to match it to, and he didn't have a record.

So, he persuaded himself, he was safe. Unless they picked him up.

Mark suddenly realized how important it was to talk to

Jeff. If Jeff had broken the golden rule and given out his real name and mobile number, the police would be able to trace him via Jeff.

He pulled up Jeff's number. It rang out four times, then Jeff picked up.

'Hey, mate, at last. Where are you?'

'Back in Edinburgh.'

'How was she?'

While Mark figured out what his answer should be, Jeff came back. 'The bitch ditched you before you got a taste?'

Mark couldn't help himself. 'Oh no. I made it into the garden all right,' he heard himself boasting. 'How about you?'

'Same.' Jeff gave an appreciative whistle.

'Seeing her again?' Mark said.

'No way. A one-off as agreed, to spice up the regular love life.' He paused. 'I take it Emilie bought the five-a-side routine?'

'No problem. Did you tell her your real name?' Mark checked.

'Treated myself to a new one. George. How about you?'

'Never got round to names, too busy doing other things,' Mark said.

'Excellent. See you next month for more of the same?'

'You bet. And, Jeff? Whatever happens, we were never in that pub. Agreed?'

'Agreed.'

Mark felt better when he rang off. Maybe he could survive this. He had tomorrow to get his head straight before work on Monday. He would avoid Emilie until next weekend. Plead too much work. Play it safe. Play it low.

The phone call had calmed him a little.

Now that he had thought it through, he was pretty sure that the sex games they'd played had never reached that room with the dolls. So, if he didn't have a hand in her death, then how did it happen?

He'd been trashed by drink, drugs and sex. Not so much asleep as unconscious. And while he was comatose, had someone else come into the flat? He'd toyed with the idea that she'd committed suicide, but it didn't fit with the way she'd acted. Why invite him there for sex then top herself?

He'd blotted out the image of her on the hook, but he forced himself to recall it now. She had been off the ground and there was no upturned chair.

So how the hell had she got up there?

Someone must have entered the flat while he was asleep. It was the only explanation. And that someone must have killed her. Did the killer realize he was in the bedroom? If so, why wasn't he killed too?

It only took him seconds to work out why.

He was the mug that would take the blame. The last one seen with her alive and the one whose DNA was all over her and the murder weapon.

Let's face it, he was totally fucked.

6

Saturday night and the pub was busy, both with regulars and, McNab could hear from the voices, tourists, come to taste the wide variety of whiskies on offer. He made his way through the throng to the bar and, showing his ID, asked to speak to Barry Fraser.

The young woman disappeared round the back and, minutes later, a tall, blond man emerged, looking worried.

McNab flashed his ID again. 'Barry Fraser?'

When the guy nodded, McNab asked, 'Anywhere we can talk in private, Barry?'

He looked unsure. 'The cellar's about the only quiet place tonight.'

'That'll do.'

Barry looked nonplussed at this, but realizing McNab was for real, lifted the counter and ushered him inside. As they passed the shelves lined with malt whiskies, McNab kept his eyes firmly on Barry's back.

A narrow corridor led to a door that opened on a set of stairs. Barry headed down them and McNab followed. The cellar was tidy and well stocked with a row of barrels attached to pipes leading upwards. There were shelves with whisky bottles all arranged by distillery. It was something a connoisseur would notice and McNab did. How the hell anyone worked here and didn't imbibe, he had no idea. Barry took up a stance in front of a barrel and waited with worried eyes for his interrogation to begin.

'I wanted to ask you about someone who was in here last night.'

Barry gave him a disbelieving look. 'Have you any idea just how many folk were in here last night?'

McNab nodded. 'This one you would have noticed.'

'Okay. Try me.'

'A young woman. Auburn hair. Green eyes. About five five. A real looker. She was with a pal. Pretty, petite, blonde. They were in here about ten o'clock?'

The barman eyed him warily. McNab guessed he had seen Leila. She would have been hard to miss and he thought Barry Fraser would be well practised at bird spotting in his bar.

Barry was considering his reply and wondering what it might lead to. Curiosity tinged with a little concern eventually decided him.

'It sounds like Leila Hardy. Why, what's happened to her?'

McNab ignored the question. 'You definitely saw them?'

He nodded. 'Sure. They were over in the corner with two lads.'

'Can you describe these lads?'

He shook his head. 'I notice the lassies, the lads don't interest me.'

It was a fair comment. Had McNab been asked to describe one of the crowd of blokes propping up the bar tonight, he would have been hard pressed to do so.

'Did you see Leila leave?'

In that split second, McNab knew his barman was about

to tell a lie. Call it police intuition or psychology in action, but he just knew.

'No.'

'What about the blonde one?'

'Leila, I noticed. The pal not so much.'

'How well do you know Leila?'

McNab already suspected the answer to that, but he was pretty sure Barry wouldn't reveal it. Not until he sussed out why the policeman was interested.

McNab decided to go for the jugular.

'Leila Hardy was found dead this morning.'

Barry's eyes widened. The shock appeared real enough for him to seek a seat on the edge of a nearby barrel.

'Jesus,' he whispered under his breath. He looked up, his face now suffused with anger. 'You bastard, you never said anything about that on the phone.'

McNab decided not to warn him about swearing at a police officer, but waited as Barry tried to pull himself together. Eventually he did and rose to his feet again. 'What happened to her?' he said, genuine concern in his voice.

'That's what we're trying to establish.'

Barry searched McNab's expression. 'You mean she was murdered?'

'She was found hanged in her flat.'

Barry looked as if he was trying to compute and couldn't. 'Leila committed suicide?'

When McNab didn't respond, Barry came back. 'No way. Leila had everything going for her. She really enjoyed life.'

'So,' said McNab, drawing the conversation back to where he wanted it to be. 'When did she leave the pub and who was she with?'

This time Barry thought. Hard. 'I came down here to

change a barrel sometime after ten. When I went back up she had gone and the blonde was on her own.'

'You were keeping an eye on Leila?' McNab suggested.

'I wasn't stalking her if that's what you mean,' Barry declared.

'Just taking a keen interest?' McNab smiled. 'I take it you two were once an item?'

Judging by Barry's expression, he was contemplating another lie, then thought the better of it. 'No, but we did get together on occasion.'

'You had sex with Leila *on occasion*?' McNab said.

'Sometimes she asked me back to her place,' Barry said defensively.

Lucky you, McNab thought. 'But not last night?'

'No. Not last night.'

'The guy she did take home with her. What did he look like?'

Now that Barry knew that Leila was dead, he was more forthcoming about his rival. 'Tall, maybe six foot. Late twenties, early thirties. Blond. Worked out by the shape of him. Was wearing a blue striped shirt with short sleeves and jeans. By the clothes, the Gucci watch and the wallet, I'd say he wasn't short of cash,' he added.

The description, McNab noted, was a close match to Shannon's, although she hadn't mentioned that he'd looked affluent.

'What about the mate?'

'Dark hair, not as tall, dressed the same, but he never came near the bar. They moved in on Leila and the blonde quite quickly after that.'

'You don't know Shannon?'

He shook his head. 'Leila came in a lot, living round the corner.'

'What about security cameras?' McNab said.

'One on the front door, one on the side.'

So they might have footage of Leila and the guy leaving, if they weren't obscured by a crowd of smokers. McNab thanked him.

'Someone will be round for the security tapes.' He handed Barry a card. 'If you remember anything else, give me a ring.'

McNab fought a desire to reward himself with a dram and headed outside. As he suspected, the entrance was encircled by smokers all within sight of the security camera. He took a look in the back lane and discovered the fire exit standing wide open. Just inside was the Gents, so the mate could have exited here when he'd deserted Shannon on the pretext that he was going to the toilet. If so, there was a chance that the back camera had caught him.

McNab left the lane and took the short walk between the pub and Leila's flat. There were plenty of revellers about the city centre at this time on a Saturday night. No doubt there were folk about last night too, who might have spotted the auburn-haired Leila and her tall blond companion walking the short distance home.

Once the post-mortem was over, they could get down to the business of looking for witnesses, unless the pathologist decided McNab's intuition was suspect and that Leila Hardy had simply taken her own life. That was a possibility, of course. Suicides were extremely adept at carrying out their wishes, often against the odds. If their aim was a cry for help, that was usually evidenced by the method they chose and the circumstances in which they made the attempt, which often had a 'way out'. A bit like driving down the wrong side of the road until you met an approaching car, then swerving to avoid it. Alternatively, courting death could be used to make life more exciting or maybe just bearable.

A condition McNab had been known to suffer from himself.

Tonight, the real and present danger presented itself in the form of numerous bars, from which music, chatter and female laughter escaped to surround him in a warm embrace.

McNab walked with a determined step, eyes forward, fighting the desire to say 'Fuck it!' and head into the next one he passed. He hadn't drunk alcohol in the last three weeks and planned a month at least, just to show that he could. Relieved to find that he could function without it, he'd convinced himself that although he'd been drinking heavily, he was not, yet, dependent on it.

Back at his own flat, he contemplated how to pass the midnight hour, alone and sober, knowing that tomorrow, Sunday, wouldn't be any easier. He phoned out for a pizza and put the recently purchased coffee machine on. While the coffee was brewing, he stripped to his boxers and did fifty press-ups. Anything to keep his mind off the open bottle of whisky in the cupboard near the sink. Kept there undrunk, it had become a symbol of his success.

Sex would have helped, but staying away from pubs had meant the only females he met were the ones he worked with. He'd long ago made his way through the fanciable ones, apart from Janice, and was pretty sure none of them would welcome a return visit however fit and sober he was now.

Janice had suggested, as they parted company, that now he was no longer a DI, he might like to come out for a drink with the team again. McNab was secretly pleased by her suggestion, but didn't trust himself to do that, yet.

Then there was his Rhona obsession.

He may have kidded himself in the past that they might get back together *on occasion* but he knew that wasn't going to happen. Ever. He was like the barman, with one eye on the object of his affection and a constant hope that she might just, in a weak moment, ask him back to her place.

Sad bastards, the pair of them.

McNab slipped on a T-shirt and answered the buzzer for his pizza delivery.

Sitting on the couch now, feet on the coffee table, a double espresso already drunk, he was reminded of another night, when Rhona had sat opposite him, sharing a pizza. They'd exchanged words over the girl he'd been bedding at the time, young enough to be his daughter.

Rhona had been less than impressed, and she'd been right.

But the memory of those sexual encounters with Iona were as difficult to forget as the bottle of whisky. McNab abandoned the remains of the pizza and headed for the shower.

Ten minutes later, reddened by the force of the hot, then cold shower, the bullet scar on his back glowing, he poured another coffee and carried it through to the bedroom. The room was stuffy and warm, so he opened the window a little, then lay down naked on top of the bed and listened to the siren sound of his fellow officers dealing with the fallout from too much alcohol on a Saturday night.

Staring at the ceiling, McNab set his caffeine-buzzed brain to figuring out what had happened to Leila Hardy after she left the pub and headed home for sex with the unknown blond guy.

In all the possible scenarios he came up with, not one, but two men figured.

One thing his gut told him.

Leila Hardy hadn't died by her own hand.

7

It wasn't a requirement for the investigating officer to attend a victim's post-mortem and many simply chose not to. Seasoned officers, well acquainted with the variety of terrible ways that humans dispensed with one another, often found viewing the systematic surgical dissection of a body too difficult to deal with.

Familiarity with the aftermath of murder, however messy and horrific that might be, was not the same as actually being present when a knife sliced its way through flesh, and an electric saw cut its way through bone. The variety of noises alone were often hard to bear, although earplugs could be employed, and often were.

When Rhona arrived in the changing room, DS Clark was already there.

They'd exchanged pleasantries as they'd donned the overalls, both managing to avoid mentioning McNab's recent demotion. Rhona gained the impression that Janice was more relaxed about working with McNab as an equal, which suggested that he was definitely making an effort.

This pleased her.

When the object of her thoughts arrived, he wasn't hungover, which had often been the case in the past. Glancing from one woman to the other, you could see what he was thinking, so Rhona put him straight.

'We weren't talking about you.'

McNab's feigned expression of indifference made Janice smile.

'So what were you talking about?' he asked airily.

Rhona ignored the question and posed one of her own. 'How did you get on with the barman?'

McNab located a forensic suit and began to pull it on.

'He saw Leila leave with a man fitting Shannon's description. He admitted that he had the hots for Leila himself and that he and she were an *occasional* item.' He threw Rhona a swift glance which she ignored.

'What about the suicide angle?'

'He was as adamant as Shannon that Leila wouldn't kill herself.'

'Well, let's see what the pathologist has to say,' Rhona said, pulling up her hood and raising her mask.

Dr Sissons didn't glance up on their entry. His usual behaviour was to simply ignore the presence of others at the post-mortems he conducted. He and Rhona had an unspoken understanding that they did not cross the boundaries between their specializations unless absolutely necessary. Sissons did not like his judgement questioned. Like a surgeon in an operating theatre, he gave out orders and did not take them. To break into his train of thought would probably result in being told to leave.

All three of them were aware of this, and stood in absolute silence as he recorded the bodily measurements and condition of the body, then the signs of rapid anoxial death.

Anoxia, the scientific term for a lack of oxygen, could develop over a long period of time, due to a variety of illnesses, where the lungs and the heart weren't working properly. Rapid anoxial death was an entirely different matter. If the flow of oxygen from the atmosphere to the tissues was interrupted suddenly, then rapid anoxial death occurred. Classification of such deaths included suffocation, choking, strangulation, compression of the chest, cyanide poisoning, drowning and hanging. Some of these methods were swifter than others. In very rapid deaths, the oxygen supply to the body and brain was cut off and the victim immediately became quiet and pale, and passed swiftly into unconsciousness then death.

Such a quick death usually caused little disturbance at a scene. In more slowly progressing rapid anoxial death, the situation was quite different. Once anoxia had started, the victim fought for breath, often lashing out at an attacker. The result was the obvious signs of a death struggle, evidenced by bruising on both victim and attacker, and DNA exchange often through scratches and blood transfer.

When Sissons stated that he was about to remove the cord from round the victim's neck, Rhona asked permission to record this and Sissons gave a curt nod. From observation, she had deduced that the main knot was a slip knot or simple noose. Watching it being unravelled would confirm this.

Now that the neck was free of the cord, it was clear that there were no pressure fingermarks or bruises associated with strangulation. As was common in hanging, the mark of the ligature was incomplete, evident only at the front. The mark was depressed, pale and parchment-like, the pattern of the plaited cord evident.

Dr Sissons recorded this evidence in his usual dry tone. As he did so, McNab's eyes met Rhona's above the mask.

'I found some fibres in her mouth,' Rhona said.

Sissons acknowledged this with a nod and went in for a

look himself, extracting a further fibre from deeper in the throat, suggesting, as Rhona had surmised, that a cloth of some sort might have been put in the victim's mouth or even pushed into her throat to cut off the air supply.

Gagging was common in homicidal suffocation, along with plastic or wet material covering the nose and mouth, and in some instances shoved down the throat.

Rhona could feel McNab's growing impatience; Sissons wasn't known for speed in post-mortems, even when the cause of death appeared obvious to everyone round the table.

But Sissons got there eventually.

In the pathologist's estimation, the victim had something wedged in her mouth, causing her to pass out. This had then been removed and the cord tied round her neck while she was unconscious. She had then been hung on the hook.

He finished this by stating, 'There is, of course, the chance that all of this was done as part of auto-erotic hanging, which she may have consented to.'

Now back in the changing room, all three stripped off their suits and dumped them in the basket.

'So she was gagged,' McNab said. 'What with?'

'The fibres I extracted were a cotton synthetic mix. I sent Chrissy back to the flat to check for anything that might match.'

'I don't buy the auto-erotic bit,' Janice said. 'If she was into all that, we would have found other stuff in the flat. Plastic gags, blindfolds.'

'There's something else to consider,' McNab said.

'What?'

'I believe the other guy left the pub immediately after Leila and her man. I have a feeling he followed them.'

If that were true, it could change everything.

'We're checking the security cameras.' McNab turned to Janice. 'Any luck with the next of kin?'

'The brother's band, the Spikes, are on tour in Germany. I've emailed the manager but he hasn't come back to me yet.'

'Did you ask Shannon about the dolls?' Rhona said.

'She says she was never in that room,' McNab said. 'You still think the dolls are significant?'

'Who hangs twenty-seven dolls from their ceiling unless it means something?'

'Put that way,' McNab agreed. 'I take it you never discovered the secret of nine?'

'What's this about the number nine?' Janice came in.

Rhona explained about the nine knots in the cord and the pattern of dolls. 'Any ideas?'

Janice shook her head. 'But it's intriguing.'

'I thought I might run it past Magnus. He's back in Glasgow.' Rhona had been planning to drop that suggestion into her conversation with McNab the previous night, but had decided not to, in view of the circumstances.

'Good idea,' chimed Janice.

McNab had opened his mouth, no doubt to protest, but changed his mind and shut it again.

'I'll give him a call,' Rhona said. 'And let you know what he has to say.'

Back now at the lab, Rhona logged the arrival of the cord, then surveyed the sea of dolls laid out in rows on the table.

She had filled her Sunday with work, preferring to spend time at the lab to wondering if Sean would get in touch. It seemed, however, that he'd got the message. There had been no phone calls, no texts, and when she'd returned home early Sunday evening, she'd found no evidence he'd been back in the flat, despite still having a key. Rhona had found herself mildly irritated that he had taken her at her word and a little sorry not to encounter the scent of a cooked meal waiting for her.

Nevertheless, Sunday had been fruitful. A deserted and peaceful lab had resulted in a considerable amount of work being done. She'd established from the swabs that the victim had had sex before she'd died. There had been no bruising in the genital area, which Dr Sissons had confirmed at the PM, so the sex appeared to have been consensual.

More interestingly, fine fibres plucked from Leila's navel matched those of the red silk cord, suggesting it had also been round her waist. From sweat on the cord, she'd extracted samples of two different strands of DNA. One from the victim and the other matching that taken from the semen.

So her sexual partner that night had also been in contact with the cord.

Examining the red cord in more detail, Rhona found that the nine knots were identical and, from the chirality of each, she deduced they'd been tied by the same person, since the direction of movement was consistent.

Now she replayed the short movie she'd taken as Dr Sissons slowly untied the knot that had fixed the cord round Leila's neck. Rhona had suspected a slip knot or simple noose and this was proved to be right. After replaying a couple of times, she retied it herself to make sure.

It wasn't possible to definitely determine whether the person who tied a knot was left- or right-handed, but it became apparent that replicating the chirality of the slip knot felt awkward, and since she was left-handed, she suspected whoever had tied the slip knot wasn't. As for the nine knots, they were too simple to be certain. The post-mortem hadn't established whether Leila was left- or right-handed. That was something McNab would have to find out from Leila's pal, Shannon.

Rhona was tackling the knots in the dolls' cords when Chrissy appeared and waved through the glass, indicating it was time to eat.

Abandoning the dolls, she joined Chrissy in the office where the warm scent of baking emanated from a paper bag, reminding Rhona how hungry she was.

Chrissy busied herself spooning coffee into the filter and unpacking what turned out to be four large sausage rolls.

'Help yourself.'

Rhona did as commanded.

Coffee machine on, Chrissy plonked herself down next to Rhona with a bottle of ketchup and proceeded to dollop some on her sausage roll before attacking it with gusto. It was clear there was to be no conversation until her forensic assistant had satisfied her hunger. Rhona had to wait until Chrissy had demolished two sausage rolls and half of Rhona's second one.

Settled back at the desk with her coffee, Chrissy finally said, 'I've brought a few items back that might match your fibres. How did the PM go?'

Rhona relayed what Sissons had said.

'Okay, but I don't think she was a gasper. I double-checked all her belongings. There's no evidence she was into erotic asphyxiation unless it's on the laptop the Tech guys took along with her mobile.'

'Except for the hanging dolls,' Rhona reminded her.

Chrissy made a face. 'I used to love my Barbie. Wasn't so fond of Ken though. He always seemed a bit of a wimp.'

'I'm going to give Magnus a ring. See if he has any ideas about the pattern of nine and the dolls.'

Chrissy considered this. 'McNab won't like that.'

'He agreed,' Rhona assured her. 'Or at least Detective Sergeant Clark thought it was a good idea.'

'And McNab didn't bite her head off?'

'No.'

Chrissy looked impressed. 'Changed days, eh?'

But for how long? Rhona wondered.

8

Professor Magnus Pirie was a typical Orcadian, if such a thing existed. He had grown up surrounded by the sea, spent a great deal of time battling against the wind that stripped the islands bare of trees, made his own home-brewed beer (a dying art). He spoke with an Orcadian accent when at home in Houton Bay and had mixed ancestry with the Inuits of Northern Canada via the Hudson Bay Company. Apart from these typical characteristics shared by many of those who inhabited the windy northern isles, he also had a powerful sense of smell which, at its best, was a blessing. At its worst, a curse.

Today it was a curse.

The train back from Edinburgh, packed as it was with teatime commuters, had developed a fault which prevented it from regulating the temperature in the carriage. The resultant heat was accentuating every aftershave, perfume and not-so-pleasant bodily odours that radiated from his fellow travellers.

He'd survived the journey so far by focusing on the book he'd brought to read en route. A prescribed text for his students of forensic psychology, they were currently studying the chapter on 'Police Psychology', in particular the section entitled 'Canteen/Cop Culture'. The term 'canteen culture' had been coined to differentiate it from the more general police culture, since rank-and-file officers' cultural norms rarely matched those of their management.

Magnus's own experience of police work had brought him into contact with many of the features of 'cop culture' discussed. Cynicism, conservatism and suspicion being just three of them. Most working officers didn't take kindly to a forensic psychologist being foisted on an investigation, his arrival being seen as an indication that senior management didn't trust the judgement of its detectives.

Rank-and-file officers regarded forensic psychology as nothing more than unproven mumbo jumbo. Forensic science had been accepted over time, particularly if it helped convict 'the bastards'. Psychology, on the other hand, was not regarded as a science and had no basis in reality, as far as most cops were concerned.

It was often bracketed with social work, and social workers were known to try and get people off by relating some sob story about a perpetrator, just as psychologists strove to understand and explain the criminal mind.

As far as the majority of front-line officers were concerned, bad people did bad things and must be stopped. End of story. At times, Magnus found himself in complete agreement with them.

He closed the book and slipped it in his bag as the train approached Queen Street Station. He always enjoyed his trips to Edinburgh. Much as he loved the vitality and 'in-your-face' nature of Glasgow, a trip to its sister city, so different in manner and architecture, reminded him of the eternal dichotomy of the Scottish psyche.

Built on seven hills, always breezy and rather fond of its own importance, Edinburgh's outward appearance was of douce respectability. Industrial Glasgow, on the other hand, having known real hardship, preferred to lace life with irony and dark humour.

The trip east had involved a visit to Edinburgh University to give a guest lecture on his criminal profiling work. The lecture theatre had been packed with eager students, who, in the main, were there to ask about his involvement in the high-profile *Stonewarrior* case, which had set their social media sites alight, involving as it did an alternative reality game, which, it appeared, the whole student world had been eager to play.

The case having never reached court, because of the death of the perpetrator, Magnus had been free to give some indication of the role he'd played in apprehending the killer, although he deemed it to be a small one.

He'd also been perplexed and not a little perturbed to discover from one student that a well-known gaming company was already putting the finishing touches to a new game entitled *Stonewarrior Unleashed*.

Thus the fiction of the original *Stonewarrior*, which the perpetrator had played out as fact, was to become the new fiction. Something, Magnus suspected, the perpetrator would have relished from his prison cell, a desire for notoriety being a psychological feature of his personality.

Emerging from the station into the noise of traffic circling George Square, Magnus caught the vibration of his mobile in his jacket pocket. Retrieving it, he found Rhona's name on the screen and immediately answered.

'Rhona. How are you?'

'Good. And you?'

'Fine. Back from Orkney and in downtown Glasgow as you can tell by the noise.'

'I wanted to run something past you, but now doesn't sound like a good idea.'

Magnus immediately came back. 'I'll be at my flat in twenty minutes, if that helps?'

Rhona was silent for a moment, then said, 'Might I come round? I'd like you to take a look at some photographs.'

'Of course,' Magnus said, trying to keep delight from his voice.

When Rhona rang off, Magnus upped his pace. If he was quick he could pick up some food on the way home and perhaps persuade Rhona to stay and eat with him after their discussion. They'd had no contact since the *Stonewarrior* case and he hadn't been called on to do any further police work. Initially this had suited him, and he'd immersed himself in his university tasks, but now he was ready for another challenge, especially one brought to him by Dr Rhona MacLeod.

Half an hour later, having welcomed Rhona into his riverside flat, Magnus found himself regarding a photograph on her laptop that deeply disturbed him. The image was of a room, bare of furniture, but festooned with naked Barbie-type dolls, attached to the ceiling via cords round their necks.

The grotesque image reminded him of another case he and Rhona had been involved in that had also featured dolls. Then, the baby dolls had been much more realistic. Termed *Reborns*, they'd been beautifully fashioned replicas of real babies, who had died shortly after birth. The man who had created them had been a psychopath.

The dolls before him now were hard plastic imitations of an impossibly shaped female body. Skinny catwalk models with pert breasts, bright eyes and avid smiles. Not to mention too much hair.

Rhona's voice interrupted his thoughts. 'There are twenty-seven of them, arranged in three rows of nine,' she said.

Magnus drew his eyes from the grotesque nature of the image and checked what she'd said.

'So there are,' he noted with interest. 'And arranged in threes by hair colour,' he added.

Rhona changed the image on the screen. 'This was behind the curtain of dolls.'

A young woman, naked, hanging on a hook, her eyes staring, her mouth and tongue swollen. If the dolls were bad, this was much worse. Magnus couldn't prevent himself recoiling in horror from such a death scene.

Rhona immediately apologized. 'I'm sorry, Magnus, I should have warned you.'

Composing himself, Magnus brushed her concerns away. 'I take it she was murdered?'

'We believe so.'

Rhona gave Magnus time to absorb the scene and recover from its impact, before continuing. 'The pattern of nine and three is continued in the cord used to hang her. It consisted of three strips of red silk, plaited, and had nine knots tied in it, evenly spaced out along its length.'

A series of facts Magnus found intriguing.

'And this pattern of nine is what you wanted to ask me about?'

'That and the possible significance of the dolls.'

Magnus reviewed the images as he considered Rhona's question. 'Nine is significant in mathematics, for lots of reasons. It also features in most religions.' He caught Rhona's eye. 'But you know all that, I take it?'

'I did spend some time researching online,' she said with a smile.

'But nothing you read seemed to fit?'

She nodded. 'There's forensic evidence to place the cord round the victim's waist, as well as her neck. And she had sex before she died. The DNA from the semen also matches a sample taken from the cord, which suggests her sexual partner also handled it.'

Magnus gave her a keen look. 'Are you saying that the death may have occurred during a sexual encounter?'

'Or shortly after.'

A flood of thoughts raced through Magnus's mind. He attempted to slow and order them.

'What do we know about the victim?'

'The night she died, she was drinking in a pub with a friend where they picked up two men. The victim left with one of them, according to her friend. She says the intention was to go back to the flat for sex.'

'Did the friend know about the dolls?'

'She says not. However, she did tell McNab that the victim was into New Age stuff.'

It appeared Rhona had sparked an idea. She watched as Magnus went over to the bookshelves and began a search. Some minutes later, he pounced on a book on the top shelf. Withdrew it and brought it across to her.

'Medieval Orkney had a fearful reputation as a haven for Witches and warlocks,' he said. 'I did some research on this a few years ago.' He leafed through the large blue book, which was entitled *Complete Book of Witchcraft*, eventually stopping at a chapter headed 'Magick'.

'How long was the cord?' Magnus said.

'Approximately nine feet. Is that important?'

'It could be a cingulum.' Magnus began reading out loud. *'Three times three makes nine, the perennial magick number. It should be red, the colour of blood, the life force, and nine feet in length,'* he looked to Rhona, *'made with three lengths of red silk if possible.'*

'What about the knots?' Rhona said.

Magnus read on in silence for a moment, then said, 'It seems the nine knots are storage cells for the magical energy required to make a spell.' He turned to the next page. 'And here we have the sexual aspect.'

The illustration he indicated featured a couple having sex and bound together by a cingulum tied round their waists.

'Looks like your victim may have been dabbling in Witchcraft.'

'And the dolls?'

'At a guess, something to do with the importance of the Goddess in the Wiccan religion.'

He surrendered the book to Rhona.

'Take a look while I make us something to eat, unless you have other plans?'

'Food would be good,' she said.

'Sex magick is one of the most potent forms of magick, for we are dealing here very much with the life forces.' The more Rhona read of the chapter, the more it seemed that Magnus might be right and that the coupling before Leila's death, using the red cord or cingulum, might have been, for her at least, a *magick* ritual.

Magnus's voice calling Rhona to table broke into her thoughts.

'It's just pasta, I'm afraid, but it is fresh and the sauce is my own.'

'I was planning a takeaway, so this is an improvement.'

The last time she'd eaten with Magnus had been at his house on Orkney, overlooking Scapa Flow. Back then, he'd cooked her fresh scallops and served home-brewed beer. The memory of that meal came swiftly back to her. She'd been unsure about accepting his offer of a room for the night. A deluge of midsummer tourists, combined with a stream of police personnel come to investigate a murder at the famous Ring of Brodgar neolithic site, had filled all available accommodation, so she'd had little option but to stay with Magnus, despite her misgivings.

Initially things had been awkward, on her part at least. She and Magnus had history, not so much romantic as tragic. Thrown together on a case that had changed their lives, the memory at that time had still been raw.

'How much do you know about the Wiccan religion?' Rhona asked when they'd reached the coffee stage.

'Not much,' Magnus admitted. 'The research on Witchcraft was more about the past than the present, but I found that book fascinating and informative. It's difficult to find covens and speak to members about their beliefs and practices. They tend to keep very low key. There's still a great deal of prejudice and misunderstanding about Wiccans – and Pagans, for that matter.'

'The Wiccan Rede doesn't sound very murderous,' Rhona said.

'"An' it harm none, do what thou wilt,"' Magnus quoted. 'Present-day practitioners deny any cavorting with the devil. It's more New Age tree hugging and eco-friendly, but then again, maybe it always was. I think burning Witches was more about gaining sadistic sexual gratification from torturing women than a desire to rid the world of evil. There were psychopaths back then too.'

A thought struck Rhona.

'Maybe that's why she died,' she said. 'Maybe she was killed because she was a Witch.'

'Well, after burning, hanging was the most popular method of dispensing with a Witch. Followed by drowning.'

'Is that true?' Rhona said, surprised.

'It is. So maybe your theory has some validity.'

'Or maybe she made the mistake of taking a sadistic psychopath home with her.'

'An equally valid theory.'

Rhona glanced at her watch, sensing it was time to go.

'There's a strategy meeting tomorrow about this. I take it you would be willing to attend, if asked?'

'I look forward to hearing what Detective Sergeant McNab makes of the Witchcraft angle.' Magnus gave a wry smile.

'I'll run it past DI Wilson first.'

'A wise move.' Magnus walked her to the door. 'Well, good luck with the investigation. And if there's anything else I can help with, feel free to call me.'

The subway was quiet and her journey to Byres Road swift and uneventful. The short walk that followed brought her to the jazz club by nine. As she descended the steps to the cellar she heard the sound of Sam on piano.

Sam, an Ibo from Nigeria, was close to completing his medical degree at Glasgow University. He and Chrissy had been an item long enough to produce a son who had inherited, as was often the case in a mixed relationship, the most attractive qualities of both parents, which made him perfectly beautiful as well as good-natured.

Chrissy had proved herself to be a rather good mum, without losing her essential 'Chrissyness'. Her relationship with Sam had brought an end to her own parents' marriage, because her father found he didn't like the idea of a 'black' grandchild. Her mother had disagreed. The resultant split had been no bad thing, according to Chrissy. In fact, she'd declared that she'd wished it had happened years earlier. Chrissy's mother, finally free from having to deal with a domineering and often drunken husband, was thoroughly enjoying being a 'hands-on' granny.

So, there were people like Chrissy who could form lasting relationships in the most difficult of circumstances, thought Rhona.

Just not me.

Rhona made for the bar and ordered a glass of white wine. She'd half-expected to find Chrissy there. She often came in on the nights that Sam was playing. That way she got to see him, their paths rarely crossing during the day. But there was no sign of Chrissy tonight. Mildly disappointed by this – she had hoped to get Chrissy's take on Magnus's revelations – Rhona made a swift decision. Lifting her glass of wine, she headed through the back to Sean's office to find the door closed and the low sound of voices inside.

Once upon a time Rhona would have walked straight in and expected a welcome. Now, things being different, she hesitated before knocking on the door.

The voices inside fell silent, then the door was flung open.

Sean's surprise was evident, but he quickly masked it with a smile.

'Rhona, to what do I owe this pleasure?'

Rhona wasn't often stumped for an answer, but she was now. When she didn't immediately reply, Sean waved her inside.

The woman in the room was in her twenties, pretty and a little put out by Rhona's appearance. The feeling, Rhona decided, was mutual.

Sean, seemingly unperturbed, made the introductions.

'Rhona, Merle. Merle, Rhona.'

The two women eyed one another. By Sean's expression, he was rather enjoying the moment.

'Merle is our new singer. Rhona is . . .' he hesitated, then opted for, 'an old friend.'

Rhona didn't relish that description of herself.

But what could he say? *Rhona and I are old news, resurrected now and again when sex is required.*

'Hi, good to meet you.'

'And you.' Merle's voice was melodious and husky, as a jazz singer should sound. She glanced at Sean. 'I'd better go through. I'm due on shortly.'

Rhona smiled a goodbye as Sean ushered Merle to the door with words of encouragement. Rhona felt like following her out, but couldn't.

Sean shut the door.

He regarded her for a moment, then approaching, removed the glass from her hand and set it down on the desk.

'So, why *are* you here?'

Rhona didn't have an answer, at least not one she was willing to give.

When nothing was forthcoming, Sean brushed her cheek, his eyes meeting hers. It was a gentle gesture that led to nothing more. He dropped his hand.

'Are you planning on staying?'

Every ounce of sense she possessed screamed *no*. Yet she almost nodded her agreement, before a sense of reality regained the upper hand.

'I have to prepare for a strategy meeting in the morning.'

'That's a pity.'

They stood in silence for a moment, before Sean said, 'I'd better go in and catch Merle's spot.'

'Of course.'

If only he had tried just a little harder.

Rhona followed Sean to the door.

9

Shannon tensed as she heard the main door open below, and waited as the voices and footsteps passed by on their way upstairs. Normally, she liked hearing the comings and goings of her neighbours. It made her feel safe to be surrounded by people, but since Leila's death, she'd jumped every time the buzzer had sounded and viewed all approaching footsteps as a possible threat.

Tonight, she'd turned on the news at ten only to discover Leila's face staring out at her. Unnerved before, she'd crumpled in shock. Despite being adamant when speaking to the policeman that Leila would never have committed suicide, Shannon had secretly wished that might be the explanation, however unlikely, because the alternative was so much worse.

Plus I lied to the policeman when he asked about the dolls.

It had been the preservation instinct that had provoked her reaction. The first rule was to tell no one what they really were. So she'd blurted out that Leila was a New Age believer.

How stupid was that?

The news item had given details of the man Leila had left the pub with, which was of course the description Shannon had given to the police. So, she reasoned, the man who had killed Leila would know that she, Shannon, was able to identify him.

Which puts me in danger too.

That fearful thought had driven her through to the bedroom.

Unrolling the circular mat, she spread it out on the floor at the foot of the bed.

Having cast a circle around her and lit the four candles, setting them at north, south, east and west as required, Shannon felt a little better, but not safe enough. Leila had always been the strong one, the sure one. The one who had faith in all the rituals.

I was only a follower.

The insistent ringing of her mobile eventually forced her to break the circle. The number was withheld but she knew who it would be.

'You didn't tell them, did you?'

'No.'

'If you do, I'll know.'

'I won't, I promise,' she insisted, but the caller had already gone.

Shannon dropped the mobile and crawled back inside the circle, chanting the words to help reseal it. Hugging her knees, she watched as the dark shadows cast by the candle flames danced about her.

10

Mornings minus a hangover were beginning to become a habit.

McNab swung his feet out of bed, relishing the non-pounding of his head, a mouth that didn't taste like a cat had pissed in it and eyes that could face daylight without splintering pain.

Likewise, his morning shower felt less like an attempt to wake the dead, and a look in the mirror didn't involve squinting and images of bloodshot eyes. All in all, he decided, being sober had its plus points. The negatives, however, also had to be faced.

His bed had been empty of female company since the alcohol had dried up, so no good memories of wild coupling the previous night and no repeat performance in the morning to set him up for the day. In fact, craving sex had now taken over from craving drink. If he didn't get laid soon, McNab feared he would seek religion, if only to satisfy his desire to have something to get ecstatic about.

Then there were the nightmares.

Whisky had aided sleep to the level of unconsciousness. If he'd experienced bad dreams, he rarely remembered them. Now, however, his sleep was often like a night at the movies, of the horror genre. The latest serial dream replayed the finale of his last case in glorious Technicolor, accompanied by smell, the overpowering nature of which made him even sympathetic to Professor Pirie. Something he would admit to no one, even himself.

So apart from bad dreams and no sex, he was doing okay.

Dressed, coffee machine on, McNab contemplated visiting Shannon Jones, who wasn't answering her mobile. He'd tried three times the previous night, only to be diverted to the messaging service.

They'd not yet succeeded in contacting Leila's brother Daniel in Germany. Shannon wasn't a relative, but McNab would rather have let her know they were treating her friend's death as murder before she heard it on the news, though it was probably too late for that now.

He swallowed down the remainder of his coffee and headed out, having decided to call in at Glasgow University library on his way to the meeting. He owed Shannon that, at least.

In general, McNab preferred to avoid the university precinct. True, the female talent on show there was good, but definitely too young. He'd learned his lesson on that score. As for the guys, they were way too clever and confident for his liking.

Needless to say, McNab's route to his present position had not been via a university degree. His mother would have liked it to be, but money was tight and McNab decided not to make it any tighter. He'd briefly contemplated the army, but didn't fancy returning in a body bag, so he'd joined the police instead.

In the end he *had* seen the inside of a body bag and had lived to tell the tale, evidenced by the bullet scar on his back, not to mention the damage done to his internal organs.

It had turned out, for him at least, that fighting crime was every bit as dangerous as combat duty in some foreign land.

The only college he'd attended had been police college, where, it seemed, most of his fellow recruits had come via university, after studying forensic and criminal psychology and, of course, sociology. A fact that had irked McNab and which probably accounted for his distrust of such subjects, and those who taught them, like Professor Magnus Pirie.

Irritated with himself for thinking about Pirie again, McNab flashed his ID at the reception desk and asked to speak to Assistant Librarian Shannon Jones.

The man peered at him over his spectacles.

'I'm not sure Shannon's in yet. Let me check.'

He abandoned McNab and headed for a desk phone. Moments later he was back.

'Shannon's not in, I'm afraid. She wasn't in yesterday, either.' He gave McNab a searching look. 'Is this to do with Leila's death? I saw it on the news last night. A terrible business.'

McNab ignored the question. 'Did Shannon call to say she wasn't coming in?'

'I have no idea, I'm sorry. She doesn't work in this part of the building.'

'Where does she work?'

'Archives.'

'Can I speak to someone in Archives?'

The man looked nonplussed. 'I can't leave the desk, but I'll get someone to take you there, if you'll wait a moment.'

The student queue forming behind McNab was growing restless. McNab turned and gave them the police eye, which shut them up long enough for his guide to appear. At a guess, she was in her mid twenties, with long brown hair, and very presentable.

'Detective Sergeant McNab.' He presented his ID, hoping she might give him her name in return. She didn't.

'If you'll follow me,' she said.

It took five minutes to get to their destination. During the journey in lifts and corridors, McNab asked if she knew either Leila or Shannon, and was rewarded with, 'Not really.'

'So you didn't socialize?'

She shook her head.

'Or drink in the same pubs?'

'Everyone drinks in Ashton Lane at some time or another.' She gave him a scrutinizing look. 'Maybe that's where I've seen *you* before?'

'Could be,' McNab said casually, hoping he hadn't been inebriated at the time.

She opened a door and stood back to allow him entry.

'Grant!' she called to what looked like an empty room apart from multiple rows of stacked shelves.

A man McNab guessed to be in his fifties appeared, a frown on his face at being disturbed at whatever one did in Archives.

'This is Detective Sergeant McNab,' his guide announced. 'He wants to talk to you about Shannon.'

'She isn't here,' Grant said, the frown lines deepening.

'I know,' McNab said patiently.

'Get Grant to call reception when you're finished and I'll come back for you,' his guide offered.

McNab thanked her.

After she'd gone, he asked Grant for the young woman's name.

'Freya Devine. A post-graduate student in medieval history.'

Perfect name McNab thought, and definitely too brainy for him.

Sensing this wasn't going to be over quickly, Grant asked McNab to follow him between the shelves into a small office. There were two desks, one of which he indicated was Shannon's.

'I can offer you a coffee?'

'Great. As strong as possible, please,' McNab said.

Grant indicated that McNab should take Shannon's seat, before spooning three scoops of instant coffee into a mug and adding hot water from a thermos.

'Milk, sugar?'

'Just as it is, thanks.'

Grant handed it over and, retrieving his own mug, sat down opposite McNab.

'Shannon phoned in yesterday. She said she was ill. It sounded as though she'd been crying. Then I saw the news last night and realized what was wrong.'

'You knew Leila Hardy?'

'Only really by sight. She works elsewhere in the building, but I knew that she and Shannon were friends.'

'I'm having difficulty getting in touch with Shannon. She's not answering at the number she gave me,' McNab said.

'Really? Maybe she's too upset.'

Or she doesn't want to talk to the police again.

'Could you try her for me?' McNab said.

'Of course.' Grant checked a pad next to the phone for her number and dialled. McNab heard it ring out, but no one answered. Eventually Grant hung up. 'Should we be worried?'

McNab showed Grant his notebook. 'Is that her current address?'

'Yes. You're going to check she's all right?'

McNab assured him he would. He gulped down the remainder of his coffee and asked if his guide could be called, to direct him back to the entrance.

'Of course. It is a bit of a warren.'

Freya appeared a few minutes later. McNab was aware that he had only five minutes to make her acquaintance properly, before she ushered him out the front door. He wondered if it was worth the effort since she was, he feared, out of his league.

'Could we have met in the jazz club in Ashton Lane?' he offered as they wound their way towards the lift.

'You're a jazz fan?' She sounded surprised.

'Sometimes,' he hedged his bets.

'Me too,' she offered.

'The piano player, Sam Haruna. Have you heard him play?'

'No, I haven't. Is he good?'

'Very.' McNab decided to go for it. 'He's on tonight.'

'Really?'

'Maybe I'll see you there,' McNab tried.

'Maybe.'

Well, at least it wasn't a no.

When they reached reception he handed her his card. 'If you think of anything that might help me, however small, give me a call,' he said.

Her face clouded over at that and McNab thought he might have overstepped the mark.

She left him at reception, but with a farewell smile. McNab had the feeling those intelligent eyes could see right through him and they weren't sure they liked what they saw. Still, he had tried.

Once outside the building, he called DS Clark.

'Where are you? The strategy meeting's in fifteen minutes,' she said.

'At the university library looking for Shannon.'

'Well, I suggest you get here, and fast.'

11

Detective Inspector Bill Wilson swivelled the chair round to face the window just to hear it girn – a Scottish term for which he could find no English equivalent, but which described the sound perfectly, while endowing the seat with character.

How many cases had he attempted to solve while sitting in this seat? He didn't dare count. And had he made the world a safer place?

That he could answer. No.

His spell at home with his wife Margaret, during her second bout of cancer treatment, had brought out the philosopher in Bill. Or, put more simply, he'd spent too much time thinking dark thoughts and questioning what the point of his years in the force had been. Whether the time wouldn't have been better spent with his family. So he had hung around at home, trying to make himself useful, until Margaret, ever the pragmatist, had told him to please go back to work, so she could have her old Bill back. And so he had obliged.

And what of his protégé?

Bill had come to the decision that we each have a place in which we do the most good. DS McNab had tried a different place, and it hadn't worked out for him. Yet, in Bill's opinion, Michael Joseph McNab was a bigger and better man than those above him in rank could ever imagine, let alone achieve.

During the debriefing after the *Stonewarrior* case, Bill had been aware that something was being left unsaid. That something had driven a wedge between McNab and Rhona. They had history already, spiky at times, tragic at others, but this was something else, and it bothered and fretted Bill like a sore that would not heal. Secrets, he knew from his job and his personal life, had a cancerous habit of growing bigger.

This morning's strategy meeting, he decided, was likely to be more enlightening regarding the investigative team than the murder they were seeking to solve. An early-morning visit by Rhona had persuaded Bill to add one more player to the game. Professor Magnus Pirie. Solid, reliable, knowledgeable, yet esoteric, he brought a questioning to an investigation that most officers felt uncomfortable with.

In this job, it was always more reassuring to regard life and the humans that inhabited it as purely black and white, with no grey areas. Thus Magnus was, in the words of Gandhi, first ignored, then mocked, then fought against by the front-line troops, before occasionally winning. McNab wouldn't like it, of course, although DS Clark would be relaxed, and Rhona, from her forensic analysis of the crime scene, deemed it necessary, which was good enough for Bill.

He turned from his view of the city and checked his watch.

It was time for the fray.

The room was packed. A murder investigation involved far more people than could be imagined by the general public. They saw only a limited number, the focus on a few faces representing the full team. The superior officer who fronted the investigation on media broadcasts was the one the public grew to recognize, although it wasn't he, or she, who did the groundwork.

Before him were those who would perform the irritatingly tedious jobs, such as watching endless hours of security camera footage, and interviewing the public, with all their prejudices, lack of observation and self-obsession. Attention to detail was everything, however long and mind-numbingly slow that might be. Success was achieved because each police officer on the case did their job properly.

The whole was only as good as its individual parts.

Then there was the digital world that now ran parallel to their own, recording and illuminating it in a way that couldn't have been imagined even five years ago. The information gathered was vast, and complex. All of it had to be sifted through and examined, registered as important or discarded. Added to this was the insatiable demand of the mainstream media, forever hungry and keen to refashion the facts to suit its own agenda.

Surveying the sea of faces, Bill noted the presence of Rhona, Magnus and DS Clark, but as yet no DS McNab. The questioning look he sent Janice brought the response, 'On his way, sir.'

Bill called the assembled company to order and directed their attention to the screen and its collection of photographs. In truth, the images had perturbed Bill in a way he found hard to explain. He had been at many murder scenes. All of them horrific. All had affected him to a greater or lesser degree. Why then was this one particularly disturbing?

He had come to the conclusion it was because Barbie dolls normally evoked a memory of his teenage daughter's innocent childhood, yet here they appeared to symbolize something else entirely – the female of the species, stripped, abused and hanged. And behind that curtain, a real female, treated in the same manner.

What did that say? What did it mean?

If Bill had learned anything from his time on the force it was that to every kill there is meaning. Not one the majority of the human race would recognize as valid, but valid to the perpetrator nonetheless. And the staged nature of the death scene screamed *meaning* at him.

At this point he would have asked McNab to come to the front, since he had been first on the scene, but as McNab hadn't yet put in an appearance, Bill asked Rhona to give her version of events.

She gave a brief résumé of the results of her forensic examination so far, together with the post-mortem findings. She then asked them to study the photographs again and raise any points they thought might be significant.

'The way in which the dolls are arranged?' DS Clark offered. 'The different hair colours together in groups of three?'

Someone else piped up. 'There are three rows of nine dolls.'

'There are,' Rhona confirmed, 'and yes, the arrangement seems precise.'

Bill had spent a great deal of time on the photographs, but he hadn't noticed the pattern of nine, or of three. Once mentioned though, it seemed obvious, as evidenced by the sounds of first surprise, then affirmation from the assembled company.

Bill watched intently as Rhona brought up an enhanced image of the cord used to hang the victim.

'The noose is plaited silk, that is, made up of three

individual strands. If you count you will see that there are nine knots in it, evenly spaced out. What I can also tell you is that the overall length of the cord is nine feet.'

This piece of information brought a gasp from her listeners and then the question that Bill too wanted to ask.

'So what's significant about the number nine to the perpetrator?'

Rhona took a moment to answer. 'I'm not sure it is significant to the perpetrator, but it may be of significance to the victim.' She went on to explain about the forensic evidence found on the cord and the probable role it had played in the sexual act prior to the victim's death. 'Professor Pirie identified the cord as a possible cingulum, which is a ritual cord used in British traditional Wicca, or what is more commonly termed Witchcraft.'

Magnus approached the front in an outbreak of excited chatter.

Now this was news as far as Bill was concerned. He wondered if McNab was party to this development.

Magnus was prone to nervousness at strategy meetings. Bill didn't blame him for that. Front-line officers in general didn't rate criminal profilers. Magnus had had some success in his work with them, but he'd also screwed up, which tended to be what was gossiped about, and remembered.

Bill indicated he wanted silence while Magnus composed himself before speaking.

'I was involved in an extensive study of Witchcraft for an Orkney project some years back and when Dr MacLeod showed me images of the cord, it triggered a memory of a cingulum. The cingulum is used in a variety of rituals and should be nine feet in length with nine knots in it. It should also be red to represent the life blood. When sexual magick is performed, the two participants are bound together round the waist by the cingulum. However, contrary to popular belief, reinforced by the Christian Church, Wicca is not satanistic. The Wiccan Rede in its briefest form says "An' Ye Harm None, Do What Ye Will."'

He continued, 'The Wiccan religion has dual deities in the God and Goddess, often represented by small statues. Unlike in Christianity, in Wicca the male and female are regarded as equals – in fact, the Goddess is often seen as the more powerful and influential of the two.'

Bill intervened at this point. 'In your opinion, did the victim's death have anything to do with Wicca?'

'There are ways it may have,' Magnus said.

'Such as?'

'Three possible scenarios suggest themselves. One, that the sexual partner reacted badly to the idea that he was being used in a spell and killed the victim for that reason. Two, they were both participants in a sexual game which went too far. However, I'm unaware of a ritual using sexual magick where auto-erotic practice is involved. And thirdly, the cingulum may have been used simply because it was available to the perpetrator, and had no significance for him whatsoever.' Magnus ground to a halt, his expression suggesting he was clear on nothing, and had therefore not been much help.

Bill thanked Magnus anyway, and moved on to dealing out jobs, which the team looked relieved about. Working out *who* had killed Leila Hardy was, in their eyes, a better proposition than *why* it had been done.

Once he'd set everyone to work, Bill asked DS Clark to get DS McNab on the phone and find out why the hell he hadn't come to the meeting.

12

McNab tried the doorbell one more time and listened to it echo in what sounded like an empty flat. It seemed that Shannon Jones was neither at work, nor at home.

Why didn't he believe that?

McNab held open the letter box and peered inside. The poor view this afforded was of a small shadowy hallway with three doors leading off, only one of which was closed.

'Shannon,' he called, trying to keep his voice friendly. 'Shannon, it's DS McNab.'

His attempt was greeted by silence.

'Shannon, please open the door. I'd like to speak to you.'

When there was no response to his second plea, McNab tried a different tack.

'I have news on how Leila died.'

Shannon had been very keen to know what had happened to her friend. If she was in there, surely that would bring her to the door, ill or not?

It didn't.

McNab checked his watch. He was now late for the strategy meeting, and he didn't have the decent excuse of a chat with Shannon Jones about her dead pal. He stood for a moment contemplating his choices, which, he decided, were limited. Either he forced entry or he walked away and faced the music back at the station. McNab examined his reason for coming here one more time and found it still valid. He was uneasy about the well-being of Shannon Jones. If he walked now, he would be none the wiser.

McNab pushed the letter box open again, and then he spotted it. A pool of water seeping from under the only shut door in the hallway.

Jesus, what has she done?

McNab put his shoulder to the door. The force he exerted rattled the door in its frame, but that was all.

Fuck's sake.

Pulling out his wallet, he fished out his Costa Coffee card. The tried and trusted method of springing a snib on a door, but only if she hadn't turned a mortice lock as well.

It took no more than a second to slip the card between the door and its frame. Another to find the right combination of angle and force, then the snib clicked free and McNab stepped into the hall. He didn't bother checking the rooms that lay open but made immediately for the third, squelching across a sodden carpet, while praying she hadn't locked herself in.

She hadn't. The door swung back to reveal the real reason Shannon Jones hadn't answered his calls.

This time, there *was* an upturned chair in the room. Tilted against a filled bath, its rear two legs were off the ground. Sitting on it was a naked Shannon, her head and shoulders submerged, tendrils of blonde hair floating in strands on the surface of the water.

Christ, girl. What happened?

McNab reached in and gently lifted her head, already knowing that Shannon Jones was long gone. The pretty face was white and puckered, the lips a mottled blue. The cold eyes that stared up at him seemed to say *Why didn't you come sooner?*

McNab checked the remainder of the flat. The main room, which also housed a small kitchen area, looked undisturbed. Entering the bedroom, he immediately caught a strong scented smell. On the floor at the foot of the bed was a circular green mat. Around its perimeter were four candles, one still fluttering, emitting the fragrance he'd caught on entry.

As McNab watched, the final candle spluttered and went out.

He had no idea what the circle and the candles meant, but instinct told him that Shannon had constructed it as an imagined place of safety. A forlorn hope as evidenced by the scene in the bathroom. McNab felt something akin to despair wash over him. Shannon had been shocked and terrified by her friend's death. That much had been plain at her interview. She'd also been adamant that Leila hadn't taken her own life.

McNab had assumed that Shannon, like him, considered the man Leila had taken home as being instrumental in her death. She'd even blamed herself for not spotting the danger.

But had that been the whole truth?

Shannon had denied all knowledge of the dolls' room, which McNab found hard to believe if they were such good mates. Then she'd blurted out that Leila had been into New Age things, as though that was nothing to do with her.

Looking at the circle and the candles suggested McNab's instinct had been right. Whatever Leila had been involved in, so too had Shannon.

With a heavy heart, McNab pulled out his mobile and dialled the station.

Janice answered almost immediately.

'Where the hell are you?' she began.

McNab interrupted her. 'Can you get a forensic team and pathologist to come to . . .' He gave her the address.

'Who—?' she began.

'Shannon Jones. I found her drowned in the bath.'

'My God.' The shock in her voice was palpable.

'Can you organize a team?' McNab said. 'I'll stay here and wait for them.'

Janice had collected herself. 'Of course. Do you want Dr MacLeod to come?'

McNab didn't answer immediately. Rhona didn't have to do the forensic but then again if it wasn't suicide, and there was a link to Leila's death, Rhona's expertise would be the best option.

'Try her first,' he said.

'Will do.'

McNab rang off. For the first time since he'd been off the drink, he had an almost unbearable craving for it. Had a half-bottle been in his pocket, he wouldn't have hesitated. If he were at home now, the bottle in the kitchen cupboard would have been out and open.

He checked his hands and found they were trembling. What he needed was the buzz of strong coffee to dull the craving, but there was little chance of that until the team arrived. He checked his pockets for any sign of a packet of cigarettes, his other habit, which he'd beaten before but which occasionally raised itself from the grave, trying to steer him into one.

Thankfully there were no remnants of his smoking days

lurking anywhere in his jacket. So McNab chose to do the only compulsive action left to him. He strode up and down in an agitated fashion.

The first cop car arrived twenty minutes later. After Janice brought him briefly up to date on the strategy meeting, McNab handed over the preservation of the crime scene to her, then took himself outside, ostensibly for some fresh air, but really to await the arrival of Dr MacLeod, which occurred ten minutes later.

'What happened?' she said as soon as she stepped out of the van.

'Shannon didn't go in to work the last two days and I couldn't reach her by phone. So I decided to come and find her. That's why I wasn't at the meeting.'

Rhona's expression told him that she could read him like a book. His thoughts, his distress, his horror at what he'd found and what she must now face herself.

'You did the right thing,' she said.

McNab didn't reply.

Rhona pulled on her forensic suit. 'Bill will be here shortly. He says to stay put, he wants to talk to you.'

'There's a coffee shop on the corner. Tell him I'll be there,' McNab said.

As he set off, he prayed that there wouldn't be a pub in the vicinity of the coffee shop, and definitely not one en route. His prayers were thankfully answered.

He stepped into the cafe and quickly ordered two double espressos. Carrying both to an unoccupied table, McNab drank one down and waited for the craving to subside.

When the caffeine hit home, he pushed the empty cup to one side and drew the full one in front of him. He then tried to order his thoughts in advance of DI Wilson's appearance.

It wasn't just the coffee that had driven him here. McNab really didn't want to face the boss while Rhona was in the vicinity. However much they may have appeared to patch things up, there was still an awkwardness between them, and he was pretty sure the boss had spotted it.

Therefore the less he saw of them together, the better.

When DI Wilson arrived minutes later, McNab was struck by how thin and tired he looked. His stint at home should have seen the boss rested, but McNab had gathered from Janice that watching his wife deal with the return of her cancer had eaten away at Bill, so much so that Margaret had ordered him back to work.

The depth of commitment between the boss and his wife was something McNab admired. At times, he thought he wanted something similar for himself, but couldn't see it ever happening. His personal relationships seemed to be motivated, for the most part, by lust. Self-sacrifice just didn't figure anywhere in them.

But if he met the right woman?

I have met the right woman. It's just that the feeling isn't mutual.

Bill acknowledged his sergeant's presence and the two espresso cups in front of him.

'Another?'

'I still have one to drink, sir.'

Bill ordered a filter coffee with cold milk and carried it over to the table.

'Has anyone filled you in on what happened at the strategy meeting?'

'I heard from DS Clark that Professor Pirie knows a lot about Witchcraft,' McNab said drily.

Bill ignored the barbed nature of the reply and continued,

'He had some interesting theories involving the Wiccan religion, which appeared to fit with what Rhona found at the crime scene.'

'There's a suggestion of something similar at Shannon's place,' McNab admitted, describing the mat and candles.

Bill looked thoughtful at that. 'Have you had any luck tracing the man Leila took home with her?'

'We have a decent description and I'm waiting for results from the security cameras.'

'And now another death. Did Shannon Jones say anything to you that suggested she was afraid for her life or that she might be suicidal?'

'She was very shocked and upset about Leila, but was adamant that Leila wouldn't have hanged herself.'

'Which we now believe to be true.' Bill paused. 'We have to pick up the main suspect and soon.'

'We will,' McNab said.

'What about the other guy?'

'The description of him isn't so good. I'm hoping he'll appear on the camera in the back lane. We think he may have left that way.'

'Could they be working as a pair?'

'It's something I've considered.'

'I want to know if Leila was a practising Witch, and if so, who she was practising with. Check with the Tech department. See what they have from the mobile and laptop.' A thought struck him. 'What about a mobile or laptop in Shannon's flat?'

McNab said no. It had been the first thing he'd checked for. 'Maybe the search team will have more luck.'

Bill observed his sergeant.

'Why did you force the door?'

McNab hesitated as though he wasn't sure how to answer that. 'A gut feeling, sir.'

That was good enough for Bill. 'I want you to liaise with Professor Pirie on the Witchcraft angle. He has the knowledge.'

McNab's expression suggested that was the last thing he wanted to do, but he didn't argue, which Bill realized was probably a first.

13

The pathologist had come and gone, required only to certify death.

The dribbling tap had been turned off, but the water still lapped around her feet, transferring any movement Rhona made into tiny waves of energy that crossed the floor tiles to break against the pile of the hall carpet.

The bathroom was small. *Not much bigger than a coffin.*

Rhona had heard about Leila's friend, who had been with her the night she'd died, but hadn't viewed an image of her. The hair floating in tendrils in the water reminded Rhona of a painting of Ophelia. Contrary to popular opinion, drowning wasn't an easy death, unless the victim was comatose to begin with.

The notion that you could enter water, deny your lungs air and not experience pain and terror, was a cruel fallacy. Which was why waterboarding as a means of torture was so widely used and successful.

She had already taken her 'before' photographs, as had the Return To Scene team. Now, they would require taking again, without the water. As the last liquid was pumped out of the bath into a container to be transported to the lab, Rhona took close-ups of the exposed face and upper body, then stepped outside and gave the Return To Scene personnel access. Their 360-degree recordings of before and after would be invaluable.

McNab had departed, due, Rhona surmised, to her presence or a desire for Bill not to engage with them together. A wise move on McNab's part. Rhona was well aware that the tension between them was tangible, despite their mutual agreement to 'let things lie'. Secrets had a habit of revealing themselves, eventually.

And Bill, she knew, was a natural detective.

Still, she reminded herself, *I made the right decision*.

Waiting for R2S to complete their recording, Rhona checked out the other rooms in the flat. A forensic team was already at work, eyes above the masks acknowledging Rhona's presence. The flat was tidy and pretty in an understated way. No room of hanging dolls, no evidence of anything but normality, except in the bedroom.

A circular mat had been laid out at the foot of the bed. Around it, at four locations, stood candles. Rhona's first thought was that Shannon had been meditating recently, soft music and candlelight being a common method of relaxation. Then again, the circular mat might have something to do with the Witchcraft angle.

With that in mind, she gave Magnus a call.

'Describe the bedroom scene to me,' he said.

Rhona did so, including the candles.

'Are they set at the points of the compass?'

Rhona tried to work out where north was via her knowledge of Glasgow landmarks.

'Probably,' she said. 'Any chance you could come and take a look?'

'I have a lecture shortly, so it will have to be after that,' Magnus said.

'Not a problem, I'm likely to be here for some time.'

Rhona rang off and headed back to the bathroom.

Roy Hunter and his colleagues at R2S had worked along-side Rhona on many jobs, including the most recent *Stonewarrior* case. Vastly experienced, particularly in some of the more forensically challenging crime scenes, Rhona always valued Roy's opinion.

'What do you think?'

'Suicide drownings usually involve slit wrists and a warm bath. So I don't buy the chair and submersion,' Roy said. 'Who would hold their own head under water long enough to drown? But, then again, she may have been under the influence of drugs or drink at the time.'

Roy's thoughts mirrored her own. If Shannon had taken her own life, then it was a difficult way to do it. McNab had reported her as very distressed and frightened by her friend's death, so there was no doubt she was in a vulnerable state. The scene in the bedroom only served to emphasize this.

Perhaps Shannon had run a bath to help her relax? The chair she sat on, painted white and made of light wood, looked as though it belonged in the bathroom. Shannon's clothes were in a pile close by on the floor. The bath water, Rhona suspected, had had lavender oil added to it, a bottle of which stood nearby.

All of which suggested Shannon was trying to calm herself.

There had been no evidence of alcohol being consumed and no evidence of drugs on the premises. They would have to wait for toxicology tests to discover if Shannon had ingested any drugs prior to her death, legal or otherwise.

Had Shannon been intent on killing herself, the easiest

way, as Roy suggested, was to ease the passing with drink and drugs and simply allow herself to sink under the water. In this case Shannon was sitting on the chair, which had been turned to face the bath and her head submerged. Either by accident or by force. Shannon wasn't tied to the chair, although she might have been at the time. Rhona checked the wrists first.

The hands were small and slim, the fingers free of jewellery. On initial inspection, there was no obvious bruising on the narrow wrists. Rhona examined the chair for evidence of anything having been tied to the legs or main body and found nothing. Using the magnifying glass, she took a closer look.

The fingernails were bleached white from the water, but there was something caught beneath them. Rhona extracted a fibre and bagged it, then swept below the nails on both hands.

She then examined the neck, finding no evidence of bruising.

The scalp was more of a problem, covered as it was by thick wet hair.

Rhona visualized a hand forcing Shannon's head underwater and where the fingers of that hand might have gripped, and was rewarded by a surface cut on the crown which could have been inflicted by a fingernail.

After sampling the head and all its orifices, Rhona called for some help to tip the chair back. Slim and undoubtedly light in life, Shannon had become heavy and waterlogged in death.

With Roy's help, Rhona set the chair upright and Shannon with it. From this vantage point, it was clear that her knees had been pressing against the side of the bath, perhaps as her head had been held under the water.

Having freed her from her watery grave, Rhona stepped outside to allow Roy to record the scene again. Once that was done, she set about cataloguing the body forensically, every square inch covered, every nook and cranny sampled. If Shannon Jones had been manhandled, evidence of her attacker was on her. It was up to Rhona to find that evidence.

Magnus arrived a couple of hours after she'd called him. He appeared suddenly in the bathroom doorway, immediately recognizable despite the forensic suit, mainly because of his height. His eyes above the mask registered his dismay.

Rhona took a moment to describe the original scene, before they'd emptied the bath and uprighted Shannon.

'Her head and shoulders were underwater while still on the chair?' Magnus said.

'The chair was tipped forward as you can see by the pressure marks on her knees, although it's not certain whether the bruising occurred before or after death.'

'So she drowned?' Magnus said.

'That's what it looks like, although we'll have to wait for the post-mortem to be certain.'

'Forced?'

'Perhaps,' Rhona conceded. 'Again, it's too early to say.'

Magnus nodded. 'Can you show me the circle?'

Rhona led him through to the bedroom.

Magnus studied the mat, bending down to sniff at the candles before asking Rhona whether a cingulum or any other Wiccan artefacts had been found in the flat.

'Only the mat and candles so far,' she told him.

'The mat is a type used to create a magic circle. The

candles are normally placed at the four points of the compass. If your victim was frightened for some reason, it would be natural for her to make a circle and stay inside it until she felt better.' He paused. 'I picked up the scent of lavender in the bathroom. I assume she'd added it to the bath water?' Magnus asked.

'I think so.'

He nodded. 'There was another scent in the bathroom, one I'm not so sure of. It's not present in here. Can we go back?'

Magnus stopped outside the third room. 'What's in there?'

'The sitting room and kitchen.'

Rhona followed Magnus in. The room was small, with the kitchen tucked into a corner. There was a single window overlooking a back court, an L-shaped settee, a coffee table, a small gas fire and a flat-screen TV. There was also a forensic officer dusting for prints. Nothing looked unusual or out of place.

Magnus exited, without speaking, and went back to the bathroom, where he sniffed the soap at the sink, then shook his head.

'Maybe it's the smell of the chemicals I'm using,' Rhona suggested.

Magnus shook his head again. 'No. I can identify them, having met them all before at various times.' He stood for a moment, eyes closed, deep in concentration, breathing in slowly through his nose.

'It could be a man's cologne, it smells astringent. Citrus, spicy.' He shrugged his shoulders in defeat, then hunkered down to look more closely at the victim.

'Was she tied to the chair?'

'Not when she was found.'

103

'But maybe?'

'There were fibres under her nails, but no obvious pressure marks on her wrists.'

'Finding her like that reminds me of a ducking stool,' Magnus said.

'What?'

'In medieval times Witches were primarily disposed of in three ways, as I said before. They were either burned at the stake, hanged or they were drowned by tying to a ducking stool.'

14

The front security camera had a good view of Leila but a rather poorer showing of her male companion. Just as he emerged, a group of smokers had gathered, obscuring the camera's sight of him. From what McNab could make out, Barry's description held. The guy was blond and tall, and looked fit. He was wearing a shirt as described, and jeans. There was even a brief sighting of his watch worn on the left wrist. His face, however, wasn't visible.

McNab asked the officer to rerun the sequence one more time, peering at the screen in his frustration. It was no good, he could be any one of hundreds of fit young males in shirt and jeans on a night out in Glasgow. The best they could do was show it on a news bulletin together with the description, and hope it rang a bell with someone.

The back-door camera proved equally useless. The only thing it picked up was a couple having a shag against a wall, oblivious to the fact they were being recorded. Then again, maybe that's why they'd chosen to do it there. If the second male had definitely left the pub shortly after Leila and his pal, the angle of the camera hadn't recorded him.

Running through the front-door footage again proved just as fruitless. In the time sequence following Leila's departure, dozens of people exited the pub, some to smoke, but plenty heading off elsewhere.

Frustrated, McNab abandoned the video and called the pub again.

His enquiry after Barry brought the response, 'I'll get him for you,' then the sound of the phone being carried elsewhere. Eventually Barry came on the line.

'Yes?'

'It's DS McNab here. We spoke before about Leila Hardy. On the night she died,' McNab added for emphasis.

'Yes?' Barry said, sounding nervous.

'You said the blond guy with Leila looked affluent by his clothes, the Gucci watch and wallet.'

'Yeah, he did.'

'How did he pay for the drinks?'

Silence.

'Did he use cash or a card?'

Pause. 'I can't remember. I served loads of people that night.'

'Try.'

'I honestly can't remember.'

'But you remembered he had an expensive wallet and a fancy watch,' McNab reminded him.

'Because he flashed them at me.'

'Did he also flash a card?'

McNab could almost hear Barry thinking out loud. What should he say? Cash or card? And what would that mean for him?

Eventually, Barry came back with his decision. 'No, I remember now. Cash. He paid cash for the drinks. His wallet was full of it.'

Bastard.

'You're sure of that?'

'Yes.'

'Okay. We'll need a list of all your card transactions that night anyway,' McNab told him.

There was a gasp at the other end of the line, which McNab ignored. 'Someone will pick them up tomorrow.'

McNab rang off, irritated that he hadn't checked the card angle when he'd first spoken to Barry. In his experience people paid by card when out on the town. Carrying wads of cash was becoming a thing of the past. Still, if you didn't want anyone to know what you were up to, cash was the better option. That way you didn't leave a trace of your transactions and their location on your debit or credit card. If Barry had told the truth, then their suspect's card details wouldn't be on that list, but they would have to go through them all anyway.

He headed for the coffee machine in the corridor and topped up his caffeine levels. What he really needed was food, but that would have to wait. Mid afternoon now, he planned to check out the contents of Leila's mobile and laptop before he finally went for something to eat.

McNab didn't like the Tech department, mainly because it made him feel inadequate, and those who did the job seemed very young, thus highlighting both his lack of digital skills and the fact that he was getting old.

The *Stonewarrior* investigation had introduced him to the digital world in some detail, wherein he had met Ollie, who looked as though he should be in the second year of secondary school. Overcoming such prejudices on McNab's part had proved difficult but he had managed it, after a fashion. And he had to admit that Ollie's skills in forensic computing had been extensive and had helped McNab to crack the case.

Entering the digital domain again, McNab sincerely hoped Ollie was still around and that he wouldn't need to forge new allegiances. In that he was lucky.

Ollie greeted him with a grin, his eyes wide behind the round glasses.

'DI McNab, good to see you again.'

'It's detective sergeant now,' McNab reminded him.

Ollie's face fell, his expression moving from pleasure at encountering McNab again, to outright anger.

'You fucking solved the *Stonewarrior* case.'

'You helped,' McNab said.

'So why the fuck did they demote you?'

McNab listed a few of the many actions that had brought him down. 'If I'd been a soldier they would have shot me at dawn.' McNab smiled. 'I put you in the shit too, as I recall.'

'It was well worth it,' Ollie said with relish.

They acknowledged the righteousness of their joint indignation.

'So,' said Ollie, 'how can I help?'

'The laptop and mobile belonging to Leila Hardy. I want to know what's on them.'

'Come this way.'

Ollie led McNab across the room between the various desks, each one a hive of digital activity, then gestured at him to take a seat alongside.

Back in front of a series of screens, McNab screwed up his eyes. How the hell these guys did this for a living he had no idea.

'Just tell me what you found,' he said.

Ollie looked sympathetic. 'Okay, your victim was unusual in that she has *no* social media presence. No Twitter account, no Facebook page. Her email account is the one for the university library and its entries are all to do with work. Basically, she's offline.'

'No personal email?' McNab was stunned. He thought he was the only one in the world not tuned in to the digital revolution. 'What about her mobile?'

Ollie handed McNab a list of contacts. It was short. A dozen at the most, at least half of them relating to university departments.

'That's it?'

Ollie nodded.

'I don't believe it. Even I have more mobile contacts than this.'

'Maybe she had another mobile. Possibly a pay-as-you-go?'

'Well, it wasn't in the flat.'

Ollie shrugged his shoulders. 'Sorry.'

'Her Internet history?'

'Limited, although she did order some stuff recently from Amazon.'

'Such as?'

Ollie pulled up a list on the screen for McNab to look through. The orders were all from the same site.

'It sells New Age stuff mostly,' Ollie said. 'Amulets, crystals, books, etc.'

McNab had to ask. 'Is there anything there related to the Wiccan religion?'

'Probably. Why?' Ollie looked intrigued.

'There's evidence to suggest the victim may have been a practising Witch,' McNab said cautiously.

Ollie looked interested. 'I knew a guy at Edinburgh University who practised Wicca,' he said.

'In Edinburgh?' Witchcraft in Scotland's douce capital city. McNab could hardly believe it.

Ollie seemed unfazed by McNab's reaction as he continued. 'Joe was really into it. Had the altar and all the stuff in his room at the halls of residence. Even performed spells to help us pass our exams and get girls,' Ollie said.

'Did they work?' McNab said sarcastically.

'Passing exams got me here.' Ollie shrugged. 'The love potions weren't so successful.'

'Join the club,' McNab said with feeling.

'Anyway, Joe's coven had a rented room in the Vaults just off the Royal Mile.'

'Are you still in contact with this guy?' McNab said. 'If so, I'd like to talk to him.'

'I can probably locate him.'

'Do that,' McNab said. 'So, how do we find out if our victim was a member of a coven?'

'Mmm. Tricky. Covens don't normally advertise in case they attract nutcases.'

McNab was about to laugh, then realized Ollie was serious.

'You get to join by recommendation. Sometimes the shops that sell the tools and gear you need know the local covens. There's bound to be at least a couple in Glasgow and Edinburgh. I could check for you.'

'Do that.'

Departing the Tech department, McNab made for the incident room, the printouts Ollie had given him clutched in his hand. Someone could make a start on contacting what few email and phone contacts Ollie had retrieved. McNab glanced at his watch. The public appeal to identify the suspect was due to be broadcast shortly, using the description and the security camera footage.

When McNab arrived, all eyes were turned to the TV screen on which DI Wilson was giving a brief résumé of events surrounding the discovery of Leila's body at her flat. An image of the pub appeared, then the CCTV footage of the couple as they exited. Leila was in clear view, her companion not so much. The identikit image of the main suspect followed, based on Shannon's written description in her testimony to DS Clark. It was a reasonable match for Barry's version, although McNab thought the suspect's height, build and general good looks were more likely to provide evidence of sightings, rather than the constructed facial image.

Then followed a request for the two men who had met Leila and her friend to come forward to allow them to be eliminated from the enquiry. No mention was made of Shannon's death, although they wouldn't be able to keep that under wraps for long. The appeal ended with the repeated image of the man they wanted to interview – tall, good-looking, blond, and sporting a Gucci watch with a black leather strap.

Where the hell was that guy?

15

Mark opened the snap pack and gently shook out a line along the black granite kitchen surface.

When he'd bought the flat six months before, the estate agent had waxed lyrical about the excellent kitchen and its incredible view over the park to the distant crags of Arthur's Seat. Mark had never cooked in the kitchen, but the granite surface had been well used, and he'd enjoyed the view on numerous occasions, including tonight, until the latest news bulletin had hit the giant TV screen and spoiled it all for him.

The bottle of cold beer, which he'd also been enjoying, had met its end on the tiled floor as the grainy video of himself exiting the pub with *that girl* had filled the screen. Jumping up, he'd listened open-mouthed to the description of himself and a request for Jeff and him to come forward and help the police with their enquiries.

Like fuck he would.

Then the killer ending with the photo-fit picture, and the mention of his bloody Gucci watch. That had brought the beer climbing back up swifter than it had gone down. He'd made the sink just in time, spewing it out like poison. After that, alcohol just didn't offer what he required for his sanity, hence the hit.

Mark gripped the edge of the sink and waited for the

panic to be replaced by something more pleasurable. Gradually, it was. With a sigh of relief tinged with excitement, he loosened his hold and turned on the cold tap, rinsing away the evidence of his fear. Then he studied the now famous Gucci watch.

The other girl, the blonde, must have noticed it.

Mark removed the offending item and laid it on the surface.

How many people know I have a watch like this? Jeff. Emilie. And all my co-workers at the bank. After all, I've flashed it often enough.

But then again, he reminded himself, the watch wasn't unique. You could buy it at House of Fraser if you were willing to spend a grand and more. So he wouldn't be the only male in Edinburgh wearing one. Or in Glasgow either.

But he had been in that pub on Friday night wearing it. And he had left with that girl, whose name he now knew was Leila Hardy.

The memory of him asking her name came surging back. *You're not here to ask questions,* had been her reply.

Fuck, that had been a turn-on. That and her ordering him to strip.

Snorting the coke, he realized, had made him high and aroused. He thought back to the mad coupling, the crazy cat smothering him, the mix of pain and ecstasy.

One thing's for certain. I didn't kill her.

He was sure of that. Or was he? The flashbacks had become more frequent and more varied. Once or twice, he thought he recalled another man in the room with them, taking part in the action. Doing other things that involved the red cord round her neck.

Could that be true?

Mark pushed the offending watch off the kitchen surface to the floor. Resilient, it bounced a little then lay unhurt, staring back up at him accusingly. He lifted his foot and stamped on it, grinding his heel into its face, hearing the glass shatter, putting all his energy, frustration and fear into its destruction.

If anyone asked, he would say it had been stolen.

He poured himself a large whisky and settled on the couch. He needed to think. Destroying the watch wouldn't be enough to cover his tracks. Emilie knew he'd been in Glasgow on Friday evening. If she saw the CCTV footage, would she recognize him from those images? The thought horrified him.

And what about Jeff? What would he do when he saw the police appeal?

They'd agreed to say nothing about that night, whatever happened. But would Jeff keep his word once he heard the girl was dead? Jeff had more to lose than a girlfriend if it got out that he'd been there that night.

They both had more to lose than a girlfriend.

16

McNab glanced at his mobile, expecting the station, only to find a number he didn't recognize. He let it ring a few more times before finally answering.

'Detective Sergeant McNab,' he offered.

There was a short silence, as though the caller thought they'd dialled a wrong number.

'Hello,' he tried again.

'Sorry, this is Freya Devine from the university library.'

'Hello, Freya. What can I do for you?' McNab tried not to sound too jubilant about the call.

A hesitation. 'I was just wondering if you'd managed to contact Shannon Jones yet.'

Now it was McNab who was hesitating. This was a tricky one.

'Why?' he ventured.

'Grant still hasn't managed to reach her on the phone. I said I could go round and check if she's okay.'

'No, don't do that,' McNab said quickly.

'Why?' Her voice had risen in fear.

McNab made his voice calm. 'I need to speak to you first.'

'Is something wrong?' she said quietly.

McNab ignored the question and asked one of his own. 'Where are you exactly?'

'Outside the library.'

'Walk down to Ashton Lane. I'll meet you there.' McNab rang off before she could question him further.

He knew he was taking a risk. Freya Devine might well decide to go round to Shannon's place anyway and spot the police activity. They wouldn't tell her anything and nor should he, but the fear in her voice had decided him. Freya had said she didn't know Shannon very well, but McNab wasn't so sure that was true.

This way he might find out.

She was standing outside the jazz club, waiting for him.

'What's wrong with Shannon?' she demanded as soon as McNab drew near.

McNab led her to an outside table and motioned her to sit down. She looked as though she might argue, then didn't.

'Do you want something to drink?' he said.

She shook her head.

The waitress appeared and McNab ordered two espressos.

When they were alone again, he said, 'I went to Shannon's flat directly after I left the library. She didn't answer the door, so I forced an entry. I'm sorry to have to tell you that Shannon is dead.'

The shock of what McNab was saying hit her and she swayed a little in the seat. McNab grabbed her arm to steady her.

'I'm sorry. There was no easy way to tell you that.'

She looked at him in horror. 'How?'

He shook his head, indicating he couldn't say.

'Did somebody kill her?' she demanded.

McNab didn't answer.

'My God, somebody killed her,' she said, shaking her head in disbelief.

McNab intervened. 'We won't know exactly how she died until the post-mortem.'

She examined his expression, those intelligent eyes missing nothing.

'Leila, now Shannon. Who's doing this?'

'Why do you think the deaths are connected?' McNab said swiftly.

'Don't you?' she challenged him.

'Why *would* they be connected?' he tried again.

He watched as she collected herself, then carefully chose her words.

'It's all over the news about the man Leila picked up in the bar. Shannon could identify him. Isn't that reason enough?'

It was a possibility, although McNab wasn't sure he bought it. Shannon wasn't the only person who could identify the chief suspect. He changed tack a little.

'It's important that you don't discuss what I've told you with anyone until it's official.'

'When will that be?'

'In the next twenty-four hours.'

At that moment the coffees arrived. McNab immediately drank his down, then eyed hers.

'Have it,' she offered. 'I don't like espresso.'

'Can I buy you a drink instead then?' he said, certain of a rebuff.

She surprised him by considering his offer, then asking if he'd eaten yet.

'No. If you're hungry we could order something here?' he suggested cautiously.

She glanced about at what was now a busy after-work crowd. 'I'd rather go somewhere quieter.'

'I know just the place,' McNab said.

*

Twenty minutes later, they were settled in a quiet corner of a small Italian restaurant he occasionally frequented on Byres Road, their order taken and a bottle of very nice red Italian wine uncorked on the table in front of them.

McNab poured her a glass.

'Aren't you having some?' Freya said.

'Tell me if you like it first,' he said, stalling for time.

She sipped a little and pronounced it very good. McNab, familiar with the vintage, knew it would be. He was just questioning whether he could stop at wine.

Well, it was time to find out.

He poured himself a small amount, then filled their water glasses, internally reminding himself *one glass of wine, one glass of water*.

'Grant said you were a post-grad student in medieval history,' McNab began on what he thought was safe ground.

It wasn't.

'You asked Grant about me?' she said, perturbed.

'A police habit,' he quickly apologized. 'So why medieval history and why Glasgow?'

'You noticed I don't come from here,' she said with a small smile.

'Newcastle?' he guessed.

'Correct.'

'Honorary Scot,' he assured her.

'Everyone says that.' She relaxed a little and took a sip of wine. 'I chose Glasgow because it's home to the Centre for Scottish and Celtic Studies and I have access to the Baillie collection, which is a prize collection of printed medieval and modern sources in Scottish, Irish and English history.'

'That all sounds good,' McNab said, as though he understood the significance of Glasgow University's medieval attributes.

She seemed amused by his expression. 'I chose medieval research because it's like being a detective, although all the cases are cold. Very cold.'

McNab smiled back. 'Now, I understand.'

As the food arrived, McNab allowed himself a mouthful of wine instead of water. After weeks of abstinence, it tasted pretty bloody good. He admonished himself silently and weakened its impact with more water.

They lapsed into silence as they each tackled their plates of spaghetti. McNab felt strangely at ease in Freya's presence, something he wasn't used to experiencing with attractive and desirable women. Wearing a plain blue dress, sporting no make-up or jewellery – he'd noted the lack of a ring in particular – she was, he decided, quite lovely.

And out of my league.

The spaghetti eaten, he offered to refill her glass.

'If you have more, too,' she said. 'Or maybe you're still on duty?'

'No,' he said and poured some for himself.

McNab was feeling better after the food and the wine, and her company, but he still had a job to do.

'May I ask you a question?' he said.

She studied him intently. 'If it will help find the person who did this to Shannon and Leila.'

'It will,' he said. 'Are you a practising Witch?'

The glass, halfway to her mouth, halted abruptly. 'What?' she said in mock amazement.

'Do you practise Wicca?'

'Why do you ask me that?'

'Do you?' he insisted.

She contemplated lying, but by her expression, lying wasn't something she was comfortable doing.

Finally she said, 'Yes,' and met his eye. 'Why?'

'Because both Leila and Shannon also practised Wicca, as I expect you already know.'

She shifted a little in her seat and he waited as she considered another lie. 'I was aware of that, yes.'

'And you didn't think it important to tell me?'

'No. If they were practising Catholics or Buddhists or agnostic, I wouldn't have mentioned that either,' she said defensively. 'Has the fact they practised Wicca something to do with their deaths?'

'There was a room of naked Barbie-type dolls in Leila's flat. Twenty-seven of them hanging from the ceiling.'

Her face, already porcelain in colour, became transparent. McNab watched the blood beat rapidly at her temple, dark blue against the white. He'd surprised and frightened her and he felt sorry for that, but he couldn't give up now.

He told her what had not, as yet, been reported in the media, although it was bound to come out soon.

'Leila was found hanged in that room, just like the dolls, with a red plaited silk cingulum round her neck.'

Her hand flew to her mouth and McNab wondered for a moment whether she might throw up. So did the waiter, who was glancing over at them anxiously.

She stood up.

Realizing she was planning on leaving, McNab said, 'I'm sorry. Please sit down and I'll explain.'

She was fighting herself. McNab also suspected that the possible link between the deaths and Wicca had just hit home, and that connection had spooked her.

'If you think there may be a link between their beliefs and their deaths, I have to know, *if* I'm going to find who killed them,' he emphasized quietly.

Her frightened eyes met his and she sank into the seat again. McNab gave her a few moments to compose herself.

'I won't spring anything else on you,' he promised.

The waiter, sensing the furore had come to an end, approached and offered them dessert. Freya declined, as did McNab, but he did order an espresso.

'Talk to me,' he said when some of the colour had re-appeared in her cheeks.

She gathered herself before she spoke. 'My research involves the practice of Wicca and the occult in medieval times. The university has a substantial collection on the occult called the Ferguson collection. Shannon looked after it. That's how I knew about her involvement with Wicca, although we never discussed it in detail. Leila was more obvious. One staff night out in Ashton Lane, she revealed that she believed in sexual magick.' She glanced at McNab to check if he knew what that was. When he shook his head, she said, 'Spells cast during sexual inter-course are believed to be more potent, because of the energy released during climax. Leila was adamant that this was true.'

'Which is why she made a habit of picking up men for sex?' McNab said.

'Possibly.'

'And the significance of the dolls?'

'That I don't know, although the Goddess is an important deity in Wicca.'

McNab tipped the rest of the wine into their glasses and drank his down, before hitting the coffee.

'I'd like to go home now,' she said.

'Of course.' He waved at the waiter for the bill. 'I'm sorry I frightened you.'

'No, you're not,' she said sharply.

McNab decided there was no point in arguing. He had done his job and by doing it had blown his chances.

Outside, they stood awkwardly for a minute, before McNab said, 'Please call me at any time, if you want to talk about this, or if anything frightens you about it.'

She nodded in an unconvincing manner, then turned and walked away.

With a stab of regret, McNab registered that Freya Devine was unlikely ever to seek him out again.

He retraced his steps to Ashton Lane, entered the first pub he came to, ordered a double whisky and carried it outside.

17

Laid out in three rows of nine, matched by hair colour, they were in the same formation as when she'd first seen them hanging from the ceiling in the murder room.

Except the last one was missing, because Chrissy held it in her left hand and in her right hand was a scalpel.

'Okay?' She looked to Rhona.

Rhona nodded.

Chrissy inserted the tip of the blade between the breasts, then cut a clean line between there and the navel, making an L-shape at top and bottom, a classic incision used in many post-mortems. Laying down the scalpel, Chrissy used forceps to pull back the plastic and reveal the inside.

'There it is,' she said, her eyes glinting in excitement.

Chrissy had spent the afternoon examining the dolls. Dusting for prints, and combing the hair for trace evidence. During the procedure she'd spotted that some of the dolls had an incision between their legs, and suspected this had been done to insert something into the body.

Now she was proved right.

Picking up a pair of tweezers, Chrissy carefully extracted what appeared to be a rolled-up piece of paper from the body of the doll.

The triumphant grin behind the mask was obvious.

With gloved hands, Chrissy carefully unrolled the paper

and laid it flat on the table to reveal an outline sketch of what appeared to be a male figure, including the genitals with the penis dominant and erect. Below the drawing was a set of symbols.

'Well, we know what the drawing represents, but what's that below?' Chrissy said.

Rhona reached for a magnifying glass and took a closer look. 'They look like runes of some sort.' She handed the glass to Chrissy. 'How many dolls have been cut in this way?'

'Nine, including this one.'

'Okay,' Rhona said, 'we'll each take four and check if there's anything inside.'

Twenty minutes later the other eight dolls had had their own post-mortems and their contents removed. All had contained a similar drawing of a man in a state of arousal, but the body shape and height of each male was different. Some had distinguishing marks on them, such as a symbol that might be there to represent a scar. The size of the genitals differed too. All of them had a different set of runes below.

'Are these replicas of the men she had sex with?' Chrissy said.

Rhona was thinking that too. 'It looks like it.'

'Maybe the sex was rubbish so she cast a spell on them,' Chrissy suggested with a laugh.

'Or maybe she had sex with them in order to cast a spell,' Rhona suggested, remembering what Magnus had said about sex magick. Rhona glanced at her watch. 'You head off. It's been a long day.'

'My mum's got wee Michael for the night. Fancy a drink?'

'What about Sam?'

'He's playing tonight, so I'm headed to the club.'

Rhona contemplated what visiting the jazz club might mean in terms of facing Sean and decided to delay her decision.

'I want to photograph the drawings and email them to Magnus first. Can I catch you up?'

Chrissy threw her a suspicious look. 'How long will you be exactly?'

'Half an hour,' Rhona promised.

Once Chrissy had gone, Rhona set about photographing the nine sketches and transferring the images to her laptop. They had made some progress since the morning strategy meeting. While Chrissy had concentrated on the dolls, Rhona had examined the cingulum in more detail. Unplaited and spread out on a lab table, shaking the silk had resulted in two hairs from the strands. A light brushing had brought forth flakes of skin. If, as it appeared, the cingulum had been used in a number of sexual encounters, then other partners may have left trace evidence of themselves behind, depending how often it had been washed.

The attempt at making the drawings particular to different shapes and sizes of men did seem to indicate they were replicas of real people. Would Leila's final partner feature among them?

She prepared an email for Bill, copy to Magnus, describing what Chrissy had found, then attached the images. Just before she sent it, she considered adding McNab's name to the recipients, then decided she would leave that up to Bill.

The more distance she kept between herself and McNab, the better.

As she logged her results and tidied up, Rhona contemplated heading for home. Chrissy would no doubt call when she didn't appear at the jazz club, but she would have her excuse ready. The post-mortem on Shannon Jones was scheduled for tomorrow morning, and it had been a long day. Whatever the excuse, Chrissy was smart enough to know the real reason for Rhona's non-appearance.

Not for the first time did Rhona regret inviting Sean back into her bed. Not because she hadn't enjoyed the experience, but because she'd enjoyed it too much. It would be easy to slide back into that relationship, but only if she forgot how it had played out the last time. Still, she should be able to go for a drink with Chrissy without agonizing over it. With that thought in mind, she turned her steps towards the jazz club.

The night was fine with a clear late-summer sky. The inhabitants of the West End were out in force, taking advantage of the pleasant weather. The outside tables in Ashton Lane were packed, the doors and windows of the various eateries and pubs standing wide open.

As Rhona made her way through the throng she spotted a figure she recognized. He sat alone, apparently deep in thought. In front of him was a glass of amber liquid that she suspected was whisky. Rhona watched as he raised the glass to his lips, then lowered it again untasted.

As she tried to make up her mind what to do, if anything, McNab glanced up and spotted her. Their eyes met for a moment, before he nodded briefly and turned away. There was something in his manner that troubled Rhona enough to make her approach.

McNab acknowledged her arrival with an enquiring look.

'Dr MacLeod. What can I do for you?'

'You can buy me a drink,' Rhona said. 'A white wine, please.'

A ghost of a smile passed his lips. 'My pleasure.'

When he'd disappeared inside, Rhona checked out what was in his glass and found it was whisky, although she suspected he'd drunk none of it, yet.

McNab appeared minutes later with a bowl of peanuts and a glass of white wine.

'I thought you might not have eaten yet.'

'I haven't,' Rhona said gratefully.

He watched as she sampled both the wine and the nuts, but made no attempt to take a drink himself. Rhona wondered how long he had been sitting there and whether this was his first drink. She realized she had little idea how to deal with this version of McNab. Their relationship before *Stonewarrior* had consisted of flashes of insight, barbed comments and occasional sexual congress. This silent, non-confrontational McNab bothered her. When he made no attempt to engage her in conversation, Rhona decided to open the proceedings.

'When Chrissy examined the dolls, we found nine of them had small sketches hidden inside.'

That caught his attention. 'Sketches of what?'

Rhona described the drawings. 'I sent image files to Bill and Magnus.'

'And me?'

She hesitated. 'I thought Bill would pass them on.'

That didn't please him and she saw a flash of the old McNab in the look he gave her.

'Fuck you, Dr MacLeod,' he said quietly.

She didn't react, because she probably deserved his anger. 'I sent them to Magnus because I thought he might be able to interpret the runes.' Which was true, but sounded like an excuse.

'And I wouldn't?' McNab gave a little snort of derision.

'I'm sorry,' she said.

'So am I.' McNab lifted the glass and drained it dry.

Rhona watched him walk away, hoping it wasn't her lack of faith in him that had broken his resolve.

McNab had done exactly what he'd vowed not to do, and it had felt good, which was why he'd left immediately after. Had he hung around he would have had another, and another. Rhona had done him a favour dissing him like that, although his anger at her failure to include him in the latest discovery had been real enough.

Christ, she could really get under his skin.

Emerging on Byres Road again, he stopped to make a call.

Magnus answered on the third ring.

'McNab here. Are you at home?'

'Yes,' Magnus said, sounding guarded.

'I'd like to come over, if that's okay? I need to talk to you about Witchcraft.'

18

The feeling of nausea that had hit in the restaurant swept over her again. Freya stopped for a moment and, leaning against a nearby garden wall, fought to quell the fear that was causing it. Focusing on the stone, still warm from the day's sunshine, she watched as a spider extended its web from an overhanging clematis, instantly trapping one of the tiny insects that occupied the evening air.

She grabbed the plant, tearing the cobweb, its sticky tendrils now clinging to her hand instead of the foliage, but the fly was already dead.

Just like Shannon.

Breathing deeply, she contemplated turning back. Seeking out the detective again. Revealing her innermost thoughts.

But did they make any sense?

Or was she just in shock at the death of a friend? Even though neither Shannon nor Leila were really friends. They had just shared an interest in Wicca.

And he thinks that's why they were killed.

Collecting herself, she walked on, heading back towards the university. The library would still be open, but that wasn't where she was going. On the crown of the hill, she turned right, entering the main gates.

The last time she and Shannon had spoken, Shannon had mentioned she had access to the room that had originally housed the famous Ferguson collection. Shannon seemed excited by this, but hadn't said exactly why.

One of the reasons Freya had chosen Glasgow for her PhD had been the Ferguson collection, something she'd mentioned to the policeman. John Ferguson, former Regis Professor of Chemistry at the university, had amassed 7,500 volumes, including 670 books on the history of Witchcraft, the subject of her own thesis. Now housed in the main library, its original home had been in the main Gothic building.

Once inside the deserted quadrangle, Freya made for the staircase to the tower and climbed to the second level. She'd been up here only once before, as a pilgrimage more than anything. Her initial interest in both this area of study and the collection had been sparked by a lecture she'd attended by Emeritus Professor of Astronomy Archie Roy.

He hadn't visited Newcastle University to talk about celestial bodies, but to discuss his other interest – psychical research. Both funny and entertaining, he'd told the sceptical audience of science students how, as a young lecturer in physics at Glasgow, he'd inadvertently visited this part of the old building only to discover a library he never knew existed. Curious, he'd entered and found numerous tomes on the occult, and realized he recognized some of the authors as eminent scientists. He reasoned that if these men wrote books on the subject, then it must be worth investigating. Freya had immediately felt the same way.

She stood for a moment on the landing, getting her bearings, then made for the double doors midway along. There was no sign on the wall or the doors to tell her she was in the right place, but memory told her she was.

The outer room was being refurbished, which was why Shannon had been called to check it out before workmen stripped out the original bookcases. Piles of old shelves sat in the centre of the room and dust danced in the late sunlight that streamed through the Gothic-shaped windows.

The door in the back wall was the one she sought. Crossing to it, Freya tried the handle, establishing it was locked. She felt in her pocket for the set of keys she'd taken earlier from Shannon's desk, and slipped the larger of the two into the lock.

With a satisfying clunk it turned. Freya pushed open the door and stepped inside.

19

Rhona took a breath, then let her body sink. Relaxing her muscles sent her arms floating of their own accord, her breasts swaying gently with the water. She thought of her pregnancy, almost two decades before. How she'd loved lying in a warm bath, the mound that was her unborn son a small island in the water. Almost twenty years ago.

I was a child, who bore a child and gave it away, to be raised by strangers.

As her brain repeated the mantra she periodically rebuked herself with, her muscles began tensing again. Rhona breathed in and this time dipped her head below the water. Despite her efforts, small bubbles of air immediately escaped through her mouth and nose.

How long before I breathe in water? Not long and even less if I panic.

She was counting now. Counting down the seconds before she would have to give up and rise to the surface. The water enveloped her and she had the sensation of being pulled deeper, reminding her of an incident when she was a child. Paddling at the edge of a loch, her feet had gone from under her and she'd dropped like a stone into the freezing water. The shock had made her gasp and she'd breathed in water. It might have been over in seconds had her father not pulled her out unceremoniously by the hair.

'Rhona?' The voice floated towards her from what seemed like an immense distance.

She opened her eyes just as a hand reached in and yanked her to the surface.

'Christ, Rhona, what the hell are you doing?'

She finally opened her mouth and sucked in air, with all the desperation of a smoker taking a nicotine hit.

Sean's expression was so furious, Rhona almost laughed.

'A scientific experiment,' she said.

'Like fuck it was.'

He hauled her upright.

'Here.' He thrust a towel at her. 'You're freezing. How long have you been in there?'

Rhona ignored the proffered towel, stepped out of the bath and took her robe from behind the door. 'A while. I was thinking about drowning.'

'What?'

'About the science of drowning. Anyway, how did you get in?'

'I still have keys, remember?' He flourished them at her.

Rhona tied her robe, suddenly conscious of her nakedness beneath, and headed for the kitchen, Sean following.

'Chrissy said you were coming to the jazz club.'

'I decided on a bath and an early night.'

'So you weren't avoiding me?'

'No,' she lied.

He didn't look convinced. 'Have you eaten?'

'Not yet.'

He opened the fridge door and took a look inside. 'I could make us an omelette?'

'I'm having a takeaway.'

'What did you order? Chinese or pizza?'

By the sceptical look on his face, it was time for the truth. 'I haven't ordered, yet.'

Sean extracted the eggs and some Edam cheese she'd bought days ago and started breaking the eggs into a bowl.

'I brought chilled white wine. A nice Italian. Two bottles.'

'I'll get dressed,' Rhona said.

'Don't bother. Relax. Pour the wine.' He gestured to a bag. 'There's olives and bread.'

She poured them both a glass, put the olives in a bowl and cut up the bread. Already the barriers were breaking down. This is what they did well. Eating, drinking and talking, although the talking usually led to sex.

'How's McNab doing?' Sean said as he whisked the eggs.

'Okay,' Rhona conceded.

'He's a one-off. Like you. A free spirit. That's why he's good at what he does.'

Rhona struggled to respond to that. 'He was demoted,' she reminded Sean.

'Who the fuck cares? McNab will never fit the mould, but he understands how people tick. Good or bad.'

It was a fair assessment. 'I thought you didn't like him?' she said.

'You don't know men, although you think you do.' Sean flipped an omelette onto a plate and handed it to her. 'I like him.'

They ate together in silence. It always amazed Rhona that Sean could conjure a meal from nothing and make it taste good. It was a skill she didn't possess. She also killed plants despite strenuous attempts to keep them alive. Why was that? Did she possess a life force that destroyed? Both plants and food, and men?

Sean, on the other hand, was a creator. Of both music

and food. She merely grazed on the fallout of life. The good and the bad. But mostly the bad. Analysing and reporting it. Not a pretty thought.

Christ, she even studied drowning while in the bath.

'Music?' he suggested when she'd cleared her plate.

'How's the new singer?' she countered, suddenly remembering the woman in his office who had looked less than impressed by her arrival.

'Good, although she's only here for a month,' Sean said as he stacked the dishes in the dishwasher.

'Why's that?'

'Her boyfriend's a musician. When he tours, she goes with him.'

Sean's mention of touring made her think of Leila's brother.

'Have you heard of a band called the Spikes?'

Sean looked surprised at the question. 'Yes, why?'

'The police are trying to get in touch with a band member, Daniel Hardy. He's the dead girl's brother. They think he's touring in Germany.'

Sean shook his head. 'No. He's in Glasgow. I saw him a couple of days ago.'

'Are you sure?' Rhona said, surprised.

'Pretty sure.'

'If he's here, he must know about his sister. It's been all over the news. Why didn't he contact the police?'

Sean looked thoughtful. 'Maybe he has and McNab hasn't mentioned it yet.'

It was possible, but unlikely. 'I think I should tell him.' Rhona rose and went in search of her mobile. Contacting McNab was an ideal way of terminating the cosy wine-drinking session in the sitting room before it progressed to other things. McNab's phone rang out a couple of times then went to voicemail. Rhona left a message relating Sean's sighting of Daniel Hardy, then rang off.

As she made her way back to the sitting room, she met Sean in the hall.

'I'm heading back to the club, if that's okay?'

She covered her surprise. 'Of course. Thanks for the meal.'

'My pleasure.'

In that moment, Rhona wished he wasn't going. This was always the way of it. If she felt Sean was manipulating her, she rejected him. If he appeared to reject her, she wanted him.

Sean dropped his set of keys on the hall table.

'You don't have to . . .' she began.

'Yes, I do.' He smiled. 'Call me.'

Rhona stood at the open door, listening to Sean's footsteps descend the stairs. Well, she'd got what she wanted. So why didn't it feel good?

20

On his arrival, Magnus had welcomed him in with no sign of animosity. That in itself had irritated McNab because Magnus's magnanimity had always been a sore point. Then, of course, Magnus had offered him a whisky, a rather good Highland Park. The taste of the earlier whisky still in his mouth, McNab had had to strive hard to turn down the offer. He was aware that his curt refusal had appeared to be more like bad grace than abstinence, but again Magnus had seemed unperturbed as he set up the coffee machine to produce McNab's requested caffeine hit.

They were now seated at the table by the open French windows, with a view of the flowing river below and the compelling Glasgow skyline above. Magnus was nursing a whisky, McNab a mug of strong coffee. Before them the big book on Witchcraft lay open, wherein McNab had read the selected passages with a mixture of interest and outright disbelief. Now they were looking through the photographs on the laptop screen. The ones Rhona had sent Magnus and omitted to send to McNab.

From the moment he had set eyes on them, McNab had loathed those dolls.

A psycho who hangs a woman from a hook, probably for sexual pleasure, was something he understood and could deal with. He didn't want the dolls to play a role in the story of her death. But it seemed they might.

He marshalled himself to ask the necessary question. 'Why would the victim place drawings inside the dolls?'

'I don't know for certain,' Magnus said. 'I'm assuming it was something to do with casting a spell.'

McNab didn't like the word 'spell' either, but he couldn't ignore it.

'A *spell* to do what?'

Magnus shrugged. 'Again, I have no idea.'

Fuck this, McNab thought, but didn't say out loud. Instead, he tried a different angle. 'What are spells used for in general?'

'Anything you desire. The Wicca code suggests you can do what you like, provided it harms no one.'

God, he would like a whisky, and that would harm no one, except of course himself. McNab held out his mug. 'More coffee?'

As Magnus went to get a refill, McNab eyed the whisky bottle.

If he added some to his coffee, did that count as drinking?

When the mug reappeared, McNab drew his eyes from the whisky and focused on the drawings on the screen.

'Okay. We know whether these guys were short or tall, well hung or not. What we need are names.'

Magnus surprised him by saying, 'I think we may have them, or at least a first name.' He indicated the symbols below the first drawing. 'These look like runes from the Seax-Wica alphabet, which is popular in occult writing.' He flipped through the Witchcraft book. 'Here are the runes and their alphabet equivalent.'

'If we exchange each rune below the first drawing with its alphabet equivalent, this is what we get.' He passed McNab

A B C D E F G H I,J K L M

N O,Q P R S T U V W X Y Z

NG GH EA AE   OE TH

a sheet of printed paper with the symbols above and the letters he recognized below.

'Are these their real names?' McNab said.

'There's no way of knowing. True Wiccan names are chosen personally by each member of the circle. They usually relate to plants, the elements, like wind, rain or fire, animals such as raven or wolf, Gods or Goddesses like Freya, or special gifts that someone might have. This list doesn't contain any names like that.'

'They could also have fed her a false name,' McNab said.

'True, but I think Leila Hardy was intelligent enough to discover their real names if that was the case.'

McNab studied the list.

One name jumped out at him and that was Barry. Could it be the barman, Barry Fraser? If so he had a scar which, by its position, might be the result of an appendectomy. According to the sketch, the barman also had a package big enough to incite male envy.

If Barry Fraser was the one named, what were the chances that the last man seen with Leila before she died was also there? McNab studied the drawings again. There were three tall figures which could match the suggested build of their suspect, but there was no indication as to their age or hair colour, so not enough to pinpoint the tall blond man that Leila had left the pub with.

McNab cautiously reviewed his earlier anger. Rhona had been right to send the drawings to Magnus. He allowed himself a brief grudging acceptance of the man observing him from across the table.

'Thanks, this has been helpful and informative,' McNab managed.

Magnus appeared momentarily discomfited by the unexpected approbation, then added, 'There's one thing more I should mention, although I'm not sure if it's significant.'

'What's that?'

Magnus drew the book forward and indicated the passage that followed the table of runes. *'To know a person's name is to have a hold over them. For to know the name is to be able to conjure with it,'* he quoted.

A shiver ran up McNab's spine, something that didn't happen often and which he didn't like.

'You think that's why the drawings are named? Leila conjured up something *with* these men?'

'Or *against* them,' Magnus said.

'You're suggesting she made sexual magick with them in order to curse them?'

McNab had been cursed by a variety of women, most, if not all of them – including Rhona – with justification. But there was a difference between being cursed at and being cursed. Even he could appreciate that.

'A revenge killing?' he offered.

'It's a possibility.'

There were too many possibilities and now too many possible suspects.

Identifying the nine men of the apocalypse would be difficult, if not impossible, especially with the death of Shannon Jones. McNab's thoughts moved to Freya. Might she recognize any of the descriptions contained in the dolls? Or maybe their best bet was the brother, the elusive Daniel Hardy.

'I should get going,' McNab said. 'Thanks for your help.'

'I'll write a report on the drawings and send you and DI Wilson a copy.'

'And Rhona.'

'And Rhona.' Magnus seemed pleased at being reminded.

Once back at street level, McNab checked his mobile messages and found one from Rhona regarding Daniel Hardy, which made him immediately call the incident room. He was surprised to find Janice still on duty.

'DS Clark, have you no home to go to?'

'I could say the same about you.'

'Okay, we're both sad bastards. I got a call from Rhona. She says Daniel Hardy's been seen in Glasgow. Has he contacted the station?'

'Not that I'm aware of.'

'Have we got an address for him?'

'Yes. Give me a minute and I'll get it.'

Janice came back on the line and quoted an address.

'Want me to come with you?' She sounded almost keen.

'No need. Go and have a drink with the team. I'll see you in the morning.'

McNab rang off and checked his watch. It was after ten now. If Daniel Hardy was set on avoiding the police, he was unlikely to hang around at home waiting for them to call. But then again, he wouldn't be expecting an unwelcome visitor at this time.

The address for Daniel Hardy was a flat in the East End, on the High Street, not far from the location of the first investigation Professor Magnus Pirie had been involved in. The East End had seen a makeover since then, the Great Eastern men's hostel refurbished, the nearby wasteland where they'd searched for bodies transformed by the erection of brightly coloured blocks of flats. Somewhere below ground the Molendinar burn still ran through its brick-built caverns, taking Glasgow's fresh water run-off from Hogganfield Loch down to the River Clyde. Thinking about what had happened in those caverns didn't bring back good memories for McNab, of Magnus, Rhona or himself.

He parked the car near the cathedral precinct and walked down the hill. The refurbishment hadn't quite reached this section of the High Street, although one or two coffee shops had opened since last he'd been here. McNab was never sure if he welcomed the infiltration of old Glasgow by the latte brigade, yet the place did look better for their arrival and suggested that at least some of the locals now had money to spend on fancy coffees.

None of the coffee shops were open at this late hour. Neither did he encounter a pub, which was a blessing in his current state of mind. He might have missed the shop, intent as he was in following the street numbers to his chosen destination. Ollie had said he would check for covens via local magick shops. McNab realized he should have recalled this one, which had been here on the High Street as far back as he could remember, although he'd always assumed it was simply selling New Age rubbish, left over from the hippy era.

Now he saw it was much more than just joss sticks and hookah pipes. The poster in the window advertised a visit by a well-known Wiccan warlock and a promise of all things required for magick inside. The proximity of the shop to the brother's flat seemed noteworthy.

One puzzling aspect of Leila's flat, apart from the dolls and the cingulum, was the singular lack of evidence that Leila had worshipped there. According to Magnus there should have been an altar complete with candles, an incense burner, various dishes and a goblet, together with figures to represent the female and male deities.

McNab noted that the window display offered a selection of such items, the Goddess being available as a picture or a statue, both of which were nakedly beautiful, with long flowing hair and voluptuous bodies.

McNab crossed the road and a couple of blocks further down found the number he was looking for. There were no names on the various entry-phone buttons, just flat numbers, which hadn't been included with the address. McNab chose a button at random and pressed it. When there was no answer, he tried another. This time he was lucky and a male voice answered.

'Daniel Hardy?' he tried.

'Wrong flat, mate.'

'Can you let me in, then?'

'Why should I?'

'Because I'm the police,' McNab said sharply.

The lock clicked free. On the way up the stairs, McNab met his interrogator at an open door. It was a man in his sixties. McNab flashed his ID at him. 'Which door?'

'Top landing on the left.'

McNab continued up the stairs, aware of the guy's eyes following him. Reaching the door in question, he registered that the nameplate wasn't Hardy but Carter. McNab rapped on the door. It took two more raps for someone to finally answer.

The door was pulled open only to the length of a thick metal chain, thus obscuring McNab's view of a frightened female face. McNab showed his ID.

'Detective Sergeant McNab. Is Daniel Hardy at home?'

By her expression she would rather he'd declared himself a mad axe murderer than a policeman.

'No,' she finally said.

'May I speak to you then?'

'What about?'

'His sister.'

Through the crack in the door he watched the pale face grow paler.

'I don't know anything about his sister.'

'I'd still like to talk to you,' McNab said, making it sound more like an order than a request.

He was rewarded by the chain being removed and the door opened. His gatekeeper was a little over five feet, with cropped bright pink hair, black rimmed eyes and a nose ring. She wore a T-shirt with the word 'Spikes' on it, which suggested she was a fan, if not a girlfriend.

McNab softened his look. 'May I come in?' he said, aware he sounded a little like a vampire requesting entry.

When she eventually nodded, McNab stepped over the threshold into a small hall with a washing line strung along one wall, on which hung a variety of garments including boxer shorts.

'Is there somewhere we can talk?'

Her eyes flitted about, unsure. She glanced at a couple of doors, dismissing them, while McNab tried to establish if there was anyone else in the flat with her. A block which housed three flats on each landing wouldn't be spacious. He decided two bedrooms at the most, or maybe only one, with the sitting room made into another. That would leave the kitchen as the only communal room.

Eventually she led him to a door, beyond which was the kitchen. In here was a table and two chairs, with a window that looked out on a small concreted back court. It was tidier than his own place, despite his increased attempts at house-keeping. She took a seat at the table and McNab joined her there.

'When will Danny be back?'

'I don't know.'

'Is he playing somewhere tonight?'

'I don't know,' she repeated.

'Yet you're a fan?' McNab gestured to the T-shirt.

She immediately folded her arms over the offending advertisement.

'What's your name?'

She'd been preparing for another question about Danny and was openly disarmed by this one.

'Maggie Carter.'

'May I ask if you and Danny are an item?'

'We just flat-share.'

McNab wasn't sure he believed her, but let it go anyway.

'We've been trying to contact Danny because of the death of his sister, which has been widely reported on the news. It's important we speak to him.'

His words seemed to shatter her defences.

'He doesn't want to. I told him to, but he won't.' She sounded and looked really upset by this.

'When did Danny get back from Germany?'

She studied the table. 'He didn't go on the tour.'

'Danny's been here in Glasgow all the time?'

She nodded.

McNab said a silent curse at the public in general, and Danny Hardy in particular, for pissing the police about. He pushed his card across the table.

'Tell Danny if he isn't in touch within the next twenty-four hours, I'll issue a warrant for his arrest.'

The alarm that caused suggested she would do her best, which is all he could ask.

Outside now, McNab contemplated his next port of call, which should be a further chat with Barry Fraser. If he was swift, he might just catch him before the pub shut. Then again, he would be visiting a pub, with a wide range of excellent whiskies on offer – a tempting thought.

21

The night was still young, Mark decided, as he stood glassy-eyed in front of the mirror. Robotically checking his watch, he found an empty wrist.

Fuck. He would have to stop doing that.

But, then again, it was a natural reaction in someone who'd recently had an expensive watch stolen. Emilie had been sympathetic and urged him to report it and make an insurance claim. He'd said he would, but hadn't, obviously. The last thing he wanted was to make his presence in Glasgow on that night known to the police with the added extra that he'd been wearing a Gucci watch with a black leather strap.

Mark wiped his nose of any excess coke and rubbed his finger along his gums.

Three days now and no one had linked him to those images on CCTV. No one at work or Emilie or even Jeff had mentioned the footage. The silence from Jeff's end had surprised Mark. He'd contemplated calling him, but had decided against it. If Jeff had viewed the police appeal, it seemed he'd decided to keep well clear of involvement. A wise move on both their parts.

Especially since it involved murder.

Thinking the word immediately replayed the image of that room and the curtain of clicking swaying dolls. Mark tried desperately to halt the rerun before it reached the view of what lay beyond those dolls, and failed. There she was. The naked body with its pink-tipped breasts, the auburn mound between the long slim legs. As his eyes rose to the cord round her neck, he felt himself harden.

Why did that happen? Was it because I killed her?

His stomach churned as the numerous vodka shots he'd swallowed threatened to resurface. No way could he do that to a woman. But if he had been out of his head? He'd watched plenty of porn, some of it rough, but that wasn't unusual among his circle of mates, including Jeff. It didn't mean he actually wanted to hurt anyone. And, Mark reminded himself, she had been the one to order him about, not the other way round. She had been the one to tie them together. Recalling that aspect of the encounter did nothing to soften his prick. In fact, it made it harder.

Fuck it. He would have to leave the Gents soon or his absence would be noted.

Mark set about imagining his father's face if he ever found out. The coke would be bad enough. HIGH COURT JUDGE'S SON CAUGHT SNORTING COKE would make a great headline. But hey, HIGH COURT JUDGE'S SON AS MURDER SUSPECT was so much better. Imagining the second headline had the required effect on his erection.

Mark washed his hands, dried them and headed out.

As he climbed the stairs to the main bar, the coke began to lighten his mood. It would be okay, he assured himself. He was sorry about the girl, but it had had nothing to do with him, and if it emerged that he'd been with her that night, a lot of people would be hurt. No, devastated. Emilie for one. His father, for obvious reasons. His mother, who he definitely didn't want upset, not in her present condition.

He had no choice, really.

As Mark weaved his way through the crowd towards his colleagues, a figure suddenly stepped out in front of him.

'What the fuck are you doing here, mate?' Mark said, his stomach dropping to his feet.

'Don't fucking *mate* me, you bastard,' Jeff blazed back at him.

'Keep it down,' Mark hissed as a couple of heads turned in their direction.

'Whatever happens, we were never in that pub?' Jeff sneered. 'Whatever happens?'

'Let's go outside,' Mark said. 'And talk.'

Jeff lifted the shot in front of him on the bar and downed it. Mark wondered how many had gone the same way. Jeff could drink him under the table, and he looked pissed as well as mad. A volatile combination. Jeff was known for his bad temper, when provoked. Mark had rescued him from a number of angry Glasgow encounters where Jeff had taken offence for some throwaway comment. But tonight he was the target of Jeff's anger.

He led Jeff past the tables out to the centre of the paved Grassmarket, where they served lunches under the trees. A cool wind from the Forth was rattling the leaves, reminding them that autumn was on its way. Mark shivered as he tried to marshal his thoughts. How much was he planning to tell Jeff? How much was it safe to tell him? Maybe a lie would be better? Whatever he said must convince Jeff to keep quiet. If neither of them came forward, the police had nothing more than that crappy video, and that would take them nowhere.

Jeff was glaring at him, his fists clenched by his side. 'What the fuck have you done?' he said.

'Nothing,' Mark said. 'Nothing,' he repeated.

'That girl's dead.'

'I know.'

'*You* were the last one to see her alive.'

'No, I wasn't.'

'You went back with her. You're on CCTV.'

'I didn't go back to the flat. She blew me off.'

'What?' Jeff looked incredulous.

'She said it was a joke to see if I'd fall for it.' Rising to the lie, Mark rushed on. 'You saw the look she gave her mate. I think they had a bet on, like we do sometimes.'

'You didn't fuck her?' Jeff said.

'No way. She blew me off,' he repeated.

Mark watched as the lie took root.

'Why didn't you come back then?' Jeff said suspiciously.

''Cos you looked as if you might make it. You were getting on much better than me. Remember?'

Jeff did remember.

'And you did get it, didn't you?' Mark reminded him.

Jeff nodded.

Mark clapped him on the back. 'I didn't want to fuck up your fun.'

Jeff eyed him. 'So what do we do now?'

'Keep schtum, as agreed.' Mark warmed to his argument. 'Someone will have seen her after she left me and tell the police. They have no way of finding us. The video's crap.'

'What about the other girl?' Jeff said.

Fear leapt in Mark's chest. 'You're not in contact with her?'

'No way.'

'Good. So, we lie low. And say nothing. Agreed?'

Jeff slowly nodded.

'Let's go back to my place. Have a drink together. The booze here is way overpriced,' he added, knowing that Edinburgh prices were a favourite gripe of Jeff's.

He watched Jeff agree, and was relieved. He would get him to stay over. Make sure everything was still okay in the morning. Besides, it was better if they weren't seen together by his colleagues. Just in case. He would make an excuse tomorrow about his disappearance. Tell them Emilie called, keen for sex.

Mark congratulated himself as he led a now docile Jeff in the direction of his flat. He'd been fucking brilliant back there. Defused the situation and convinced Jeff that he'd never been in the dead girl's flat.

It would all blow over. They would find the guy that did it, because it definitely hadn't been him.

22

As he approached his front door, a figure stepped out of the shadows. McNab, immediately on alert, felt instinctively for a gun he didn't possess, a result of undercover work he'd rather forget.

'It's only me,' Freya said apologetically as she entered the light.

To say he was surprised to see her there was an understatement. He'd given her his card with a mobile number and the station number. He had definitely not mentioned where he lived.

'How did you find out my address?'

She gave him a disarming smile. 'My job is to find out things about people who lived centuries ago. Finding you was less difficult. Besides, you mentioned where you ordered your pizza from.' She pointed across the street. 'After that it was easy.'

McNab was impressed. 'You haven't any relatives in the Italian Mafia?' he said.

'I'm from Newcastle, remember?'

He met her smile. 'Only a little less scary.'

'Can I talk to you in private?' she said quietly.

'Want to come inside?'

'Please.'

Opening the door, McNab said a silent thank you for the

fact that the place didn't smell of stale food and whisky – a definite upside to his new-found sobriety.

Freya glanced about. 'You live alone?'

'Always,' McNab said firmly, then regretted it.

When she came back with, 'Me too,' and an understanding look, something shifted inside him.

God, he was on dangerous ground.

'Fancy some coffee?'

'That would be great. Black, please.'

'Take a seat,' he said as he spooned fresh coffee into the filter.

McNab heard her settle behind him and imagined her there on his sofa, wishing the circumstances were different. Memories of Iona, his last attempt at a relationship, resurfaced. Admittedly, Iona had been about sex. Only sex. Most of their sex had been fuelled by whisky and in her case coke. Something he'd chosen not to notice at the time, preferring to believe the big pupils were all about her excitement at being screwed by him.

As the boiling water filtered through the coffee grains, McNab fetched two mugs from the cupboard, keeping his eyes averted from the whisky bottle that stood alongside. He hadn't avoided The Pot Still and Barry Fraser tonight to come home and repeat his earlier mistake.

'I wouldn't mind a tot of whisky in mine,' she said from behind him.

'Sure thing,' McNab said and lifted the bottle out.

Everything went into slow motion after that. He poured a decent measure in her coffee, then the bottle headed towards his own mug. His fumbled attempt to prevent this resulted in a spill on the kitchen surface. When the sharp scent of the spilt whisky met his nostrils, McNab fought a desire to scoop it up with his finger and lick it.

He turned away swiftly and carried both mugs over, setting hers down on the coffee table in front of her.

'Hope it's not too strong,' he said.

'My father used to make me a hot toddy when I had a cold. He swore by them. I didn't like the taste of whisky then, but I like it now.'

'A hot toddy in Newcastle?'

'My dad came from Inverness.'

McNab swallowed a mouthful of coffee. For some reason, the caffeine didn't provide its usual kick. He must be getting used to it. Just as you did with whisky, which was why one was never enough.

'What did you want to speak to me about?'

She had moved on to whisky with water. He'd finished the coffee and made another pot, stronger this time. There was a scent in the air. At least there was for him. It was the mingled aroma of a woman and whisky. Freya was, he thought, a little drunk. She was also frightened.

The tale she'd told him had been an odd one and he wasn't sure he recognized the significance she placed on it. But it meant something to her. It seemed Shannon had hinted that she'd found something in the old library in the main building which had originally housed the Ferguson collection of manuscripts on the occult.

'And?' McNab had said.

'We were interrupted at this point and I never found out any more. Then she didn't come into work and . . .' Freya's voice had tailed off in distress.

'You think Shannon found something important?'

'The Ferguson collection is world renowned,' she'd explained, then gone on to mention a selection of famous pieces it contained.

McNab had made suitable noises, at the same time thinking that writings about casting spells and turning metal into gold were about as believable as parables about turning water into wine and feeding the world on a few loaves and fishes. Eventually he came to understand that whatever Shannon had thought she'd found, it was no longer there.

'And you think this possible discovery could have something to do with Shannon's death?'

Freya had thrown him a look of exasperation at this point.

'Such documents are priceless. Someone might kill for them.'

Now those two statements did make sense to McNab.

'So Shannon mentioned finding something to you. You took the key to the room from her desk and went looking for whatever it was, after I told you about her death?'

She nodded. 'And there was nothing there.'

'Could she have been the one to move it?'

Freya shrugged. 'I don't know.'

'What about Grant?'

'I asked him. He said Shannon had never mentioned anything to him, but he'd check it out.' Freya asked McNab for another drink.

McNab took the glass from her and went to fetch a refill. There had been half a bottle's worth and there wasn't a lot left. Perhaps it was safe now for him to have one. He couldn't go out and buy another bottle at this late hour. McNab made a decision and shared the remainder. His neat, hers diluted.

When he arrived back with the two glasses, she looked pleased.

'I thought you were still on duty,' she said.

'Time to knock off for the day.'

'Good.'

She shifted along the couch towards him. That surprised McNab, but not as much as what happened next. He was used to being the one to make the first move. Often he overstepped the mark and was rebuffed. Iona had made a play for him in the pub on the night of his promotion. He'd succumbed only after Rhona had turned him down. Iona, he liked to think, had caught him on the rebound.

The lips that met his were moist and whisky-laden. The tongue that sought his even more so. She tasted good, and smelt even better. As she arched her back he felt the press of her breasts against him.

It had been a long time since McNab had experienced sober sex. The eagerness was there, but the desperate fumbling, forgotten in the morning, didn't have to be, he told himself. McNab stood up and offered Freya his hand. When she took it, he led her through to the bedroom.

He woke as dawn filled the room to find Freya no longer beside him. For a split second, McNab thought she had been no more than an erotic dream, then he spotted something on the pillow next to his. It was a figurine, a small replica of the Goddess statue he'd seen in the magick shop window. On its base was the name Freya.

Under the shower, McNab relived their encounter. With a clear head, he recalled everything in detail. He had become the perfect witness. The one the police longed for. The one who could describe a suspect in detail, down to the exact location of a freckle or a mole.

McNab could recollect the timbre of Freya's voice, the sound of her sigh, every curve and plane of her body, the taste and smell of her. If he'd walked into a crowded room, he suspected he would know immediately if she was there.

It was something he'd experienced only once before.

As he dried and dressed, McNab moved from thoughts of Freya to what she had further revealed after they'd made love. It was that moment when closeness made you say things you might come to regret.

'I rarely saw Leila or Shannon at work. Most of my time in the library is spent on research. I didn't know they were practising Wicca until I met them at a coven meeting.'

McNab had sprung to attention at that point. 'Where was this?'

'In Edinburgh. There's a meeting place in the Vaults under the Bridges. It's not a secret. Tourists who visit the Vaults during the day can look through a grille at the room. But,' she said, 'the members don't advertise their identities.'

McNab recalled Ollie mentioning his friend Joe using the Vaults for a coven meeting.

'And you three are members?' he said.

'Just visitors. Shannon and Leila were as surprised to see me as I was to see them.'

'Were they members of any Glasgow coven?'

'No. And neither am I. It's perfectly possible to practise Wicca alone or in a group of two or three.' She hesitated. 'Leila and Shannon worked together, but Leila was the leader. And I think she was using her skills as a Witch in other ways.'

'How exactly?'

'Selling sexual magick.'

'You mean casting spells during sex?' he'd said with a dismissive laugh.

Freya had pulled away from him at that point. 'You shouldn't mock something you don't understand,' she'd warned.

'Or you'll put a spell on me?'

Her hurt expression had cut McNab to the core. 'I'm sorry. That was way out of order,' he'd said, keen to make amends. When Freya had eventually nodded an okay to his apology, McNab had felt his stomach flip in relief.

Don't fuck this up, a small voice had warned him.

'What made you think Leila had been selling sexual spells?' he'd said, having finally registered the true significance of her statement.

'Because of something she said once.'

'And what was that, exactly?'

'That men were willing to pay for sex, and pay even more for sex magick.'

23

Rhona disrobed and deposited her suit in the bin. This morning's post-mortem on Shannon Jones had proved to be straightforward. In the pathologist's opinion, Shannon had in fact died of suffocation, after which her head and shoulders had been immersed in the bath water. Opening up the body, he'd discovered evidence of congestion in the lungs and the heart muscle, consistent with undue pressure.

How she was smothered was less obvious. A plastic bag over her head was a possibility. Or a pillow from the bed next to the circle which she'd hoped would keep her safe.

The small incision on her crown had been noted, together with pressure marks on the skull, suggesting her face may have been held against a pillow. Alternatively, it may have happened when her dead head was being forced beneath the water.

A heavy impact caused blood vessels to rupture even after death, particularly areas engorged with post-mortem hypostasis. Oozed blood in the tissues produced a visual effect similar to ante-mortem bruising. The most reliable way of determining whether bruising had occurred before or after death was to examine whether a large number of white blood cells had been dispatched to the area to deal with an injury. Dr Sissons's conclusion had been that the contusions on Shannon's knees had happened post-mortem.

Undressed now, Rhona stepped under the shower.

The piping hot water felt good after the chill of the mortuary. McNab hadn't shown up for the post-mortem and she'd heard nothing back from him regarding her message about Daniel Hardy. Her first thought was that he'd fallen off the wagon after their brief meeting in Ashton Lane, and, she decided, that might be her fault.

But, then again, McNab needed very little to persuade him to do what he wanted to do anyway. If he wanted to drink, he would. Yet his attempt at abstinence had appeared to be going well, although the substantial increase in caffeine had created its own edginess.

She turned her face to the spray, rinsing out her mouth, dispensing with the taste of death and chemicals. DI Bill Wilson hadn't been present at the PM either, nor DS Clark, which suggested that Bill had assumed McNab *would* be there. Yet he wasn't, and Rhona wondered why.

She turned off the water and stepped out, grabbing a towel.

In truth, she was as annoyed with herself as she was with McNab, because she was letting him get under her skin, despite her efforts not to.

Just as I'm doing with Sean. Another uncomfortable thought.

Once dried and dressed, she checked her mobile and discovered a message from Bill asking her to drop round after the PM. It could be that McNab's absence had been noted or, more hopefully, Bill wanted to discuss the drawings found in the nine dolls.

The day was overcast, the air distinctly cooler. It had been an exceptional summer in Scotland and it seemed her residents, by their apparel, were determined to pretend it would continue that way, despite the obvious change in temperature. But Glasgow was no Los Angeles, even though this summer the tans had been more real than fake. Autumn was coming. The trees knew it, even if the residents pretended not to.

She contemplated the result of the PM on Shannon Jones as she drove. As Magnus never failed to remind them, a perpetrator always had a rational reason for a kill, although it may never appear rational to a normal person. They also had a reason for the manner in which they killed, the location they chose and, assuming they weren't disturbed, the state in which they left the crime scene.

Which led to a number of questions.

Where had Shannon been suffocated? If it was in the bedroom, why transport her to the bathroom and half immerse her in the bath, if not to try and give the impression she'd drowned? Most people had no idea how drowning was actually determined, and that despite few outward signs of suffocation, a post-mortem could reveal them.

Then there was Magnus's revelation about the favoured manner in which Witches were disposed of. Hanging, drowning or burning. Could the attempt at portraying Shannon's death as being caused by drowning have anything to do with the fact that she was a practising Witch? As she parked and made her way to Bill's office, Rhona decided she was none the wiser, but hoped Bill was.

She hesitated before knocking, aware that this had been McNab's office too in the short time he'd served as DI. It couldn't have been easy for McNab to take up residence here. McNab worshipped the boss, that much was plain. Had DI Wilson been around to support him in his new position, maybe things would have gone differently.

Then again, maybe not. McNab's *don't give a fuck about authority* mode was hardly going to bode well for him in any position of seniority. Although, she reminded herself, Bill hadn't risen through the ranks despite his obvious ability, probably because he didn't care for prestige and position either.

Maybe the two men weren't that different.

You look too thin, she thought, as Bill turned from the window to welcome her. Rhona's forensic eye quickly estimated the loss of a couple of stone from a body that had been trim in the first place. She suspected he'd lost it in tandem with Margaret, as she'd entered her second bout of cancer treatment. Worry killed the appetite as much as chemotherapy.

But maybe now he was back at work?

Rhona had already spied the mug of tea on the desk, left to go cold just the way Bill liked it, alongside a plate piled high with chocolate biscuits.

'Rhona.' Bill's face broke into a smile. 'It's good to see you.'

'You too,' she said. 'How are the troops treating you?'

He indicated the biscuits. 'Feeding me up. Or trying to. You haven't brought more, I hope?'

'No, but I'm happy to help you demolish those,' Rhona said, suddenly feeling hungry.

When she accepted his offer of coffee, Bill stuck his head out the door and placed the order, his voice, unlike his body, anything but frail.

'So,' he said, indicating that she should take a seat. 'The dolls have provided a clue to their existence.'

'Chrissy's eagle eye,' Rhona said.

'Have you read Magnus's take on it?' Bill said.

'No, I was at the PM on Shannon . . .'

When she halted, Bill said, 'And?'

'Suffocation, followed by immersion.'

'So not drowned, voluntary or otherwise?'

'Apparently not.'

'You and McNab discuss it?' Bill said as the coffee arrived.

There was no avoiding an answer.

'So he didn't turn up?' Bill's expression indicated that McNab should have. 'Is he drinking?'

'A great deal of coffee,' Rhona said, honestly. 'And he's definitely on the case. Both cases.'

Bill nodded. 'He went to see Magnus last night. Apparently they discussed the drawings and Magnus came up with some interesting information regarding the symbols.' Bill pulled up an image on his screen. 'Take a look.'

Below the first photograph, Magnus had added a graphic which took each of the symbols and translated them into a letter of the alphabet.

'In his detailed email he says the symbols are those of the Seax-Wica alphabet, which is popular in occult writings.'

'Magnus thinks the runes represent the first names of possible sexual partners?'

Bill nodded. 'It's something, although with Shannon dead, we have no way of identifying these men, aside from a possible first name and rough description.'

'You've had no luck with the CCTV footage?'

'Lots of calls. None leading to a suspect.'

Rhona decided it was time to tell Bill the latest news. 'We may have more than a name and a description.'

Bill waited for her to continue.

'I found traces of semen on each of the nine drawings,'

Rhona said. 'It looks like Leila may have left a DNA marker, as well as a description and a name.'

It made sense in terms of sexual magick as described by Magnus. The power of the spell was in the seed. So the seed must be retained for the magic to continue. They could create a DNA profile for each of the nine men who had indulged in sexual magick with Leila, but if they weren't recorded on the database already, even that wouldn't be enough to find them.

Rhona encountered the elusive McNab as she exited Bill's office. He was in an animated conversation with DS Clark, a totally different man from the one she'd encountered last night in Ashton Lane.

Her first thought was that he and Janice had become an item, an idea that rather pleased her. She liked Janice, but was well aware that McNab had hit on her in a spectacular fashion when she'd first arrived. Then, when rejected, had behaved like a misogynist idiot and been duly chastised for it by the boss. Rhona had already noted a different relationship between them now they were both the same rank, but a romance she hadn't anticipated.

A closer look convinced her that McNab had definitely hit it lucky somewhere, but not necessarily with DS Clark.

'Dr MacLeod. Good to see you.'

McNab gave her his signature grin while Janice shot her a look, one that matched Rhona's reading of the situation. Detective Sergeant McNab was the tomcat who had got the cream but that cream wasn't Janice.

'You missed the PM,' Rhona said to burst his bubble.

'Let me guess. She was suffocated, then dumped in the bath?'

'You spoke to Sissons?' she said suspiciously.

'No, but I'd like to speak to you. Fancy a coffee?'

Rhona was about to suggest he would be better seeing the boss first, but a persuasive look from Janice made her agree instead.

They made their way to the room that housed the drinks machine. Luckily, the room was unoccupied. McNab immediately selected a double espresso then asked what she fancied. Rhona settled for a black coffee.

As soon as the espresso arrived, McNab knocked it back and pressed for another.

'That's a lot of caffeine,' Rhona ventured.

'Better than too much whisky.'

'How's that going?'

'Good,' he said. 'Better than good.' The smile that passed his lips wasn't meant for her, but for some thought he was having.

The question had to be asked.

'Who is she?'

'What do you mean?' McNab feigned puzzlement.

'I've seen your post-sex expression. Remember?'

The grin he bestowed on her was infectious. 'Oh, I remember all right, Dr MacLeod.'

'That's why you weren't at the PM?'

'No. I was in fact in the Tech department discussing Witches' covens with my friend Ollie. I've arranged to visit one and wondered if you'd like to accompany me?'

'What?' Rhona said, taken aback at this turn of events.

'Apparently there's an *esbat* tonight. That's the name of a regular meeting, to the uninitiated.'

He was definitely trying to annoy her with his newly acquired insider knowledge. Rhona decided not to rise to the bait.

'Where is this meeting?'

'In the Edinburgh Vaults.'

Rhona was tempted. 'Why me? Why not DS Clark?'

'If you don't fancy it . . .'

'Have you spoken to Magnus about this?'

'No, but I plan to.' McNab threw the empty cup in the bin. 'I'll pick you up at eight.' And with that McNab and his Cheshire grin was gone.

Rhona pondered McNab inviting Magnus to participate, coupled with his upbeat attitude. She should be glad of it, yet . . . McNab with a hangover was tricky to manage, but at least she had some experience of that. McNab in love would take some getting used to.

And who the hell was the female involved?

The person to ask was obviously Chrissy. Nothing got past her forensic assistant's network of informers. If Chrissy didn't know who McNab had got lucky with, no one would.

'No way,' Chrissy said later, when presented with the circumstantial evidence. 'Are you sure?'

'I know that look,' Rhona said.

Chrissy was already checking her mobile for any messages regarding McNab's love life which she may have missed. There apparently were none.

'He's not even been to the pub.' Chrissy's brow creased in thought. 'So where the hell did he meet her?'

'No point looking at me,' Rhona said. 'You're always the first to know. You must be slipping.' It felt rather good to be one step ahead of Chrissy for a change, even though the step was a small one.

Chrissy was immediately on the case. 'It must be someone

he met during the investigation. After all, he's been working twenty-four-seven, according to Janice. I'll give her a call.'

'You do that.'

Having off-loaded the detective work on to Chrissy, Rhona headed into the lab.

24

The Pot Still was a different beast at ten o'clock in the morning. No crowds wearing the whisky glow and talking the talk; it was empty apart from a young guy who wasn't Barry, bottling up.

When McNab asked for Barry, he was informed that he was due in shortly. McNab decided to wait. In the meantime he would take advantage of their breakfast menu. He ordered the biggest plate on offer, together with a pot of coffee, and, retreating to a corner table, reflected on how Glasgow had changed when you could have something other than a liquid breakfast in a pub of a morning.

He was well through the offering of square sausage, bacon, black pudding and egg when Barry arrived. McNab watched as he was cornered by his colleague and a whispered conversation ensued. Then Barry turned his gaze on the corner, where McNab had just popped the final bit of sausage in his mouth. To say that Barry wasn't pleased to see him would be an understatement.

In contrast, McNab gave him a welcoming smile. 'Barry. Come and join me.'

Barry made a weak effort not to comply. 'I have to start work.'

McNab glanced at the guy behind the bar. 'I'm sure your

colleague can manage without you for just a little longer. Take a seat.'

Barry did so grudgingly.

'The details of the card payments?' McNab said.

Barry looked a little flustered. 'I'll get them for you.'

'Later,' McNab said, pushing the cleared plate to one side and easing back in his seat. 'I have a couple of questions to ask you.'

'I've told you everything I know,' Barry protested.

'Not everything.' McNab gave Barry time to worry about what was coming next, before asking, 'Have you had an appendectomy?'

Puzzlement flooded Barry's face. 'What?'

'Have you had your appendix taken out?'

'What's my appendix got to do with anything?'

McNab pushed his mobile across the table. On the screen was the image of the drawing of the man that just might be Barry, with a stitched scar on his abdomen.

Barry stared down at the sketch in disbelief.

'What is this?'

'The rune below says it's someone called Barry. So I'd hazard a guess and say it's you, assuming the size of the genitals are exaggerated.'

Barry pushed the mobile away from him, but said nothing.

'These sexual encounters with Leila. Did they involve tying you together with a red cingulum and casting a spell when you climaxed?'

Barry's face was now a tumult of emotions. If asked to translate them into a well-known phrase or saying, McNab would have settled for *I'm fucked*.

Barry gave up. 'Okay. Okay. That's what she was into, and I didn't see any harm in it.'

'We'll require you to give a DNA sample.'

'But I was here the night she died. I have witnesses.'

McNab was about to ask Barry where he'd been on the night Shannon had died, when the door opened and a tall, slim, auburn-haired guy walked in.

Barry sprung to his feet. 'We're not open yet, mate.'

The guy turned and, seeing Barry's warning expression, immediately backed towards the door, but McNab was there before him.

'Of course they're open. I've just had breakfast,' McNab said with a smile. 'Take a seat and Barry here will serve you. Won't you, Barry?'

The newcomer hesitated, trying to weigh up the situation. There was no doubt in McNab's mind that these two men knew one another. He also suspected that the man standing nervously in front of him was Leila Hardy's brother.

'So, Danny, we meet at last.'

The impasse had endured until McNab introduced himself as Detective Sergeant McNab, investigating officer in the Leila Hardy murder enquiry. The stark announcement appeared to have the desired effect. Danny no longer resembled a colt about to bolt, although he definitely still wanted to.

McNab gestured him to take a seat and promptly ordered a worried Barry to bring more coffee.

When Barry took himself off, albeit reluctantly, McNab observed the troubled young man before him.

'I'm very sorry about your sister—'

Danny broke into McNab's attempt at sympathy. 'Have you found the bastard who did it?'

'Not yet,' McNab admitted.

'Why not? He was seen leaving the pub with her.'

'So you've been following the investigation. Yet you didn't get in touch with us?'

'I didn't need you to tell me Leila was dead.' His voice broke a little on her name.

'But we need you to identify her body.'

Danny looked shocked at the prospect. 'Shannon Jones, her mate, can do that. She saw her more often than me.'

'You and your sister weren't on speaking terms?' McNab said.

'We got on okay. We just didn't hang out together.'

'That doesn't explain why you avoided contacting us, especially under the circumstances.'

Danny turned on him at that. 'You should be looking for the bastard who killed my sister. Not trying to find me.'

Nothing is right about this interchange.

The young man before him was obviously shocked and angry about his sister's death, yet had deliberately not come forward to speak to the police. Why?

'Did you know your sister was a Witch?' McNab said.

'A Wiccan. She was a Wiccan,' Danny spat back. 'And, yes, I knew. There's no crime in that.'

'No. But she may have died because of it.'

Danny should have reacted to that announcement, but didn't. No shock. No demand to know why McNab had said such a thing. Just a closed-down expression that suggested to McNab that Danny Hardy already suspected that to be the case.

Just then, Barry arrived back with the coffee.

'Join us,' McNab ordered.

It seemed that Barry might protest, but then thought the better of it.

McNab waited until he was seated then looked pointedly from one to the other, before stating, 'Shannon Jones is dead. She was found murdered in her flat yesterday.'

Both men's shocked reaction to this announcement was instantaneous and apparently genuine, leading McNab to surmise that Barry had known Shannon better than he'd admitted up to now.

Danny, suddenly suspicious, eyed McNab. 'You fucking bastard. You're lying.'

'It's not a lie,' McNab said. 'I was the one who found her.'

Danny muttered some obscenity under his breath and stood up.

'If you're not arresting me, I'd like to leave.'

McNab realized that despite his announcement, or because of it, the discussion was at an end. He contemplated ordering Danny to stick around a while longer, but decided he would keep him until later.

'You are both required to report to the police station within twenty-four hours to give a statement and provide a DNA sample.' He turned specifically to Danny. 'You will also formally identify your sister.'

25

DI Bill Wilson and Detective Superintendent Sutherland went back a long way. The road they'd travelled together had often been a rocky one, with bad blood on occasion. Something which Bill chose not to dwell on, although Sutherland liked to allude to it now and again. The rocky and bloody patches usually featured DS Michael Joseph McNab. As it did again today.

Sutherland was a man Bill thought he understood. They were similar in age, both married, with teenage children, although their careers had not followed similar paths. Bill had always sought to stay close to front-line policing. Sutherland, on the other hand, had striven to get away from it as swiftly as possible. At times, Bill thought the super had forgotten what it really meant to be a detective. What had to be done, sometimes outside the rule book, to get results.

The image before him now confirmed this – the carefully groomed hair, the smart uniform, even the neatness of the desk, suggested someone who had forgotten that life and death was as disordered as those involved in it.

Apparently there had been some *disquiet* regarding McNab's participation in the current murder case. Bill had interrupted the doublespeak at this point, to remind Sutherland that it had been DS McNab who'd had the sense to check on Shannon Jones.

'And forced entry in the process,' Sutherland said.

'And that's what the *disquiet* is about?'

'McNab does not maintain the discipline of a police officer. He acts like a wild card with no respect for the law, which has been, I must remind you, a big contributor in his downfall.'

'He caught Stonewarrior, sir,' Bill reminded him, 'when the combined might of the UK police forces couldn't.'

'You exaggerate, Inspector.'

Bill bit back a retort. Annoying Sutherland further wouldn't help McNab's case.

'So there isn't an official complaint, just some *disquiet*?' Bill tried to nail down the reason for his summons.

'I thought it apt to remind you that DS McNab is your responsibility.'

'I am aware of that, sir.'

Sutherland shot him the look of a superior making a point of his superiority.

Bill ignored it. 'Is that all, sir?'

On Sutherland's curt nod, Bill exited.

So there was *disquiet* about the investigation. He would have put it more forcibly than that. And it had nothing to do with McNab's part in it. Bill's *disquiet* came from the fact that they had not yet picked up their main suspect, despite numerous showings of the CCTV footage. And now they were about to release details of the Shannon Jones murder.

In his opinion it was no unlucky coincidence that Shannon Jones had met her death so swiftly after that of her friend. Neither death, he thought, was random. Both had been planned, but the reason for them escaped him. True, it might be that the second killing had occurred because the perpetrator viewed Shannon as a threat to his continued freedom. But Shannon Jones hadn't been the only one to see the suspect that night in the pub. The barman McNab had interviewed had given a good description, even added to it with details of the expensive watch and wallet. If Shannon had been in danger because she'd had a close-up of their suspect, so too was the barman.

And what about the suspect's mate, who was even more elusive? If he was innocent of any wrongdoing, why hadn't he come forward? Then again, maybe the deaths were the work of two men rather than one.

Bill re-entered his office and took up residence in his swivel chair, turning it to face the window with its view over his city. He registered that he was grateful to be back here with more to think about than Margaret's illness and was then flooded with guilt that he had stopped thinking about it, even for a moment.

But dwelling on Margaret's cancer hadn't stopped it returning and wouldn't make it go away. That's what she'd said when confronting him with her demand that he go back to work. Thinking about an investigation, on the other hand, could help solve it.

His wife was a wise and courageous woman, both attributes Bill acknowledged she had in greater abundance than her husband.

On Margaret's orders, Bill now turned his thinking skills back to the task in hand.

Rhona's recent revelation regarding possible DNA identification of the nine men whose sketches were in the dolls could be a game changer, but only if they were already on the database, and that was only a possibility if they'd already been found guilty of a crime.

*

There were a number of presumptive tests used in the detection of semen which weren't dependent on the presence of sperm cells. One was the acid phosphatase (ACP) test, used both in the search for seminal stains and in their presumptive identification. ACP was an enzyme secreted by the prostate gland and found in very high concentrations in seminal fluid compared to other bodily fluids. If a stain was seminal fluid, exposure to the ACP test would result in a purple colour in less than half a minute. However, the colour also developed when other bodily fluids were present, such as vaginal fluid, although the reaction time was much longer.

The definitive test, the one Rhona had chosen to use, was the p30, which detected the presence of a protein of the same name produced by the prostate gland. Among bodily fluids, p30 was found almost exclusively in seminal liquid. Its other advantage was that the identification of semen was unaffected by the absence of spermatozoa. So if the owner of the seminal fluid had had a vasectomy, or was affected by a condition known as azoospermia, it didn't matter.

Once the existence of seminal fluid on the nine pieces of paper stored in the dolls had been established, the next step was to produce a DNA profile for each of them and run them through the database. Besides DNA profiles, they'd already amassed a sizable collection of trace evidence – hair, fibres, skin flakes, urine traces from the toilet, vomit, fingerprints and even a naked footprint. All useful in building up a picture of who had been in Leila's flat. Even the chirality of the knots used in the noose made from the cingulum provided another piece of the jigsaw.

Rhona checked the time on the wall clock. If she was going to Edinburgh with McNab, she would have to get a move on. Go home, eat, change and be ready for his arrival. Chrissy had departed already, having not yet solved the mystery of McNab's love life. Before leaving she'd instructed Rhona in the art of interrogation. Not for the first time Rhona had thought Chrissy would make a good detective.

'Why don't you just call him?' Rhona had suggested. 'After all, you two are bosom buddies.'

It seemed Chrissy had already considered doing that. 'He would see it as failure on my part that I had to ask,' Rhona had been told, with an exaggerated sigh.

Rhona had found the only way to put an end to the conversation was to go into the lab and firmly shut the door.

She eventually left at seven. On the way home she stopped at the deli and bought some cold cuts and potato salad. One thing Sean had done by intermittently reappearing in her life had been to highlight the paucity of her culinary horizons – namely, pepperoni pizza and no. 12 on the Chinese menu. Both fell short of Sean's freshly cooked food. The cold cuts and potato salad weren't freshly cooked either, but at least they offered some variety.

Showered, Rhona contemplated what should be worn to the meeting of a Witches' coven. Obviously if one had a gown, what was worn beneath, if anything, didn't matter. Eventually, having dressed as normal, she settled down to her deli meal.

The buzzer sounded dead on eight o'clock. Approaching McNab's car, Rhona found Magnus already in the passenger seat and registered that the two men looked relatively comfortable in one another's company, which was as surprising as McNab's new loved-up persona.

McNab drove in his usual fashion, reminding Rhona why she preferred to travel in the back when he was at the wheel. Judging by the stiff set of Magnus's shoulders, he was bracing himself rather than openly gripping the seat.

Once on the motorway, things improved a little. The traffic was relatively thin, the road straight. McNab cruised along at just over seventy, slowing for speed cameras where necessary. Magnus relaxed a little and Rhona decided it was time to bring both of them up to date on the sketches and the probability of DNA profiles from the deposits of semen.

'I showed Barry Fraser the sketch with his name under it,' McNab said. 'By his reaction, I would say he thought it might be him. He also admitted to the cingulum playing a role in his encounters with Leila.'

'Did he have any idea who the others were?' Magnus asked.

'I didn't reveal there were nine. I'll keep that for when he comes in for his DNA test.' McNab paused. 'I also ran into Danny Hardy, who seems to be mates with Barry.'

'Did Danny know what his sister was involved with?' Rhona asked after McNab had described their encounter.

'He knew she was a Wiccan. Said there was no law against it, and he's right.' McNab looked about to add something, then didn't.

Magnus had remained silent during McNab's story, but Rhona could tell by his expression that he was deep in thought. Her rendition of his name had no effect, so Rhona tried again.

'Magnus?'

This time he did respond. 'I wonder if the nine men involved are a defined group.'

'You mean like a coven?' Rhona said.

McNab again looked as if he would say something, then stopped.

'That's twice you've done that,' Rhona accused him. 'What is it?'

There was a moment's silence, then he said, 'A workmate of Leila's thought she was selling sex magick.'

'Someone from the library?'

McNab nodded. 'Her name's Freya Devine. She's a PhD student in medieval history and also a Wiccan.'

'So there were actually three of them?' Rhona said.

'Freya didn't know about the other two until they met at the Edinburgh coven. Like her, they weren't members, just visitors.'

'Are you sure she was telling you the truth?' Magnus joined in with Rhona's concern.

Now McNab's *yes* sounded slightly hesitant. 'They weren't close friends, not like Shannon and Leila.'

'So she couldn't be linked to them other than through the library?' Magnus said.

'No,' McNab said in a manner which indicated he no longer wished to discuss the woman in question, which immediately raised suspicions in Rhona's mind.

Was this the female Chrissy had been seeking?

'I'd like to talk to Freya Devine,' Magnus said. 'Is that possible?'

By the set of McNab's jaw, he was now regretting ever mentioning her name.

'Maybe.'

Magnus looked as though he might pursue this, but catching Rhona's warning glance, wisely decided not to.

26

Rhona had never visited the Vaults before, although she knew about them.

The series of chambers, up to 120, had been formed by the building of the nineteen arches of the South Bridge during the 1700s. Originally used to house taverns and tradesmen and as stores for illicit goods, they'd eventually become home to the poor of Edinburgh.

After they too had moved out in the 1800s, the caverns had been filled with the detritus of those who lived or worked above ground.

Now, they were a popular location for ghost tours and in this case a coven meeting.

The owner of this section of the Vaults warned them as he threw open the gates that the ground was uneven.

'Some of the caverns have power but the passage is unlit, so watch your step.'

McNab had had the sense to bring a torch, as had Rhona, but even then the going was tricky, the stone floor rising and falling intermittently.

The owner gave them a running commentary as they walked, which included a complaint about a band that had taken to practising in one of the caverns without paying for the privilege.

'The coven, on the other hand, are excellent tenants,

although they haven't met for a while due to the warlock being in hospital with gallstones.'

There was a pregnant silence before McNab ventured, 'I take it there are no spells to prevent gallstones.'

'It seems not.'

They made one stop before their destination, orchestrated by Magnus who asked why an empty cavern had a ring of large stones set out on the floor.

'The coven say the room had an evil presence which they're trying to contain within the stones,' the owner told them. 'They advise that no one steps within the circle.'

Rhona heard a muttered 'Fuck's sake' from McNab, thankfully at low level.

A few yards further on, they stopped outside a metal grille with a gate, through which they could see a room. Candlelit, with an altar, the floor had a painting of a five-pointed star and was surrounded by nine low stools with red cushions.

At first it seemed there was no one in there, until a figure in a long black embroidered robe stepped into view.

'Derek,' said the owner, 'I've brought your visitors.'

The man who came towards them was middle-aged, stout and balding. He unlocked the gate and, swinging it wide, invited them to enter. His voice was deep and melodious, reminding Rhona of a Church of Scotland minister.

McNab showed his ID and introduced Rhona as Dr MacLeod and Magnus as Professor Pirie. Derek gave his surname as White and welcomed them.

'The others should arrive shortly. Would you prefer we wait?'

'We can start without them,' McNab said.

'Of course.'

Magnus had already wandered away, apparently intent on examining the room and its artefacts. Rhona stayed close to McNab, interested in how the interchange would develop.

'I understand you had three visitors at your last meeting?' McNab began.

'Yes. As I said on the phone. Three young women.'

'Were they together?'

'Two were. The other came alone. She was a post-grad student at Glasgow who got in touch with me about her thesis on Witchcraft.'

'And the other two?'

'They were on a night out in Edinburgh and asked to drop by.'

'Were they known to anyone in your circle?'

'Not that I am aware of.'

'Then how did they get in touch?'

'There's a shop in Glasgow on the High Street. They contacted me through the owners.'

By now people were filtering in, glancing with interest at the visitors as they donned gowns and made ready for whatever was in store. They all looked perfectly normal. Most were middle-aged, although there was a younger man among their ranks who came over as soon as he spotted McNab.

'DS McNab? I'm Joe, Ollie's mate from uni.'

They shook hands.

'Great job on the *Stonewarrior* case. Ollie told me all about it, or at least what he was permitted to tell,' he added cautiously.

'We'll have to start the ceremony soon,' Derek interrupted. 'So, if you'd like to talk to the others?'

Being surrounded by a group of people dressed in star

and moon embroidered gowns wasn't in McNab's comfort zone, but he did the job admirably, giving out just enough information and getting a good response. Many hadn't picked up on the death of Leila Hardy, or hadn't linked any mention of the murder to their recent visitors. At the news of the second death, a babble of noise erupted.

McNab held up his hand for silence.

'The murder of Shannon so soon after Leila suggests that their deaths may be linked. Of course, that link may not be because of their involvement with Wicca, but the nature of both crime scenes suggests that it might.'

McNab then gave brief details of the room of dolls and of the cingulum, which caused a lot of consternation. Rhona had been studying the reactions of the group while McNab talked. All were distressed, but one man, in particular, had looked increasingly uneasy. By the sheen on his skin he was sweating, although the vaults were cool, verging on cold. On one occasion he had darted a look towards Rhona and swiftly away again when he realized she was watching him. After that he'd made a point of not catching her eye.

When McNab began talking about the men they believed Leila had performed sex magick with, the man had swiftly made an exit. Rhona followed to find him in the passageway leaning against the wall.

'Are you okay?'

'I'm a little claustrophobic,' he explained. 'The room is small and with the extra people . . .' He tailed off.

'It wasn't a pleasant story to listen to,' Rhona said.

'No. It wasn't.'

'Did you meet the women when they visited?'

He nodded. 'They were young and enthusiastic.'

'And now they're dead.'

He looked sick at that.

'Is there anything you know that might help find who killed them?'

He was struggling with himself. Rhona wasn't sure if his story of claustrophobia was true, or whether he, like most people, merely struggled with the horror of murder. She, McNab and even Magnus forgot that the world they inhabited was something unimaginable to people living ordinary lives, even if, like the man before her, they practised Witchcraft.

'I'm sorry, I didn't mean to upset you.'

'I am upset, but more because I may have been a party to what happened to those young women.'

When they'd emerged from underground Edinburgh, McNab had quickly located the nearest pub, where they were now seated in a quiet corner. The man, whose name was Maurice, had a large brandy in front of him, half of which he'd already consumed. Minus his robe, he looked more like a bank manager than a warlock. A frightened one.

'When she asked my advice, I reminded her of the creed,' he said.

'*An' it harm none, do what thou wilt,*' Magnus quoted.

Maurice looked swiftly at him. 'Yes. There was no harm intended, she assured me of that.'

'Then what was intended?' McNab said sharply.

'The men wanted something important to their future prosperity, she said.'

'They all wanted the same thing?'

Maurice shook his head as if trying to remember. 'They were in it in some way together, so it was binding on them, I think.'

'So you advised her to keep a record?'

'Yes.'

'To blackmail them?'

He looked shocked by that. 'No. Sexual magick is made powerful by the life force. Men's seed is that force. More powerful than a name.'

'To know a person's name is to have a hold over them. For to know the name is to be able to conjure with it,' McNab said, with a glance at Magnus. 'Did she say how many men were involved?'

'No, she didn't.'

'Did *you* suggest she sketch them?' Rhona asked.

'I suggested a drawing would serve in place of a clay model.' He drank the remainder of his brandy, his hand shaking as he raised the glass to his mouth.

'Who was party to this discussion?' McNab said.

'Only Leila. She asked to speak with me alone after the ceremony.'

'The other two weren't involved?'

'The one called Freya left first. The other two stayed until the end. That's when Leila spoke to me.'

'Why you?' McNab said.

'She'd read a pamphlet I'd written about sexual magick.'

Rhona suspected he was telling the truth. Magnus's expression suggested he did too. McNab, ever the detective, worked on the assumption that everyone was lying until proved otherwise.

'Would you be willing to give a DNA sample?' Rhona said. 'To prove you weren't one of the group?'

Maurice looked surprised by the request, then relieved.

'Of course. Can I give it now?'

'If Detective Sergeant McNab is okay with that, we can do it now.'

McNab nodded and stood up, masking the general view while Rhona swiftly donned gloves, took a mouth swab, slipped it in a container and put it in her bag.

Now that he had seemingly proved his innocence, Maurice relaxed, going so far as to offer to buy them a drink. McNab said thanks, but no thanks. They had to get back to Glasgow.

They left him there at the bar buying himself another. Confession and forensic science had seemingly restored him to his former innocent self.

The journey home was memorable mostly for its silence. What had happened had given them all food for thought. Rhona was glad she'd come with the two men, but wasn't sure her presence had achieved much, apart from one DNA sample.

Magnus, whatever his thoughts, had chosen not to share them. McNab was keyed up. Rhona could tell that by the nerve that beat in his cheek, but he too remained silent.

On entering Glasgow, McNab headed for Rhona's place first. She'd hoped to talk to him in private about Freya Devine, but that wasn't to be.

As the car drove off, Rhona had the distinct impression that McNab was determined on a private conversation, but not with her.

27

McNab waited until he'd dropped Magnus before calling Freya. Almost midnight, he decided to only let it ring three times. If she didn't answer, he would assume she was asleep and wait until the morning to get in touch with her.

Freya answered on the second ring.

'You're still up?' he said.

'I'm a Witch, remember? I'm contemplating the full moon.'

She sounded pleased to hear from him, at least McNab let himself think so.

'Where are you?' she said.

'In the car, heading home.'

'Come here instead.'

When he didn't immediately answer, she said, 'It's late, I know.'

'I don't care about the time.'

'Then you'll come?'

'Yes.'

She told him the address.

'I'll be there in ten minutes.'

McNab did a great deal of thinking in those ten minutes. Mainly around the question: *What the hell am I doing?* Regardless of how he might try and persuade himself otherwise, Freya was part of the investigation and he was pursuing a relationship with her. Not professional and not wise. But what worried him more was the concerned reaction of Rhona and Magnus to Freya's existence. True, Maurice had confirmed that the three women hadn't come together to the coven, which meant Freya had told McNab the truth about that. *But*. And this was the big but. The three women were connected by Wicca, and whatever he might think of that, it might place Freya in danger.

Which is why I need to watch over her.

It was a good line to feed himself, he thought, as he pressed her buzzer. She answered immediately and freed the door. She was waiting for him on the first landing. There was a moment's hesitation as neither of them knew quite how to greet one another.

Freya settled for a smile and ushered him inside.

McNab followed her through to an open-plan room with a sitting area and kitchen combined. A large bay window gave a distant view of the university towers.

'Coffee?' she said.

McNab answered in the affirmative, although he would have preferred alcohol.

She was dressed in tracksuit bottoms and a T-shirt and he thought she looked beautiful. While they waited for the coffee, he told her he'd been at the coven meeting in the Vaults.

She registered this with surprise. 'Tonight?'

He nodded. 'That's where I was coming from when I called you.'

Her open look suggested she wasn't worried about what he'd discovered there, because she'd told him the truth about her visit. McNab was so used to people lying to him, or at the very least avoiding the truth, he found her honesty disconcerting.

'Was it helpful?' she finally said.

'It was.' McNab took a mouthful of coffee. 'Do you know anything about a pamphlet on sexual magick?'

She thought for a moment. 'I've seen incunables on sexual magick.'

'What's an incunable?'

She smiled at his confusion. 'A book or pamphlet printed in Europe, before the year 1501.'

'This pamphlet is more recent. Written by a man called Maurice Wade. A member of the Edinburgh coven.'

She shook her head. 'I haven't seen it. Is it important?'

'That's why Leila was there, to speak to him about it.'

She looked thoughtful at that. 'So what I said was true? She was performing sex magick?'

'According to Maurice, yes, she was.'

'And you think that's why she died?'

McNab was suddenly weary of it all. He didn't want to talk about violent death with this woman. He wanted to be here for a different reason.

As though reading his mind, Freya said, 'Shall we go to bed?'

McNab hadn't been invited into a woman's bedroom for what felt like forever. His sexual encounters, even with Rhona, had not been at her place. Iona had turned up at his unkempt, unpleasant-smelling flat and seemingly hadn't cared. But then, if you're high on drugs and drink, who does?

McNab was stone cold sober now, and he cared.

This time *she* led him through to the bedroom.

The scent of her was here in abundance, encompassing

him, heightening his senses. He had the buzz, but it wasn't from drink.

She chose to undress him first. Her gentle moves excited him more than any mad tearing off of clothes. Standing before her was a revelation. He had never felt so naked before, physically or emotionally. The feeling both frightened him and flooded him with pleasure.

Undressing Freya, he was seized by an overwhelming need to protect her.

No one will frighten or hurt you while I'm here.

McNab imagined he only thought the words, but realized by her reaction that he must have said them out loud.

She touched his cheek and it felt like fire.

When he woke she was beside him. That in itself filled McNab with wonder. If he was honest, most of his couplings involved himself or the woman leaving in the middle of the night. In truth, he often preferred it that way. No awkward morning silences. No uncomfortable goodbyes. No lies about calling them.

Freya was still asleep, her expression content, her breathing quietly even.

He took time to study her in detail, feeling wonder that someone so lovely would invite him into her bed. Perhaps sensing his attention, she opened her eyes.

'Good morning,' he said.

She smiled and drew him to her.

He stayed to breakfast, which was another first. Minus a hangover, loved up and verging on happy, McNab felt like a stranger to himself. The more cynical side of him muttered an occasional internal *It won't last*, which he did his best to ignore.

Freya pottered about, brewing fresh coffee, toasting bagels and spreading them with honey. Watching her eat one, her tongue licking the honey from her lips, was an erotic experience. McNab realized if he didn't leave soon, he was unlikely to leave at all.

He stood up.

'You have to go to work,' she said, sounding sorry.

'Don't you?'

She nodded. 'I have a thesis to research and write.'

'On Witchcraft.'

She smiled. 'Does that worry you?'

'I spend my days chasing killers. Does that worry you?'

A shadow crossed her face, making him want to take back the words. They had said nothing of the case from the moment she'd led him to her bed. He wanted to keep it that way.

'Can I phone you later?' McNab said.

'Yes, Michael.'

McNab was unused to being called by his first name, but found he liked it. When Freya said it, he forgot for a moment that he was Detective Sergeant McNab. The feeling didn't last long. He was barely out of the building when his phone rang.

'Dr MacLeod. This is an early call.'

'Can you come by the lab?'

'Not if you intend interrogating me,' he said, keeping his voice light.

'There's something you should know.'

'Okay,' McNab said, noting her serious tone. 'I'm on my way.'

His first instinct was that the secret he shared with Rhona was no longer a secret. That would account for her obvious concern. Also, she wouldn't want to reveal this in a phone call, hence the request for his lab visit. McNab's joie de vivre evaporated and he was back in the real world.

She was in her office when he arrived. Security had buzzed him in, commenting on his early visit, to which McNab had feigned a jocular reply. A mood he was no longer in. Dread had descended again. The dread he used to experience when he first opened his gritty eyes and knew he had another day to face, half of which would involve a hangover. The light mood with Freya had gone so quickly, McNab questioned whether it had really happened or whether it could ever happen again.

Seeing Rhona only served to heighten this feeling.

Her studied look reminded him that Dr Rhona MacLeod was the only woman who had ever come close to *knowing* him, and not just in the biblical sense.

'It's Freya Devine,' he said, seeing no point in hiding the fact from Rhona.

She smiled and he thought it was from pleasure on his behalf. 'I thought so.'

'I went to see her last night.' His confession rolled on like a Catholic who'd just found a long-sought-for priest.

She nodded, although he detected her thoughts were elsewhere.

'So why am I here?' he ventured.

She caught his look. 'It isn't about your love life or about . . . the other matter.'

McNab registered relief.

'What is it then?'

28

Her intuition had been right.

The results were in for the first samples she'd dispatched last night before heading for Edinburgh. Of the five she'd sent, four had registered against the Scottish Database as a no show, which meant the men involved had not been convicted of a crime north of the border. The fifth result was rather unexpected.

Rhona handed McNab the printout. 'This one found a match, but the details have been withheld. From me, at least.'

McNab scrutinized the paper. 'Has this ever happened to a search you've done before?'

'No, but I did have forensic evidence removed from the lab fridge once. A dismembered foot found on a beach in Skye. The Ministry of Defence decided they preferred to deal with it themselves.'

'The MOD interfered with your investigation?'

'They took it over in the interests of national security.'

It was a long and sorry tale, which had happened before she and McNab had met, but the memory of the mishandling of the case and its aftermath still rankled.

McNab was studying her. 'You think this is something similar?' he said.

'I think that someone in a position of authority doesn't

want this particular person to be *openly* identified as part of the investigation.'

She watched as McNab processed what that might mean, something Rhona had done already. Just because your details were currently on the database didn't mean you were guilty of a crime. You may have given a DNA sample voluntarily in an investigation for the purposes of elimination, just as Maurice had done last night.

It might be that the case you were attached to hadn't yet reached a conclusion. Under Scots law, your details would be removed from the Scottish Database once the case was decided, or you were not charged with an offence. They only remained there if you were found guilty. There was one exception to this, which involved sexual offences, where a suspect, not convicted, would have their details retained for three years.

English law was different. Once on the database you stayed there, even if innocent of any crime. All profiles on the Scottish DNA Database (except volunteers for intelligence-led screenings) were exported to the National DNA Database, which gave all police forces throughout the UK the ability to search for profile and crime-scene matches. But once you were removed from the Scottish Database, you then had to be removed from NDNA.

McNab was well aware of all of this, so Rhona didn't remind him. The true consequence for the investigation of being denied access to the details of the match, he got immediately.

'If Magnus is right and we do have a group of nine, then having a lead on one of them could take us to the other eight,' McNab said.

'My thoughts exactly.'

'We can't let this go unchallenged.'

'I agree.'

'So?'

Rhona took a moment to savour the fact that McNab was asking for her advice. Her first instinct when she'd viewed the printout had been not to show it to McNab. The old McNab would have acted first and thought about the consequences later, but this wasn't the old McNab.

'I think you should take this to the boss,' Rhona said.

All leads should be followed and all possibilities eliminated – that was the rule of an investigation. Bill had said exactly that when he'd sought an interview with Superintendent Sutherland to ask why details of the search match had been denied to the submitting forensic scientist, Dr MacLeod.

Now that he had been granted leave to state his case, Bill continued, 'DS McNab's work with Professor Pirie leads us to believe the nine men may form a group. Identify one and we may be able to identify them all.'

Sutherland interrupted before Bill could continue.

'The person you refer to is not a suspect, and their connection with the case will be dealt with at a higher level.'

Bill felt his anger rising. 'Who is this special case?'

'You don't need to know,' Sutherland said curtly.

'If you want me to explain why this is necessary to my team, *I* need to know who we're shielding and why.'

Sutherland considered this, then appeared to come to a decision.

'The owner of one of the DNA samples presented himself to a senior officer as soon as the case hit the news. He met the victim briefly, some months ago. I repeat, he is not a suspect.'

'That's for me to decide,' Bill retorted.

'On the contrary, Inspector, it is for me to decide.' Sutherland's tone had turned icy.

So the identity of someone currently on the database had to be kept secret. Those who worked in crime enforcement and were therefore likely to visit crime scenes had their DNA recorded for elimination purposes. In fact, so did anyone visiting a crime scene in an official capacity. His was on there, as was McNab's and Rhona's.

Bill took a calculated guess. 'He's one of ours.'

When Sutherland didn't respond, Bill tried a few possibilities. 'A serving police officer? Someone working undercover? Or just someone very important?'

The only evidence that he might have hit home was a blink at the final suggestion on his list. Hardly evidence that would hold up in court, but intriguing nonetheless.

Sutherland suddenly gave full attention to some papers on his desk. 'Thank you, Detective Inspector, that will be all.'

Summarily dismissed, Bill took his leave, accepting he'd met a dead end. Besides, he had other ways of discovering the truth. He didn't command a room full of eager detectives for nothing.

The thought briefly occurred that Sutherland's earlier concern about McNab's role in the investigation had been occasioned by this development. McNab had a reputation for ferreting out information which many of those in positions of power would prefer to keep out of the public eye.

Politics and policing – a shit sandwich, but one that was served up all too frequently in his opinion.

Bill glanced at his watch. It was time to talk to the troops.

29

The nightmare had been sudden, vivid and frighteningly realistic.

The green-eyed girl's intonations as she tightened the cord that bound them together. His determined thrusts and the resulting ecstasy which became the sole reason for his being.

Then the hand stuffed something into her mouth, silencing her words.

But whose hand?

Then she was choking, the green eyes bulging with fear, as he fell into the sweet abyss of climax, where nothing and no one mattered more than his own release.

Mark had woken at that point, launching himself upright, bathed in sweat, gasping for air, his heart banging painfully against his ribs.

Jesus.

He'd taken a deep breath and willed his heart to slow. When it hadn't, he'd risen and gone through to the kitchen. Throwing open the freezer door, he'd upended an open bag of ice on the kitchen surface, sending cubes slithering to the floor.

Grabbing some, he'd shoved them in his mouth. The instant and shattering cold had stunned him, but he'd known it would work. Apparently there was a nerve in the roof of your mouth. If you froze it, your heart slowed. He'd learned the trick from his mother, although her galloping and erratic heartbeat was a symptom of her illness and owed nothing to over-indulgence in coke and alcohol.

Or to guilt-ridden nightmares.

As his heart had finally begun to slow, the tight pain in his chest had loosened its grip. Mark had turned and spat the remains of the ice in the sink.

I'm doing too much coke. That's the reason.

He'd opened the balcony doors and stepped outside. In the distance, the imposing shadow of Arthur's Seat had been a blot on a midnight horizon. Up in the penthouse flat, he'd always considered himself on a par with the rock, with the scattered lights of Edinburgh spread out below him.

Which was why he'd bought the flat.

Thinking of buying the flat had immediately brought his father to mind, because a large chunk of the deposit had come from him, and Mark hadn't wanted to think about that.

He'd turned from the view then, and gone back inside. As he'd closed the patio doors he'd tried to relive his earlier success with Jeff. Jeff had definitely been contained for the moment. If Mark went to the police, Jeff's presence that night would also be revealed. And no upwardly mobile young lawyer would want to be associated with a suspect in a murder enquiry.

At that point Mark had congratulated himself. He'd been so convincing with Jeff, he'd almost believed it himself. Until an internal voice had reminded him yet again . . .

You did have sex with the girl and she died while you were in that flat.

On re-entering, he'd picked up his mobile from the coffee table and had noted an unread text from Emilie and, worse, a voicemail from his father.

The text he'd left unopened. The voicemail was another matter.

His heart speeding up again, Mark had listened to voice-mail service.

The call had come in at eleven, shortly after he'd passed out on the bed.

'I want to speak to you, Mark,' the cultured Edinburgh voice said. 'Come to my club at eight, tomorrow night.'

Mark had dropped the mobile at this point as though it was red hot.

Shit! Why did his father want to see him? What had he done wrong now?

Then a terrible thought had struck. Had his father seen the CCTV footage? Had he recognized his only son?

Jesus fuck.

He'd immediately started thinking of a list of possible excuses not to go. None of which, he knew, would be accepted. What his father wanted, his father got.

He will know something's wrong. He will know I'm lying.

A High Court judge for twenty years, his father could spot a liar with ease.

The rest of the night had brought little sleep, but he had made it into work at the bank this morning, although there wasn't much actual work being done.

Mark tried to take his mind off the meeting with his father and concentrate on the task in hand. The presentation was due to be given tomorrow and he'd prepared less than a third of it.

Who the fuck cares?

I'll care when I have to stand up in a room full of people and talk about it.

When his attempt to focus didn't work, Mark considered a trip to the Gents for a line of coke. Maybe half a line would be enough to get his enthusiasm going. If he finished the presentation by the end of the day, he could meet his father with a feeling of success.

The truth was, the *only* way he could face his father tonight was via a line of coke coupled with a very stiff drink, and if he did indulge his father would know. He'd seen too many drugged-up individuals in the dock. Sent many of them down. Including murderers.

I'm not a murderer. I had sex with a girl I met in a bar. It was consensual. In fact, she was the one in charge. I woke to find she wasn't in the bed. I vomited and, embarrassed by this, I went home.

He'd spent the hours awake last night rehearsing his confession. Always missing out the trip through to that room and the image of the girl hanging on the hook behind the swaying dolls.

Mark froze at the memory. Jesus, he couldn't go on like this. It was screwing with his brain.

Maybe I should go to the police? Tell them I was the guy on CCTV. Explain what happened. After all, my father is a High Court judge. That has to count for something?

His mobile pinged, bringing his mind back from that terrifying scenario.

Mark checked the screen to find a photo message from a number he didn't recognize. His first thought was to delete it, but curiosity won instead.

When it opened he stared at the screen for a moment, unsure what he was looking at. It was like one of those puzzle pictures taken at a strange angle to confuse you. Then he made out the plaited red cord. Just as he realized what it was, the image began to move, revealing it as a video clip.

It only lasted seconds, but Mark knew the male in the clip was him and the female most definitely the dead girl, bound together in a heart-stopping embrace until . . .

A hand – his hand? – stuffed a cloth in her mouth.

Mark made a dash for the Gents, causing consternation among his colleagues. Entering a cubicle, he immediately rid his stomach of a part-digested lunch of chicken and salad wrap.

A cold sweat swiftly followed. He pulled himself to his feet and flushed the toilet with an unsteady hand. His nightmare was fast becoming a reality. Someone else had been in that flat, in that room, while he was with the girl. They'd even filmed him fucking her. Had filmed him stuffing something into her mouth.

So it *was* true. He *had* made her choke.

Mark couldn't face that thought, or the one that followed on from it. Not without help. He felt in his pocket for the coke and shook out a line on the cistern.

He would say he was feeling ill. A stomach bug. Go home. Try and think this through. He stood, hands gripping the cistern, waiting for the coke to take effect. Then he heard someone enter and Campbell, the guy on the next desk to him, shouted, 'You okay in there, Mark?'

'Not so good, mate. A stomach bug, I think.'

'Go home. I'll tell the boss what happened.'

Mark thanked him. He would leave work, but he wasn't sure if he would go home. If the third person that night knew his mobile number, chances were they knew his address too.

Ten minutes ago, he'd thought he was in deep shit.

Now, Mark acknowledged, it was much worse than that.

30

The two young men waiting in Room 1 stopped their argument immediately she entered, unaware that she'd been listening to it through the door.

The one with dark auburn hair she knew to be Leila's brother without an introduction. The similarity in eye and hair colour was striking. Leila had been beautiful, her brother equally handsome. According to McNab, there was only ten months between them, Leila being the elder. An only child herself, Rhona had no experience of the closeness of siblings, but imagined that with less than a year between them, the brother and sister must have felt like twins. Yet according to McNab, Danny had claimed that he and his sister weren't close.

The argument raging as she'd approached the room had suggested the two men were at odds over Leila's death. How exactly, Rhona wasn't able to make out, except for the fact that they both blamed each other.

As Rhona introduced herself, she was acutely aware of Danny's appraising glance. Barry kept his eyes averted.

'So you're a doctor?' Danny said with a smile.

'Of science,' Rhona replied.

'Still, a bit too important to be taking swabs?'

Rhona let that one go and asked him to open his mouth. From the corner of her eye she noted that Barry looked decidedly worried about what she was doing. Danny on the other hand was gallusness personified. He even gave her a wink as she circled the inside of his mouth with the swab.

When it came to Barry, she saw fear in his eyes, but then again McNab had run a drawing past him which suggested his DNA might have already been found at the scene of crime. If this sample was a match to the semen found inside the doll, then Barry was one of the nine.

'So,' said Danny as she prepared to leave, 'will I see you again, Dr MacLeod?'

Rhona met his challenging look with one of her own.

'Unlikely, unless it's in court.'

Danny didn't like that answer. A cloud suddenly covered those handsome green eyes.

He immediately came back at her with, 'Why would I be in court?'

'To see your sister's killer brought to justice.'

'If you lot ever fucking find him.'

Rhona wanted to say, 'We'll find him, all right,' but chose not to, which she decided irked him even more.

DS Clark and McNab were waiting outside for her.

'Well?' McNab said.

'Barry's worried about the swab, Danny not so much,' she told him.

'Looked like Danny was chatting you up.'

'He *is* very handsome,' Rhona said, with a glance at Janice.

'And knows it,' Janice agreed.

McNab intervened. 'If you have the hots for Danny, I'd better do his interview.'

'Barry's not bad either. He definitely works out,' Janice said.

McNab looked from one woman to the other.

'You're shitting me.'

'Took you a while to work that one out, Detective,' Rhona said as she departed.

Back at the lab she found Chrissy eager to tell her the news regarding McNab's love life. Rhona decided not to burst her bubble by revealing that she knew already. Her plan failed, as she suspected it might. Chrissy McInsh had an eye for a lie.

'You know,' she said accusingly.

'McNab told me himself, first thing this morning.'

'He did?' Chrissy looked taken aback. 'Why would he do that?'

'Confession's good for the soul?' Rhona tried.

Chrissy, the Catholic, didn't go for that. 'He wanted to make you jealous.'

'Why would he want to make me jealous?'

'Were you?'

'No.'

Chrissy eyed her speculatively. 'Is it the real thing?'

'I believe he likes her. Very much,' Rhona said truthfully.

Chrissy seemed at a loss for words at this, but only briefly. 'Well, good on him. He deserves it.'

Rhona couldn't have agreed more.

Danny had been in Glasgow when his sister had died. His excuse for not going on tour was that he'd been ill.

'Ill with what?' McNab said.

'Flu.'

'You went to the doctor?'

'No. I sweated it out and got better.'

'When did you last see your sister?'

Danny threw him an evil look. 'In a drawer in the mortuary twenty minutes ago.'

McNab didn't rise to the bait. 'Before that?'

'I don't keep a diary. Maybe three weeks ago.'

'What did you talk about?'

'She talks. I don't listen.'

'What was the room of dolls in her flat about?'

'Never saw it. Don't go there.'

'Where do you meet then?'

'We have coffee some place.'

And so the conversation had progressed mainly into dead ends. The most important question was where Danny had been on the night his sister died and that was one that demanded an answer.

'I told you. I was ill. So I was in bed.'

'Anyone vouch for that?'

Danny nodded, and McNab could swear he was very pleased with his reply.

'Maggie Carter.'

So the plan was for Maggie to give him an alibi.

'Funny she didn't mention that when I spoke to her.'

'You didn't ask,' Danny said with a smirk.

'Been conducting your own interview?' McNab said.

'A policeman comes to the door, I want to know why.'

McNab had left it there, for the moment. Danny was cocky and confident. Maggie not so much. He had a feeling she had a greater respect for the truth than her flatmate, or lover. Did he think Danny might have killed his sister? Most murders were committed by someone known to the victim. Few were carried out by a stranger.

McNab had a strong feeling that Danny and his sister's

lives were far more intertwined than he had been willing to admit. He also thought Danny had a plan. To do what, he didn't know. He would love to put a tail on Danny if he could convince the boss that it would be worth the man hours and the money. And McNab didn't have anything other than a feeling, yet.

Once he'd finished with Danny, he checked on DS Clark. The room she'd occupied with Barry was empty, so he went to top up his caffeine levels at the machine before seeking her out. This was the time in an investigation when you were bombarded with spurious bits of information, possible witnesses and false leads. It could sometimes feel like you were wading through treacle.

And still no pointers to the man Leila had left the pub with.

McNab was beginning to believe the guy wasn't local. Both Shannon and Barry had maintained he was Scottish, but that didn't mean he lived in Glasgow, or even Scotland. If one or both of the men had been up in Glasgow for the weekend, and departed swiftly afterwards, they had little chance of locating either of them.

If McNab had been a praying man, he would have prayed for some luck.

As he downed the double espresso, a call came in from Ollie.

'Hey, Ollie.'

'I have some good news for you. We found Shannon's mobile.'

'Where?

'Tossed in a litter bin not far from her flat.'

Somebody had just made a big mistake. McNab said a silent thank you to the God he hadn't prayed to.

'It's been damaged, but not badly enough. Want to come and see?'

McNab very much wanted to come and see.

31

As she headed home through Kelvingrove Park, the rain came on. The dark clouds amassing on the horizon as she left the lab should have been enough to warn Rhona of the impending deluge. The first drops were large, although infrequent. They sent the summer-clothed Glaswegians scurrying onwards along the path, or heading for the nearest tree to take shelter.

A flash of lightning split the sky above the Gothic grandeur of the university main building. Seconds later, they were treated to an exaggerated roll of thunder that might have heralded the entry of that master of horror, Boris Karloff.

Then the rain began in earnest.

The force of it on her head and shoulders drove Rhona, like the others, to seek any kind of shelter. Advice about not standing under a tree during a thunderstorm was heeded by no one. Getting soaked was a certainty, being hit by lightning less so.

The panic changed to screams of laughter as the group under the tree squeezed together in an effort to give house room to those who still needed to get under cover. Beside her, a pram, with hood up, provided the best refuge of all, the baby inside gazing out with saucer eyes at the antics of the grown-ups.

The deluge lasted a full fifteen minutes. Tropical rain rather than that usually experienced in Glasgow. Even the term 'pelting' didn't do it justice. Eventually her fellow shelterers grew bold and stepped out into it. Glasgow folk were used to rain, after all, and at least the stuff coming out of the sky today was warm.

Rhona added herself to the departing throng.

Strangely, getting soaked had put a spring in her step. By now the rain had lessened to a warm shower, pleasant and invigorating. The grass steamed and the park turned into a scene from *Avatar* minus the wild beasts and gangly blue inhabitants.

Her mobile rang as she exited the park gates. She hesitated when she saw the name on the screen, but answered nonetheless.

'Where are you?' Sean said.

'Coming out of the park.'

'You're wet?'

'Very.'

A distant roll of thunder emphasized what had just happened.

'I called to ask you out to dinner.'

That foxed her. Rhona played for time. 'When?'

'Tonight.'

'Where?' Rhona suspected it would be his place. Sean considered himself a better cook than most chefs. In that he was probably right.

'You choose,' he said, surprising her even further.

Rhona named a popular restaurant in Ashton Lane.

'We might not get a table, but I'll try,' Sean said. 'I'll text you the time.'

Ringing off, Rhona found herself rather pleased by the

call, and the invitation. Not to mention the prospect of a proper meal, and some male company, unconnected with the investigation.

On entering the flat, she was immediately besieged by Tom, desirous for food and affection. She dealt with both demands, then took herself off for a proper shower, which also involved soap and shampoo.

Dressed and ready, she awaited the promised text. When it finally arrived, she had ten minutes left until the allotted time. According to Sean, he'd waited in her desired restaurant foyer for a full hour in the hope of a no-show or a cancellation, and had finally struck it lucky.

Rhona immediately called herself a taxi. As she headed for the door, she spotted something on the floor. Tom had a habit of bringing in dead things from the roof, where he spent a lot of his time. Her first thought was that it was the remains of a bird.

She considered ignoring it and dealing with it on her return, but that would give Tom time to dissect the carcass, leaving bits scattered throughout the flat for her to step on. Rhona bent for a closer look and discovered it wasn't a dead bird, but a small stick figure made of twigs. It was lying close to the wall under the coat rack, next to a pool of water from her dripping jacket.

How did that get there?

Her first thought was that it had to have been brought in by Tom, but he only had access to the roof. How could such a thing have got on the roof? Rhona glanced at the letter box. Had it arrived that way? Had it been there when she'd first come in?

Her mobile rang a warning that the taxi had arrived.

She could either leave it where it lay and trust Tom not

to dismember it, or take it with her. She opted for the latter, creating a makeshift evidence bag using a couple of clean paper hankies.

The taxi driver, having had no response from the mobile call, was now ringing her buzzer.

Rhona slipped the stick figure into her bag, already aware that her planned evening of no thought of work wasn't to be. A figure made of sticks in her hall she might have contrived to find an explanation for. One with what looked like human hair glued to its head and a red thread wound tightly round its neck would be more difficult.

Double-locking the door, Rhona headed downstairs to the waiting taxi.

The rain having cleared, the people of Glasgow were back out in force to enjoy the evening. During the journey to Ashton Lane, Rhona pondered whether it would have been better to have cancelled the outing in the wake of her find. If she'd done that, Sean would have rightly asked for an explanation and what could she have said?

The deaths of Leila and Shannon had hit the news now big time, especially the Wicca aspects. Although nothing about the Witchcraft angle had been officially released by the police, the tabloids had managed to ferret out that aspect to the story. Passing a newsagent on their way up Byres Road gave evidence of that, the latest headline in the evening paper declaring SECOND GLASGOW WITCH FOUND DEAD.

They were on the third course when Sean finally asked her what was wrong.

Arriving at the restaurant, she'd resolved to put the stick figure out of her mind for this evening at least. There would be time enough tomorrow to consider its implications.

Meeting Sean like this for a meal was bizarre enough, so she'd concentrated in dealing with that, and then found herself enjoying both the food and the company. When Sean was in the mood to entertain the ladies, he couldn't be faulted. The only thing missing in what was obviously a courtship meal, was a serenade on his saxophone. Maybe he had plans to do that later.

But despite Sean's best efforts, he'd found himself with a non-attentive companion.

'This was a bad idea?' he suggested quietly.

In a sudden rush of emotion, Rhona remembered all the reasons why she'd been with Sean. His kindness, the fact he was non-judgemental, and his support when she'd chosen to search for her son, Liam. And when they'd finally met, Liam had taken to Sean in a big way.

'No,' Rhona said. 'It wasn't a bad idea. I just have something on my mind.'

Sean accepted that and didn't ask what the something was. He knew her well enough not to.

Just at that moment the coffee arrived, along with two Irish whiskeys.

When the waitress departed, Sean reached over and took Rhona's hand. That small gesture ruined her resolve. She reached into her bag and placed the parcel on the table, opening it up to expose her find. Against the white of the tablecloth, the twig figure, with its wisps of hair and holes where eyes should be, was a disturbing image.

Whatever Sean had been expecting, it hadn't been this. Rhona watched as he tried to assess what he was looking at.

'May I pick it up?'

'Better not touch it,' Rhona said.

'Where did you find it?'

'In my hall, near the front door, as I was about to leave.'

Sean absorbed her answer and read its implication. 'Has it something to do with the Witchcraft case?'

'I don't know.'

'It's female?'

'I'd say so.'

'And the string round the neck . . .' Sean said.

'Leila Hardy was found with a cingulum round her neck.'

'Cingulum?'

Rhona explained the meaning of the term and what a cingulum was used for.

'So this is a representation of her death?'

'Maybe,' Rhona said.

She placed the stick figure inside a clean napkin and put it back in her bag.

Sean started asking the questions she'd been asking herself.

'Was the lower door open when you got home?'

'No, but by using the common buzzer anyone might be let into the close.'

'How would the person who delivered it know where you lived?'

Rhona shrugged. If someone was determined to find out an address, they probably could.

'Were you followed through the park, maybe?'

Rhona cast her mind back to the torrential rain and standing in close proximity with dozens of others under that tree. It had been like the subway at peak time. Someone could have slipped it in her pocket in the crush, and it could have fallen out when she'd hung up her jacket. She said as much to Sean.

'I think the more important question is why was it delivered?' Sean finally said the words Rhona had been avoiding.

Rhona lifted her whiskey. Having spoken of the figure, she now wanted to forget it, how it had got into her hall and definitely why.

Sean read her expression and interpreted it correctly.

'I'll come back with you.'

32

The New Town Club didn't open its doors to just anyone. Mark Howitt Senior was a member. His son was not. He could be signed in as a guest, but was only allowed access to certain public rooms, such as the one he was in now.

Having already consumed a couple of good measures of high-strength Russian vodka in a pub on the Royal Mile, Mark had also ordered a vodka tonic from the waiter, while awaiting his father's arrival.

Seated in a high-backed leather chair, with the drink on a polished table next to him, he contemplated the thick-carpeted, wood-panelled room, which hadn't changed since the first time he'd been allowed entry to the hallowed halls. It struck him that this stuffy room resembled his father. Both, in Mark's eyes, had always been old.

His father had consistently looked, and acted, the same throughout Mark's childhood, adolescence and early adult-hood. A formidable figure, he had always seemed remote, even when at home in the large town house in central Edinburgh which the family had shared.

Mark had never seen his parents kiss or even embrace in public, or at home, except for a peck on the cheek. As an adolescent, he'd spent a lot of time wondering if they ever had sex. They'd definitely had it once because he was here, but there was a phase when he thought he might have been adopted, because he felt sure he was in no way genetically connected to his father.

On the other hand, Mark loved his mother, quite fiercely at times. He couldn't have said why, but she generated an affection in him which he found worrying, because it was seldom repeated in his other personal female relationships. His mother was kind, loving, thoughtful and wished her son well. She didn't cling to him, but almost pushed him away, so that he might 'find his own feet'.

Mark sometimes thought it was because she wanted him away from his father. But why? His father wasn't a cruel or bad man. He was supportive of his son. Interested in his future. He supplied Mark with money when necessary, but Mark knew the difference between his parents. His mother loved him unconditionally. His father, on the other hand, was disappointed in his only son.

And disappointment was harder to deal with than dislike.

At this thought, Mark attacked the vodka tonic, swallowing down half of it. He considered heading to the Gents, then remembered he'd left the line of cocaine at the flat as a precaution, having decided vodka would be his only prop.

The waiter was hovering nearby, so Mark emptied the glass and indicated he would like another. Should his father enter now, it would look like his first drink.

As it was, his order and his father appeared at the same time.

A big man, both in girth and height, Sir Mark Howitt Senior QC was a striking figure. Mark had seen him in action in court and been impressed, despite himself. His own inability to be certain about anything seemed entirely at odds with his father's view of the world and those in it.

His father glanced about and, spotting Mark, immediately headed in his direction.

Mark stood to attention like a soldier in front of a commanding officer.

'Mark.'

The handclasp his father offered was cool and firm, the opposite of Mark's warm, nervous, damp one. Mark withdrew his offering as quickly as possible.

'Good. I see you've ordered,' his father said as the vodka tonic was placed on the side table. 'I'll have my usual,' he told the waiter.

The usual was, as Mark knew, a double measure of his favourite single malt, served with a small jug of water. That, too, hadn't changed over the years.

His father sat down opposite him, his figure dwarfing even the voluminous high-backed leather chair.

'How are you, Mark?'

'Fine,' Mark said. 'Work's going well.'

'Good.' His father looked down for a moment as if squaring up to reveal the real reason why Mark was there, which definitely wasn't to enquire about Mark's job.

There was a pause in the proceedings when the waiter arrived with the pale malt in the crystal glass and the jug of water. His father thanked him, then waited until they were alone again, before speaking.

His father had always been forthright, a feature Mark had not inherited. Whatever his reason for bringing Mark here, it would be said clearly and unequivocally. Mark waited in silence for his nightmare to begin.

'I asked you here to tell you that your mother is dying. She has at best two months, but I don't believe it will be that long.'

The words Mark heard and attempted to process were not the ones he'd expected. Tensed and ready to spill lies as necessary, he was suddenly faced with the clear words of a truth too terrible to contemplate.

'What?' Mark said stupidly.

'She didn't want me to tell you, but I felt you should know.'

When rehearsing his confession, Mark had consistently heard his mother's voice, telling him he was right to go to the police and she was proud of him for doing so. It had been his 'get out' clause. His safety net. Whatever he did, his mother would still love him.

'I haven't been to see her,' Mark said, suddenly aware of how long it had been since his last visit.

'But you've spoken on the phone,' his father reminded him.

Mark realized his father was simply repeating his mother's words, and her excuses for his infrequent visits.

'I'll come home with you now.'

'No,' his father said swiftly. 'The nurse is with her and she'll be asleep, anyway.'

A tidal wave of emotion threatened to drown Mark. 'When, then?'

'I'll have to break it to her that I've told you. Then I'll call and let you know when to come.' His father lifted his glass and swallowed the whisky down. In that moment he looked vulnerable and bereft. Something Mark couldn't bear to behold.

'Why didn't she want me told?' Mark said.

His father contemplated him for a moment.

'Your mother has been courted by death for most of your life. She didn't want you to be courted by it too.'

The job done, his father rose. 'If you'll excuse me, I have another matter I must deal with before I go home.'

Mark followed his father's glance. A man had just entered the room. With a jolt Mark realized he recognized the man's face, but from where? Not sure his legs would support him, Mark stayed seated as his father approached the man, greeted him, then ushered him into a side room.

Mark lifted his drink with a shaking hand as the memory of where he'd seen the man came flooding back. It had been on television at a press conference about the Glasgow Witch murders. The man meeting with his father was the detective in charge of the investigation.

33

The rest of the Tech team had gone home, the main lights had dimmed, yet the machinery still hummed and blinked, giving the impression of a spacecraft automatically piloting itself through the outer darkness.

McNab didn't like this room, and felt inadequate when in it. What value had instinct, intuition and years of experience when faced with the vastness of the digital mind, the ability to process at a rate approaching the speed of light, cross-referencing and calculating?

Ollie, on the other hand, resembled a child with a toy, playing a complicated game. No fear. No trepidation. No lack of confidence in his abilities to master the digital world. That made Ollie a proper scientist.

What does that make me?

McNab suddenly recalled the term 'urban warrior' had been used by his superiors and definitely not in a complimentary way.

'Shannon received a single short phone call that evening, from this number,' Ollie said, bringing McNab back to the task in hand.

'Who was it?' McNab demanded.

A name appeared on the screen.

Jesus fuck. No wonder the bastard had looked so frightened

*when he'd been told about Shannon's death. Or maybe he'd known
already? Maybe he'd been the one to kill her?*

'Barry Fraser,' he said softly.

'You know him?' Ollie said.

'I know him, all right.'

Ollie moved on to the list of contacts and the more recent
texts he'd retrieved. The university library number was
among them, as too was Freya's mobile number. Seeing
Freya's name on the list gave McNab a jolt.

'How many calls or texts from, or to, that number?' He
pointed to Freya's name.

Ollie did a quick check. 'Eleven in total. There's a call
from it the day you found the body, which wasn't answered.'

McNab experienced a sense of relief that Freya's version
of events and the level of her friendship with Shannon
appeared to be true, at the same time admonishing himself
for ever doubting her.

Daniel Hardy was also on the list, as often as Barry. When
McNab had first interviewed the barman, Barry had been
quick to deny he'd even noticed Shannon in the pub, only
admitting to knowing Leila. For someone he didn't know
he was on the phone to her a lot, including speaking to her
the night she'd died.

It was time to talk to Barry Fraser again.

The earlier rain clouds had disappeared, leaving a clear sky
and a rosy sunset. McNab toyed with the idea of saving
Barry for the morning and calling Freya instead. The police
had revealed to the press that Shannon's mobile was missing,
but hadn't updated them with the news that it had now
been found. So assuming Barry was following the investigation, he wouldn't be currently concerned about his call being

discovered. Barry Fraser, McNab decided, wasn't going anywhere.

He contemplated going by The Pot Still just to check on the guy, but if he was seen it might alert Barry to what was to follow. No, McNab decided. Let the bastard do his shift and go home. They would bring him in tomorrow, and he would take great delight in tearing Barry's story to shreds.

McNab pulled out his mobile and called Freya's number.

This time he let it ring longer than just three times, but still she didn't answer. McNab was a little taken aback by the degree of his disappointment. He checked his watch, only now taking note of the time. He should have called earlier, before he met up with Ollie.

Maybe she'd given up on him and was out somewhere she couldn't hear her mobile? Alternatively, she'd spotted the name of the caller and decided not to answer. A thought that didn't go down well.

Eventually Freya's voice asked him to leave a message. McNab said, 'Hi, moon lady. Sorry it's so late. Call me, please.'

What to do now? In past times, he might have headed for the jazz club. Had a drink there and talked to colleagues. Maybe he would catch up with Sam, if Chrissy wasn't about. It was a tempting thought, but a dangerous one.

He would go home. Pick up a pizza on the way and watch some TV. He hadn't replaced the half-bottle of whisky he and Freya had shared. Hadn't even thought of doing so, until now.

A hole had opened up in his evening. A place he'd assumed would be filled by Freya, but now a bottle of whisky was vying for second place. In that moment his self-belief went, his conviction and determination with it. He knew he would buy a bottle of whisky on his way home. The off-licence was next to the takeaway. It was too easy.

McNab tried to persuade himself that that particular scenario wouldn't necessarily happen. That he'd made a commitment and would stick to it. Then he thought of Freya and his resolve evaporated. He tried to raise it again by checking his phone. But there was no answering message. No request that he come by.

I cannot depend on this woman to stop me from drinking.

But if not her, then who?

The answer came in the form of a phone call. McNab almost missed it, so intent was he in his approach to the pizza place and, of course, the off-licence. He didn't even glance at the screen, so hopeful was he that it was Freya calling back.

The voice that answered wasn't Freya, but it was the voice of a lost love.

'Dr MacLeod,' he said.

'Why don't you call me Rhona?'

'Because you told me we could never be friends again,' he said, knowing he sounded pathetic.

'What's wrong?'

'Nothing,' he lied.

'Have you been drinking?'

'Not a drop,' McNab said with honesty.

'Come over,' she said. 'Please.'

McNab had waited a long time to hear those words spoken by this woman.

'Why?'

There was a moment's silence. 'Because I'm asking you to.'

Her voice sounded worried and sad and evasive all at the same time. McNab knew he would agree because he'd never been able to say no to Rhona MacLeod, except that one night, in the stone circle.

'I'm on my way.'

Their history was as complex as the numerous investigations they'd worked on together. When he was being honest with himself, McNab knew exactly what Rhona thought of him. The term 'infuriating' came immediately to mind. She'd called him many things in the time they'd known one another; most of the terms used or implied had been less than complimentary. He also knew that she cared about him. Deeply and loyally. McNab would trust Rhona MacLeod with his life, as she could trust hers to him.

When he arrived, the flat was a blaze of light, every window facing the street lit up. When he buzzed, Rhona didn't free the door until she'd heard his voice. As McNab climbed the stairs, the thought occurred that something had spooked Rhona. This in itself spooked McNab, because one thing he knew about Rhona was, she didn't frighten easily.

When she opened the door to him, he was surprised to find her dressed as though for a date. He gave her an appraising look, which was quickly quashed by an unspoken warning from her.

The words, 'You didn't have to get dressed up for me,' died on McNab's lips.

She led him into the kitchen. No subdued lighting here either, every corner free of shadow. The window which normally stood open to allow the cat access to the roof was firmly closed and, McNab suspected, locked.

'What's going on?' he said.

She gestured to the table. On it lay a clear evidence bag with something inside. McNab picked the bag up and checked out its contents. The bundle of sticks it contained took shape and became a woman with long hair, wearing a red thread round her neck. There was no mistaking the image the figure conjured up.

'Where did you get this?' he said.

'I found it in the hall when I got back from work—'

He interrupted. 'Why didn't you call me?'

'I just did.' She sounded exasperated.

'Four hours later.'

'I had a date. I decided to keep it.'

McNab wondered who with, but didn't ask.

'Can I look at it out of the bag?'

She brought him gloves and a pair of tweezers.

'Who's touched it?' he said.

'Only me, and maybe the cat.'

She handed him a magnifying glass. 'There's something scratched on the body.'

At first McNab didn't see what she was talking about, so faint were the marks.

'What are they?'

'Runes,' she said.

'Fucking runes.' McNab felt his exasperation mount.

Rhona pushed a piece of paper towards him. On it was the alphabet table he'd seen in Magnus's book on Witchcraft. McNab expected her to translate for him. The fact that she didn't, worried him.

'What does it say?' he demanded.

Rhona hesitated for a moment. 'I think it says Freya.'

At the utterance of the name, McNab's stomach dropped like a stone.

Rhona immediately added a proviso. 'Freya is the name given to the Goddess in Wicca, so it's not unusual to see it on replicas.'

McNab remembered the little statue the real Freya had left on her pillow. He'd carried it with him since that morning. He produced it now and showed it to Rhona.

She studied the little green figure, noting the name on the base.

'Freya gave you this?' she said.

McNab nodded. 'That's a true depiction of the Goddess and there isn't a cingulum round her neck.'

'Have you spoken to Freya recently?' Rhona said.

McNab had his mobile out and already on fast dial. 'I tried calling her earlier. She didn't pick up.' He felt his throat tighten as his call rang out unanswered. Eventually Freya's voice came on asking him to leave a message.

'I'm on my way round to your place,' McNab said, trying to keep his voice even.

He pocketed his mobile.

'I'm not convinced this has anything to do with your Freya,' Rhona said. 'I called you as a precaution.'

He understood that. 'Thanks.'

'If she's stayed late at the library, her mobile may be switched off,' Rhona offered.

'I'll check there too.'

Rhona went with him to the door.

'You'll let me know?'

'Yes.' McNab suddenly remembered. 'We have Shannon's mobile. Barry Fraser called her the night she died.'

As he descended the stairs, he heard Rhona shut and double-lock the door behind him.

*

Rhona turned as the sitting-room door opened and Sean emerged.

'How did it go?' he said, concerned.

'He's going round to check on Freya.'

'You did the right thing.'

Rhona wasn't sure she had. She'd interpreted the runes as reading 'Freya', but even with the magnifying glass it wasn't clear that they did. She hadn't announced the name at first because she'd wanted McNab to attempt his own translation, to reinforce her own reading of the runes. Tomorrow, under a proper microscope, she could be more certain. But she hadn't wanted to wait until tomorrow.

'The doll might not be a threat,' Sean said.

'What could it be, then?' Rhona said sharply.

'A plea to find Leila's killer?'

Rhona halted the retort in her throat. Sean was right. She'd had pleas before, some by letter, some via email. When people realized she was forensically involved and the crime was personal to them, they sent her messages, either castigating her efforts or encouraging her to do more. The general population had great faith in the power and truth of forensics, mainly because of watching TV crime shows. It was both humbling and worrying.

'Freya is an established name for the Goddess,' Sean reminded her. 'And McNab's Freya wasn't a friend of the dead women. Just an acquaintance, like all their other colleagues in the library.'

'They weren't Wiccan,' Rhona said.

'How do you know?' Sean smiled. 'If I suddenly revealed that I practised Wicca, what would you say?'

He had her there. 'You *are* joking?' she said.

'I was brought up an Irish Catholic, worshipping a man

227

who died a couple of thousand years ago. According to my teacher and the local priest, women were temptresses, destined to bring a man down. I find I'm rather drawn to the Wiccans, with their female Goddess.'

'There's a male God too,' Rhona reminded him.

'Equality between the sexes. Who would have thought?'

He had lightened the moment, which of course had been Sean's intention.

'Freya has a champion in McNab,' he reminded her. 'She can trust him with her life.' Sean smiled. 'Now will you come to bed with me?'

34

The library building was in darkness as he drove past on his way to Freya's flat. If Freya had been working late, as Rhona had suggested, she wasn't there now. Approaching the traffic lights at the foot of University Avenue, McNab ignored the red signal and drove straight through, taking a swift left up into the grid of streets behind the university union.

The arrival of the stick figure had initially annoyed rather than worried him. The papers had hyped up the Witch aspect of the killing of the two women. Black magic and sex sold newspapers and the tabloids were making the most of it. That sort of coverage attracted nutters, who liked to get involved. There had also been outrage from so-called Wiccans, defending their beliefs, accusing the police of a witch-hunt. Delivering a token like the stick figure to a member of the investigating team was on a par with all of that.

He'd been singled out on numerous occasions by angry members of the public who thought he wasn't doing his job properly, as had Rhona. McNab suspected the real reason she'd waited four hours before calling was because she hadn't initially spotted the faint runes or translated them. Once she had, she'd felt compelled to tell him, especially in view of the blurted confession in the lab about his love life.

Turning the car into Freya's street, McNab saw a figure

exit the main door to her set of flats and walk swiftly away. It was a young man, tall, slim, his back towards McNab, hood up, his face unseen, yet there was something recognizable about him. McNab was momentarily tempted to follow the guy, just to check him out, then he spotted a light on in Freya's place.

To say his heart lifted would have been an understatement.

With no empty spaces on the narrow street, McNab parked alongside a wheelie bin, despite the police warning notice that he would be towed away if he committed that particular crime. As he turned off the engine, his mobile rang and the name he'd longed for lit up the screen.

'Freya.'

'I just got your messages. When you didn't call earlier, I went to the library to work and forgot my mobile.'

McNab said a thousand silent thank yous. 'I'm sorry, I got held up at work.'

'Are you home now?' she said.

'No. I'm standing outside your flat.'

There was a moment of surprised silence. 'How long have you been there?'

'I just arrived.'

Another short silence. 'Are you planning on coming up, or staying on sentry duty outside?'

'I'll come up,' he said.

The door buzzed open.

She met him in the hall, already naked. The fear he'd striven hard not to acknowledge drove McNab now, and he swept her into his arms, lifting her high in delight. Freya responded by encircling him with her legs. McNab carried her through to the bedroom, their laughter and desire colliding.

Laying her carefully on the bed, McNab undressed.

Before he could lie down, she moved to the edge of the bed and took him in her mouth. The action was unexpected and explosive. But McNab didn't want this. He gently caught her head in his hands and drew her up. He wanted to cradle the face that was coming to mean so much to him. He wanted to kiss her. To make every nerve in her body sing. Freya was alive. She was safe. McNab hadn't known until this moment just how much that meant to him.

He lay and watched her sleep. McNab had rarely done that with a woman before, except perhaps Rhona MacLeod. The opportunities to do so with Rhona had been rare, and precious, to him at least. For her, he knew, not so much. There had been genuine affection in her responses, even passion at times, like the day he'd reappeared from the dead. That was the encounter he liked to remember most.

Would this relationship be any different?

McNab removed a wisp of hair from Freya's cheek, so that his view of her face was unimpeded. She was younger than him, by ten years at least. Was that a problem? He was a detective sergeant destined to go no further than that. Her career, on the other hand, was only just beginning. If they were together, could she cope with his strange existence, his brushes with drink and his obsession with work?

The boss had a wife and a family, McNab reminded himself. Bill and Margaret had been together almost as long as the woman before him had been alive. Now that was a sobering thought.

But he wasn't Bill Wilson. If McNab had been asked to

liken himself to anyone, it would have been Rhona, although her obsessions were better controlled than his. Neither of them had truly committed to one partner. McNab had accepted long ago that there was only one man who stood a real chance with Rhona MacLeod, and it certainly wasn't him.

But maybe his chance of happiness lay facing him?

What future did this woman, Freya, Wiccan goddess, and he, Detective Sergeant Michael Joseph McNab, recently demoted, have together?

As he contemplated this, Freya turned in her sleep and McNab was met with her back. In view of his current thoughts, it was an uncomfortable image. Women had a habit of turning their backs on him.

McNab lay down behind her, craving again the warmth and touch of her skin. She moved a little to meet him. The closeness of her sprung him into action again. McNab retreated, not wanting to impose himself on her when she was so obviously asleep.

Just then his hand touched something protruding from under her pillow. He found it and took hold, sliding it free from its hiding place. McNab knew what it was, even before he saw it. He could feel the shape of the plaited silk and judge its long length as it uncurled. Had she intended using the cingulum tonight? Had she planned to wrap it round them, tightening it as they reached climax?

The idea both disturbed and excited him.

Freya had made no secret of the fact that she was Wiccan, he reminded himself. She had been, McNab believed, completely honest with him up to now. If she'd wanted him to take part in sexual magick, she would have asked. His answer, McNab wasn't so sure of.

At that moment Freya stirred into wakefulness, moving close to press herself against him. It was the signal McNab had been waiting for.

35

He stood in the darkened room, the cold damp smell of disuse enveloping him. Gone was the warm scent of incense, the glint of candlelight and the soft music of her chanting.

In vain he searched the shadows for any sense of her presence, and found none.

Then it hit him. If Leila's spirit was absent from this place, then she *had* truly gone.

The finality of this struck with a terrible intensity that stopped both his breath and his heart. Seeing her lying in the mortuary, white and cold, the shining hair already dull, the green eyes closed, he hadn't recognized that lifeless mannequin as his sister. He'd been angry to have been forced to look at it. To pronounce it as his sister.

At that point hate had taken possession of him and he'd directed that hate at the detective, because Danny couldn't face the truth – that Leila was probably dead because of him.

In this place, surrounded by her altar and candlesticks, her robe and wall hangings, her God and Goddess statues, he knew it was true.

His beautiful, wonderful sister had gone from him.

Where are you?

He shouted his thoughts and his voice hit the concrete walls and echoed back at him unanswered.

What use is your magick now?

Danny sat down on the circular mat, with his back against her altar, put his arms about his knees and wept.

Sometime later, he stood up and lit all the candles and the incense burner, then topped up the dishes, one of salt and one for water. Finally, he filled the goblet with wine.

Her book of spells he placed at the back between the statues of the God and Goddess. Danny thought of the red cingulum, which should have been here, but was being kept by the police as forensic evidence.

I don't need forensic evidence to find out who killed my sister.

He lifted the green Goddess and turned her upside down. Made of china, the figure had a small hole in the base. Below the hole, the name Freya was etched. He lifted it to the candlelight and tried to see inside.

If the other Freya was right, this was where he might find it.

Danny stepped back a little and, swinging the hand that held the statue, struck it hard against the surface. It shattered, sending sharp shards to litter the altar. One sliced the palm of his hand, breaking the skin, sending a trickle of blood to fall on the salt dish, quickly colouring its contents red.

There was nothing hidden in there.

Freya had been wrong. There was no contact list. Nothing to help him track down Leila's killer or killers. All he had were three video clips and without being able to identify the men in them, he had failed.

In Wicca there was no retribution after death. No hell and damnation awaiting the wicked. Witches believed you got your rewards and punishments during your life, according to how you lived it. Do good and you will get good back. But do evil and evil will return.

What had Leila done to deserve such evil?

'Give of yourself – your love; your life – and you will be thrice rewarded. But send forth harm and that too will return thrice over,' Danny intoned.

That part of the Wiccan Rede, he did agree with.

Danny lifted the sacrificial knife and the Book of Shadows from the altar and blew out the candles.

36

When his father had disappeared into the side room with the policeman, Mark had waved the waiter back over and ordered another double vodka, then pulled out his mobile and called Jeff, despite the disapproving look from an elderly man sitting two chairs away.

Jeff had answered after three rings. 'I thought we agreed—'

Mark had cut him off. 'Listen. It's important.'

The tenor of Mark's voice had had the desired effect on Jeff. 'Okay?' he'd said cautiously.

'I'm coming through to yours. Now.'

'Why the fuck would you do that?' Jeff had sounded genuinely perplexed.

'I've had a video message on my mobile. It's of me . . . and the girl.' Mark hadn't been able to bring himself to say the name because that would have made her real.

'Where was it taken? In the bar?'

At that point, Mark had suddenly remembered he'd told Jeff he'd never had sex with her. *Jesus fuck.* The lies just kept mounting up.

'In the street, near her place, just before she told me to fuck off,' he'd lied again.

'Can you see your face in it?'

'A bit.' Another lie because in the video you couldn't see his face, just most of his naked body.

'Who the hell sent it?'

'I don't know, do I?' Mark had said, thinking what a stupid bastard Jeff could be at times. Christ, if he got a lawyer like Jeff on his case, he'd be done for.

'Maybe the killer?' Jeff had said in a frightened voice.

'That's why I want to lie low for a bit at your place. In case he knows where I live, as well as my number.'

'How could he know your number? You didn't give it to the girl, did you?'

'No.' Mark had asked himself the same question and didn't like the answer he'd come up with. He'd been out of his head on coke and drink that night. He didn't remember anything after fucking the girl. Didn't remember passing out. Didn't even remember if he'd smothered her. But somebody had seen all of it and no doubt when Mark *had* passed out, had taken his mobile number for future reference. But to do what?

'Maybe they're planning on blackmailing you. If they find out your father's a judge—'

Mark had interrupted him at that point and told Jeff he was catching the next train. 'Meet me in the Central Hotel bar.' He'd rung off then, not keen to get involved in any further discussion, especially one involving his father and blackmail.

Now at Waverley Station, his mobile rang again. Checking the screen, he saw Emilie's name. Mark ignored it. He would text her once he was on the train. He could tell her he'd been sent home ill, but then she might come round to see him. No, he decided, he'd make some excuse about being away on a course for a couple of days. She might buy that.

The train to Queen Street was busy. Mark found himself sharing a table with three young women, all dressed up for a night out clubbing in Glasgow. No drink was allowed on the trains after nine o'clock, but that hadn't thwarted them.

Mark soon discovered that the Costa Coffee cups they'd carried on didn't contain coffee, but a pink alcoholic concoction. Their subterfuge worked well, probably because, although chatty, they didn't appear drunk and behaved impeccably when the inspector arrived to check their tickets. When he left the carriage, the girls offered to 'share' their lethal cocktail with Mark and he accepted readily. Even better than the booze and chat, the one opposite, a dark-haired brown-eyed beauty, removed her shoe and used her foot to massage his crotch under the table, which helped Mark forget the mess he was in, for the length of the journey, at least.

Hanging back as the train drew into Queen Street, he let the giggling girls get off. His crotch nuzzler delayed long enough to pass him her mobile number. Mark gave her a grateful smile in return.

He watched the three of them clip clop their way up the platform, either the ridiculous heels or the cocktails they'd consumed contributing to their unsteady gait. As they exited through the barrier, his admirer turned back and gave him a wave which Mark returned, wishing with all his heart that it had been her he'd met on that fateful night out.

The hour of pleasure over, reality came back with a vengeance. Not only that, his bladder seemed suddenly keen to get rid of the vodka tonics he'd downed in his father's club, augmented by the cocktail potion. His mobile buzzed as he jumped the turnstile into the Gents. Mark expected to discover Emilie's name on the screen again, having totally forgotten to contact her on the train. However, the text wasn't from Emilie, but from the unknown number.

Mark's first instinct was to stamp on the mobile and throw it in the nearest bin. Then the bastard couldn't contact him, ever again.

But that might prompt his tormentor to contact the police instead.

Mark made for a cubicle, went in and shut the door. Feeling unsteady, either through drink or fear, Mark lowered the lid and sat down.

Then he opened the text.

The buzz of drink and cocaine was wearing off and stark terrifying reality settling back in. He was still high as evidenced by the enhanced colours and sharp vibrant sounds, but the fall was coming and fast. He'd planned to be high when he met his tormentor, but had timed it wrong.

Anger split through the sudden despair and he shouted a litany of silent abuse at the girl who had so fucked up his life. Why had the bitch taken *him* home? Why not Jeff or any other stupid fucker in that bar? A rush of nausea swept over him and he thought that he would throw up, there on the street.

He stopped and waited, cold sweat popping his forehead.

Gradually the inner swell subsided, but it had brought a flashback of that morning when he'd stood in his own vomit in the dead girl's bedroom. God, would he never rid himself of these images?

Go to the police and tell them what happened.

The cool, calm voice that appeared in his head was that of his mother. It was so real, so clear, that Mark could have sworn she was standing there beside him.

He straightened up and came to a decision. He would meet his tormentor as planned, but he would tell him that he was going to the police. If he had choked that girl, then it had been an accident. And he definitely hadn't hung her on that hook.

Buoyed by his new-found flicker of courage, Mark upped his pace.

The rain came on as he approached the meeting place. He stood at the entrance and looked down the narrow, dark, rain-splattered lane. The last time he'd come here, *she* had been leading the way. All he could think about as he'd walked behind her was the sex that was to follow. Now, he had no idea what awaited him here.

37

Despite heading out early, McNab found the council had been true to their word and had removed his car. He called the appropriate number, but his excuse that he'd abandoned the car to chase the perpetrator of a crime didn't wash with the man on the other end. In fact, he sounded delighted to have shafted a police officer.

'You'll have to pick it up from the pound, like everyone else, *Detective Sergeant*. But maybe you can claim the fee on expenses and make the good citizens of Glasgow pay for it,' he added for good measure.

Normally McNab would have given him a mouthful in return, but not this morning. He headed back upstairs to say a proper goodbye to Freya.

'You can stay for coffee, then?' she said in response to his announcement.

McNab didn't see why not, and besides, he'd decided to broach the subject of the stick figure. He didn't want to frighten Freya, just encourage her to be vigilant and to report any unexpected visitors or deliveries.

When he'd finished his brief description, Freya immediately asked if the figure had been given a name. That threw McNab a little and he contemplated saying no, then decided against it. If Freya was being honest with him, he had to be honest with her.

'There were runes scratched on it. When translated, we think they said Freya.'

'So that's why you came by last night? Because the runes said Freya? You were worried for my safety?'

'That, and to see you again.'

She looked touched by this, then glanced down and studied her coffee for a moment.

'I did have a visitor last night, just before you arrived,' she said.

Now McNab was the surprised one. 'Can I ask who?' he said cautiously.

'Leila's brother, Danny.'

It was the last name McNab had expected to hear. 'Danny Hardy?'

In flashback, McNab remembered turning into the street and glimpsing the man emerging confidently from her main door, then the sensation that he recognized something about the guy, despite not seeing his face. He now knew what it had been – the bloody swagger of the man.

'Why was Danny here?' he said, striving to keep his voice calm.

In an instant McNab suspected Freya was about to lie to him, and he desperately didn't want her to. As she avoided eye contact, a terrible series of thoughts hit McNab. She'd asked him on the phone how long he'd been outside, because she wanted to know if he'd seen Danny. When she'd met him in the hall, she was already naked. And the worst thought of all – the red cingulum below her pillow hadn't been there for him, but for Danny.

McNab recalled the way Danny had looked at him in the interview room, as though he was revelling in some secret

McNab didn't know about. Maybe the secret was that he was shafting him?

Jealousy and suspicion bloomed, then grew exponentially. The detective in McNab took over and with it the belief that everyone is a liar until proved otherwise. Including Freya.

'You're sleeping with him.' The words were out before he could stop them.

She flinched as they hit home. McNab found himself interpreting her non-answer as guilt and convinced himself he was right. When she didn't respond to his accusation he tried again.

'Are you sleeping with Danny Hardy?'

'I'm sleeping with you,' she said quietly.

McNab ignored her response because the thoughts were coming too rapidly, and all of them were bad. 'You were telling the truth when you said you didn't know Leila that well, but what you didn't say was that you knew her brother. Intimately.'

'Michael,' she tried.

His look as she uttered his name silenced her.

'I'll have to ask you to come down to the station and give a statement regarding the deaths of Leila Hardy and Shannon Jones, and your relationship with the deceased's brother Daniel Hardy.'

The face he'd watched in sleep last night, drained of colour. Freya looked as though she might protest, or try and explain, then chose not to.

Now McNab saw sadness in Freya's eyes, rather than guilt, and knew that whether he was right or wrong, what had happened in the last few moments was irreparable.

'I am not having sex with Daniel Hardy. He came here last night to talk to me about Leila. What he told me, I want to tell you.'

Seconds had elapsed since McNab's outburst, but it felt like hours. He'd messed up. Big time. He hadn't given her a chance to speak. He'd failed to trust her, because he didn't trust himself.

They sat on either side of the kitchen table, the warm coffee pot between them. McNab could still smell its aroma and with it his feelings about having breakfast with her. But the man who'd shared her bed and looked so tenderly on her sleeping face was no more. He knew it and she knew it. Whatever she said now wouldn't change that. He'd screwed up whatever had been possible between them, just as he'd feared he would.

She waited for him to acknowledge what she'd said before she continued. McNab took refuge in his detective demeanour. It was a shabby thing to do, but once he thought of her as a suspect or a liar, he found himself incapable of moving away from that premise. This, he decided, is why I cannot sustain a relationship in this job.

'Leila was performing sex magick, according to her brother, almost exclusively for a group of men who occupy positions of power,' Freya said. 'She had been sworn to secrecy about this. One night when high or drunk she told Danny. He was worried, so he decided to film what was happening, to safeguard his sister.' She paused to let the words sink in. 'Barry knew about it.'

Her words drifted over McNab, not really registering, because he couldn't draw his emotions away from what had just happened between them. Eventually his brain engaged and analysed what she'd been saying. 'There's footage of her meetings with the Nine?' he said.

'According to Danny, there's some footage, but not of all the men in the group.'

'Why did he tell you?' McNab said.

'Danny wants to find his sister's killer. He thinks you . . . the police aren't doing enough. He asked what I knew about the covens and Leila's place in them. And did I know anything about the Nine.'

'And do you?' McNab said.

'No. What I told you is true. Leila, Shannon and I were work colleagues who shared a similar interest. That's all. It was a coincidence that we were all at the Edinburgh coven that night.'

McNab wished she hadn't used that word. One thing the boss had taught him was not to believe in coincidence.

'Why didn't Danny tell me about the video footage in his interview?'

'He said you didn't like or trust him, and you didn't want to listen.'

Both could be said to be true, but McNab didn't buy it. Danny Hardy had a mission and McNab wasn't convinced it was the one he'd assigned to Freya.

'What's he planning?'

'I don't know. He had a call, probably around the time you arrived downstairs. He said he had to go. That's when I called you.'

McNab recalled Danny's swift exit from the building, plus the fact that he'd avoided looking in the direction of the arriving car. McNab's detective heart told him that Danny had been warned of his imminent arrival, and not by an external call. That heart shattered as he formed the words, but he said them anyway.

'I don't believe you were at the library. I don't think you forgot your mobile. I think you didn't answer because you and Danny were fucking. When you got the second message, you knew I was on my way, so Danny had to leave, and fast. That's why you were naked when you opened the door to me.'

Freya stood up, that lovely face white, sad and furious.

'I want you to go. Now,' she said.

McNab deliberately drank down the remains of his coffee before standing up.

'Be at the station sometime this morning. Detective Sergeant Clark will take down your statement.'

He waited a moment on the landing after she'd shut the door on him, listening to the sound of her weeping, knowing if he was wrong, then he'd just fucked up the best thing that had ever happened to him.

38

So he didn't need whisky to press the self-destruct button. He could do that when stone-cold sober.

As he walked towards town, McNab relived every word he'd said, and saw his expression as he'd said them. It wasn't a pretty sight or sound. He'd conducted the conversation like an interview with a known criminal – with sarcasm, innuendo, accusation and cruelty.

McNab felt his chest tighten and his throat close. He had been a bastard to her. Then he remembered Danny's expression in the interview room when he'd been coming on to Rhona. His manner while McNab was interviewing him. The arrogance. The sense that Danny had something on McNab and was very pleased about it.

Then, to crown it, an image of Danny and a naked Freya came into his head.

Had there been an object he could punch at that point, McNab would have done it.

He forced himself to think about what Freya had told him. The Nine were important men and Danny had footage of some of them with Leila. McNab's first instinct said it wasn't true and she'd said it to deflect him from his rant about Danny's visit. Why would Freya tell him something like that? Did Danny tell her to?

None of it made any sense.

If only he'd stayed calm and not let suspicion take over, he might have learned more. But, he reminded himself, suspicion was at the heart of being a detective.

Everyone was a liar until proved innocent.

For once the mantra didn't work. He'd conducted himself badly. He should have asked more questions, instead of throwing accusations. Janice would make a better job of it – that is, if Freya turned up at the station as ordered.

He would call and warn Janice that Freya was on her way. Bring DS Clark up to date on what he'd been told about Danny. He would also ask for a warrant for the arrest of Daniel Hardy. Barry Fraser, he would keep for himself.

A brisk walk and a phone call later, he was outside The Pot Still.

Last time he'd been here, Barry had turned up ten minutes from now, just as McNab had finished his breakfast. The thought of anything other than a liquid breakfast didn't appeal at the moment. McNab stood for a moment, composing himself, rehearsing the word 'coffee' rather than 'whisky' before heading inside.

The same guy was bottling behind the counter. His expression when he spotted McNab's entry was anything but welcoming.

'He's not in,' he said before McNab could ask after Barry. 'Didn't turn up last night either. I had to come in and cover for him.' He didn't include *bastard* in the complaint, but McNab got the flavour of it.

'You have his number?' McNab said.

'I've tried it twice already this morning. He's not answering.'

McNab gave his order and went back to his table in the corner. As he waited for the coffee to arrive, his mobile rang and DI Wilson's name lit up the screen. McNab hesitated before answering, aware he'd been off the radar for a while, and would have to explain his reasons.

'Boss?'

'Where are you?'

Another hesitation. Should he tell him he was in the pub?

McNab came clean. 'The Pot Still, looking for Barry Fraser.'

'Get round to Bath Street Lane. Now.'

McNab rose to his feet, just as the pot of coffee was plonked on his table.

'What's up, sir?'

'A council worker just called in to report the body of a male, behind the Lion Chambers.'

He lay curled in a corner, his face and knees close to the wall, a thick pool of congealed blood seeming to cushion his head against the cracked concrete. From the back, McNab estimated him as around six feet tall. Dressed in shirt and jeans, his broad muscled shoulders stretched the cotton. Blond, twenties to thirties, worked out – a description of plenty of the blokes who may have frequented the Hope Street area last night.

McNab would have given anything to have checked out the face, but knew that wasn't possible. With the forensic team not here yet, he couldn't step any closer to the crime scene without contaminating it.

The tape was already up cordoning off entry to the lane, two uniformed officers on sentry duty. The bloke who had found the body had been told to stay put until someone interviewed him. His anxious face sought McNab over the barrier, seemingly keen to tell all.

McNab departed the body and went to talk to him.

Up close, the man had a pinched look, the voluminous yellow jacket dwarfing his thin frame. His face was pale and sickly, not surprising when he'd come to clear up rubbish and found a body instead.

McNab introduced himself and showed his ID. 'What's your name?'

The man looked surprised to be asked. 'Tattie McAllister.'

'Your real name?'

He looked taken aback by the question. 'That is ma real name.'

'Well, Mr McAllister —' McNab couldn't bring himself to say 'Tattie' — 'tell me how you found the body.'

'I came in to pull out the wheelie bin for emptying and he was lying there.' He gestured at the corner, but averted his eyes.

'Did you touch the body?'

He shook his head. 'No way. I knew he was dead, so I kept away.'

'What time was this?'

Tattie checked his watch. 'Half an hour ago.'

'Any sign of a weapon?'

'Naw, but it might be in the bin,' he suggested helpfully.

McNab hoped so. Just then he saw the team arrive, including the forensic van. He thanked Tattie and said he could go, but to leave his contact details with one of the uniformed officers at the cordon.

'I haven't emptied the bin,' the man said, looking worried.

'We'll do that,' McNab assured him.

McNab recognized Rhona's figure despite the shapeless forensic suit. McNab joined her and began kitting up himself.

'Any ID?' Rhona said as she taped her gloves and pulled on a second pair.

McNab explained about the position of the body. 'I haven't got close enough to check.'

Back inside the cordon, Rhona followed McNab along the cobbled lane, round the Lion Chambers building and into the rear concreted area behind a wheelie bin, passing the door into Leila's flat en route. Rhona stopped six feet back and studied the scene. The body lay close in to the corner, where the back of the Lion Chambers building met a neighbouring block of flats. The cramped location would make securing a tent a problem. Something she didn't have to tell McNab, who'd been crime-scene manager on a number of incidents.

Rhona approached with caution, trying to assimilate and question as she did so.

The smell was of warmth and rotting refuse near the bin, but as she got closer to the body she also picked up a faint scent of male cologne.

The position had struck her as odd from six feet away. Now nearer, it seemed even odder. Why was he so close to the wall, almost hugging it? Had his assassin pulled him into the corner to hide him from view of the few windows that did look down on the lane? Or was it to make it difficult to see his face? The pool of blood didn't look disturbed and there was no evidence of him being dragged into the corner.

Rhona hunkered down and began to check the accessible pockets of the jeans. All of them were empty. If he'd had a wallet or a mobile phone, they appeared to have been taken.

At this angle, she couldn't see his face without moving his head. Remaining crouched, she took some shots to indicate the exact angle of his head, then handing her camera to McNab, she gently turned the head enough to expose the face.

Any hope of instant recognition was immediately quashed, although the method of death became apparent. The eye sockets had been pierced and gouged out by a sharp implement. Both cheeks and the forehead had been cut in the shape of a cross, in what looked like an attempt to make the victim unrecognizable.

McNab crouched beside her. 'Jesus, God.'

'You know him?' she said.

McNab shook his head. 'I thought it might be the barman, Barry Fraser, but there's no telling from that face.'

'Why Barry?'

'He and Danny were apparently filming some of Leila's encounters with the Nine, supposedly as a safeguard for Leila. Then again, maybe it was for blackmail. The Nine are apparently pillars of our society.'

'Who told you all this?' Rhona said.

McNab gave a little shake of his head, indicating he wasn't willing to divulge his source. 'I'm not saying it's true, but if it is . . .' McNab reached over to double-check the pockets, then said, 'There's no watch.'

'Maybe he didn't wear one,' Rhona suggested.

McNab stood up as though he'd just realized something. 'I think the bastard took his watch,' he said, amazed.

'Who, the killer?'

'No, the guy who found him. He swore he didn't go near the body, but he looked shifty about it.'

'What about the wallet and mobile?'

'Maybe he got the whole lot before we arrived.' McNab cursed himself. 'I'd better locate Tattie McAllister before he gets rid of his plunder.'

'Before you go, what happened about Freya?' Rhona felt she had to ask.

'She was fine,' McNab said curtly.

The difference in his demeanour from that of last night suggested Freya might be fine, but McNab definitely wasn't, and neither was their relationship.

Rhona wanted to say, 'What happened?', but settled for, 'That's good,' instead. When McNab's expression closed down, it was better not to probe too deeply.

In the end, with rain threatening, Rhona had made the decision to move the body away from the wall in order to raise a forensic tent. Once enclosed, with the heavy patter of rain on the roof, she'd continued with her forensic examination in situ.

A police pathologist had come and gone. Expecting a knife crime but not in the manner it was presented, he'd been a little taken aback at the gouged eye sockets and slashed face, and had stayed just long enough to pronounce death.

Judging by the knees of the victim's jeans, it appeared he'd been kneeling prior to his death. The walls that met on that corner were green with slime from a leaking drainpipe which ran down the back of the Lion Chambers building. The corner also housed some rather artistic graffiti, perhaps as a tribute to the Chambers' former use as a set of artists' studios.

There were deposits of green fungus on the victim's palms and under the fingernails. Rhona imagined him on his knees facing the wall, his hands on the stone. Whoever had killed him had made him a supplicant first. If that had been his position, then why not slit his throat? Easy to do and less chance of blood on your clothes. Why bother with the messy business of stabbing out the eyes, unless it had some meaning for the perpetrator?

The state and temperature of the body suggested he'd been killed the previous night, which matched McNab's story of the missing Barry. Having been with him for such a short period of time to take a mouth swab, her one abiding memory of Barry Fraser was the fear in his eyes. And now those eyes were gone.

When her mobile rang, she'd already finished work on the body and was in the process of writing up her notes. Outside, she could hear the movements and calls of the forensic team scouring the lane. Chrissy had worked the area inside the tent and had now joined her colleagues who were decanting the contents of the wheelie bin, looking for a possible murder weapon.

Rhona fished inside her forensic bag for her mobile, assuming it would be McNab to give her news on the missing items, but the call came from an unknown number.

'Dr Rhona MacLeod?' a voice said hesitantly.

'Yes. And you are?'

'Freya Devine. I'm a research student at Glasgow University.'

McNab's Freya.

'How did you get this number?' Rhona said.

There was a moment's embarrassed silence. 'From Detective Sergeant McNab's mobile.'

By the tone and manner of her reply, it seemed clear to

Rhona that McNab knew nothing of this acquisition. She waited for an explanation for the call and it eventually came.

'There's something I need to speak to you about. Will you meet with me?'

'If it's to do with the current case, then you should contact the police directly,' Rhona told her.

'It's about Michael.'

Hearing McNab's first name spoken in that concerned manner, coupled with McNab's earlier demeanour, decided Rhona.

'Okay, let's meet.'

39

The video clip had arrived on his mobile shortly after McNab had left Rhona at the crime scene. He'd barely had time to contact the council and get details for Tattie McAllister, who it appeared had knocked off work early because of his shock at finding a body in Bath Street Lane.

McNab thought it more likely that Tattie was disposing of his loot and with it the identity of the corpse. Of course, he could be wrong. Tattie could be an upright citizen who, after a bad experience, needed a lie-down. Experience and intuition suggested otherwise.

The message that heralded the video clip immediately caught his attention.

It said, 'This is the man you're looking for,' followed by a mobile number.

McNab launched the video.

There was a moment when he could make out nothing but flickering candlelight and dancing shadows. Then he saw them. They were seated upright on the bed, Leila straddling the man. Around their waists was fastened the red cingulum. There was no sense from their actions that they were aware of a camera recording them, but then again, maybe they were acting for the camera. Leila's face was in clear view. The male's face was barely visible and only briefly.

257

The shoulders were broad, the upper body toned. The chest hair suggested he might be blond.

On the top right-hand corner of the recording was a date and a time. If they were correct, this had happened the night Leila had died. There was no sound on the recording, but it was clear that they were approaching climax as Leila reached down and began tightening the cingulum.

McNab realized that the *thump thump* was the sound of his own heart in his ears. He had a sudden and overwhelming desire to shout *Stop*, then the video jumped as though it had halted on his command then started again.

Now he saw only Leila's face, her eyes wide with excitement or maybe the beginnings of fear, as a male hand appeared to push a cloth into her mouth.

Without sound, the image of panic in her bulging eyes was even more horrific.

McNab waited for her hands to appear to pull the cloth free, but they never did.

The screen went black. It was over.

Around McNab life continued. Pedestrians stopped and checked out the yellow tape and were moved on. A bus trundled past, those on this side craning their necks to see why so many police were about. A young woman appeared with a pram. She and McNab exchanged glances as she realized something bad had happened behind that tape.

'I'm sorry,' she said as she walked past, as though she could do anything about it.

McNab didn't answer, intent as he was on what he had just viewed.

Freya had said that Danny had footage of some of Leila's encounters.

If that were true, was this one of them?

He dismissed that as a probability. If Danny had shot this video, then surely he would have prevented his sister's death?

So if Danny hadn't taken it, who had? And who was the guy in the video?

McNab rang Ollie and warned him he was forwarding him the clip and message.

'I want to know who sent it and who owns the mobile number in the message. The guy in the video could be our prime suspect. See if you can match him with the CCTV footage. I'll call in after I've spoken to the boss.'

'Will do.'

McNab checked the time. The boss was expecting a report in person, and he certainly had plenty to tell him.

The rain that had given them problems earlier had eased in the interim, although judging by the thick mass of dark clouds, they could look forward to another downpour soon enough.

McNab headed off on foot, aware he should have done something about his car. That something was to turn up at the pound and pay the fine. For that he needed to borrow a vehicle and a driver to transport him. All of which took time. Something he didn't have.

The incident room was working full out – on the wall board photographs of Leila and Shannon, alive and dead, plus a myriad of other material. Despite everything being recorded on Return To Scene software and accessible by all, there was still a demand to see it up there – to watch the placing of each piece in what seemed like a giant jigsaw puzzle. If the recent victim was Barry Fraser, then they had yet another death to add to the puzzle.

At least now he could walk into the boss's office and tell him that they might have a lead on the perpetrator.

DI Wilson was in his seat facing the window. When he heard the door open he swivelled round to face McNab. The face was still too thin, but there was a light in his eye and a firm set to his mouth. A look that McNab knew only too well. That look was usually present when he or some other member of the team had screwed up and let the boss down. McNab had met that look often and deserved it.

Surprisingly, when DI Wilson realized that it was McNab, the look changed.

This time McNab was waved to a seat.

'I'm sorry, boss, about being out of touch,' McNab began.

DI Wilson shook his head, dismissing McNab's opening line of apology.

'Tell me about the Bath Lane body.'

McNab described the scene, and the possibility that the victim might be Barry Fraser.

'Has his home address been checked?'

'Someone's gone round. I'm still waiting for the officer to get back to me,' McNab said.

'Why do you think it might be Barry despite the injuries to his face?'

McNab decided it was time to reveal what Freya had told him. Even as he outlined what she'd said about Danny and Barry being involved in taking footage of Leila's sexual encounters with the nine pillars of the establishment, he could hear all the things he should have asked her resound in his head. The boss was looking at him with a questioning air, no doubt wondering the same thing.

'I told her to come in this morning and give a full statement, sir,' he finished.

There were a few moments of silence, then the question: 'Were you aware that Freya Devine was in contact with Daniel Hardy?'

'No, sir. Not initially,' McNab added.

The eyes were boring into him now.

'And when did you become aware of this, Sergeant?'

McNab's throat closed and he covered it with a cough. This was turning into an interrogation with him on the receiving end, and the boss was ace at scenting a lie.

'Daniel Hardy was at her place, just prior to my arrival, sir.'

'And you were there, why?'

Now he was on tricky ground. He could come clean and admit he was sleeping with a possible witness, or lie. He never got the chance to do either.

'Since when, Sergeant?' DI Wilson said, a hard glint in his eye.

'I met her at the university library. She turned up one night at the flat, frightened about the death of two of her colleagues. That's when she told me about their visit to the Edinburgh coven.'

The boss had risen as McNab talked, and walked back to his spot by the window, so that McNab was addressing his back.

'Did you learn nothing from the *Stonewarrior* case, Sergeant?' the voice said.

'I learned to curb my drinking, sir.'

The boss turned to face him. 'But not yet to vet your sexual partners before bedding them?'

'She's a post-grad student from Newcastle working part-time at the library. She's not a criminal,' McNab said defensively.

'But she *is* a possible witness.'

McNab couldn't refute that. Freya hadn't appeared to be when they'd first met, but that excuse wouldn't wash with the boss.

'I severed my relationship with Freya Devine as soon as I realized that might be the case, sir.'

If the boss did the maths, he would know the timeline didn't quite match his pronouncement. McNab didn't wait for that to happen. He took out the mobile and laid it on the desk.

'I received a video recording a short while ago accompanied by a message stating that this is the man we're looking for for Leila's murder, together with a mobile number.'

McNab set the video in action.

DI Wilson had sat back down and was now staring at the mobile screen. When the video ended, he played it again.

'I've already given it to the Tech department,' McNab said. 'They should be able to trace who sent it.'

DI Wilson nodded. 'We need to pick up Daniel Hardy. If he took this video, he was there when his sister died. If it wasn't him, I want to know who it was.'

'Yes, sir.'

McNab made to rise.

As he did so, DI Wilson surprised him by saying, 'I called in a favour on the missing DNA report.'

McNab waited in anticipation.

'My source confirmed that one of the Nine is a serving officer.'

40

'You should be telling this to a police officer,' Rhona said.

'I don't want to get Michael into trouble.'

McNab was already in trouble, Rhona thought, but didn't say so. The young woman looked worried enough.

She'd arranged to meet Freya Devine in The Pot Still, which seemed appropriate, considering its role in the investigation and its proximity to the crime scene. When Rhona arrived, Freya had been sitting in a corner alone, a pot of tea in front of her.

Rhona had approached and introduced herself.

'I'm very grateful that you agreed to see me,' had been the reply.

Rhona had ordered a coffee and taken a seat across the table from her. Freya was young, but definitely not as young as McNab's previous disaster of a relationship that had nearly cost him his career. She also looked and sounded intelligent, another improvement on the previous one.

Rhona had waited for her coffee to be delivered before she'd encouraged Freya to tell her why she'd asked to speak to her. Then it had all come tumbling out. Freya's original meeting with McNab at the university. Her shock at Leila's death. Her conversation with Leila about sexual magick. Then Shannon's non-appearance at work.

'I wanted to go round and check on her, but Michael

stopped me. He already knew by then that Shannon was dead.' A shadow crossed her face, then she pulled herself together and went on. 'He was very kind to me.' She looked as though she might say more on that, but didn't. 'He came to check on me after you received the stick figure. Told me to be careful of visitors or deliveries, and to inform him if anything odd happened. So I told him about Danny Hardy's visit.'

Rhona waited for her to continue. When she didn't, Rhona said, 'And that didn't go down very well with McNab?'

'He thought that Danny and I were –' she paused and looked directly at Rhona – 'which we aren't. Danny told me he didn't trust the police to find Leila's killer, and he knew that Leila had kept a list of the men she was performing sexual magick with, but he didn't know where it was. He thought I might know.'

'And did you?'

'No, but I suggested a possibility and he said he would look there.'

'Where?'

'On her altar in her Goddess statue.'

'Where is her altar?' Rhona said.

Freya looked surprised. 'I thought she worshipped at home.'

'There was no altar in her flat.'

'That's strange. I got the impression Danny knew where it was.'

'He didn't mention a location?'

Freya shook her head. 'Shannon would have known . . .' She stumbled to a halt.

Which was probably why Shannon was dead, was left unsaid by either of them.

'If Leila didn't worship at home, then where might she choose?' Rhona persisted.

Freya inclined her head a little as though in deep thought. 'My mother had a little hut in our garden. I use a box room in my flat.' She thought again. 'Somewhere quiet where she was unlikely to be disturbed. A basement maybe, easily accessible.'

'The university somewhere?' Rhona tried.

'I thought Shannon might have been using one of the rooms that originally housed the Ferguson collection.'

'On the occult,' Rhona added.

Freya seemed surprised she should have heard of it.

'Professor Pirie, who works with us as a profiler, spoke about it,' Rhona explained.

'I found a set of keys in Shannon's desk.' Freya produced a simple ring with two keys on it, one large, the other much smaller. 'The bigger one opens a small back room there. Shannon had let slip something. I thought . . .' Freya hesitated.

'Thought what?' Rhona urged.

'Shannon said something about a Wiccan secret.'

Rhona waited for her to continue.

'I thought she might have unearthed a manuscript left behind when the collection moved to the main library. Or maybe she'd been using the room to worship in. But there was nothing there.'

'Shannon's bedroom had a circular mat but she didn't have an altar either,' Rhona told her.

Freya looked at her, wide-eyed. 'So maybe she and Leila were worshipping together?'

Rhona suspected so. 'But where?' she said.

Freya shook her head. 'I have no idea.'

'I suggest you go down to the station and give a full statement. Tell them everything you've told me,' Rhona said.

Worry crossed Freya's face. 'It was me who came on to Michael. I don't want him to get into trouble because of it.'

'Just tell them the whole story. That's the best thing.'

Freya didn't look convinced but eventually nodded. 'You're right. That's what I'll do.'

'Why did you contact me in particular?' Rhona had to know.

'Michael gave the impression . . .' Freya seemed to want to choose her words carefully, 'you were someone he trusted.'

Who can I trust?

In answer to the internal question, two names immediately sprang to mind – Bill and Chrissy. At one time she would have also said McNab, but since the *Stonewarrior* case, she wasn't so sure. Sean's name hadn't occurred, and she questioned why.

Perhaps it wasn't possible to truly trust a lover? Then she thought of her adoptive parents, who'd been both friends and lovers until death had finally parted them. Bill and his wife Margaret were the same.

As to Chrissy and Sam, Rhona wasn't so sure. The cracks in that relationship were already showing. Sam, Chrissy believed, would go back to Nigeria when his training as a doctor was complete. Chrissy had already declared that she wouldn't go with him. She was also determined that their child, named after McNab, would stay in Scotland with her. Circumstances had drawn her and Sam together, and it appeared that circumstances would break them apart.

As for McNab and Freya . . .

Rhona recalled how upbeat McNab had been since he'd met Freya. Seeing McNab joyous had been a revelation. One that hadn't lasted long. He'd always said, in his job, everyone was a liar until proved otherwise. It seemed McNab had decided that was also the case with Freya.

But maybe he was wrong?

Freya hadn't asked Rhona to plead her case with McNab, but Rhona decided she just might, given the opportunity.

Had she registered the padlock in passing, even subconsciously? *No.* Her focus had been on the body and its immediate vicinity. Searching the surrounding area had been the prerogative of the crime-scene manager.

She hadn't considered the padlocked door at all, not until Freya had shown her the key ring she'd found in Shannon's desk and stated how the larger key opened a door in the previous Ferguson library in the old building, but what the smaller key was for, she had no idea.

At that point Rhona had asked if she could have the smaller of the keys to study and Freya had handed it over without argument.

Rhona retrieved the said key from her pocket and approached the door on the lane side of the Lion Chambers, yards from where the latest body had been discovered. This entire section of the building reeked of damp, its crumbling concrete sprouting glossy green growth, fed by a broken drainpipe further up the narrow eight-storey property.

All the metal on the door and the security-grilled windows was corroded, including the thick chain, but strangely not the padlock itself, where the area around the keyhole gleamed clean with use.

Rhona eyed the small key.

If Freya was right and Shannon and Leila had worshipped together, might it not have been near Leila's flat?

It just could be.

Rhona whispered a silent *please*.

As though in answer, the key turned swiftly to the right. The padlock clicked and fell open.

According to the two officers sent to check out Barry Fraser's flat, there had been no sighting of him in the last two days. Apparently he lived alone but entertained frequently, often after the pub shut.

'No music, no noise, no nothing, according to his downstairs neighbour, who sounded pretty relieved about that,' the uniforms had told McNab.

They hadn't forced entry, unlike McNab with Shannon's flat. Mainly because McNab was of the opinion that the body currently on the mortuary slab was Barry Fraser. He was just awaiting DNA comparison with the mouth swab taken in the interview to prove it. McNab anticipated that the same swab would prove that the barman, although an occasional sexual partner of Leila's, wasn't one of the nine 'important' men featured in the dolls.

The method used to kill him, a sharp implement shoved into his eyes, had a ritual feel to it. Knives were often the weapon of choice in Glasgow, but the eyes weren't the usual entry point. McNab couldn't help but feel that stabbing someone's eyes out indicated that the killer hadn't liked what Barry had viewed with them. If what Freya had said was true – McNab could hardly say her name even to himself without feeling pain – then Barry and Danny had truly pissed off Leila's important customers.

En route to the Tech department, McNab stopped at the coffee machine for a double espresso. He drank it down and pressed the button for another, aware that coffee had been his only sustenance apart from anger since he'd risen from

Freya's bed that morning. He'd assumed he'd have to go hungry for a while longer, but cheered up as he approached Ollie's cubicle and spied what awaited him on the desk.

Ollie grinned round at him.

'I took the liberty of ordering a double helping, seeing as you ate most of mine the last time.'

McNab eyed the giant filled roll with delight.

'Sausage, bacon, egg and tattie scone special,' Ollie informed him. 'And strong black coffee. Is that okay?'

McNab's mouth watered in anticipation. 'Better than okay.'

Ollie waved him to a seat and pushed the plate and cup towards him. McNab set about the roll with vigour, while Ollie retrieved the display he'd obviously had planned for McNab's visit.

A name appeared on the screen alongside the number sent to McNab's mobile phone.

'The number belongs to a Mark Howitt. I did some research on him. He's on LinkedIn, has a Facebook page and tweets now and again.'

Ollie pulled up a photograph.

'He works for RBS in Edinburgh, a trader of some sort. Aged twenty-seven. Has a penthouse flat built in the grounds of the former Royal Edinburgh Infirmary overlooking the Meadows, so not short of money. Went to Edinburgh Academy, which is a fee-paying school, followed by Edinburgh University, where he studied law.' Ollie paused here, while McNab polished off the remains of the roll and had a slug of coffee.

'Now the really interesting part.' Ollie paused for effect. 'It appears that Mark Howitt has an illustrious father. Sir Mark Howitt Senior QC.'

'Jesus,' McNab said as he registered the name. 'His old man's a High Court judge?'

'Assuming the lead you were sent is true.'

Now came the crunch. 'Is he the guy in the video with Leila?' McNab said.

'Probably,' Ollie said.

'What do you mean probably?'

'According to the software there's a sixty per cent probability that the partial view of the face in the video is a match for Mark Howitt,' Ollie said. 'However . . . the video jumps just after the climax scene and before we see the hand approach the victim's mouth.'

He ran it again for McNab, stopping it at the spot mentioned.

'When it starts again, only the female's face is visible. I'm not sure where her hands are.'

McNab remembered waiting for Leila to pull the cloth from her mouth.

'The two slices of video are taken at different times?'

'I believe so. Unfortunately, we don't have a good shot of the man's hands during sex, so we can't compare them to the hand at the end. I've been trying to find clear images of Mark Howitt's hands but no luck so far.'

'So we bring him in,' McNab said.

'That would be good.'

'And if we have the ID wrong . . .' McNab imagined the fallout if that were the case.

He took a mouthful of coffee. His heart was already beating rapidly and he didn't need the caffeine, but the coffee felt the equivalent of a celebratory drink.

'What about the judge?' Ollie said.

McNab acknowledged they would have to tread carefully. He could approach the boss and give him the news. Let DI Wilson decide. Alternatively . . .

'Can we forget you discovered Mark Howitt's *possible* illustrious connections for the moment?' McNab paused. 'Just long enough for me to check out the suspect.'

Ollie gave him a long, slow smile. 'Sounds like a good plan to me.'

Back in the incident room, McNab looked for DS Clark only to be told she was taking a statement from a friend of the two female victims. The elation he'd experienced in the Tech department fell away and was replaced by a dull anger, whether at himself or Freya he wasn't sure.

He checked which room they were in, then went to take a look.

From the observation point next door, he studied the two women sitting across the table from one another. Janice looked calm and assured, Freya nervous and distressed. McNab's stomach flipped as she inclined her head to the right, a gesture he realized he'd come to love about her. It was something she did when thinking deeply.

In that moment, McNab wished the previous twelve hours had never happened. That he'd arrived ten minutes later at Freya's flat and, as a result, had never seen Danny Hardy leave.

Would that have made a difference to his reaction when Freya told him of Danny's visit?

Yes, because he wouldn't have immediately linked her nakedness to Danny's exit.

McNab wanted to listen in, but found himself incapable of doing so. He'd lost all confidence in his ability to analyse, accept or reject anything Freya said. He would have to leave that up to Janice. McNab left the viewing room and shut the door firmly behind him.

It was time to do something he *was* capable of.

41

Rhona stood for a moment considering her next move. Already kitted up, she could enter alone or wait and locate McNab. There were still a couple of SOCOs further down the lane, but Chrissy, she knew, had accompanied the evidence retrieved from the body back to the lab.

Rhona pulled at the chain and it rattled through the double handles and fell free.

As she pushed the door inwards, the scent of incense wafted out, faint but recognizable. Water dripped somewhere, each plop echoing back at her from the concrete walls.

A sudden mad fluttering saw a trapped pigeon avoid the glare of her torch and escape upwards through a hole in the ceiling, seeking the windowed and brighter upper level. In return, daylight drifted down, exposing the emptiness and dereliction of the room, with its covering of concrete dust and bird shit.

Yet she could still smell incense – of that she was certain.

According to Magnus, the area required to perform the rituals and work magick could be a whole building, a room or just part of a room. A place kept solely for rituals, in perhaps an attic or basement, like the vaults they'd visited in Edinburgh, would be ideal.

The room had to be clean and would have been scrubbed out with salt before the temple was constructed. Rhona checked the floor again. If there was a room, then there should be a noticeable pathway through the dust that led to it. She switched off her torch and stood for a moment, accustoming herself to the grey light.

Then she spotted it.

Rather than head across the room, the path snaked left. The room had been a shop at one time, as evidenced by the long counter and shelved back wall. Rhona followed the path behind the counter to an abrupt end at an old-fashioned wooden stool that stood between the counter and the shelves.

Rhona moved the stool back to expose a small brass handle embedded in the floor, signalling the existence of a trapdoor. She slipped her finger through the ring and pulled upwards. With a sigh the wooden door released itself and rose.

Immediately the scent, she recognized now as sandalwood, escaped.

Glancing down, she saw a steep ladder of perhaps a dozen or more steps.

Minutes later, Rhona was standing in the temple.

Entering at the north-west corner of the basement room, she faced the altar, which stood in the middle of the circle. To the east was the opening on the circle. The walls were painted the magickal symbolic colours: the north wall painted green, the east yellow, the south red and the west blue. On the south wall, which faced her, stood a couch draped in red. Above, black writing on the red wall read:

Here do I direct my power
Through the agencies of the
God and Goddess.

Directionally opposite, smoke still drifted from the censer that stood on the altar. According to Magnus, a special charcoal briquette was lit and sprinkled with incense, then placed in the censer, allowing it to burn slowly. Hence the lingering scent. Around the circle and in all four corners of the room stood a burnt-out candle. Only one remained alive, fluttering its way to extinction. The candles and censer suggested someone had been in here recently, maybe only hours before.

As Rhona approached the altar, she spotted the broken pieces of what looked like the Goddess statue scattered among the other ritual items, which included the statue of the God.

Freya had said she'd told Danny to check Leila's Goddess statue and it looked like either he or someone else had done just that. Rhona studied the altar and came to the conclusion that it wasn't only the Goddess that was missing. Salt and water dishes were there, as was a beautifully inscribed horn for wine. Two goblets for the God and Goddess stood on either of the altar. On the floor before it stood two further goblets for participants, confirming that two Witches used this temple for worship.

Magnus had said that every Witch has a personal knife, called an *athame*, or in the Scottish tradition, a *yag-dirk*. Usually made of steel, it was a double-edged blade. A ceremonial sword lay on the altar, normally used for marking the circle, but there was no knife, although there was clearly a place for it.

Rhona recalled the body outside with its gouged eyes. A double-edged knife would have been a perfect implement to achieve such a result.

If Danny had come here to search for the list, had he taken the knife?

Freya had told McNab that Danny and Barry had both been involved in taking videos of Leila and her sexual partners. If the victim in the lane was Barry, was it possible Danny had killed him? If so, why?

Rhona retreated upstairs. Back in the lane, she called McNab.

'Dr MacLeod?'

'I've located Leila's temple,' Rhona told him.

'Where?'

'In the Lion Chambers building.'

'That's been checked.'

'They missed a basement in the downstairs shop on the lane side.'

'You're fucking kidding me, right?'

She didn't answer the rhetorical question but asked one of her own. 'Can you come down?'

'I have something I have to do first. Are there SOCOs still about?'

'Chrissy's gone but I can bring her back,' Rhona offered. 'And I could ask Magnus to take a look?'

'Do that.'

His swift agreement surprised Rhona.

'Are you okay?' she said.

'Fine. Why shouldn't I be?'

Rhona could think of at least one reason. She decided to come clean.

'I found the temple because of Freya.'

She broke the loaded silence that followed. 'She showed me the keys she found in Shannon's desk. One looked like a padlock . . .'

McNab cut in, his voice a splinter of ice. 'You had no business interviewing Freya Devine.'

'I didn't interview her,' Rhona said. 'She called and asked to speak to me about Shannon.' That wasn't exactly true but . . .

'How did she get your number?' McNab asked sharply.

'I'm not sure,' Rhona lied. 'But I think what Freya told me was the truth.'

'Really?'

Rhona ignored the sarcasm. 'I'll let you know if we find anything.'

'You do that, Dr MacLeod.'

He rang off before Rhona could tell him about the missing knife.

Stupid, argumentative, stubborn bastard. No wonder he made a piss poor DI.

But, a small voice reminded her, *that stubborn bastard never gives up, no matter what it might cost him.*

And in this case, it looked as though it might have cost him Freya.

McNab threw the mobile on the passenger seat and tried to concentrate on the road. Having commandeered a vehicle, he was now on the M8 heading east. The afternoon traffic was steady which meant he wasn't going anywhere fast. McNab thought about putting on the blue light and hitting the accelerator. He would relish a burst of speed and some serious driving right now. On the other hand he was so angry, he was probably a danger to the public as well as himself.

He forced himself to stay in the left-hand lane at a steady sixty and tried to think things through. He'd done it again. Cut Rhona off with sarcasm, instead of questioning her about her find. And it was a find, one that he or his team had failed to achieve. The main search had made use of the front entrance to the Lion Chambers. All rooms had been checked but no one had spotted the basement entrance. Congratulations should have been in order and instead he'd given Rhona grief.

Was he a worse bastard sober than when he'd been drinking? Or was he just a bastard?

And what had Freya told Rhona that she believed? He hadn't even asked. So much for being a detective.

When he pulled in at Harthill services for petrol and a coffee fix, he found a text message from Ollie. It seemed the mobile used to send the video was a pay-as-you-go, which had since gone quiet. No surprise there. The next bit of news was more interesting. Mark Howitt had made a call in the last hour *to* Edinburgh *from* the Glasgow area. If true, then McNab was heading in the wrong direction if he wanted to speak personally to his suspect.

'Where in Glasgow?' McNab asked when he rang Ollie back.

'City centre area.'

'Who did he call?'

'An Emilie Cochrane.'

'Do we know anything about her?'

'Quite a lot.'

'Tell me.'

McNab listened to the details of Emilie's life, including her place of work, which was a high-end fashion store on George Street.

'Okay, keep a trace on Mark. I'll get back to you.' McNab rang off and finished up his coffee. If Emilie was the girlfriend then chances were she knew exactly where Mark was.

McNab began to wish he'd taken the train as he entered the city centre. Glasgow traffic was bad enough with its one-way system, which inevitably meant you went round the block while trying to get to your destination. Edinburgh had its own unique problems, including the addition of the trams on Princes Street and the rule on buses only. Running in parallel, George Street was wide with two-way traffic but getting a parking place was no easy matter. He finally located one at Charlotte Square and, paying his dues via the meter, began his walk, fetching up outside a rather smart clothes shop that had no prices in the window.

McNab headed inside.

The scent in here was not of incense or candles but of money. It was funny how money had a smell. A very pleasant one. McNab enjoyed the aroma for a moment before taking a look around for a possible Emilie.

Mark Howitt was by all accounts a tasty and well-heeled bloke, even if he might be a killer. McNab imagined a girlfriend would be his equal. He spotted who he thought might be Emilie moments later. She emerged through plush blue curtains and came walking towards him, although walking was an inadequate word to describe the movement she made.

She was tallish, blonde and very classy. McNab gave her a silent ten out of ten.

'Can I help you?' she said with a coquettish smile.

McNab killed that smile when he produced his ID and introduced himself. She observed him in a puzzled, defensive manner. Dealing with the police would be like dealing with riff-raff, is how McNab read it.

She collected herself and assumed a caring, bewildered look.

One McNab had met many times before, usually among those who thought themselves above and beyond the law.

'I'm investigating the murder of a young woman in Glasgow last Friday night.' He paused to allow that to sink in. 'And I'd like to speak to a Mark Howitt who I believe is a friend of yours.'

Whatever she'd expected, maybe a parking offence or a burglary in the vicinity, it hadn't been death, or a mention of Mark.

McNab barged straight ahead. 'We know he was in Glasgow at that time. We have him on CCTV leaving the pub with the female in question. We'd like to know where he is now.'

The lovely face became a turbulent mass of emotions, including outright shock, but McNab could see the calculations behind them. How much to say? How much to get involved?

'Can we go somewhere and have a quiet coffee?' McNab suggested with a reassuring smile. 'No one need know why I'm here.'

She saw and immediately clung to that smile and its reassurance. Image was everything here. If she was linked to a murderer, he suspected the job and quite a few other relationships might be over.

'I'll just tell them I'm popping out.'

McNab told her he'd wait for her outside.

She appeared moments later having donned a jacket to match her outfit. In the interim she'd collected herself and her look was now one of steely determination. McNab suspected she was about to shaft Mark Howitt, whatever their relationship had been.

She suggested a nearby cafe and chose to sit inside in

the darkest corner she could find. McNab went along with her desire for anonymity. Edinburgh was a small place, and he presumed George Street and its environs were even smaller.

When the waiter, decked out in long black apron, approached, McNab ordered his usual double espresso. Emilie asked for chamomile tea, to settle the nerves, no doubt. Left alone while they waited for their order to arrive, McNab asked Emilie what her relationship with the suspect was.

'We go out together – now and again,' she added, making it immediately impermanent.

McNab accepted that to put her at ease.

'Were you aware he was in Glasgow on Friday night?'

By her expression, this was a tricky one for her. If she revealed the truth, it might be construed that she knew Mark better than she wanted to admit.

Eventually, she said, 'He told me he was playing five-a-side football with Jeff in Glasgow.'

'Jeff?'

'Jeff Barclay. They went to university together. I've only met him once when he came through to Edinburgh. He and Mark get together once a month—' She came to a sudden halt, aware she was giving the impression that her relationship with Mark was long-standing.

McNab smiled again to further reassure her.

'Do you have Jeff's phone number?'

'No, but he's a lawyer for a big Glasgow firm.'

'Where is Mark now?'

'He said he's on a course for the next few days, in Glasgow.'

'When did he tell you this?'

She hesitated. 'He called this morning.'

'When did you last see him?'

Another hesitation. 'Saturday. He took me out to lunch.'

'How did he seem?'

She didn't like this, that was plain to see, as every answer indicated that she knew Mark better than she wanted to admit.

'Hungover, and –' she went in for the kill – 'he had a bad scratch on his right shoulder. He said he got it at the football.'

McNab thanked her and handed her his card.

'If Mark gets in touch again, you'll let me know?'

She stared at the card. 'I don't want to talk to him,' she said, shaking her head.

'Just let me know if he calls, or tries to see you.'

She didn't relish the thought of either possibility.

'Am I safe?' she said.

'We don't know that Mark's guilty of anything yet,' McNab said. 'That's why we need to talk to him.'

She wasn't sold on that. Mark was plainly guilty of lying to her and picking up other women. Her expression said as much.

'The sooner we contact him the better,' McNab said. 'So anything you can do to help would be much appreciated.'

Mollified by this, she slipped the card into her jacket pocket.

'I'd better get back,' she said.

McNab offered his hand and thanked her again for all her help.

When she'd gone he called the waiter over and ordered another espresso, this time to go. Emilie's chamomile tea was left untouched.

McNab picked up the car and headed up the Mound, intent now on checking out Mark's pad. He didn't have a search warrant, but that didn't necessarily mean he couldn't glean some information from a visit. Leading to the Royal Mile, this was the part of town most tourists flocked to. Crossing the Mile, he spotted the university in the distance and, to the west, the old Royal Infirmary.

Just inside the main gate was a reception area for those interested in purchasing a property on this prime site. According to Ollie, Mark's penthouse wasn't in the older building, but part of the new block which overlooked the extensive parkland known as the Meadows.

Parking in one of the many residents' bays, McNab headed for the block in question. The view even from ground level was pretty spectacular and the location was only a fifteen-minute walk from Princes Street. McNab thought of his much more modest backstreet flat as he gazed upwards at the structure that rose in turrets of glass. If the view was ace down here, what must it be like in the penthouse?

He turned in at reception where he was pleased to find a concierge on duty. McNab introduced himself once again and flashed his badge, which caused some interest.

'Aye, how can I help you, officer?'

'Mr Mark Howitt. The penthouse flat? Is he home?'

The man lifted a phone and pressed a number, which turned out to perform much like the buzzer in McNab's own less palatial residence.

'He's not in.' The concierge waited on the next development.

'Have you seen him recently?' McNab said.

'No. Why? Is something wrong?'

McNab assumed a serious expression. 'We're concerned for Mr Howitt's welfare. Is there any way we can check the flat just in case he *is* in there?'

'Well,' the man mulled this over, 'if you think something might be wrong with the bloke, I could use the pass key.'

'Thanks.'

Mission accomplished, they proceeded to the glass lift which sped them swiftly skywards. The door opened with a swish and McNab was presented with a bird's-eye view of the volcanic crag that was Arthur's Seat. The view alone must have added a hundred grand to the asking price.

As the concierge unlocked the door and pushed it open, McNab took his arm.

'If you could wait here, sir. Just in case.'

The concierge looked as though he might argue, so McNab added, 'We were alerted to the fact that Mr Howitt was suicidal. Better that you should stay out here.'

The 'suicide' word did the trick.

'I'm not supposed to leave my desk, officer. I'll head back down. I hope the bloke's all right.'

McNab waited until the lift sped downwards, then entered and shut the penthouse door behind him.

The smell of money was in here too, just like in the fancy clothes shop.

He stood for a moment admiring the wide open space that stretched from the glossy kitchen area to the floor-to-ceiling windows, which occupied three sides of the room. The furnishings were all black leather, the flat wall-mounted TV as big as a small cinema. Mark Howitt had *the pad*, all right.

McNab noted the whisky bottle and the glass on the granite kitchen surface. Next to which was undoubtedly a film of white powder. McNab rubbed his finger in it and tested it on his tongue.

So last time Mark was here, he'd indulged in some coke washed down with whisky.

Next stop, the bedroom.

Colours here were the same. Black bedding, leather headboard, white rug on the polished floor. Above the bed was a mirror, another on the ceiling, just like in Leila's apartment. The doors stood wide on the wardrobe, a couple of the drawers disturbed, suggesting Mark had maybe packed for a journey.

McNab checked Ollie's information for Mark's work number and gave it a ring. There was only one way to determine if Mark was actually on a course and that was to ask.

It took a few minutes to get through to his department where the call was fielded by someone called Cameron. This time McNab didn't mention police but just asked to speak to Mark Howitt.

'He's off sick, I'm afraid. May I help?'

McNab said he preferred to deal with Mr Howitt. 'Any idea when he'll be back?'

'I'm afraid not.'

McNab thanked him and rang off.

So Mark Howitt Junior had definitely flown the coop and McNab suspected his hideout to be pal Jeff's place. Jeff hadn't come forward as a witness despite the nationwide appeals featuring the CCTV images, suggesting he and Mark had decided to keep quiet together.

McNab took a last look round, then exited and shut the door. Emerging from the lift, he bestowed a reassuring look on the concierge.

'He's okay?'

'He's been located in Glasgow,' McNab said. 'Thanks for your help in this. Much appreciated.'

'You're very welcome.'

Once back at the car, McNab retrieved the whisky glass with the nice clear fingerprint on it and popped it in an evidence bag, then he called Ollie and asked him to seek out one Jeff Barclay who worked for a big firm of Glasgow lawyers.

'His home and work address,' he said, then added 'please' as an afterthought, to keep the troops happy.

'I take it this is about the Mark bloke?' Ollie said.

'He's hiding out in Glasgow. You did a good job tracking down the girlfriend. Now I need you to track down the mate.'

42

The temple was laid bare, the mystical nature of it dispersed by the harsh entry of the arc lights. Rhona shivered a little, and wished she'd put another layer on under the boiler suit. The cellar wasn't damp, not like the upper floors, but there was a definite chill down here which crept into your bones.

She'd called both Chrissy and Magnus, both of whom would appear shortly. In the interim she would take her own set of stills and a video recording, before embarking on a forensic examination of the room.

From the layout of the altar and the couch, this may have been the most likely place for the sex magick to occur. If that were the case then Leila's encounter with the man in the bar seemed random and perhaps nothing to do with the Nine.

Rhona recalled McNab's assertion that Danny had been filming some of the encounters in secret. If that was true, then here would be a better place to do it than Leila's bedroom, but where exactly in this room might a camera or a person with a camera or camera phone be hidden?

It took her thirty minutes to work out what she believed was the best possible location. Once decided it seemed obvious. The altar under its long white tablecloth consisted of a circular stone tabletop balanced on a wooden frame. It stood tall enough for someone to crouch beneath.

When Chrissy and Magnus arrived, Rhona ran her theory past them. Chrissy's response was that they should try it out.

'If Danny or Barry took the video they would have to fit under there. Both of them are tall, maybe not as tall as Magnus . . .' Chrissy eyed Magnus speculatively.

Under Chrissy's intense scrutinizing gaze, Rhona could swear he winced.

Chrissy snatched Rhona's mobile from her hand and gave it to a reluctant Magnus.

'Okay, you get under the altar.'

Magnus, seeing he had little choice other than to agree, dropped to his knees and did as commanded. It was a tight squeeze for a man of his height and build, but he managed it.

'Right, boss, now's your chance with me on the couch,' Chrissy said with glee.

After much laughter and many sexual innuendoes, the deed was accomplished.

Rhona played back the video. It was clear that the location under the table was a good vantage point should someone want to capture anyone using the bed for sexual magick.

With the fun over, Chrissy set to work on the room while Rhona and Magnus discussed the altar. Rhona explained her thoughts on the missing knife and the wounds on the most recent victim found in the lane.

'There should be a *yag-dirk* here,' Magnus agreed. 'And it would be capable of inflicting damage like that, but there's something else missing too.'

'What?' Rhona said.

'Leila's Book of Shadows. There's a chance she might

have brought it with her each time she came to the temple, but if that was the case, I assume you would have found it in her flat.'

'What would it look like?'

'It's the Wiccan equivalent of a Bible. Witches will create their own. They're often bound and very ornamental.'

'There was nothing like that in her flat.'

'Assuming Leila and Shannon were worshipping together here, the Book of Shadows would contain the rituals they practised and the spells they performed.'

'Including the ones cast with the Nine?' Rhona said.

Magnus nodded. 'It might give you a clue as to what the Nine were involved in, and what their desires were.'

'Which makes you wonder who removed it, and the knife?' Rhona said.

'From a profiler's viewpoint, nothing feels right,' Magnus said. 'Leila met the main suspect for the first time the night she died. She took him home and they had sex. In her flat, *not* here. If he did kill her, the act would appear to have been random, perhaps fuelled by drink or drugs, or as a reaction to the idea that she was putting a spell on him via the cingulum. So why hang her on a hook in that room? Why not just get out of there and fast?' He shook his head in consternation. 'This isn't the profile of a random killer. It does, however, fit the profile of a serial offender or,' he paused here, 'someone who is intent on wiping out everyone who might identify him.'

'One of the Nine?' Rhona said.

'Or all of them. Killing as a group makes it far more difficult to pin the blame on anyone.'

'If Leila threatened to expose them,' Rhona began, 'or Danny tried to blackmail them with the videos he'd taken, and your theory is correct, then maybe McNab is right, and the latest victim is Barry Fraser.'

'Which means Daniel Hardy is the only one left alive who's able to testify to any of this.'

An uncomfortable thought reared up in Rhona's mind. 'Danny made contact with Freya Devine recently. It was Freya who suggested he look in the Goddess statue for the list.'

From Magnus's expression he didn't like that piece of information one bit. 'I believe anyone who may have a link to this case will be considered a threat to the perpetrator *or* perpetrators,' he said. 'Can you ask McNab to keep a watch over Freya?'

43

'He's not here.'

'I'd like to take a look inside to confirm that, sir,' McNab said.

Jeff Barclay appeared about to refuse, then caught McNab's eye and decided to back off. As a lawyer, he must have been aware how things would go if he obstructed a police officer in a murder hunt.

McNab was permitted to enter and the door shut behind him. No doubt Jeff didn't fancy his neighbours knowing his business. He waved his arms in a dismissive manner. 'Go right ahead, Sergeant. Search the place. He's not here, as you'll see.'

McNab soon did see. The place, though not as expensive a pad as Mark's, was definitely upmarket. Situated in the Merchant City area of the city centre, McNab suspected this had been the place Mark had made his last call from. At the top of a renovated building, it had a view of Glasgow Concert Hall. With a similar layout to the penthouse, minus the floor-to-ceiling windows, it didn't have many places to hide.

McNab checked them all and found nothing.

Returning to the kitchen, he spied a bottle of Russian vodka and two shot glasses standing next to the sink, one of which had traces of vodka in it. McNab pointed and asked who Jeff had been entertaining.

The response was swift. 'My girlfriend, Carla.'

'And where is Carla now?'

'She left before you arrived.'

'How soon before I arrived?'

'Ten minutes.'

'She didn't finish her shot.'

'She's not a big drinker.'

It seemed to McNab that Jeff was growing more confident with every passing second, which suggested he felt safer now than when McNab had entered. McNab wondered why.

Then he saw the swift glance he wasn't supposed to see, and knew.

McNab lifted the bottle and checked it out as though he recognized good Russian vodka when he saw it. Meanwhile he calculated how he planned to play this out.

The long window on the street side sported what appeared to be a narrow ironwork balcony only big enough to house a couple of pot plants. Then again, maybe not.

McNab set the bottle down, strode swiftly across the room and opened the window. Behind him, he could swear he heard an intake of breath, but no warning shout. So maybe he was wrong.

The glass door now open, the noise of the Merchant City swept in. McNab stepped out and took a look round. The railing was four feet high. Beside it was a drainpipe that ran up to a flat roof which was surrounded by a low stone facade. A fit guy could make his way up there, no problem.

McNab re-entered to find Jeff looking even happier.

'I told you he wasn't here.' He could hardly keep the delight from his voice.

'We have witnesses who saw you and Mark Howitt at The Pot Still the night Leila Hardy died. I don't need to remind you that it appears you have been withholding information in a murder enquiry.'

Jeff's smirk dissolved and he produced a concerned and earnest expression to replace it.

'I *was* with Mark that night in the pub, but he left with a girl. I don't watch TV and had no idea what happened to her until now. If I had, I would of course have gone to the police.'

McNab listened as the man before him slithered like a snake round the truth. Lawyers in his opinion could be very good at bare-faced lies, or telling the truth as their clients perceived it. McNab chose to nurse his anger. He would fan the flames when he was ready.

'I want you down at the station to give a statement and a DNA sample. If Mark Howitt gets in touch, I want to know.'

Jeff gave a small smile of success. 'Of course, Detective Sergeant. Now that I'm aware of the circumstances, I'd be delighted to help.'

McNab could have cheerfully spat in his eye, but he'd already decided to save Mr Smoothie for later. An hour in an interview room with Jeff Barclay was a prospect he would relish.

On exiting the flat, McNab fired his next shot.

'I'd like to take a look on the roof.'

The satisfied smile slid from Jeff's face.

'That's not possible,' he said swiftly. 'There's no access.'

McNab pointed at the trapdoor in the ceiling above the top landing. 'If we pull that down, there will be steps. You should have a pole with a hook on the end to do that.'

Jeff quickly shook his head.

'I don't have anything like that,' he insisted.

'Then bring a chair.'

Jeff took so long to comply with the request, McNab suspected the bastard was texting his mate, so he went for a look. It turned out Jeff had taken refuge in the toilet, obviously stalling for time.

McNab took a chair from the dining table.

As he suspected, the freed trapdoor revealed a set of pull-down steps.

In minutes he was on the roof. From this vantage point it was obvious that anyone emerging here could make their way along the building and choose to exit via one of the other stairways in the L-shaped block of flats. If Mark Howitt had come up here, he was long gone. McNab chose to walk the roof anyway, checking behind the redundant chimney stacks, just in case.

Ten minutes later he was back in the flat. Jeff had emerged from his sojourn in the toilet and awaited him, the self-satisfied look he'd worn earlier back in place.

McNab stood for a moment in ominous silence, then said, 'Did you know that if someone drinks from a glass of water, by the time they've drunk two thirds of it, the remainder is pretty well all DNA from their saliva?'

Jeff blanched, having an inkling of where this might be going.

'You made a statement to a police officer, captured on my mobile, that you had been entertaining your girlfriend Carla. Let's see if that was true.'

McNab produced a pair of forensic gloves, two plastic evidence bags and a mouth swab. He donned the gloves, sampled the vodka with a mouth swab and, lifting each glass, placed them in a separate bag.

Jeff suddenly remembered he was a lawyer and began protesting.

'Also,' McNab interrupted him, 'if you made a call to the suspect while in the toilet, our Tech team will have logged it.'

This wasn't strictly true, but it was worth it to see the effect his announcement had.

McNab made that his parting shot, before he headed down the stairs.

44

Freya had been nervous and jumpy all day. Having spoken to Dr MacLeod and given the police her statement, she should have felt better by now, but didn't. From her high vantage point by the window in the library, she watched as dusk fell over the university grounds and a grey mist crept in to envelop the towers of the main building.

Never did this ancient seat of learning look more like Dracula's castle than it did at this moment.

Tucked in a corner, encircled by shelves of manuscripts and ancient tomes, her laptop open on the desk before her, Freya had written nothing. How could she think about anything other than the deaths of Shannon and Leila and what had happened between herself and Michael?

It had stung her that Michael believed she'd lied to him, but it stung even more that he had been right. When Grant had asked her to fetch the detective from reception, little did she know that the chance meeting would have such a profound effect on her life. At first glance, she'd been intrigued by the tall, auburn-haired man with the bright blue eyes. It appeared to her that the interest had been mutual and she'd found herself flattered by that. He was both intriguing and scary, an exciting combination.

In the aftermath of Leila's death, Detective Sergeant Michael McNab had also made her feel safe. So, when

Shannon hadn't turned up again for work, Freya's first instinct had been to call him. Listening to the tone of his voice when he'd asked her not to go round to Shannon's flat, she'd known something terrible had happened.

That's when everything changed.

That's when she'd forged the lie that had come between them.

She and Danny had never been an item, but she had met him before the previous night when McNab had seen him leave her flat. He and Leila shared many characteristics, to the extent that they might have been twins. Both extremely attractive, charismatic and openly sexual, it wouldn't have been difficult to fall for Danny's advances.

But she hadn't, so in that McNab had been wrong. She should, of course, have told him the truth, but the hurt and suspicion that had radiated from him had stopped the words in her throat, so she'd chickened out and insisted she'd never met Danny in person before that night.

And once a lie had been told, it immediately multiplied.

McNab, good detective that he was, would discover that she'd met Danny before, because he would eventually meet up with Danny and he would simply ask him.

She recalled Dr Rhona Macleod's quiet expression this morning as she'd listened to Freya's tale. She hadn't told the entire truth then either, although she'd hoped by explaining to someone McNab obviously trusted that she'd helped in some way.

And what of the key Rhona had taken?

'Freya?' A quiet voice brought her back from her tumultuous thoughts.

She looked up and found Grant standing there. 'Sorry. I was miles away.'

'How's the thesis progressing?' He eyed the pile of books beside the laptop, all of which were unopened.

'Not so well,' she admitted. 'Can't seem to concentrate.'

He smiled an understanding. 'Could you spare a few minutes then for a visitor?'

'Who?' For a moment she hoped it might be Michael, however improbable that might be.

'A benefactor of the library, who's interested in the Ferguson collection and your work on it.'

Freya's heart sank, but how could she refuse?

'Sure, Grant. I'd be happy to speak to them.'

'He's waiting for you over at the old building where the collection was previously housed.'

She looked at him, puzzled. 'What about the workmen?'

'They've gone until Monday. It'll be nice and quiet there to chat. Use the back room. You'll find a key for it in Shannon's desk.'

Freya opened her mouth to say she already had the key, then shut it again.

'Okay. Who am I looking for exactly?'

'Dr Peter Charles,' Grant said. 'Don't worry about the books. I'll put them back for you.'

'Thanks, Grant.' Freya slipped her laptop into her bag and lifted her coat from the back of the chair. 'I'll see you tomorrow, then?'

'See you tomorrow.'

Freya took the lift down to the ground floor and said a goodnight to the guard on the door. Buttoning her coat against the evening chill, she set off across the road and through the main gates. Anything happening in the main building would already be over, but there were still a few students wandering the echoing cloisters on their way to the exit.

Freya headed for the tower that had housed the old library.

As she did so, a text arrived. She stopped to read it, hoping it might be from Michael, but it was Danny's name on the screen. Did she really want to make contact with Danny again? Maybe if she ignored his calls and texts, she could extract herself from this entire mess? Good sense told her that, but she still didn't heed it.

The text was brief.

Barry's dead. Be careful.

'Barry's dead,' she repeated, stunned.

She had never met Barry, but she was aware he was somehow involved in all of this. And now he was dead? Like Shannon and Leila? And why did she have to be careful?

With trembling hand Freya pressed the call button. It rang out, shrill and insistent.

'Why don't you answer?' she pleaded.

At that point a figure appeared from the shadows. Tall, distinguished, suited, with grey hair and a kind face, he quickly approached her.

'Freya Devine?' He held out his hand. 'Peter Charles. Thank you for agreeing to meet with me.'

Freya slipped the mobile in her pocket and grasped his proffered hand.

'Grant said there's somewhere we can chat about your thesis on Witchcraft?'

Freya pulled herself together. 'He suggested the old library where the Ferguson collection used to be housed.'

'Excellent idea,' he said with a smile.

As she led her visitor up the winding stone staircase, Freya made up her mind to contact Rhona immediately after Dr Charles left. Her first thought had, of course, been Michael, but that was no longer possible.

As she opened the door to the inner room, she recalled Michael's promise that night in her bed: 'No one will frighten or hurt you while I'm here.'

But you're not here, Michael. Not any more.

She turned and invited Dr Charles to follow her inside.

45

The question, 'Is she a danger to us?' hung in the air, awaiting its answer.

Dinner had been served and enjoyed and the brandy and whisky glasses recently filled. The waiter, having completed his duties, had exited, closing the double doors on the private dining room behind him. No one else would enter until called.

The meal had been eaten by candlelight as it always was, no man's face exposed to the glare of electric light. The faces flickered in the shadow, indistinguishable, but the voices they could recognize.

Over the years, they'd indulged in a variety of entertainments since the group had been formed. None of which had quite grabbed their attention as much as that which had been put before them the last time they had met.

No one believed in magic, but one of their group had a great deal of knowledge of its practice in both medieval and modern times. At this point in the proceedings he'd handed round a number of images of sexual magick being performed. Some came from ancient tomes he and they were trading in, some were present day.

The images had provoked what could only have been described as a frisson of excitement, even more powerful than making money had. They'd questioned him avidly, particularly about the photograph featuring the red-headed Witch, Leila Hardy.

'She would be my choice,' the promoter of sexual magick had said, satisfied at their response. 'It would of course be up to each of you to decide which spell you would demand of her.'

'And she's willing?' The voice came from the far end of the table.

He'd confirmed she was. 'On condition that the spells you choose fit the Wiccan Rede.'

'Which is?' a rich baritone had asked.

'"An' Ye Harm None, Do What Ye Will."'

An explosion of laughter had followed the quotation.

And so the fun had begun and the spells cast.

Back then it had been exciting; now it had become problematic. It was time to deal with the fallout from their forage into magick.

He looked round the circle of faces. These men were not friends, but they were bound together and, provided they kept faith, they would both survive this and continue to prosper.

'Gentlemen,' he began. 'It is time to put our affairs in order.'

301

46

As she approached the steps to her front door, Danny Hardy appeared from the shadows and smiled at her. The smile held a promise of something . . . but what exactly? Rhona had encountered that smile in the interview room, when she'd taken the swabs from him and Barry. During the interchange, Daniel Hardy had indicated that they would meet again, somewhere at sometime.

It seemed that time and place was here and now outside her flat.

'Can we talk?' he said, then added a 'please'.

Daniel Hardy was effectively on the run, with a warrant out now for his arrest. She suspected he'd probably been the last person to visit Leila's temple. The one who had broken the Goddess statue and maybe removed the Book of Shadows and the knife. He was also a man in mourning for his sister, with possible revenge on his mind. For his sake, and McNab's, she should accept his offer. She should also endeavour to keep him talking until the police might be called.

If she could persuade him to go to a cafe nearby, the encounter would be in full view of the clientele, thus guaranteeing her safety. There might also be the opportunity to visit the toilet and, once out of sight, contact McNab.

'Where?' Rhona said, realizing if she was too firm about the location of their discussion, he might anticipate why.

Danny hesitated, her immediate agreement having surprised him.

'Your place?' He looked up at her window, indicating that he knew exactly where she lived.

Rhona suddenly realized something. 'It was you,' she said. 'You posted that stick figure through my letter box.'

Danny looked as though he might dispute the accusation, then nodded.

'Why?' Rhona prompted.

'You lot needed to get your act together,' he said angrily. 'If you had, Barry wouldn't be dead.'

'You think the body in the lane is Barry?'

'You don't fucking know?'

'There was no ID on the body and his face had been mutilated. We're awaiting the DNA results.'

It was obvious from his shocked expression that Danny knew none of the gory details but had simply assumed it had been Barry.

He shook his head. 'If it isn't Barry, where the fuck is he?' he demanded.

Rhona ignored the rhetorical question. 'Come on. There's a coffee shop round the corner.'

At close quarters, Danny's eyes suggested sleep had evaded him for some time, and access to washing and shaving had been minimal. Rhona was aware McNab had put a watch on Danny's flat and wondered where he'd been sleeping, then remembered the couch in Leila's temple.

If that had been his place of refuge, it was no longer available.

Danny quickly drank half the contents of the large cup of strong black coffee he'd ordered, making Rhona think she should have offered to buy him food as well. While standing at the counter, waiting for them to make her latte, she'd considered trying to text, but the table Danny had chosen had been picked for a reason. That reason being its clear view of the queue at the counter.

Rhona sipped her coffee and waited. Eventually Danny spoke.

'Have they got the guy who went home with Leila?' His voice broke a little on his sister's name.

Rhona shook her head. 'Not yet.'

'I don't think he killed her,' Danny said.

'Then who did?'

'One of the Nine.'

'You have proof of that?'

'Maybe.'

It was what she wanted to hear. 'Then give it to the police.'

'No way. They won't touch the bastards.'

'Why do you say that?'

Danny gave her a withering look. 'All are establishment figures. One's something to do with the law. They killed my sister to cover their tracks. Just like they killed Shannon and Barry. No doubt I'm next.'

'Then hand yourself in. Give the police everything you have on them.'

'And watch it disappear?'

Rhona thought back to the DNA sample to which access had been denied. There was no way Danny could have known about that.

'Then what do you propose to do?' she said.

The look he gave her was penetrating. 'Can I trust you?'

'You must have thought so, otherwise I wouldn't be here.'

He shook his head. 'No, it's Freya who trusts you.'

Rhona felt compelled to ask. 'How long have you known Freya?'

'A while. Why?'

'Were you ever an item?' If she was going to divulge any of this to McNab, she would have to be sure.

Danny was weighing up her question before responding. 'The detective saw me that night at her flat and got pissed off?'

'You could say that,' Rhona said.

'We never fucked. That night or any other. Will that do?'

It would.

McNab stood undecided. *What next?* Mark Howitt was proving as elusive as the truth. He checked his watch and realized he hadn't eaten since early morning. The thought of heading home to an empty flat didn't appeal, although entering the off-licence en route did.

He decided instead to seek out one of the many eateries Glasgow city centre had to offer. The Merchant City dwellers had already finished work and were duly at play. He didn't feel like staying in this quarter. He'd had enough of mixing with Glasgow's wealthier citizens.

So he headed west, then up towards Sauchiehall Street and the Italian restaurant Shannon had identified as the location of her last meal with Leila. This wasn't his first visit to the restaurant and he was duly noted in the queue that was beginning to form in the doorway and waved inside. One of the perks of being a police officer.

Guiliano ushered him to a tiny cubicle next to the kitchen door.

'You look like a policeman,' he told McNab. 'I don't want to put off my diners' appetites.'

McNab took this in good spirits. He was happy to be incognito and out of sight.

He ordered a pizza, a small carafe of red wine and a jug of water. Guiliano brought him the wine, water and some bread and olives.

'On the house,' he said. 'You look hungry.'

He was right. McNab fell on the bread and olives with gusto. By the time the pizza came, he'd ordered a refill on the wine and was beginning to feel mellow. Something he hadn't experienced for some time.

Before eating, he'd set his mobile on the table beside him. Halfway through the three-cheese pizza, it came to life. McNab checked the name on the screen before abandoning his knife and fork and answering.

'Dr MacLeod?'

'Where are you?' she said, the note of suspicion in her voice suggesting she thought the noisy location might be a pub.

McNab told her.

'I'll come to you,' she said, and rang off.

McNab returned to his pizza. Rhona was either coming here to lecture him about Freya or to tell him something she didn't want to say over the phone. When she hadn't arrived by the time he ordered coffee, McNab toyed with the idea of having a single malt to go with the espresso. He would have to down it and get rid of the glass before Rhona appeared, to avoid that look of hers.

He realized, with a pang, how furtive that would be. He told himself that he was in control of his drinking and should he want a whisky, he saw no reason not to have one. Waving

Guiliano over, he ordered a double out of defiance, then purposefully left it there untouched for Rhona to see.

From his location, his line of sight to the main entrance was constantly interrupted by the opening of the kitchen saloon doors as the waiters exited with piled-high plates. The buzz of the place and the lively chatter was the first semblance of normal life McNab had experienced since he'd sat across the kitchen table from Freya in what seemed a lifetime ago, but was actually only that morning.

He was eyeing the whisky glass, eager to taste its contents, but still testing his resolution, when Rhona appeared and slipped into the seat opposite.

'Daniel Hardy did not have sex with Freya, either last night or previously,' she immediately told him. 'They were never an item.'

'He told you that?'

'He did.'

'And you believed him?'

'Yes.'

McNab eased himself back in the chair and met her look head on, then lifted his whisky glass. 'I'll drink to that,' he said.

When the spirit hit the back of his throat, it tasted even better than he remembered.

'And that's what you came here to tell me?' His voice, he knew, dripped with cynicism, yet inside his head a small flame of hope had been ignited.

'In part.' She paused. 'Danny says Leila let slip that one of the Nine is something to do with the law, and that he – Danny – has short video clips which feature three of them.'

McNab took that in. 'The boss said he believed the denied DNA match was a serving officer.'

He watched as the implications of that hit home.

A small smile played at the corner of Rhona's mouth. McNab had seen that smile before and welcomed it at that moment.

'If that's true, then whoever it is must be on the database because they're involved in a current case. Once the case comes to court, their details will be removed.'

McNab nodded. 'So we identify and locate everyone currently in that situation. That's a tall order.'

'But not impossible,' Rhona said.

'I believe the boss would be up for that, but we can't broadcast what we're doing or Sutherland will be on to it like a shot. Would Danny be willing to surrender the video clips?'

'He doesn't trust the police to expose one of their own.'

'With good reason.' McNab thought about an alternative. 'Could you tell him what we plan to do and get him to meet with Ollie in the Tech department? A fair exchange, wouldn't you say?'

'He didn't give me a way of contacting him and won't hand himself in anyway,' Rhona stressed.

'We could meet at Ollie's place.'

'That might work if we can figure out a way of getting a message to Danny,' Rhona said.

McNab felt the flame of hope leap a little higher. 'Would you be able to check for any officer who's been entered on the DNA database recently because of a current case?'

When Rhona indicated she would, McNab could have hugged her.

He took out his mobile and showed Rhona the video he'd received. Her response after watching it a couple more times was, 'The hand at the end looks different.'

'Ollie agrees. The person who sent it gave us what he claims was the first guy's mobile number. His name is Mark Howitt. His girlfriend confirms he was in Glasgow on the night Leila died.' McNab told her about his meeting with Emilie Cochrane.

'What is it?' he said, reading Rhona's expression.

'You said Mark Howitt?'

'Yes.'

'Could he be related to Mark Howitt QC?'

'His son,' McNab admitted.

'Jesus, McNab, does the boss know?'

'Not yet.'

'And when were you planning to tell him?'

'When I bring Howitt in.' Seeing Rhona's doubtful look, McNab rushed on. 'If Sutherland finds out you know, what will happen?'

'Your career or what's left of it will be dead in the water,' Rhona said.

'But if I bring him in and charge him, it can't be hushed up.'

Rhona looked troubled. 'That video isn't proof he killed Leila. Danny doesn't think he did. He maintains it was one of the Nine. And he blames himself for his sister's death, because of the videos.' Then she told him Danny's suspicions about the identity of the body in the lane, something McNab didn't need to be convinced of.

'Is that everything?' McNab said, sincerely hoping it was.

By the look in Rhona's eye, it wasn't. Then she told him about Danny's fears for Freya's safety.

47

'Michael?' Freya said in disbelief.

When his name had appeared on her mobile screen she'd thought she was imagining it. Then she'd hesitated, worried he might still be angry with her, still unforgiving. The words that followed convinced her that neither was true.

'Are you okay?' His voice, although not as warm as it had been prior to their argument, gave her hope.

'I am,' she said, feeling that she now was, because of his phone call.

'Rhona spoke to Danny,' he began.

Freya interrupted him. 'He texted me to be careful. He said that Barry was dead.' Fear suddenly swept over her again, all consuming.

'We don't know for certain the body in the lane is Barry.'

Freya knew by Michael's tone that he was trying to reassure her.

'But it probably is,' she said.

'There's a strong chance.'

'Then Danny was right. He and I are the only ones left directly connected with Leila and Shannon.'

'You weren't involved with the Nine?' He hesitated, as though he wanted to check that was true.

Freya came in swiftly. 'I knew nothing about the Nine.'

He went quiet for a moment before saying, 'I believe you.'

Those three words opened a floodgate in Freya.

'I should have said that I'd met Danny before with Leila, but you were so angry, I couldn't. But I never slept with him, and we were never an item.'

'It doesn't matter if you were. I'm the one with the problem. In my line of work everyone is guilty until proved innocent.'

They were both silent as each absorbed the other's confessions.

'I want you to take Danny's advice,' he said. 'Lock up well and be careful.'

'I will.'

There was a moment when she thought the conversation was over, then he came back with, 'I could come round, if it makes you feel safer.'

'Please,' she said, her voice breaking.

His voice was bright when he answered. 'I'll text you when I'm on my way, but it might be late.'

'It's a full moon tonight and I'm a moon lady, remember?'

She rang off, her heart soaring. Michael would solve this. Once it was over they could start again. She found herself imagining Michael meeting her at the library. The two of them going out to dinner together. His presence in her flat. In her bed.

There were two things she knew she must do now, for Leila and Shannon and for herself.

Up to this point she had not been able to say goodbye to her fellow Witches. Now was the time. She headed to the small box room she'd transformed into her temple. Donning her moon lady gown, she filled the various dishes and lit the incense, then used the sword to draw her circle. Stepping within, she experienced an immediate sense of safety. She sounded the horn. The low warm note filled the room and resonated within her own body. Her skin prickled with energy, warm blood bringing a flush to her face.

She took up her stance before the altar and spoke, her voice no longer her own but that of the Wiccan priestess she had become.

'I, moon lady, sound the horn for Leila, known by her magick name of Star, and for Shannon, known by her magick name of Rowan. They are no longer in this Circle, which saddens me. I send forth my good wishes to bear them both across the Bridge of Death. May they return at any time should they wish to be with me again.'

She pointed her *athame* at a spot behind the altar and imagined Leila and Shannon standing there. The power of suggestion was strong enough to visualize them as they had been at the Edinburgh coven, Leila wearing her bright star robe, Shannon's patterned by rowans rich with red berries.

'I wish you all love and happiness. Let you both be at peace.'

Satisfied that she'd done what was required to celebrate those who had passed, Freya now turned her attention to the future. On this occasion she would choose the priapic wand. Twenty-one inches long, the final nine inches were carved in the shape of a phallus to symbolize the continuation of life. A life she hoped to share with Michael, for as long as he chose to share it with her.

She pulled her robe over her head and dropped it at her feet. Now naked, her skin glistened in the candlelight. Where her voice had spoken of loss in the first instance, this time it would speak of joy and affirmation.

312

Pointing the priapic wand towards the statues of the God and Goddess, she visualized a naked Michael standing before her, just as he had been that night in her room. She smiled, drinking in the memory of him and what had followed. It was as though he were there with her, his fingers burning her skin.

She took a deep breath and spoke the words:

'*Thus runs the Wiccan Rede.*

Remember it well. Whatever you desire;

Whatever you would ask of the Gods;

Whatever you would do;

Be assured that it will harm no one – not even yourself

And remember that as you give

So shall it return thricefold.'

McNab rose from the table.

'I'm going to head round to Freya's.'

Rhona smiled. 'So I heard. This time if Freya tries to tell you something, please listen to her.'

'You're giving me relationship advice?' He grinned. 'Well, here's mine to you. Give Sean Maguire a call.'

He left her there in the booth. Glancing back as he exited, he noted that Rhona was studying the menu, and didn't appear to be following his advice.

Waving down a taxi, he took great pleasure in instructing the driver to take him to Freya's flat. In his mind's eye he saw her, naked, waiting for him in the hall. He imagined how he would gather her in his arms. The mental picture almost stopped his breath. When his mobile rang, he answered without checking the caller's name, believing it to be Freya.

In the next moment, his dream for tonight evaporated.

'There's a man at the station who wants to talk to you,' Janice said.

'For fuck's sake,' McNab exploded in exasperation. 'It's after ten.'

'He says his name's Mark Howitt and that *you* would know why he's here?'

The news stunned McNab into silence for a moment, then he said, 'Keep him there, I'm on my way.'

He rang off and knocked on the intervening glass.

'Change of plan.' He told the surprised driver to take him to the police station.

He would have to text Freya rather than call her, because he couldn't bear to hear the disappointment in her voice.

'I take it you're a cop?' the taxi driver said knowingly.

'Always,' McNab announced.

He's very like Barry Fraser. In height, build, even the bloody hairstyle. Is there a fucking mould they use to fashion these guys? Like a plastic male mannequin. Or is it all down to gym membership?

Despite the smart clothes and handsome face, Mark Howitt looked like shit. Guilt and fear oozed from all his pores. Across the table from him, McNab was getting wafts of it. For a moment his sense of smell seemed the equal of Magnus Pirie.

Howitt's face was pale, the sheen on his skin suggesting acute stress, or perhaps he was coming down from a high. In that respect McNab had some sympathy with the man before him. Like cocaine, the highs of whisky were good, the downtime hellish.

McNab considered how he should conduct this meeting to get what he wanted. He didn't have a degree in psychology, but had enough experience to recognize a soul ravaged by guilt and despair. He'd been there himself, too often to recall.

'You were at Jeff Barclay's flat when I visited. You went up on the roof to avoid me.'

'Yes.' The voice was low, almost eager.

McNab had the sense he was the priest in the confessional. If he played this right, he would get everything. Maybe even the truth of that night. McNab sat back in the seat, creating more space between them. Give the man air. Give the man support. Let him talk. Let him release his soul.

The story poured out like liquid gold. How he and Jeff had gone on a drinking spree, looking for sex. How they both had partners, but wanted the excitement of something different. Even as he spoke, McNab could feel the thrill that had fed that night. Something out of the ordinary. They'd had no luck until The Pot Still and the two women. One auburn-haired, sexy, exciting. The other blonde, more accessible and pretty.

'Jeff went for the blonde. He always does. She seemed to like him as much as I can remember. Me, I had to persuade the other one.' He halted as though recalling.

'I didn't think I had a chance,' he went on. 'She was so beautiful, but I didn't think she fancied me. Jeff was playing a better game. He looked a cert. Then she suddenly invited me home with her.'

He stopped there, exhibiting his amazement at what had happened.

'A set-up?' McNab asked.

He thought about that. 'Maybe,' he said reluctantly.

'And?' McNab encouraged him.

'She lived nearby. We were there in minutes. She practically pushed me into the bedroom. Then she ordered me to strip.' He wiped a drip of sweat that threatened his eyes. 'I thought she was going to tell me to fuck off because I wasn't good enough. I was high and drunk. It was the most exciting thing ever.'

McNab understood his pleasure. Recognized the intense desire spurred on by drink and drugs. He'd been there himself.

'She ordered me to lie on the bed, then that bloody cat sat on my face and clawed at my shoulder. I tried to push it off but she stopped me. After that . . .'

'What?' McNab said.

'We had sex and she tied a red cord round our waists.' He paused, remembering. 'I must have passed out. When I came to, she wasn't there. Then I was sick. I got out of bed, my head still swimming, and stood in the vomit. I just wanted out of there. The weird sex, the cat—' He stopped in full flow and shuddered.

'Go on,' McNab said.

'I went into the hall, but there were all these fucking doors . . . I opened one and the cat tripped me up and started screaming. Those dolls clicking and clacking. Hitting my face.' He blanched at the memory. 'Then I saw her.'

He shook his head as though to dispel the terrible image of what had hung beyond the dolls. An image McNab could share with him.

He produced a mobile and pushed it towards McNab.

'Someone sent me this.'

McNab knew what he was about to watch, but viewed it anyway.

The same snippet of video. The two figures tied together by the cingulum. Then the climax and the terrible finale.

'Is that me?' Mark said when it finished, his face as white as a sheet.

It was something McNab wanted to know as much as Mark.

'Put your hands on the table,' McNab ordered.

'Why?'

'Just do it.'

Ollie's program would compare those hands with the one in the video, but McNab didn't need a program to tell him what was plain to the naked eye.

'That's not your hand,' McNab said.

Mark looked from his own hands to the one now frozen on the screen.

'It isn't my hand,' Mark repeated, relief flooding his face.

'But that doesn't mean you weren't there when it happened,' McNab said, wiping that look of relief away. 'The person who sent you this. Have they been in contact again?'

Mark shifted uneasily in his seat. Whether he was contemplating a lie or uneasy at the thought that what McNab had said might be true, McNab wasn't sure.

Eventually Mark came to a decision. 'Yes.'

McNab scanned the texts he was shown.

'You met him?'

'I went into the building as directed, but no one appeared.' Mark looked relieved at this.

'Has there been any mention of blackmail?'

'No.'

'Then why send the video?'

'To frighten me?'

'Or to use against your father?' McNab suggested.

That obviously hadn't occurred to Mark.

'They never mentioned my father. Not once.'

'But that doesn't mean they don't know who he is.'

Mark tried to raise the coffee McNab had supplied him with to his mouth, but his hand was trembling too much, so he set it down again.

McNab stood up. 'You did the right thing coming in and giving a statement. We will of course require your mobile to trace whoever sent the video.' He signalled to the duty lawyer that the interview was over.

'I suggest you make contact with your father. I'm sure he'll want to hire a defence lawyer for you.'

Mark shook his head. 'I don't want to speak to my father.'

'Considering your father's a respected QC, my superior officer will want to inform him as soon as possible.'

Mark shrugged. 'I'm dead to him now.'

48

The door of the cell shut with a clang. Mark stood for a moment in the silence that eventually followed, realizing this was the first time he'd stopped running since that terrible night.

He took a seat on the bed, his knees drawn up, back against the wall. The only light now was the emergency one above the door. He was finally alone.

Or was he?

One thing he hadn't told the detective. Something he could hardly admit to himself. But now here in the dark silence of his cell, he would have to.

The girl Leila had died, but she hadn't gone from him.

Her presence had grown stronger with time. The more and further he ran, the stronger it had become. No amount of coke or alcohol had silenced her voice in his head. From whispers in his subconscious, her voice had become a torrent.

He had no memory of her saying the words when they were together, so why did he hear and recognize them now?

Give of yourself – your love; your life – and you will be thrice rewarded. But send forth harm and that too will return thrice over.

Like a chant it never stopped, the phrases overlapping one another so that at times it became a cacophony.

He was stressed, he knew that, but having now confessed to his role in the night she'd died, he had hoped, even prayed, that Leila's voice would be gone.

But now, here in the absolute silence, he realized that it hadn't and perhaps never would.

In that moment he made his decision. He would do what was required of him and bring this thing to an end.

Mark retrieved the paper and pen he'd asked for and, taking a seat at the small table, began to write by the emergency light.

His confession to the detective had been heartfelt, but it hadn't been complete. He hadn't killed Leila Hardy, but he was responsible for what followed, because he hadn't gone to the police. Had he done so, Shannon and the barman would still be alive.

That's what the man had said. The man he hadn't told the detective about. The man in the Lion Chambers.

And something much worse: the fact that his father was somehow involved with the group of men Leila had been partnering in sexual magick. Something that would become common knowledge if the Nine were exposed. Mark had refused to believe this at first. His father visiting Leila for sex? But the man had seemed so certain and knew so much about his father.

'Your mother, I understand, has only weeks to live. Wouldn't you rather she spent them with your father?' the man had said.

That was the question that had troubled him the most. The question that had decided him. He didn't want his father exposed, even if he had done what was claimed.

I've hurt my parents enough.

'No one else will die?' Mark had asked.

'No one,' the voice had reassured him.

Mark picked up the pen.

49

Rhona stared into the darkness, much-needed sleep eluding her. In her self-imposed solitude she hoped that McNab and Freya were together. In a way she felt Freya held the key to all of this, because she was the only one who truly understood the two worlds they were dealing with.

On the other hand, there was nothing magical about death. She'd met it often enough to know that. If Danny was right, his sister had died because she'd become a threat to men with the power to remove her. But had they done it themselves or paid for it to be done? Had Mark Howitt been chosen as a scapegoat? The man who would be blamed for Leila's murder? But they'd taken things too far, linking the manner of Leila's death with her activities as a Witch. So Shannon had become a threat too and had to be disposed of. Danny had claimed both girls' deaths as his fault, believing he had spooked the Nine by taking the videos.

If he was right, ironically, trying to protect Leila may have resulted in her death.

Giving up on sleep, Rhona rose and went through to the kitchen where the wall clock informed her it was half past midnight. She wished now she'd taken McNab's advice for once and called Sean. Too late now. Or was it?

She settled for a text. If he was on stage or the club was

busy, he wouldn't hear it anyway. If he responded, she could always change her mind.

In the meantime she made herself a coffee and, bringing through her laptop, logged on to check on possible updates on the R2S software file.

It seemed that the remainder of the DNA samples from the dolls had come back without a match. With Barry having been eliminated as one of the possible nine samples, that meant only one of the Nine was on record, but they weren't permitted to know who that was, which made Rhona all the more determined to find out.

The DNA from the body in the lane had found a match with the swab she'd taken from Barry Fraser. McNab had been right all along on that one, as had Danny. Which meant – as Danny had pointed out – that he, and to a lesser extent Freya, were the only ones left alive who could be linked to Leila and her practice of Witchcraft.

That thought discomfited Rhona, but she reassured herself that McNab had taken the warning on Freya's safety seriously, and was with her now.

At that point her mobile screen lit up with Sean's name.

She let it ring three times before she made up her mind to answer.

'Have you eaten?' were Sean's first words.

Rhona laughed. 'You always ask me that.'

'I always have to. Well?'

'I thought about Italian but instead stopped at the chippie on the way home.'

'What about company?'

'I'd welcome some,' Rhona said honestly.

'Will I do?'

'Yes.'

'I'll bring my supper with me. I'm always hungry when I've been playing, as well you know.'

'I remember.'

'Okay. I'll see you in fifteen minutes.'

The relief she felt at the prospect of company that didn't involve work, surprised her. Or maybe McNab's happy expression as he'd departed the Italian restaurant had inspired her to forsake the lonely menu, however tasty, and head for home.

Hunger pangs had made her stop at the local chippie. There she'd chosen Chrissy's favourite, a smoked sausage supper. She'd managed the sausage but not the chips. The resultant feeling of hunger unsatisfied made her wonder what Sean would bring with him in the way of food and wine.

Rhona discovered soon enough.

Sean arrived with a covered dish and asked her to put it in the oven for fifteen minutes at 180 degrees.

'I could microwave quicker,' she offered.

The look he gave her silenced any other suggestions on that front.

'A white for you. A red for me.' He plonked the two bottles on the table. 'It's chilled,' he added, also producing a French stick that smelt hot and very fresh. 'The new bakery close to my flat. They try and catch the late-night brigade.'

'Like us,' she offered.

He set the table, moving about the kitchen as though it were his own. Rhona had no wish to argue. Sean had come when she called, which put them on an even footing as far as she was concerned. He could use her kitchen as he wished.

'Should be ready now.' Sean swept the dish from the oven and placed it on the table. Peeling back the foil, he revealed three giant stuffed mushrooms oozing scents that Magnus would have loved.

'Two for me. One for you. Or if you're not hungry, three for me.' Checking her expression, Sean scooped one onto her plate, then offered her bread to dip in the sauce.

They ate in comfortable silence. At moments like this, Rhona wondered why she'd asked Sean to leave, but the truth was, she needed her own place free from emotional involvement and, she suspected, Sean needed the same.

As he served them coffee, Rhona tackled one of the reasons she'd invited him here.

'Danny Hardy was outside the flat when I came home earlier.'

Sean looked concerned. 'And?'

'He told me things about the case, which I've duly told McNab,' Rhona said. 'However, I need to get a message to Danny from McNab.'

'This isn't a police trap to take Danny into custody?'

'No. Quite the opposite,' Rhona said.

Sean raised a quizzical eyebrow. 'McNab's playing off the park again?'

'You could say that.'

Sean considered her request.

'Give me the message and I'll do my best.'

'Thank you.'

'Is that all?'

'Not quite.'

Something had changed between them. The sands on which their relationship had been built had shifted. Imperceptibly perhaps, but Rhona had experienced a sense of it on the previous two occasions Sean had been here.

And she felt it even more strongly now as she lay in his arms.

She thought back to the beginning, when she'd been searching for her son. How Sean had gone to Paris, asking her to go with him, but she'd refused.

She had eventually joined Sean there, when she had found her son, or when he had found her. Stepping off that train in Paris, her joy at seeing Sean had matched the intensity of her emotions at finding Liam. It had been a moment to savour and hold in her heart.

Maybe this was how it could be?

Rhona allowed herself a moment of happiness before she closed her eyes and drifted off to sleep.

50

The interview over and report written, McNab made for the coffee machine. Already one o'clock, he wondered if he should really visit Freya. Exhaustion had taken over from his earlier elation and his mind seethed with the story Mark Howitt had just told him.

He checked his mobile but there was no response to his earlier message.

He drank the espresso and pressed the button for another. When it failed to appear, McNab punched the machine in frustration.

At that moment a uniform appeared at the door of the waiting room. McNab shot him a warning look, assuming his arrival had been occasioned by his argument with the coffee machine.

It hadn't.

'Sir . . . can you come down to the cells?'

McNab read his shocked expression. 'Why?'

'It's Mark Howitt, sir. He's dead.'

I, Mark Howitt, confess to the killing of Leila Hardy, Shannon Jones and the barman Barry Fraser. I killed Shannon Jones and Barry Fraser because they could identify me as the man who left the pub with Leila that night. No one else will die now.

McNab threw the confession down on DI Wilson's desk.

'This is shite, boss. Mark Howitt had sex with Leila Hardy, then ran away when he found her dead in that room. He didn't kill her and he didn't kill the others.'

'You're sure about that?'

McNab hesitated. He was sure, but it would take more than his word to prove it. 'Forensic results should show he wasn't in Shannon's flat or anywhere near the body of Barry Fraser.'

'What if that's not the case?'

A wave of anger broke over McNab. He'd chased Mark Howitt but had never caught him. Mark had given himself up in the end and last night had told his story. A story that had rung true to McNab.

'The hand in the video wasn't his,' he said.

'That doesn't mean he wasn't there,' Bill countered, just as McNab had done earlier with Mark. 'Way back when we discussed this, we contemplated that there might be two perpetrators involved. What about the friend?'

'I ordered him to come in and give a DNA sample and a statement.'

'Has he done it?'

McNab ran his hand through his hair. 'I don't know, sir.'

DI Wilson gave him a sympathetic look. 'You've been here all night. Go home, Sergeant. Get some sleep.'

McNab laughed. 'Like that's going to happen, sir.'

'A death in custody is a serious matter, especially the death of the son of a prominent QC.'

McNab grimaced. 'Mark's last words to me when I mentioned contacting his father were, "I'm dead to him now".'

The duty doctor examined the prisoner Mark Howitt and found
him to be in good physical condition, although low in mood.
He had not been put on suicide watch, although a police officer
had checked him at half-hourly intervals. He had surrendered his
valuables and had been deemed as having nothing on his person
which might be used to harm himself or others.

He had requested paper and a pen to write to his parents,
which had been duly supplied. He had been seen shortly after
this, writing at the desk. At the next check he was on his bed
apparently asleep with his face turned to the wall.

The next time he was checked, he lay in the same position
but there was a smell from the cell which suggested that he may
have soiled himself. On entering the cell the officer found that
the prisoner had taken off his socks and wedged them deep into
his throat. The doctor then called tried to resuscitate the prisoner
but failed. He was pronounced dead at 12.55.

Bill had phoned Mark Howitt Senior in person that morning
to tell him the news of his son's suicide in custody. Bill chose
not to elaborate on the circumstances until he met him in
person. He owed him that much at least.

He and Mark Howitt Senior were friends from way back,
when Bill had been at the police college and Mark a defence
lawyer. They'd kept in touch over the years, although spor-
adically. As QC and detective inspector they did not move
in the same social circles, but that didn't mean they didn't
appreciate the role each of them played in upholding the
law. Bill was aware that, though unsaid, Mark Howitt Senior
had little time for Superintendent Sutherland, although they
were often required to be seen together. In that, as in other
things, they shared a common bond.

Despite his exalted position and wealth, Bill regarded

Mark Howitt as a man he could deal with. A man he could trust. A man who deserved to be told the whole truth about his son, as far as Bill was aware of it.

The formalities of the identification of his son over, Bill suggested they go somewhere quiet to talk.

'I'd prefer outside the station,' said the man who'd appeared to age ten years in the last half an hour. 'I don't want to be away from Sarah for long. I've chosen not to tell her. I hope I may not have to.'

Bill had no words to say what he felt at this moment.

'Can we talk somewhere in the open? A park perhaps?'

Bill had led him to the nearby square and they were seated there now. The morning sun played on the trees that were already showing signs of autumn.

Bill spoke slowly and quietly, aware that what he was about to say would be difficult to take in, even for someone of the intelligence and discernment of the man before him. He explained how Mark had come into the station and confessed to being the man who'd left The Pot Still with Leila Hardy on the night she died.

'He admitted he was high on drugs and drink and had sex with Leila, but insisted he didn't kill her. My detective sergeant believed him and there is some video evidence sent to Mark's mobile which suggests he was being pressured into believing he had suffocated the girl. This has been proved false, although he could have been present when it happened.'

The face before him had become etched in stone, each line deepened like scores on granite.

'I suspected something was wrong when we met to discuss his mother. The news of her impending death was a shock to him. He wanted to come and see her but I forbade it. That was a mistake.'

'Mark left a statement admitting to all three murders. He insisted that he killed Shannon Jones and the barman who served them that night, because they could identify him.'

'Is that possible?'

'It could be if we have forensic evidence to put him at those crime scenes.'

Mark Howitt Senior stared straight ahead.

'I don't believe we should discuss this any more. I thank you for giving me the details of Mark's death and the circumstances that led up to it.'

He rose and held out his hand to Bill. The handshake was as firm as ever.

'Let me know when I can have the body of my son.'

Bill watched him walk away, a broken man who had lost his son and, it seemed, would soon lose his wife. But Bill had read something else on that granite face. His old friend had wanted to tell Bill something, but found he couldn't. Or not yet, anyway.

He brought out his mobile and called home. Margaret answered almost immediately.

'Bill, what is it?' she said, sounding worried.

'Nothing,' he lied, 'I just wanted to hear your voice.'

51

McNab stepped into the shower and turned it to the power setting. The impact on his skull felt like a pneumatic drill pounding his brain. He stood like that for all of five minutes, then moved the impact to his neck and shoulders.

After this he would eat, he promised himself, even if his stomach wasn't asking for food.

He stepped out after fifteen minutes, finishing with a blast of cold water. If he'd been asleep on his feet before, he was awake now.

Dried and dressed, he went through to the kitchen and put on the coffee machine, doubling the required number of spoonfuls of fresh coffee for the amount of water he poured in.

He'd purchased enough ingredients for breakfast in the local corner shop on his way home. He could have stopped at a cafe en route but feared that he would fall asleep, his face in whatever they served him.

He fired up the gas and, adding oil to the pan, set about frying the big breakfast pack of sausage, bacon, black and white pudding. Once cooked, he slipped the slices into the oven to keep warm and fried himself two eggs to go with it.

Once he began the process of eating, hunger took over and he demolished the food in record time. Wiping the plate clean with bread, he poured himself another coffee. Feeling human again, he said a silent thank you that he was not facing a hangover. He'd survived last night probably because he hadn't taken to whisky.

Opening the window wide, he stood in the draught of cool air and took a deep breath of Glasgow oxygen.

Now he would go and see Freya. She had to be told what had happened last night that had stopped him going round there, and it was better he did that in person. Trying her number, he heard it ring out unanswered. Well past nine o'clock now, he told himself she would be at the university library, and that's where he should head first. He left a message on voicemail to that effect, apologizing for not coming over due to an emergency at work, which he would explain when he saw her.

McNab then put his dishes in the sink, ran some water on them, fetched his jacket and set off.

The food and the shower had brought a clarity to his thinking that had escaped him in the long hours of the night. His gut feeling told him that Mark had lied. Not about the night he spent with Leila, but about his contact with the person who'd sent him the video clip.

That someone had in some manner persuaded Mark to kill himself. 'No one else will die.' That phrase had jumped out at McNab. His own initial response to it had been positive, because he wanted to believe that now Freya would be safe. But who had said, 'No one else will die'?

McNab didn't think those words had come from Mark, but from someone who'd persuaded Mark that if he confessed, that would be the case.

Mark had sacrificed himself, but for whom and for what?

The image of the Nine reared again in his head. Power, money, influence. That's what the men Leila had performed sexual magick with all had.

'Fuck them,' McNab said out loud. 'I'm going to fuck them, if it's the last thing I do.'

Rhona had risen to the drill of her mobile.

Sean, on the other hand, slept on. This time Rhona didn't resent his peaceful sleep but merely acknowledged it. She thought about placing a kiss on his forehead, but decided against it. He might stir and envelop her in his arms and she would succumb. She must save dessert for a later date.

The caller was Chrissy, her voice high with excitement or shock.

'Mark Howitt handed himself in and confessed to the three murders then suffocated himself in his cell.'

A stunned Rhona asked Chrissy to repeat this more slowly.

'A mate called me. When she went on duty this morning, the station was alive with the news. Mark Howitt, the QC's son, gave himself up last night. Confessed to McNab that he was the man who'd taken Leila Hardy home. Then wrote a further confession in his cell. He claimed that he also killed Shannon and Barry Fraser to cover his tracks.'

Rhona called a halt at this point.

'We have no forensic tests to prove that the man with Leila that night was also present at the other crime scenes.'

'Well, we'd better prove it or not, soon,' Chrissy said in her usual forthright manner. 'My bet's on a false confession.'

Rhona was inclined on instinct to agree.

'Why would he do that?'

'He said that no more killings would happen,' Chrissy told her.

'Has this hit the news?'

'Not so far. Want to take a bet how long it takes? Witch

killer and son of QC confesses all, then commits suicide. He promises in his confession that no one else will die.'

'You should be a reporter,' Rhona said.

'I'd write a damn good headline,' Chrissy retorted. 'But seriously, you need to get down to the mortuary.'

There are some places in life that are necessary. There are places necessary for the dead too. A room full of drawers of dead people sounded like something from a horror film, yet here they were. As necessary as air was, to those who lived.

The scent of death was masked in here by the presence of cold. Deep, penetrating cold that halted, or at least suspended, the organic disintegration of the human body that was both inevitable and essential.

Dust to dust, ashes to ashes, or rather decomposition, which didn't sound so philosophical, but did sound less messy. In her time, Rhona had had her hands in gloop consisting of human remains, mud and blood, so looking on cold marbled bodies could be thought of as easy in comparison.

Except it wasn't.

The young man before her was a perfect specimen of a male human body. Sculptured. Bone and sinew in complete harmony. Handsome even in death. The enormity of the loss of possibility was there to view.

Mark Howitt had gone out for a night of fun. The penis that lay there cold and flaccid had driven him to pastures new. Excitement heightened by cocaine and alcohol. But at the end of the day he was driven by a male's need to have sex. Primeval, maybe, but nevertheless the reason why humans continued to exist. Without that drive, there would be no future. No future generation.

It seemed that Leila had responded to this need, matching

it with her own desire. There had been no coercion, except perhaps on her part.

Neither of those two young people had wished evil, but nevertheless it had been visited on them.

An' it harm none, do what thou wilt.

How did following such a creed end in such evil?

There would be a post-mortem, but the result was already known. Mark Howitt had died by his own hand. So determined had he been to end his life that he had stuffed his socks so far down his throat that it would have been impossible to stop his own suffocation.

He had died as he thought Leila had died. A fitting retribution.

Or was it?

Rhona indicated that she'd seen enough and the mortuary assistant shut the drawer.

Bill was seated in his usual place at the window, the mug of cold coffee or tea on the desk beside him. Rhona waited while he turned, the resultant girn sounding like an old friend reappearing in difficult circumstances.

'You saw him?' he said.

'Yes.'

'I broke the news to his father. We know one another from way back.' He halted for a moment. 'It was Mark Howitt QC who I consulted about the denied access.'

'My God,' Rhona said.

'Strange how circular life is.'

'And now his son is implicated.'

'Do you believe his confession?' Bill said.

'The DNA sample I took from his body will indicate whether he was with Leila the night she died,' Rhona told him.

'What about the other crime scenes?'

'We should know in forty-eight hours.'

'How would you feel if your son was a murderer?' Bill said to the air, but also to Rhona. 'Would it be your fault?'

'There must be a time when a child becomes an adult and makes their own choices.'

'That sounds like Magnus talking,' Bill said. 'Do we not make the child that becomes the adult?'

'You and I both know that no matter how good and loving a childhood might be, psychopaths still exist.'

'Was Mark Howitt a psychopathic killer or a daft boy who found himself caught up in something terrible?' Bill said.

'That's what we have to find out.'

Forensics were a way of mapping out what happened in intricate detail. There was no emotion involved, only science. The science of who, where and when.

There was a cleanness in that. A certainty. Yet nothing was certain. In the past, the present or the future. It was how you viewed it that mattered.

Imagine a fence post above a ravine where a body lies. Whose DNA was on it? Those who had placed their hand there as they climbed over the fence to take a closer look at what lay below? The man who had cut the post? The man who had hammered it into the ground? All had imprinted their person on it. Only one DNA sample belonged to the person who'd held on to that post as he'd tossed his victim into the ravine.

DNA wasn't enough, but in Mark's case, it might be sufficient to make the authorities believe the man who made the confession was in fact guilty of all three murders.

On the other hand, DNA could also be purposefully placed

at a crime scene to implicate the innocent. In Rhona's opinion, Mark Howitt's confession hadn't cleared up the mystery, but only added to it.

Rhona told Bill what she thought.

'I'll request Magnus watch McNab's interview with Mark,' Bill said, 'and also examine his written confession. Maybe he can give us some insight into the thought processes that led to his suicide.'

As she made to leave, Bill added, 'You and McNab sort out your differences over the *Stonewarrior* case?'

The sudden question had caught her unawares, but Rhona answered as honestly as she could. 'McNab and I will always have differences of opinion. But we're okay, I think.'

'Good.'

The text came in as she pulled up in her parking space at the lab. Seeing it was from Danny, she said a silent thank you to Sean. The answer to her message about meeting with Ollie was short and sweet.

I'll be there.

The second task McNab had allotted her, of helping identify a list of police officers currently on the DNA database, would take a lot longer. In that, she had DI Wilson's help. Bill had surprised her by bringing up the subject himself just prior to her departure from his office. His message had been suitably oblique, but she knew Bill well enough to believe that he too was on the case.

52

Freya had chosen to sleep within the magick circle. After receiving McNab's text, she'd resigned herself to the fact that he wasn't coming, tonight at least. She'd fetched a pillow and duvet and, wrapping herself in it, had lain down before the altar. The smell of incense and flickering candles comforted her and had eventually lulled her to sleep. That and the sense that both Leila and Shannon were there with her.

The box room had no window and therefore no daylight penetrated the space. Eventually the distant sound of cars outside roused her and she'd woken to the lingering fragrant smell, but a thick darkness, as the candles had all burned themselves out.

She rose, groaning a little at the stiffness of limbs that had spent the night on a hard floor. Every morning since Leila's death, she'd woken with a tight knot of fear in her stomach. This morning it had lessened, although hadn't disappeared altogether.

She showered and put on the coffee machine.

Checking her mobile, Freya listened again to McNab's voicemail just to hear his warm tone of concern for her, but wishing too that there was a further message from him.

He's a police officer, she told herself. That's his life. If I want to be with him, I'll have to get used to it.

She left the flat just after nine and began her walk to the university library, determined to make proper use of her day. The deadline she'd set herself on her thesis wouldn't be met if she didn't start applying herself again. Grant had been kind to her over the whole business, checking up on how the thesis was going, encouraging her to talk to him about the investigation and her place in it. He'd even allowed her to skip a few of her shifts in Archives to allow her more time with her research.

She'd discovered in their talks just how well informed Grant was on the Ferguson collection and on the occult in particular. It was easier to ask him a question sometimes than to go searching the catalogue for the answer. He could often point her to the exact pamphlet or volume to refer to. Considering there were 670 books in the collection on the history of Witchcraft, Grant's recall was considerable.

Freya knew Grant was aware of her Wiccan beliefs and respected them. She found their talks on the subject re-assuring and often enlightening. He'd apparently had similar discussions with Leila and Shannon.

Dr Peter Charles had been equally interested in her work. They'd spent an hour in the old library together. He'd revealed he'd been a chemistry student at the university and since the Ferguson collection had originally been under the auspices of the chemistry department, he'd seen the old library in its original form. He'd voiced his disappointment that the precious collection was now housed 'in that soulless glass tower block'.

'But it's safer there,' Freya had remonstrated.

His smile at that point had been thoughtful and not a little sad. Afterwards, they'd walked together through the cloisters, but rather than head for the exit he'd urged her to accompany him to what she'd always considered the front of the building, the Gothic face that overlooked Kelvingrove Park and the art gallery below.

He'd walked her round, describing the meaning and purpose of the elaborate carvings and statues.

When they'd eventually reached the gates again, he'd held her hand in his and thanked her kindly for taking the time to talk to an old man much obsessed with 'what we don't yet understand'.

Her reply – 'Is that not what a place of learning should be obsessing about?' – had brought a grateful smile.

When he'd departed down University Avenue, Freya had crossed to the Wellington Church, whose doors stood open. It wasn't a place for her religion, yet from the moment she'd come here to Glasgow and the university precinct, she'd admired its splendour. With its neoclassical portico, complete with a full colonnade of Corinthian columns, it stood in direct contrast to the Gothic splendour of the university across the way.

Standing there in the entrance had reminded Freya that Wiccans needed no stone palace in which to worship, but only the magick that came from acknowledging their place in the eternal cycle of being. Freya had had the feeling that Dr Peter Charles would agree.

This morning as she approached the library entrance, she spotted a figure she knew was waiting for her. Had the auburn-haired man been Michael, she would have run towards him and thrown herself into his arms. When she realized it was Danny, Freya stopped, her desire to turn away and hope he hadn't seen her uppermost in her mind.

But he had seen her and there was to be no escape. From

Danny or from the stomach-churning fear his reappearance had brought her.

'I need to talk to you.'

Freya registered the sunken eyes and ashen skin.

'You look terrible,' she said.

Danny brushed her concerns away and indicated the rucksack he had over his shoulder. 'There wasn't a list in the Goddess statue, but I have Leila's Book of Shadows.' Before Freya could respond, he rushed on. 'Leila recorded all the spells she cast with the Nine. I think we can work out who they are.'

'Then you have to give the book to the police,' Freya said.

He read her determined expression. 'I will, after we figure it out.'

Freya wasn't convinced.

'If I hand it over now, what will they do? These people don't understand what's in there. And they don't believe in magick. Leila did, Shannon did and you do.' Danny looked imploringly at her. When she didn't respond, he added, 'Chances are they'll come to you anyway.'

In that he might be right.

'Okay,' Freya said. 'I'll take a look, but that's all.'

Relief flooded Danny's face. 'Thank you.'

'Let's go inside. I can find a quiet corner for us in Archives. Then if Leila made reference to anything in the collection, we can check it out.'

Freya knew she should ask permission from Grant to bring Danny into the library, but was pretty sure he wouldn't object, not if he thought it might help. She signed Danny in as a visitor and led him to the lift. Minutes later they were ensconced in her usual corner at the desk near the window.

'We're not allowed coffee in here,' she apologized, 'although you look as though you could do with one.'

'I'm okay,' Danny said. He pulled up a chair and sat down, shielding the contents of the desk from anyone who might suddenly appear from beyond the shelves that enclosed them. Once he seemed certain there was no one in the vicinity, he withdrew the Book of Shadows from his rucksack and placed it on the table.

It is quite beautiful, Freya thought, *like Leila*.

Fashioned from green leather, the surface etched with a pentagram held in the hands of the Goddess, it was fastened by two beautifully fashioned brass clasps.

Traditionally, a personal Book of Shadows should be destroyed on the owner's death. Seeing it here before her made Freya feel that Leila was still alive.

Danny unclipped it and, as he began carefully turning the pages, Freya glimpsed elegant and intricate writing and drawings, all in Leila's hand.

'What's in here will mean more to you than it does to me,' Danny said, 'although I can sense my sister when I touch it.'

He leafed through, eventually finding the section he was looking for, entitled 'The Nine'. 'There's a page for each of them,' he said, his voice bristling with anger.

Freya ran her eyes over the first entry, which consisted of a full-body sketch of a man and a date, which looked like a date of birth. Alongside this was what she guessed was a reduced version of the date of birth resulting in a single digit – the owner's birth number.

Below were two paragraphs of dense script written in what looked like the Seax-Wica runic alphabet, the first of which was in couplets.

'What does it say?' Danny said eagerly.

'I think the first part may be the spell, but it'll take time to decipher both sections,' Freya explained.

'How much time?'

'I'll have to get a copy of the runic alphabet and see what I can match up.'

Danny looked exasperated.

'I thought you would know.'

'I'm sorry. I will try, but I'll need to concentrate.'

Danny seemed to accept that. He glanced at his watch. 'I have to be somewhere. Can I call you later? See how you got on?'

Freya was relieved at the suggestion. She certainly couldn't focus with an impatient Danny there beside her. As he rose to leave, a figure popped his head round the shelves.

'Freya?' Grant said in surprise. 'I didn't know you were in.'

Freya, flustered, stood up. 'I'm sorry. I was planning on coming to talk to you but got a little waylaid.'

Grant's glance had fallen on the book, despite Danny's attempt to shield it.

'What have you got there?'

Freya didn't see any reason to lie, but still she hesitated to tell the entire truth.

'It's a Book of Shadows, my friend found. He thought I might be interested in taking a look at it.'

Grant was scrutinizing Danny, and Freya realized with a jolt that of course anyone who'd known Leila would recognize the likeness between them.

Danny took the initiative and held out his hand. 'I'm Danny, Leila's brother.'

Sympathy flooded Grant's face as he took Danny's hand.

'I'm so sorry about your sister. She was such a lovely young woman.'

Danny nodded his appreciation.

'Is that Leila's Book of Shadows?' Grant said.

'It is.'

'I understood that it was normal practice for a Witch's book to be burned on her passing?'

'There's nothing normal in the way my sister died.'

Grant looked aghast at having upset Danny. 'I apologize. That was an inappropriate thing to say.' He turned to Freya. 'If you need any help deciphering the contents – I assume that's what you're doing – then I put myself at your disposal.'

'Grant knows a lot about the various Wiccan alphabets,' Freya said.

'I'd rather it was kept between Freya and me,' Danny said. 'It's all I have left of my sister.'

Grant nodded. 'Of course. I understand. I'll leave you to it.'

When Grant disappeared, Danny looked at Freya.

'Can he be trusted?'

'Leila trusted him. Shannon too. He knew they were Witches. He knows I'm one.'

'I don't want him looking at the book.'

'Okay,' Freya said. 'If you like I'll take it home to study.'

Danny looked relieved when she didn't argue. 'I'd rather you did.'

'I'll need to check out a couple of reference books to help.'

Danny nodded. 'I'll call you later.' He turned back as he remembered something else. 'I've spoken to the forensic woman. I think she's on our side.'

His words were unexpected, but nevertheless made Freya's heart lift.

'I hope so.'

53

Danny's decision to come to Ollie's flat had forced McNab to change plans, so he never made the library and still hadn't met up with Freya.

Instead he was now seated beside the man who, after Mark Howitt, he'd sought the most. Danny Hardy looked even more like his sister than McNab had previously registered, but then he'd never seen Leila alive, only some photographs. He had no wish to recall the terrible image of her corpse hanging in that room.

McNab was glad Danny had never witnessed that, although seeing his sister laid out in the mortuary was bad enough.

Danny Hardy was clearly a man in mourning, who also had revenge on his mind. McNab could empathize with that. He'd made his own vow to expose the Nine. Mark Howitt's death had only strengthened his resolve on that front. So he and Danny shared a common goal. McNab just had to make sure they played their cards as close to the law as was necessary, to avoid any of them paying a heavy price for actions such as the one they were involved in now.

'Okay.' Ollie peered at them through his trademark specs. 'I've uploaded the three video clips and enhanced the quality. I can do more work on them, frame by frame, but that will take time.'

'Who took these?' McNab asked Danny.

'I set it up beforehand and Leila agreed to start the recording, secretly of course.'

'Which goes some way to explain the quality, and why the camera isn't always focused on the right spot,' Ollie said as he set the film running.

Initially there was more sound than image, but eventually two figures appeared in the camera's line of sight. McNab felt the tension in Danny's body as the lens found Leila's naked back. In this instance, Leila's body shielded the man's face, but they did have a partial view of the left hand.

'Stop,' McNab ordered. 'Can you zoom in there?'

Ollie selected the area and did as asked.

'That's a pinkie ring. Is there a crest of some sort on it?'

Ollie eased in further. 'A horse or maybe a unicorn?' he suggested.

'Any views of his face?'

The male had his back against the raised end of the sofa, Leila astride him, continuing to block their view.

'Did she do that on purpose?' McNab said, exasperated.

'I had a hard time persuading her to let me film it at all. From Leila's point of view I was messing with the spell,' Danny explained.

It was clear when they reached the end of the clip that their only means of identifying the first male was by the ring.

The man in the next video was just as hidden, although there was a good shot of his right ear.

'Ears are pretty unique and identifiable, provided we come up with a suspect,' Ollie assured them.

Number three was the best of the bunch. This man was tall and broad, so that even though Leila was astride him, she wasn't totally blocking his face. Ollie paused the video at the appropriate moment and zoomed in.

The hairline was grey, the dark eyebrows distinctive, as were the brown eyes.

'That's better.' Ollie voiced what McNab had been thinking. 'Particularly having access to the eyes.'

Danny regarded McNab. 'What happens now?'

McNab didn't want to promise something he couldn't deliver.

'It's a start, but it's not enough. Not until we have suspects to compare them with.'

'What if one of the men in the video clips is a police officer?'

'Did Leila say he was?'

'She hinted it,' Danny said.

'If that's true, that would help.' McNab explained why the DNA of serving officers was stored during a live investigation.

'So you have access to details on this group, even images of them we could compare to?' Danny said excitedly.

'In theory, yes, although they'll probably be in the hundreds and they'll cover all of Scotland.'

'If I run their photos through the comparison software . . .' Ollie began. 'We might get lucky.'

A glimpse of a hand, a bit of an ear – McNab only wished he had Ollie's faith it would be enough. The Nine had been scrupulous about keeping their identities secret up till now. He believed they had killed to keep it that way. And all he had were three video clips that showed almost nothing and the vague hope of outing a policeman, against the express orders of their superiors.

'What spooked them enough to kill your sister?' McNab said.

Danny didn't like the question, that much was plain from his face.

'Well?' McNab insisted.

'I think they found out about the recordings.'

'So they know they exist?'

'I'm not sure. Leila may have given the game away.'

'You didn't try some blackmail?'

Danny shook his head vehemently. 'No.'

'What about Barry?'

'He was keeping an eye on Leila for me. Who she met in the pub, that sort of thing.'

So Barry had been watching out for Leila at her brother's request. McNab eyed Danny. 'You've definitely told me everything?'

'Yes.'

Danny's expression was set on stubborn, so McNab let it go, for the moment. His gut feeling was telling him there was something else, maybe just a thought Danny had had, but he wasn't willing to divulge it at the moment.

'Both Ollie and I are going out on a limb on this,' McNab told him firmly. 'By rights I should be interviewing you under caution, asking where you were on the night Barry Fraser died, maybe even charging you with withholding evidence.'

'You know I had nothing to do with Barry's death. And maybe I should be in custody. I'd feel fucking safer.'

Danny was right up to a point. He had brought the video recordings as requested.

'We're evens,' McNab said, 'for the moment, but as soon as we have something on these guys, I want you at the station giving a full statement.'

'When will you have a result?' Danny said.

'Forty-eight hours,' McNab said. 'Keep out of sight until then.'

54

Freya nestled the backpack against her shoulder, feeling the weight and significance of its contents. Grant had been right. A Witch's Book of Shadows should be burned on her passing.

She imagined how they might do that, she and Danny, when this was all over, then suddenly realized it would never truly be over for Danny and that Leila's precious book would become a piece of evidence handled by scores of people.

Such a thought brought her deep disquiet.

Leila's spells were hers alone, their potency dependent on her power as a Witch. Their exposure, the secret of her thoughts and wishes, might mean she would enjoy no peace in the afterlife.

For that reason, the Book of Shadows should be burned.

Taking the Book of Shadows home now seemed wrong. Leila's place of worship felt the lesser violation but, as far as she was aware, the police were still in there.

Then a thought struck.

If she couldn't gain access to Leila's place of worship, perhaps access to Leila's flat might be possible? There she would be close to Leila, maybe even gain her spirit guidance in what she was about to attempt. Wiccans believed in reincarnation, but there was also 'the time between', the length of time spent between lives, when those who had passed became spirit guides or guardian angels for those left behind. That comforting thought grew in Freya's mind until it was the only one.

Rhona was in the midst of checking all the forensic results received. It was as yet a sporadic picture and she had no clear indication that Mark Howitt's confession had any forensic basis in the truth.

One thing was certain, however. She believed the person who'd tied the knots in the cingulum used to hang Leila was right-handed and she now knew that Leila and Mark Howitt, the chief suspect and the man she'd taken home that fateful night, were not.

Neither Leila nor Mark had tied the slip knot that had been used to hang her.

Added to that, the video McNab had shown her of the hand inserting the material into Leila's mouth had been of a right-handed man.

People didn't lead by the right if they were left-handed.

She was also running a search on the DNA database, identifying police officers currently involved in a case. It was a valid search on her part and hadn't as yet caused any disquiet. How she would deal with the list this achieved was something Rhona wasn't yet sure of.

Her mobile rang around eleven and Rhona was pleased to see Freya's name on the screen.

'Freya?'

'I'm sorry to call on a Saturday.'

'No worries. I'm at home, but working.'

The voice on the other end hesitated.

'What is it?' Rhona said encouragingly.

'I have Leila's Book of Shadows.'

It was obvious by her manner that Freya thought Rhona would know what she was referring to. Thanks to Magnus, Rhona did.

'May I ask how you have it?'

'Danny brought it to me this morning.'

So it had been Danny who'd removed the book from the altar. Rhona waited, giving Freya time to continue.

'It may contain references which might be useful to your investigation,' Freya said.

'How can I help?' Rhona immediately offered.

'This may sound strange,' Freya rushed on, 'but I think it would be easier to interpret the writings if I felt closer to Leila.'

'How?'

'Could you and I gain access to the place she died?'

'Her flat?'

'Yes.'

As Chief Forensic Scientist, Rhona could request to revisit the crime scene, but should she take Freya with her?

'What do you want to do there?'

'Decipher what Leila wrote about the Nine.'

A sense of death still lingered here. The smell of it had dissipated, replaced by chemicals used in the forensic examination, plus dust and disuse. Rhona imagined she could hear the steady beat of her heart in the depth of the silence and could see from the rapid pulse in Freya's neck that her heart was racing.

'Which room would be best?' Rhona said.

'Where did Leila die?' Freya was struggling to hold her voice steady.

'Probably the room with the dolls.'

Freya was looking at her, puzzled. 'What dolls?' she said.

Rhona pointed at the closed door, her memory of the last time she'd opened it as powerful as ever.

'There were twenty-seven Barbie-type dolls hanging in there, in rows of nine and split by hair colour, red, blonde and brunette. We found Leila's body behind them.'

After hesitating about whether she should reveal this fact at all, Freya's reaction was the last thing Rhona expected.

Freya gave a little laugh.

'The pattern of three and nine is very powerful in Wicca,' she explained, 'and the dolls I believe represented the Goddess Freya. This was Leila's way of making the room powerful. They shouldn't have killed her in there.'

'I don't understand,' Rhona said.

'Wiccans believe if you give of yourself – your love; your life –you will be thrice rewarded,' Freya said. 'But send forth harm and that too will return thrice over.'

55

'I would suggest you get the advice of a handwriting expert,' Magnus said. 'But in my opinion this is a false confession.'

'Why?' Bill said.

'I've watched the taped interview with McNab. The suspect wants to confess to what he remembers happened and by his mannerisms, his voice, the words he chooses, I would say he's telling the truth. He feels enormous guilt, which of course might also be present if he had killed Leila, but the honest detail he gives convinces me that he didn't. The relief too, when McNab points out that the hand in the video isn't his.'

'So what changed between that interview and the written confession in the cell?' Bill said.

Magnus indicated the copy before him.

I, Mark Howitt, confess to the killing of Leila Hardy, Shannon Jones and the barman Barry Fraser. I killed Shannon Jones and Barry Fraser because they could identify me as the man who left the pub with Leila that night. No one else will die now.

'Compared to the examples you have of the suspect's normal handwriting, this script suggests he's doing this under duress, like a confession looks when given under torture. And the last sentence: *No one else will die now*. Who's saying that? I don't believe it's the suspect. It sounds to me like a repeat of something he's been told.'

Bill nodded his agreement. 'DS McNab believes Mark met with the man who sent the video, although as you saw he denied this in the interview.'

'Something was done or said to cause Mark to both confess, then commit suicide.'

'Mark's father is a well-respected QC with a terminally ill wife, who isn't expected to live much longer.'

Magnus contemplated this. 'So, the psychological pressure on the suspect was even greater than I was aware.' He paused. 'Were Mark and his mother close?'

'Apparently so, although she'd kept the extent of her illness a secret from him. When his father revealed it, Mark wanted to go and see his mother, but his father refused to allow that.'

'Can I ask why?'

'Apparently the mother had forbidden her husband to tell Mark how close the end was.'

'Yet he did?' Magnus said. 'May I ask what you plan to do about this?'

'Make sure that Mark Howitt's confession and his suicide do not close down this enquiry.'

It was a meeting that had to be faced, yet Bill wasn't sure it was quite the time to do it. If he revealed he'd been conducting his own private enquiry into the identity of the police officer who'd had sex with Leila Hardy, that search was unlikely to be permitted to progress any further.

Superintendent Sutherland might be persuaded into giving his reasons for keeping the name of the officer under wraps, but Bill didn't hold out much hope that he would. There could be many reasons for doing so, one of which stood uppermost in Bill's mind, namely that by making the officer's identity common knowledge, it might endanger his life.

Having made his decision, Bill knocked on the door and awaited permission to enter.

When that didn't happen, Bill chose to walk in anyway. He found Sutherland on the phone. When he was shot a warning glance, Bill chose to stand his ground, which essentially meant the phone call had to come to an end.

'Sorry, sir, I thought I heard a "come in".'

'You didn't, Detective Inspector.'

'Then would you prefer me to come back later, sir?'

'No.'

Sutherland didn't wave him to a seat, so Bill continued standing. He preferred it that way because he got to look down on his superior officer rather than meet him eye to eye.

'Go on, Inspector. What did you wish to say?'

'We believe the confession from the suspect Mark Howitt is a false one, made under duress.'

Sutherland was immediately on to that. 'What duress?'

'We believe he met with the person blackmailing him about his involvement with the victim and was persuaded to help end the killing by taking responsibility for it.'

'Why would he do such a thing?'

Bill said what he had expressly come to say. 'I believe either his father or his mother were threatened, sir, and that tipped him over the edge.' As he spoke, Bill studied Sutherland's expression. Always closed, never giving anything away, except perhaps irritation, Bill detected a flicker of surprise in his eyes. Sutherland, he decided, had not seen that one coming.

'And your evidence for this?'

'His interview with DS McNab was viewed by criminal psychologist Professor Magnus Pirie. He suggested that when Mark used the words "No one else will die" in his confession, he was repeating the words of his blackmailer.'

Sutherland swung his chair round at this point, blocking Bill's view of his expression. It was a tactic Bill used himself and he understood the reason for it. He waited quietly for Sutherland to turn to him again.

'I believe you and Mark Howitt QC are old friends, and that you spoke to him personally about the death of his son,' Sutherland said.

'I did, sir.'

'Did you run this theory past him?'

'No, sir. I hadn't formulated it by then.'

'Did he give any indication that he thought he might be under threat?'

'No, sir, he did not.'

'Clearly this will be a distressing time for him. I would like him shielded from the press as much as possible, particularly since his wife's death seems imminent.'

'I agree, sir.'

'And where are we in identifying the Nine?'

It was a question Bill didn't expect to be asked, so wasn't sure how to answer. Eventually he went for the truth. 'No further forward except for the serving officer.'

Sutherland looked slightly taken aback at this. 'You have identified him, Inspector?'

'I have a list of possibilities,' Bill said honestly.

'Then we should discuss them.'

56

She'd helped Freya carry a small writing table and chair from the bedroom through to the dolls' room. There Freya had reverently laid the green leather Book of Shadows and the volumes on runic script, the ones she'd checked out of the library.

Rhona was keen to view the contents of Leila's book, but got the impression that Freya didn't want her to. Yet.

'A Witch's Book of Shadows is very personal. It shouldn't be handled by others. I promised Danny to keep it safe,' Freya said. 'Once I do what he asked, then he says he'll hand it over to Detective Sergeant McNab.'

It was a reasonable request and, Rhona decided, one she could comply with. So she took herself into the kitchen and set up her laptop there. From what Freya had said, McNab wasn't yet aware of the book's existence and that Freya now had it.

Rhona contemplated warning him of this, then decided not to.

She had a feeling he would find out soon enough.

The quiet in the flat continued unbroken. Had she been asked to describe it, Rhona would have said it was the silence of the dead. Wandering through to the bedroom, she had a sense of what the flat must have been like when Leila lived there. One thing was obvious: Leila had loved bright colours and pretty things. She had been a vibrant, intelligent woman who should have had a long life ahead of her. A life someone had stolen.

Two hours passed before Freya called out to her.

On entering the room, Rhona discovered the table and chair had been moved to the place Leila had been found hanging. The hook itself was now stored with the other forensic evidence taken from the flat, and Rhona hadn't mentioned the spot's significance.

'This is where she died, isn't it?' Freya said.

'Yes, it is.'

'Where are the dolls now?'

'Stored with the other forensic evidence.'

'Did the dolls tell you anything?'

'Nine of them had a sketch inside, together with semen samples.'

'There's a sketch of each of the men in here too.' She gestured Rhona over. 'But I haven't been able to translate the runes. They don't match what's in the books I brought.' Worry and exhaustion etched Freya's face. 'I'm sorry.'

Freya pushed the open book across for Rhona to view.

This time the drawings were more detailed, making the others hidden in the dolls mere pointers to their entry here.

'Is that a date of birth?' Rhona said.

'I think so. The following number is their birth number derived from it. Then I think it's the spell she cast, and a paragraph maybe about the outcome of the spell, or further details of the subject associated with the spell.'

'Which would be very useful,' Rhona said.

'I know.' Freya looked dejected.

Dusk had fallen outside and the room was filled with long shadows. The view across the lane was of the curved windows of the upper floors of the Lion Chambers, and the empty rooms beyond.

'Shall we call it a day?' Rhona said. 'Get something to eat and try again tomorrow?'

Freya thought about that.

'Can you fetch something in and some coffee? I'd like to stay a little longer.'

'You'll be all right here on your own?' Rhona asked.

'I'm not alone,' Freya assured her.

When Rhona departed, Freya took out her mobile. Keen not to be disturbed, she'd switched it off on her way here. Two texts pinged in. One from Michael suggesting they meet up. The other from Danny asking what was happening with the Book of Shadows.

Freya dialled a different number.

'Grant, I need some help with the runic alphabet in Leila's Book of Shadows.'

57

Danny pressed the buzzer again, keeping his finger on it longer this time.

Freya had said she was taking the Book of Shadows home, therefore she must be here.

Eventually someone from a different flat let him in just to stop the noise.

Danny took the stairs two at a time. When he'd got no response from Freya's mobile, he'd assumed she was concentrating and didn't want to be disturbed.

Now he wasn't so sure that was the reason.

I shouldn't have left her.

I should have taken her home. I should have made sure she was okay.

When he reached her door, Danny stood for a moment, determined to calm himself, not wanting Freya to see his fear.

He rapped and waited.

When there was no response, he tried again, louder this time.

The third time he banged and shouted through the letter box: 'Freya, it's Danny!'

At that point a door opened on the upper landing and a guy's head appeared above him.

'For fuck's sake, mate, give it a break. She's either not in or she doesn't want to speak to you.'

Danny quashed his desire to shout abuse back.

'Have you seen Freya this morning?'

'No. And she's not in now.'

As Danny had one more go at the door, the guy started down the stairs. Tall and muscled like a rugby player, Danny got the impression he intended tipping him over the banisters if he didn't leave of his own free will.

Danny stepped back from the door.

'Okay. Okay. I'm going.'

Muscleman stood three steps up and waited, a determined look on his face.

Danny had no alternative but to leave.

Back out on the street, he considered his options. Having tried once again to call Freya, with no response, he decided to head back to the library. Maybe Freya had remained there after all. Maybe the books she needed to decipher the runes couldn't be signed out.

Calmed by this thought, Danny set a course for the university.

Why don't you answer?

McNab flung the mobile on the table. He'd thought Freya had forgiven him, but it seemed he'd screwed up again. He should have been round to her place by now. Or should at least have spoken to her.

But that wasn't going to happen. Not for some time yet.

He lifted the espresso cup and drained the contents.

He and the boss were about to interview Jeff Barclay, who'd just presented himself at the front desk. But before that he needed some time alone with the boss. There was the little matter of the video clips to discuss.

McNab headed to the Gents first. The shower and decent

breakfast had perked him up earlier, and he wanted to keep that wide awake feeling. Hence the double espresso. He made use of the urinal first, the result no doubt of too much caffeine, then spent a few minutes splashing his face with cold water. Examining himself in the mirror above the sink, he acknowledged the bloodshot eyes and the rather too bristled chin, something he should have taken account of earlier.

It was always better to look smart and awake when about to go into the confessional.

The confessional had been a big feature of his Catholic upbringing. That and the implicit belief that as a Catholic he had a guardian angel. Something McNab was pretty sure wasn't available to Protestants. But back then, let's face it, there was a lot of pish talked. Most of which he'd now discarded, except the guardian angel, who'd saved his life more than once. McNab hoped he was still on side.

Refreshed, McNab approached the boss's office and knocked.

The voice that told him to come in sounded upbeat, which heartened McNab.

On entry, things continued to look good as he was told to take a seat.

McNab did so.

Now they were face to face across the desk, DI Wilson appeared to be waiting for McNab to begin the proceedings. Not sure how this meeting would pan out, McNab was keener that he not serve first. So he waited.

Eventually DI Wilson said, 'I believe you've been withholding information, Detective Sergeant.'

Rather taken aback by this announcement, McNab came in quickly with his denial. 'Not exactly, sir. I asked to see you so that I might *present* information.'

The boss sat back in his chair.

'Present away.'

McNab began with a brief résumé of how Mark Howitt had appeared on his radar and how he'd asked Tech to check the mobile number.

He was interrupted at this point, 'When were you aware that Mark Howitt was the son of a High Court judge?'

'Not *immediately*, sir.' McNab crossed his fingers. 'I contacted the girlfriend and she told me about Mark and Jeff's night out in Glasgow. She also mentioned the scratches on his shoulder.'

'So you thought you had your man?'

'Not right away, sir,' McNab said. 'I then checked Mark's home address and was granted access by his concierge.'

The boss's left eyebrow was raised at this point which flustered McNab a little. He raced on to counteract this. 'It looked as though he'd left in a hurry, taking some clothes with him. His work said he'd been signed off sick, so I thought I'd check the mate's place in Glasgow.'

The boss was listening intently now, so McNab carried on.

'Jeff Barclay denied Mark was there, but when he let me enter there were two glasses on the kitchen surface with a bottle of vodka nearby.' McNab explained about his search of the roof and how he'd taken the two shot glasses for fingerprint and DNA analysis.

'And that led to Jeff Barclay presenting himself here?'

'Yes, sir.' McNab relaxed a little.

Maybe things were going okay after all.

'What about the tapes you've been viewing?'

How the fuck did he know about that?

'I was just about to mention them, sir. Danny Hardy

brought the tapes and they were viewed by myself, Danny and someone from Tech,' he said, trying to keep Ollie's name out of it.

'And?'

'There are only partial views of three men. A set of hands. A right ear. And the upper part of a face to include the hairline, eyebrows and eyes.'

'So not distinguishable without comparisons?'

'No, sir.'

McNab thought he was through the worst, until the next question arrived.

'I take it Daniel Hardy is now in custody?'

The boss would be fully aware he wasn't in custody, so it was crunch time.

'I asked him to get back in touch in twenty-four hours and he agreed at that point to hand himself in,' McNab was swift to answer.

'And you believed him?'

McNab decided to come out fighting this time. 'Danny didn't kill his sister or Shannon or Barry Fraser, sir. In fact, he's probably the one most in danger now.'

'Which is all the more reason why he should be in custody, Sergeant.'

McNab had no good answer to that.

58

'He looks worse than me,' McNab thought, not without some pleasure.

Jeff Barclay was definitely outside his comfort zone. That much was obvious. Where McNab had been the intruder in Jeff's upmarket Merchant City apartment, now he was on McNab's home turf. One, McNab surmised, Jeff had not visited before. He suspected the man in front of him was about to see a slice of life he wasn't familiar with, and wouldn't enjoy very much.

As DI Wilson went through the usual routine of setting up the recording and advising Jeff of his rights, McNab kept a beady eye on his opponent, who kept a close eye on the tabletop.

'When was the last time you saw Mark Howitt?' Bill said.

'He stayed at my place on Thursday night.'

'What about yesterday?' McNab intervened. 'When I arrived.'

'I told you he wasn't there and he wasn't.'

'You called his mobile while you were in the toilet.'

Jeff looked as though he might deny this then thought the better of it.

'Okay, I did call Mark, but it was to tell him to hand himself in to the police.'

'Which he did,' Bill said.

Jeff looked taken aback at this. 'Mark's here? I didn't know that.'

'So you haven't been in touch?'

'No. He never answered his phone.' Jeff was observing their faces. 'He's handed himself in. That's good, isn't it?'

Bill answered swiftly. 'I'm sorry to have to inform you that Mark Howitt took his own life last night.'

'What?' Jeff shook his head. 'No. No way. Mark would never do that.' As he rose from his seat, Bill commanded him to sit down.

A brief silence fell as Jeff took to examining his hands as though they might explain what he had just been told.

Eventually Bill spoke, his voice low but firm.

'Mr Barclay. You have already admitted lying to a policeman in pursuit of a suspect. As a lawyer, you must be aware how serious that is?'

Jeff nodded. 'I'm sorry.'

'Let's get back to the night in question. The night Leila Hardy died.'

It took an hour to extract the whole story.

According to Jeff, he had departed the pub after Mark and the girl, using the excuse that he was going to the toilet. When questioned as to why, his reason had been that he'd felt sick through too much drink and decided to go home.

'I left by the fire exit.'

'When was that exactly?' McNab said.

He shrugged his shoulders. 'I have no idea. I was very drunk by then.'

'You must have crawled out, because you're nowhere to be seen on CCTV in the back lane and, believe me, I've watched it all,' McNab said. He looked to the boss, who nodded.

'Please put both your hands palms down on the table,' McNab said.

'Why?'

'Just do what Detective Sergeant McNab says,' Bill urged.

When Jeff laid his hands as requested, McNab took a photograph of them.

'Hey, what's that for?' Jeff protested.

'To eliminate you from our enquiries. We will also require a mouth swab.'

59

'Where are you?'

'At Leila's flat,' she admitted. 'I thought it might help to be in the place she died.'

'Oh, Freya. I'm so sorry.'

There was a moment's silence during which she thought Grant might let her down, but he wasn't about to.

'I can't help you decipher over the phone. You'll have to come back to the library.'

When Freya didn't respond, Grant continued. 'I think I know the volume you need. Leila expressed an interest in it a while back. It contains a variety of the less common runic scripts. Maybe that's the one she used.'

Grant was right. She would have to go back.

'Okay,' Freya conceded. 'I'll be half an hour.'

'I'll look it out and have it ready,' Grant said.

Freya repacked her bag, taking particular care of the Book of Shadows. She'd been so certain if she came here, the place where Leila died, that she would be able to decipher what was written there. She'd been wrong.

Rhona hadn't arrived back with the coffee yet.

Rather than wait, Freya decided to leave a note instead. *Rhona can't help me with this anyway.*

Freya stood for a moment in the ever-darkening room, wishing she could hear Leila's voice again. Watch her bright figure in the library. Hear her laugh with Shannon, the blonde and auburn heads close together.

She recalled the intensity of Leila's expression as she'd spoken of sexual magick and the power of the spells it generated. She'd been intoxicated by it. Had she in casting those spells forgotten the Wiccan Rede? Had she been courting the darker side of magic?

As she moved to close the window, opened earlier to aid her concentration, Freya heard a movement behind her and turned to discover a pair of green eyes observing her from the doorway.

The big black cat held her in its gaze for a moment, before opening its mouth and emitting a high keening sound that cut Freya like a knife. In that moment she was back in the room Rhona had so vividly described with the twenty-seven dolls clicking and clacking against one another in the draught from the open window, all eyes focused on her as they swayed like the pendulum of a clock. Telling Freya that time was running out and that she must hurry.

60

'You left her in that flat on her own?' McNab couldn't believe what he was hearing.

'I went out to buy us coffee and something to eat,' Rhona said. 'She was having difficulty translating the runes, she thought being there would help.'

'That wee bastard Danny said he wasn't withholding any more evidence. Now I find both you and Freya were keeping this book a secret too.'

'Keeping secrets is something we're both good at. Remember?' Her retort was below the belt, but Rhona still enjoyed saying it.

The silence on the other end was deafening.

'This Book of Shadows will be full of pish, Dr MacLeod. Wiccan pish. What the hell were you thinking, exposing Freya to it?'

'In case you've forgotten, Freya believes in the pish, as you call it. And maybe if you'd treated her better, she would have asked you for help instead of me.'

'For fuck's sake, as if you always do things right. You fuck me in extremity, you fuck Sean Maguire when you fancy a decent dinner. Who are you to give relationship advice?'

The stand-off between them came to an end when McNab said, 'Where is Freya now?'

'She said she was going back to the library.'

*

Returning to Leila's flat with coffee and sandwiches only to find Freya's note had frankly worried Rhona. Freya was fragile and frightened, yet determined, something Rhona admired. She didn't believe in 'the pish' either, as McNab had called it, but locations created strong emotions. She was well aware of that. For her, standing in this room again conjured up all the images she'd encountered the first time she'd been here.

Not just images, but smells: incense and death and the sound of the cat wailing for the dead. Even now, standing in this room devoid of swaying dolls, Rhona could hear that cry.

After their spat on the phone, McNab had indicated he was at the station, having just completed an interview with Jeff Barclay.

'I don't trust the bastard,' had been his interpretation. 'He said he left the pub by the fire exit, but we have no evidence to confirm this.'

'You have a DNA sample from him?'

'Yes, and a photo of his hands.'

At that point McNab had explained about the videos.

'We're getting closer,' Rhona had said.

'Too close,' McNab retorted.

'What do you mean?'

'That serving policeman on the list? Turns out he's not as low level as we thought. In fact, *much higher*.'

'Do we have a name?' Rhona said.

'No. *We* don't, but I suspect the boss does.'

'So what happens now?'

'We find out which of the Nine did the three murders and the remaining establishment figures will be protected.'

'That's the plan?'

'You've been here before, Dr MacLeod. You know how the world works.'

Rhona took a last look round before locking up. She'd left the table and chair in the dolls' room. There seemed little point in moving them back. She had no idea what would happen to Leila's flat once the enquiry was completed. She didn't know whether Leila owned it or whether it was rented. Either way, eventually Danny might remove some of his sister's things and let it go.

Re-entering the hallway, she was struck by a sudden and strong smell of cat urine.

Rhona stood for a moment, perplexed. The smell hadn't been there when she'd entered the first time with Freya. Had a stray cat found this place and taken up residence here?

She recalled Leila's cat and its determination to protect the body of its mistress. But it had been taken away by the SSPCA. No doubt it was still with them, if it hadn't already found a home elsewhere.

An image of the cat's angry spitting face returned, making Rhona wonder if it could ever find a new home. If it had been deemed unmanageable, then the only recourse the charity had was to put it down, simply a more oblique way of saying 'kill it'. Not an outcome Rhona liked to consider.

She decided to go back through the flat and check the windows, just in case a stray had found its way inside.

The window in the dolls' room was the only one left open a little. Rhona was about to shut it, then changed her mind.

At least you can get out again, she thought as she locked the front door.

61

Freya caught the subway at Buchanan Street. She'd felt bad at not waiting for Rhona's return, but the vision of the dolls and the cat had persuaded her not to hang around any longer.

Seated next to the door, Freya hugged the backpack close to her. Even now in the crowded carriage, she could hear the terrible sound of the cat crying. Her upset that Leila hadn't visited her in the flat had dissipated. Leila *had* been with her, was *still* with her. Freya was convinced of that now. The Book of Shadows was the answer to all of this. And she would decipher it, because Leila wanted her to.

Exiting Hillhead station onto Byres Road, she cut up through Ashton Lane. Passing the jazz club where she'd met with Michael, she had an urge to call him, but quashed it. She should talk to no one, not Michael, not Danny, until she'd accomplished her task. She didn't want to have to explain her actions or her reasons. No matter what they said, neither men understood what it meant to be a Wiccan. Michael had joked about it. Danny had tolerated his sister's beliefs, but they didn't understand how deeply and profoundly they were held.

On the final stretch to the library a text arrived. Glancing at the screen, Freya saw that it was from Grant, so she opened it.

Have taken the book to the old Ferguson room for privacy – not strictly off campus! You'll have peace there to work on it. Grant.

'Thank you,' Freya said quietly.

Entering by the main entrance to the old university, Freya registered what sat astride the gates. A unicorn on the left, a lion on the right. She recalled what Dr Charles had told her when they'd walked the surroundings together and viewed the magnificent stone figures on the ancient staircase next to the memorial chapel on the west side of the old building.

'The unicorn symbolizes Scotland, the Lion England. This staircase comes from the old College building on the High Street. It was transported to Gilmorehill in 1870 when the University of Glasgow moved to its new West End site.'

The image of the unicorn seemed portentous to Freya, and positive.

Freya was pleased to be back amid the empty cloisters. Glad of her thoughts as she moved through them.

Every sound seemed magnified as she climbed the stone steps to the old Ferguson library. She was approaching the place where it had all begun. Her interest in Wicca had been sparked by the lecture by Professor Roy at Newcastle University. His own interest as a young physics lecturer had been awakened by finding this place.

Freya emerged on the landing. Ahead of her was the set of double doors that led into the Ferguson room.

She pushed open the right-hand door and entered.

*

'She doesn't answer my calls.'

'She's okay,' McNab said. 'Dr MacLeod is in touch with her. She went back to the library to consult another book.'

Danny's reaction to this wasn't what McNab expected.

'I don't fucking trust that guy.'

'What guy?' McNab said.

'He creeps about, popping up when we're examining the Book of Shadows. Definitely wants a look. He was like a man smelling a sexed-up pussy. Believe me, Freya should not trust that guy.'

The image was ripe, but one McNab appreciated and understood.

'Okay. I take your point, but they're at the library. Freya's safe enough there. I've been inside. It's like a police station in its security.'

'People die in police stations,' Danny reminded him.

'Where are you?' McNab said.

'Headed to the library.'

'I'll be with you shortly.'

Life sometimes moved in slow motion. It had happened to McNab on numerous occasions, usually when things got tough. Maybe it was life's way of reminding you what was important. What was memorable.

Danny's call had unnerved him.

He had met Grant, the library guy. Nothing about him had made McNab wary. But he had been wrong before. And he would no doubt be wrong again. People hid themselves, often in the trappings of their professions. Jeff had tried that, on occasion quoting them lawyer speak, but his actions had belied his weasel words.

What about Grant?

McNab realized he didn't even know the librarian's second name. His fault. He should have asked. He should have interviewed him. After all, he had known both deceased women. Had known about their Wiccan beliefs.

He should have asked.

He should have asked the entire fucking world.

McNab wanted a drink now more than he had wanted anything in his life before.

He was in Ashton Lane again. Location of his initial meeting with Freya and, he reminded himself, his subsequent meeting with Rhona. Neither had gone that well and both relationships, if he was honest with himself, were on the rocks.

Sooner or later, I always rub people up the wrong way.

McNab did a quick left turn on that thought and entered the jazz club. Heading downstairs, he found himself in a busy space. Early Saturday evening jazz was proving popular in the West End of Glasgow. McNab almost turned away and headed back up the steps. Would have done had a voice not called his name.

McNab turned, knowing the voice and welcoming it.

They had been rivals more often than friends, but Sean Maguire had proved his worth on more than one occasion. McNab hated the Irishman at times, as much for his knack of enticing Dr Rhona MacLeod into his bed as his ability to play sexy music on his saxophone.

'What's up?' Sean said, his tone suggesting his concern.

McNab didn't answer.

'Fancy a drink?' Sean asked. 'We could use my office.'

McNab had used that office as a bedroom once. That room and a camp bed had provided him with a place of safety and sanity.

When McNab nodded, Sean led him through the crowd, who were listening to a female singer McNab had never heard before. She was tidy too, oozing sex from the way she handled the microphone as much as through her voice and the words she sang.

'She's only here another week,' Sean said when McNab expressed his opinion. 'Heading to Europe after that.'

'More's the pity,' McNab ventured.

'Rhona doesn't think so.'

'Jealous?' McNab ventured.

'Distrust. Rhona thinks I'm liable to stick it in any woman who looks and sounds like that.'

'Is she right?'

'She's not totally wrong,' Sean admitted.

There was a bottle of Irish whiskey on the desk and a couple of glasses. McNab almost salivated when he saw it.

'You don't have to,' Sean said. 'I can give you something soft.'

McNab laughed. 'When people say that, I always imagine a soft prick. Which is strange since mine's never been harder since I eased up on the booze.'

Sean poured a couple of shots. 'Like everything in life. Whiskey should be enjoyed in moderation. Are you able to do that?'

McNab eyed the glass as Sean handed it over. 'Let's hope so.' He examined the golden liquid. 'I was very rude to Rhona on the phone. Told her not to give me advice on relationships. Said some rough things.'

Sean gave him a wry smile. 'You screw up. I screw up. Rhona screws up. The important thing is we care enough to face up to that.'

'The wise old man of Ireland talking.'

'We Irish can talk the talk right enough.'

McNab set the untouched whiskey firmly on the table. 'Thanks for the chat. And good luck with Rhona.'

'I fear I need more than luck.'

McNab finally crested the hill and made his way up to the library. His sojourn with Sean had made him even more resolute about progressing things with Freya. He had no idea what Leila's book of spells might reveal. Based on what had happened up to now, he didn't think it would be much, but if Freya believed in it, he would try his best to support her on that.

In McNab's opinion, they needed to expose the Nine and what the boss was doing was perhaps more likely to achieve that than studying spells.

At the front desk, he showed his badge and asked to speak to Freya. A couple of phone calls ensued, before he was informed that she wasn't in the building. A subsequent enquiry after Grant revealed his surname as Buchanan and that he wasn't in the building either.

'Do you know where they are?' McNab demanded.

'It's Saturday evening. I assume they're at home,' the woman said, as though she too wished to be there.

'But I understood that Freya was coming here.'

The woman behind the desk shrugged. 'She checked in first thing, then left. Grant was in earlier too, but checked out about an hour ago.'

McNab emerged to find Danny approaching.

'Well?' he demanded.

'Freya isn't here,' McNab told him.

'What the fuck?'

McNab's sentiments exactly.

'And the Grant guy?'

'He's not here either.'

'I don't like this,' Danny said.

McNab could not have agreed more.

'You're the detective. What do we do now?' Danny demanded.

62

Freya set the Book of Shadows out on the table beside the book of runic alphabets Grant had signed out of the library for her. He'd also supplied coffee and biscuits, just as he used to do for Leila and Shannon.

'Thank you. I really appreciate this.'

Grant nodded. 'What else do you want me to do?'

Freya observed his worried face and decided to come clean.

'Danny thinks Leila's Book of Shadows contains information about the nine men she was performing sexual magick with. He wanted me to try and identify them.'

'Has he shown the book to the police?' Grant asked.

'Not yet, but he will once I've deciphered it. Danny believes one or more of these men may have been responsible for Leila's death, and Shannon's, and even the death of the barman who served them that night.'

Grant looked perturbed. 'But I heard the guy Leila left the pub with has confessed to all three murders.'

Freya was taken aback. 'When did you hear that?'

Grant shook his head. 'I'm not sure. I think it was on the rolling news this morning.'

'So they've got the guy?' Freya said, relieved.

'Looks like it.'

'Oh, Grant, that's wonderful, if it's true.'

'So maybe you don't need to translate after all. Maybe Leila's Book of Shadows can be laid to rest.'

Freya thought about that. 'I'm not so sure. When I was in her flat something happened.'

'What?'

'Her cat was there crying to me and I saw an image of the hanging dolls in the room where they found Leila.'

Grant looked askance at this.

'I know you're not a believer, Grant, but it was very real. It seemed Leila was asking me to do this.'

Grant nodded. 'Okay. Let's find out the truth.'

It was as Grant had suggested. The writing Leila had used was obscure, mainly because it was a mixture of alphabets, each symbol intricately drawn as though Leila had intended that anyone striving to interpret it shouldn't find it easy.

But before she tackled the translation, Freya spent some time on the drawings. There was one in particular she kept returning to, because there was something familiar about the figure of the man. He was naked but with no obvious discerning features on his trunk. Slimly built, he appeared tall in comparison to some of the others. He also had hair which Leila had shaded in as grey. The eyes were blue.

None of his features struck a chord with Freya, except perhaps the hands – on the left one of which was a pinkie ring. Using the magnifying glass Grant had brought her from the library, Freya examined the ring more closely and eventually decided that the engraving on the gold was of a tiny unicorn.

The last time she'd seen a ring like that, it had been worn by the man who'd visited her here. Dr Peter Charles. Freya thought back to his kindly face, his interest in her work, his fascination with the unicorn statue in the west quadrangle of the university.

Grant had indicated Dr Charles was a benefactor of the university library, in particular the Ferguson collection, which was why he'd been keen to talk to her, and was probably the reason for the signet ring.

Freya moved to look more closely at the details beside the drawn figure.

What she'd assumed to be the date of birth was given as 7/7/1949, which made his sign Cancer, his birth colour green, indicating finance, fertility and luck. His birth number involved adding all the digits together to reduce them to a single digit, in this case coming eventually to 1. A single runic word followed this, which might be his magic name, usually chosen to match the birth number.

There were numerous alphabets used in writings on Witchcraft. Seax-Wica alone had many variations in the runes used – Germanic, Danish, Swedish-Norse, Anglo-Saxon. Added to that there was the Theban script, popular among Gardnerian Witches, referred to incorrectly as the Witches' Runes, as it wasn't runic at all.

Some covens used Egyptian hieroglyphics, others the Passing the River alphabet. Then there was the Angelic alphabet and the Malachim, the language of the Magi. The PectiWita, in the Scottish tradition, had two interesting forms of magickal writing. One was a variation on runes, the other based on the old and very decorative Pictish script.

In the past Magicians often worked alone and jealously guarded their methods of operation, not from the Christian Church, but from other Magicians. Contemporary Witches continued this practice for the same reason of secrecy, but also for another motive.

One way to put power into an object is to write appropriate words on it whilst directing your energies into the writing.

Writing in everyday English didn't require the same amount of intense concentration. Creating runic script directed your energies, your power, into what you were working on.

Freya understood this, because it demanded the same energy, concentration and power to decipher the words Leila had written. It appeared that she'd chosen to mix alphabets, dropping from Anglo-runes to Angelic script with a sprinkling of Pictish thrown in. As solitary Witches, Leila, Shannon and herself could manage their faith as they chose. There were no rules, no requirement to ascend through the rankings of an Order or coven. They were as free as the first Witch. Leila had chosen to be as varied and free in her writings, choosing what suited her best.

She'd also divided her Book of Shadows into three sections, the final one being the pages concerning the Nine. The preceding page to this section consisted of a sketch of the Goddess in the form of a Warrior Queen with a shield and spear. Unlike the version on the leather cover, this Goddess bore a strong resemblance to Leila herself, the hair being short and auburn, the face bearing the same small tattoo as Leila had worn.

As Freya began the laborious task of identifying each symbol and transposing them, a strange thing happened.

Grant had gone to fetch fresh coffee, promising to be back soon.

He had shut the door behind him, but at this moment it chose to blow open. The swirling draught that entered caught Freya by surprise, almost whipping the paper she was writing on from under her pen. She rose and, fighting the sucking draught blown up from the windy cloisters below, she reshut the door.

When she returned to her seat to resume her task, she discovered that the pages of the Book of Shadows had flipped back, returning to the page featuring the Goddess.

Now Freya noted a continuous line of runic text running round the circular shield of the Warrior Queen. Intrigued, she wrote down the symbols and began to translate them.

This time the pattern came easily, each rune swiftly finding its English equivalent.

I've finally cracked the code, Freya thought.

She regarded the long string of letters, beginning at the top of the circle and moving to the right. It took only moments for her brain to break up the string into nine words that brought a chill to Freya's heart.

If you are reading this then I am dead.

63

McNab and Danny had adjourned to the nearby student cafeteria.

McNab's impression that Danny, in his quest to nail his sister's killers, hadn't been able to work and therefore had no money for food, was proved right. When McNab came back with two coffees plus two of the largest burgers on offer, Danny attacked his with a vengeance.

McNab was hungry too, but for inspiration rather than food.

He was more studied in his eating while he tried to work out what to do next. The most obvious move was to inform the boss about this latest development, although that in itself would not produce a lead on where to look for Freya. He could ask DI Wilson to send a uniform round to her flat and to force entry if necessary.

Something ice cold attacked the pit of his stomach at this thought. He quashed it, because he already knew she hadn't been there when Danny visited as she'd been with Rhona in Leila's flat.

His next and better move would be to eat humble pie and contact Rhona. She'd been the last person to see Freya and would know her state of mind. She might also have an idea where Freya would go if not to the library.

Both moves were required. One would be easier than the other.

McNab chose the easy one first.

The boss listened quietly, then agreed to have someone sent round to Freya's flat.

'You believe this book Leila left is important?'

'Who knows? It's Wiccan stuff, but Danny says it holds information on the men involved with Leila. I'll have to take his word for that because I haven't seen it.' McNab wanted to make sure the boss knew he hadn't been withholding information this time round.

The boss rang off then, with strict instructions to McNab that he was to be kept informed on the search for Freya.

McNab couldn't stomach the rest of his burger. When Danny realized this he asked if he could have it.

'Go ahead. Take the chips too.' McNab pushed the plate across. 'I'm going outside to make a call.' The last thing he wanted was for Danny to be party to his next conversation.

She had come here as though it were a place of refuge. Maybe it was. Her reason for coming was more complicated than a way to spend leisure time or even a love of jazz, which she didn't possess.

She fully understood McNab's anger and vexation, and why he'd voiced it, some would say truthfully, over the phone. She too was concerned about Freya's well-being, which was why she'd agreed to take her to Leila's flat.

It hadn't worked, but it had been worth a try.

Now, Rhona decided, she would await news and have a drink.

She ordered white wine and took a seat at the bar. Sam was doing a stint serving, having played earlier. Chrissy, he informed Rhona, was staying over at her mother's with young Michael. He sounded sorry about that and Rhona sensed an end in sight for that relationship, despite their mutual love for McNab's namesake.

At that moment the end of any relationship seemed almost inevitable.

She hadn't sought Sean but he found her anyway, news of her arrival having travelled swiftly to the boss of the establishment.

'It's quieter in the office,' he offered.

Rhona wasn't in the mood for a get-together, a dark impenetrable cloud having descended on her thoughts, but rather than argue, she followed him through. Sean ushered her inside, closed the door behind them and turned the key.

'We need to talk,' was his explanation for that.

Rhona spied the two glasses and bottle of whiskey on the desk, and interpreted Sean's remark and the evidence of a drinking buddy in the same scenario.

'McNab's been here?' she said.

'Briefly.'

'How brief?'

'One drink's worth,' Sean said. 'He told me you fell out.'

'That's an understatement.'

'He said some bad things?'

'Bad, but truthful. As did I,' Rhona admitted.

'He seemed very worried about Freya.'

'She was with me earlier at Leila's flat, which he didn't like. I went out to get us some coffee. When I got back, she'd disappeared. The message said she'd gone back to the library.'

'Where he was heading when I saw him.'

'If he was in a hurry, why stop for a drink?' Rhona said.

'You're worried, and you came here for one.'

'Piss off.'

'If you want me to.'

There was no point taking her frustration out on Sean. It wasn't his fault. She said so.

'It *is* possible to have a personal life outside work,' Sean declared firmly.

'Do you really believe that?' she said, her cynicism obvious.

'I do, although I know you and McNab don't.'

'The Irish have a fine way with words,' Rhona countered.

'Exactly what McNab said. You're more alike than you're prepared to admit.'

Rhona was grateful when her mobile rang. Despite Sean's look suggesting she ignore it, she answered, even though it was McNab's name on the screen.

'She's not at the library and neither is Grant Buchanan, the guy in charge of the Ferguson collection. Apparently he checked out a book earlier on runic scripts in Witchcraft.'

Rhona could taste McNab's concern. What he really wanted to ask her was where the hell they had gone to study it. A question she might be able to answer.

'Freya has a key to the old Ferguson collection library. She took it from Shannon's desk. There were two keys. One for Leila's altar in the Lion Chambers. The other to the old library.'

'You think she's there?' McNab said eagerly.

'It's a possibility,' Rhona said.

'Where is it?'

'Somewhere in the main building. That's all I know.'

64

If you are reading this then I am dead.

There was no doubt what the message on the shield said, and no doubt in Freya's mind that Leila had hoped, or even intended, that someone should find this message in the event of her death.

The fact that it was placed here on the drawing of herself as the Goddess and in the foreword to her section on the Nine seemed also significant.

Freya checked the Warrior Queen again in case she'd missed anything else, then flipped over the page and began on the spell cast for the first of the Nine.

So deep in concentration was she that she didn't hear Grant's entry.

'Coffee's here.'

Freya caught the aroma at the same time as she heard the words.

The door opening had brought another blast of wind from the spiral staircase that led from the cloister to the tower. It flapped at the pages of the Book of Shadows, sending them scurrying towards the end.

Grant forced the door shut.

'Have you got the key? We may have to lock it to prevent it blowing open again.'

Freya pointed to her rucksack. 'It's in the front pouch with my mobile.'

The door secured, Grant handed over her coffee.

'How's the translation going?'

'Quite well,' she told him. 'I've figured out the mix of scripts Leila used and, since she's been pretty consistent about the pattern of usage, I'm getting a little faster in translation now.'

'Good,' Grant said, offering her a biscuit. 'How long will this take? I'll have to head home soon.'

'You've been great, Grant. Go home. This may take some time. When I finish, I'll call DS McNab and hand the book and the translation to the police as you suggested.'

Grant nodded. 'You could leave the other book in here and I'll pick it up in the morning.'

'One thing,' Freya said.

'Yes?'

'I think Leila believed herself to be in danger.'

'What makes you say that?'

Freya explained about the shield. 'The translated message said, "If you are reading this then I am dead."'

Grant's face paled. 'That's not good. Maybe she had a premonition.'

'Maybe. One other thing?'

'Yes?' Grant was staring out of the window, where the rising wind was tearing at the trees.

'One of the nine figures Leila drew is wearing a signet ring engraved with a crest featuring a unicorn. I wondered about its significance.'

Grant turned. 'Was it the unicorn alone or the unicorn and the lion?'

'Only the unicorn.'

'When they're together, Scottish Unicorn on the right, English Lion on the left, they symbolize the union of the crowns of Scotland and England on the marriage of James VI of Scotland to Margaret Tudor. Dr Charles wears one like that. Maybe he's related to royalty.' He smiled. 'If the unicorn is on its own, it's probably merely decorative.'

'Okay,' she said. 'Thanks.'

'I'd better get going. Will you be all right here alone?'

'I'll be fine,' Freya assured him.

'I'll see you on Monday, then. And good luck.'

The main gates were shut and locked, but the right-hand side gate still stood open. With no sign of anyone they could ask to direct them, they had no choice but to head into the main building and trust to luck that they would meet someone who knew their way around. McNab had visited Rhona's lab on a number of occasions, but that wasn't in the old building and he had no idea of the geography of the place.

They eventually found their way into the cloisters, fighting the wind that seemed to be coming from all directions, but every door into the main building they met was firmly locked.

McNab came to a grinding halt and pulled out his mobile.

He'd tried Freya's number three times since leaving the cafeteria. Surely eventually she had to pick up? He let it ring until it went to voicemail, then simply begged her to tell him where she was.

He made a second call, this one to the station to check the outcome of the watch on Freya's flat, and found she hadn't been there. This time when he rang off, he turned his wrath on Danny.

'If you hadn't given her that fucking book, this would never have happened.'

Danny didn't have an answer to that. 'So what do we do now?' he said.

'We find whoever looks after this place at night and get them to let us in.'

Rhona had night access to her own block at the foot of the hill, but had no access to the main university building after hours.

Eventually, after a few calls, she was passed to one of the caretakers, who arranged to meet her at the gate, provided she could produce her ID.

When they finally met up, the man was pretty flustered by being called out at this late hour, and even more perplexed at being asked to direct her to a place he didn't know existed.

'The old library where the Ferguson collection was held before it was moved to the main library,' Rhona tried again.

He shook his head. 'Never heard of the Ferguson collection.'

'I think it was in one of the towers.'

'We can check the towers, but it'll be pretty dark by now. No one's supposed to be in the building.'

'My colleague, Detective Sergeant McNab, is somewhere around here,' Rhona said.

'Not to my knowledge.' The caretaker looked affronted.

Rhona rang McNab's number again, grateful when he answered.

'I'm here and I have a caretaker with me,' she said. 'Where are you exactly?'

'In the west quad,' came the reply.

'Stay there.'

*

Freya wasn't aware of the surrounding darkness or the circling wind that buffeted the thick stone walls and lattice windows of the tower room. She had just completed a translation of what she thought might be the final spell, and had discovered it was more of a declaration.

> I am the Warrior Queen!
> Defender of my people
> With strong arms do I bend the bow
> And wield the Moon-axe
>
> I am sister to the stars
> And mother to the Moon
> Within my womb lies the destiny of my people
> For I am the Creatrix
>
> I am also she whom all must face
> at the appointed hour
> Yet am not to be feared
> For I am sister, lover, daughter
> Death is but the beginning of life
> And I am the one who turns the key.
>
> Should I die, I ask the first reader
> To burn my Book of Shadows
> For its death will avenge my own.

Freya sat back, and rubbed her eyes. Outside the window, all was dark. In here she had only a desk light to work by. But she'd translated enough to know what Leila had been doing. And to know that she'd taken risks with her worship that might well have threatened her life.

Grant's revelation that the chief suspect had confessed, Freya hoped was true. Otherwise, she believed, one or all of the Nine were implicated in Leila's death.

She was ready now to talk to Michael about this. To show him the translated notes and to give him at least the magic names Leila had allotted to the members of the group, their birthdates and therefore their age. That and the spells they'd requested Leila to conjure up.

All of which may have gone against the Wiccan Rede.

Now she understood why Leila was asking her to burn the book. It was traditional that the Book of Shadows be burned on the owner's death, but that wasn't why Leila wanted it to happen. Her desire was for vengeance on those who had taken her life and Shannon's.

Whether there was a possibility of that happening, Freya didn't know.

She rose from the table and went in search of her mobile. She would arrange to meet Michael at the jazz club and hand the Book of Shadows over. She had promised Danny she would tell him the result of her translation first, but she now feared what he might do with her findings.

It was better for everyone if she handed the book directly to Michael.

As she searched in vain for her mobile in the front pocket of the backpack, then in the main pouch, she caught the faint scent of smoke. Setting the bag down, she saw the first trail of it coming under the door.

Then she heard a crackling sound from the outer room, like kindling sticks sparking and catching alight. The room, she knew, was still filled with the debris of old, dry, varnished shelves, stripped from the walls.

A veritable tinderbox.

Freya grabbed at the door, remembering that Grant had left and she hadn't locked it behind him. When it wouldn't open she was seized by confusion.

Had she locked it after all?

The curls of smoke were increasing, rising to the ceiling of the small room, catching the back of her throat.

She must have locked the door against the wind. What had she done with the key? Now the light was no longer enough, illuminating as it did only a portion of the desk.

Frantic now, Freya dropped to her knees and began feeling the floor around the desk. When that didn't produce the key, she up-ended the backpack and shook it, to no avail.

By now she was coughing, the acrid taste of smoke deep in her throat.

She had to get out of here.

Freya tried the door again, using all of her remaining strength. When that didn't work, she took off her jacket and laid it along the foot of the door to try and slow the flow of smoke. A solution that would prove only temporary.

Coughing and spluttering, her eyes on fire, she moved the chair close to the window and stood up on it. If she could open the window, then maybe she could breathe again.

The catch was stiff but manageable.

Freya flung open the window and the wind surged in, scattering her papers from the desk, flapping the pages of the Book of Shadows. As the oxygen surged into the room, helping Freya to take a breath, it also rattled the door, forcing its way round the edge and beneath, giving sustenance to the flames in the room next door.

Freya heard a roar as the fire beyond the door gained momentum, and a crash as a window exploded.

As she slumped in the furthest corner from the door, she

saw the first sparks arrive, whipped in on the wind, landing on the flapping pages of the Book of Shadows.

Freya knew she should try to save it, shelter it between her body and the wall. Make it survive, even if she didn't. But another voice told her to *let it burn*. That way those responsible would pay the price.

Freya began her own chant, echoing Leila's words because all three Witches, she, Leila and Shannon, would soon be reunited.

> *'I, moon lady*
> *Salute my sisters*
> *Of the stars and the trees.*
>
> *We are She whom all men must face*
> *At the appointed hour*
> *Yet I am not afraid*
> *Death is but the beginning of life*
> *And I am the one who holds the key.'*

They were crossing the west quad when McNab picked up the scent, faint but immediately recognizable. In moments they saw flames coming from the nearest tower.

The caretaker began babbling about dialling 999. McNab grabbed him by the scruff of the neck and told him to open the lower door first and let him in.

The man thrust a set of keys into his hand. 'It's the one marked "tower2",' he said, then pulled out his mobile and began his emergency call.

McNab thumbed his way through the keys, cursing the lack of light and his own ineptitude. Eventually he thrust a key into the lock and tried to turn it, outwardly praying it was the right one. There was a moment's hesitation as the lock resisted. In that moment McNab found himself praying to any god that was willing to listen that it would work.

'Thank you!' he shouted as the key turned and his prayer was answered.

McNab pushed the door open and smoke billowed out, engulfing them. As he headed inside, Rhona's hand caught his arm. 'The old library is on the second floor.'

McNab sensed Danny behind him as he darted upwards through the swirling smoke. By the first-floor landing he could hear the crackle and spit of the fire. Running up the staircase had taken its toll and McNab instinctively took in air, regretting it immediately as his lungs and throat objected, sending him into a paroxysm of coughing.

'Cover your mouth and nose,' Danny shouted at him.

McNab copied Danny as he took off his jacket and held it to his face.

Now Danny darted ahead, disappearing up the spiral staircase that led to the next level. McNab raced after him through the thickening smoke and the increasing noise from above. He found himself mouthing, 'Please don't let her be up there. Please God she's in a different tower. Please let her be alive.' And all the time he could picture Freya, already comatose, her smoke-filled lungs no longer taking in oxygen to pump her precious heart.

McNab threw himself onto the second level, to find no sign of Danny.

Ahead a set of double doors flapped madly in the gusts that whined up the stairwell from the open door below and blasted in through the shattered windows of the old library. Beyond the doors, as seen through the missing glass, the fire raged like a mad red beast intent on devouring everything in its path.

Freya can't be alive in that.

Horror engulfed McNab as he tried to breathe through the jacket, his eyes streaming. Pushing open the door, he could see that the fire had taken hold among the discarded timber of old shelves. Like a fifth of November bonfire, it blazed in the centre of the room but hadn't yet engulfed the high ceiling, although it was already licking the right-hand wall.

This couldn't be the room Freya had been working in, but he had to be sure. Entering, he heard Danny screaming Freya's name. McNab lowered his jacket and joined in, desperately trying to raise his voice above the roar of the fire.

Then he saw her or thought he did. A female figure through the flames looking directly at him as though challenging him to come to her.

'Freya!' McNab shouted, fearing his voice had been snatched and devoured by the din.

'In there,' he heard Danny shout in return, pointing to a door in the right-hand wall.

As they both moved towards the door, McNab from the right, Danny from the left, another window suddenly burst in the heat, shooting shards of glass like confetti in Danny's direction. McNab saw Danny try to cover his face with his arms but not speedily enough. He crumpled and fell, his face a mess of blood.

'Danny!'

Danny urged McNab onwards to the door as he tried to right himself. 'Get Freya.'

McNab hesitated, but only for a moment, then darted round the bonfire which licked at his legs and feet. He stumbled at its touch and, reaching out a hand to steady himself, met the blistering heat of the right-hand wall. The burning pain of the connection seemed to belong to someone else as McNab grabbed the door handle and tried to turn it. For a split second it appeared to give, before a sudden halt.

'Fucking bastard!' McNab screamed.

This time he put his shoulder to the door. He'd done this before. Many times. Forced a door with his shoulder. He could do it again now. The flames were licking from behind as he retreated to harness more power. He felt the burst of heat on the bullet wound in his back, and he remembered with sudden clarity what it meant to die.

That couldn't happen to Freya. Not Freya.

His first attempt shook the door on its hinges. His second attempt, he knew, had torn the lock. Once more and he would blast the fucking door from its frame. McNab retreated one more time, backing further into the heat and flames. This time he had to do it.

He launched himself at the door. As he slammed against it, he felt his right arm exit his shoulder with a sickening pop, but not before the door had sprung open.

McNab fell into the room, his right arm now hanging uselessly from its socket.

'Freya? Are you in here?'

He strove to focus in the darkness, his eyes blurred by the biting smoke. The fire, having eaten its way through the intervening wall, was now licking its way across the ceiling.

'Freya! Where are you?'

A series of sparks as the flames met the varnish of the bookshelves suddenly lit up the room like fireworks and for a moment McNab caught a glimpse of the layout. Shelves, a desk and chair, and nothing else.

She's not here. She's not in here.

As McNab stood, sensing defeat, but not yet willing to accept it, there was an explosion behind him, its force propelling him further into the room. Then he saw it laid open on the desk, the pages already curling in the heat. The Book of Shadows.

If it's here, so is Freya.

At that moment, the book flared like a paper taper and began to burn before his eyes. In its cold green light he saw her tucked under the desk, her arms about her legs, her head resting on them.

McNab dropped to his knees beside her.

'Freya.' This time his voice was as soft as a caress, as desperate as a wish he dared come true.

'I'm here, Freya. I've got you now.' As he took her arm, it dropped free and limp and she fell towards him, her body as heavy as death.

'No!' McNab shouted, tugging at her with his left arm, his right one useless. 'Please, Freya, come to me.'

When there was no response and unable to move her, McNab sat down and drew Freya to him, cradling her head against his chest, shielding her from the smoke and heat with his body.

Accepting that there was nothing he could do except stay here with her, McNab planted a kiss on Freya's head and told her he loved her and that he was sorry. It seemed to him that she stirred at his words, shifting a little against him. McNab closed his eyes, blotting out fire, replacing the image with one of his own. Freya laughing, naked, as he'd swept her off her feet and carried her into the bedroom.

Before, when he'd faced death, he had done so alone. Not now. Not ever again.

The cocoon they shared rocked as something fell across

it, tossing the burning Book of Shadows to the floor in front of him. McNab gazed on it, hatred foremost in his mind.

You fucking did this to her, Leila. You and your fucking book of spells.

His exploding anger rolled him out of their hiding place.

He wasn't giving up. He would get Freya out of here somehow or die trying. McNab got onto his knees and, dragging Freya up with only his left arm, succeeded in pulling her over his shoulder.

Now all I have to do is stand up.

He extracted his right knee. Unbalanced now, he leaned against the desk and, steadying himself with his left hand, tried to get up. Painfully slowly, every sinew striving to raise himself and the precious cargo he carried.

Then he was upright, or as upright as he would ever be. His right arm flapping uselessly beside him, he stumbled with Freya over his shoulder towards the doorway and out into the inferno.

McNab had no idea how far he walked through the hell that was the Ferguson room before he heard and felt the force of cold water as a fire hose reached the shattered window of the room, hissing and spluttering as it met the flames and turned them into steam.

Then the figure of a firefighter loomed before him, and in moments Freya was plucked from his shoulders and carried away before him down the stairs and into the night air.

Relieved, McNab turned, searching now for Danny in what was left of the room.

65

Rhona turned to face Sean's back and curled herself against him. He slept the sleep of the angels, undisturbed by her sudden warm presence. She imagined that was what he was, in waking or sleeping . . . undisturbed by her presence.

She rose, leaving him there in his slumber.

Her own sleep had been short. After they'd made love, brought on by the instinct for survival, Rhona had dozed fitfully. Sean, on the other hand, had rejoiced in Freya's survival, and celebrated it through sex then deep sleep.

Rhona envied him his ability to do that.

Now in the kitchen, she set the coffee machine up and switched it on. Tom didn't even open an eye at her early arrival in his domain.

Would you stand and howl at my grave like Leila's cat did? I think not.

Rhona walked to the window. Not yet dawn, the light on the statue of the Virgin was still distinguishable in its rosy glow. Warm, but not the flash of red fire.

The terrible memory of what had happened only hours before suddenly engulfed her. A blur of noise and soaring flames, McNab like a man possessed, diving up that stairwell. Being pulled away herself by a burly firefighter and ordered to stand as far away as possible and let them do their job.

She'd shouted at him that three people were in there,

not knowing if she'd been heard through the frantic bustle and noise. Then the terrible wait, the seconds as long as hours until the firefighter had finally reappeared with Freya in his arms. Her joy when she saw them, and then the swift despair when no one else followed him out of that door.

'He's dead,' she'd heard herself say, knowing she'd been in this place before, when McNab had died in front of her.

She'd spotted Danny first, the glow of the fire setting his own auburn head ablaze, his face a mass of blood. Then she realized that he was supported by a stumbling McNab.

Rhona had stood back as all three were loaded into an ambulance and the screaming siren had taken them from her and the burning tower.

Freya had survived, but it seemed the Book of Shadows had not, although no one – forensic expert or otherwise – was to be allowed inside the tower room to check that was the case until it was deemed safe.

All three survivors were currently in hospital, smoke inhalation being the main reason, although Danny had also been badly cut about the face and McNab had had to endure the agony of having his right shoulder put back in. Despite his obvious discomfort, McNab had opted to sit with Freya, his blistered hands forgotten in his desire to be with her when she opened her eyes.

Rhona hoped she would open them soon.

66

'He wore a signet ring with a unicorn on it. Grant said it was a unicorn and a lion but it wasn't.'

Freya had gripped his blistered hand, but McNab refused to react to the pain, so happy was he to see her awake and alive.

'Who?' he said, trying to make sense of what appeared to be ramblings.

'The man who wanted to talk about my thesis. Dr Peter Charles. We met in that room.'

'Last night?' McNab said, confused by the timeline.

She shook her head. 'No, on Friday. Then I saw the drawing.' She looked wildly at him. 'I think it was him in the drawing.'

'You met a man on Friday in the old library and you think he was in the Book—'

She interrupted him: 'The Book of Shadows. What happened to it?'

'The room was gutted. It can't have survived.'

McNab expected Freya to be upset by this, but instead she said, 'Good.'

He wondered if it was the drugs talking. 'I don't understand,' he said.

'Leila wanted that to happen.'

When she'd fallen into what appeared to be a peaceful sleep, McNab had disengaged his hand gently from Freya's and gone to check on Danny. His final memory of last night had been pulling Danny upright and helping him down the stairs.

'Hey,' McNab said, 'you're awake.'

'How's Freya?' was Danny's immediate response.

'She's going to be okay.'

Relief swept Danny's face. 'What happened? How did she get locked in there?'

'She thinks she locked the door after Grant left to prevent it blowing open in the wind, then couldn't find the key.' McNab explained the rambling story about the signet ring in the drawing and the man she'd met last week, Dr Peter Charles. 'He's a benefactor of the Special Collections in the university library. He was supposedly interested in her thesis on Witchcraft.'

Danny halted him. 'Freya never saw the video. The guy with the signet ring?' he reminded McNab.

Jesus. How could he have forgotten?

'Grant wanted to find out what Freya knew,' McNab said, suddenly understanding.

Danny nodded. 'I would say so.'

'If I go and check this out, will you keep an eye on Freya for me?'

'Sure thing.'

On McNab's departure Danny dressed and, as requested, went to check on Freya.

He stood for a moment in the doorway, observing her. She was, he decided, still in that place between sleep and wakefulness. He hesitated to disturb her by entering the room, but perhaps sensing his presence, Freya opened her eyes.

Her smile reminded him of Leila.

'McNab sent me to look after you. He had to report for duty.'

'I guess it's always going to be like that.'

Danny pulled up a chair. 'He told me about the drawing and the ring. What you didn't know was that a ring like you described appears on one of the three video clips Barry and I took.'

Freya pulled herself up in the bed. 'So he may have been one of the men who visited Leila?'

'How did he get in touch?'

'Through Grant. He arranged for us to meet at the old library to discuss my thesis.'

Danny's heart missed a beat.

'Grant introduced you?'

'Not exactly. He set up the meeting and I went along. Dr Charles was completely charming and very knowledgeable.'

Danny's conjectures were fast falling over one another.

'Did Grant suggest the old library last night too?'

'I called him from Leila's flat and asked him for help. He said he would take the book I needed there for me.'

'So he *did* suggest the old library?'

'He said it was quiet there and we wouldn't be interrupted.' She halted, her expression suggesting she didn't believe where this was leading. 'You can't think Grant has anything to do with all of this?'

'He was ultra-keen to take a look at Leila's Book of Shadows,' Danny reminded her.

'Of course he was. Anyone with his interest in the occult would be.' Freya stopped, remembering something. 'Grant told me the man Leila met that night had confessed to all three murders. Is that true?'

'It is, but he couldn't have known that. Not last night.'

'He said it was on the news.'

Danny shook his head. 'It wasn't. I only know because McNab told me.'

'Maybe Grant was mistaken,' Freya said hesitantly.

'Maybe,' Danny said carefully, although he was thinking the opposite. He swiftly changed the subject. 'How much can you remember of the translation?'

A shadow crossed her face. 'A fair bit. One thing in particular.'

Danny listened as Freya told him of a circular message on the shield that seemed to predict his sister's death. Then the final words Leila had written:

> Should I die, I ask the first reader
> To burn my Book of Shadows
> For its death will avenge my own.

Danny didn't believe in Witchcraft, in spells, rituals, chants or incense. He didn't believe in Gods and Goddesses or any of the other artefacts that had adorned Leila's altar. But he did believe in revenge, and he wasn't willing to leave its enactment to a spell cast by his dead sister.

67

'Mark Howitt Senior was found dead beside his wife this morning. It's not confirmed, but from initial reports it appears he decided his life would end when hers did,' Sutherland said.

Bill sank down on the nearest chair, his legs no longer able to hold him up.

Sutherland waited, giving Bill time to compose himself.

'I believe you and he were old friends?'

'We were,' Bill acknowledged.

'Then maybe that's why he left a letter addressed to you at the scene.' Sutherland slid a white embossed envelope towards Bill.

Bill hesitated before picking it up, unsure how to react to this. Sutherland, he could tell, was keen to know the letter's contents. Bill, on the other hand, had no wish to either open the letter in his presence, nor share what was inside unless he had to.

He rose, letter in hand. 'If you'll excuse me, sir?'

Sutherland gave a reluctant nod, before adding, 'Obviously, if the contents have any bearing on his son's case . . .'

Bill didn't bother answering as he exited the room.

Seated now in his chair, the letter still sealed lying on the desk in front of him, Bill pondered what he should do. The last time he'd met with his old friend had been at the city mortuary where he'd come to identify the body of his son. It was a task no parent should ever have to do. After that Bill had had to explain that his son had been implicated in the deaths of three people. Had in fact confessed to all three murders.

For an ordinary man, that would have been tragic. For a High Court judge, who'd spent most of his life presiding over such cases, it must have been catastrophic.

All his own life in the police force, Bill had had one overriding fear. That a close family member might become a victim of a serious crime, or even a perpetrator. The idea that only evil people were driven to do bad things was, of course, a fallacy.

We are all capable of murder given the right circumstances.

Bill recalled their conversation in the park and the sense that his friend had wanted to reveal something, yet could not, at that time.

It seemed the time had now come.

Bill slit open the envelope, extracted the letter and began to read.

There is a catharsis in telling the truth. You and I both know that. We have seen it in interviews and in court. When we met I wanted to tell you this, but wasn't brave enough to do so. Funny how we, you and I, have spent our lives urging others to confess, yet when it came to it, I was unable to do so. At least face to face.

I became aware of Leila Hardy when seeking alternative treatments for Sarah. We had been through every available medical procedure possible. As you know, none of them worked. She was dying and I was desperate. Suffice to say that Leila Hardy was my last resort. She was kind to me. Kind and persuasive. She offered me her strongest magic and I'm ashamed to say I took it. Perhaps as much for myself as for what it promised for Sarah.

Like all other routes, it led nowhere except death.

I was the undisclosed DNA sample found in her flat. I had recently visited a crime scene with a jury and had been recorded. Immediately I heard of Leila's death, I contacted Superintendent Sutherland and explained about my indiscretion. He advised me to wait. Again I took the coward's way out and did so, convincing myself that such a revelation might destroy Sarah's remaining time alive.

My biggest failure I think was not to have faith in my son. Sarah always did. Mark sensed my disappointment, when he should have sensed my love.

For what it's worth, I knew nothing of the group you term the Nine, although I suspect they had found out from Leila about me. When you said you thought Mark might have been blackmailed into confessing, my first thought was that I might have been the tool they used to manipulate him.

If that was the case, then I think he died to protect Sarah, and perhaps even me.

I sensed when we talked that you believed Mark to be innocent, as do I. I hope you can clear his name, but even more I hope you can apprehend the person, or persons, who killed Leila Hardy and her friends.

McNab looked up from the letter, his expression sombre.

'We'll get Buchanan,' he said. 'But not the Nine,' he added bitterly.

'The wheels of the Lord grind slowly, but they grind exceedingly fine,' Bill quoted a favourite saying of his late mother's.

'You believe that?' McNab challenged him.

'In a religious sense, no. But we've made a start, and the case can't be closed until we find the other members of the group.' Bill examined McNab's demeanour. He looked like a man still on the wagon, with maybe even some joy in his life, despite the frustration of the Nine.

'How's Freya?' Bill asked.

A small smile played McNab's mouth, something not often seen, Bill thought.

'She's okay, thank you, sir.'

McNab indicated the letter.

'Do you intend making this public knowledge, sir?'

'The super already knows. I'd like you to inform Rhona. I believe that's enough for the time being.'

'Thank you for telling me, sir.'

68

After the preceding forty-eight hours, the quiet of the lab felt like heaven. Having done her best to bring Chrissy up to date, Rhona had chosen to be alone, the quiet study of science a welcome relief after the psychological turmoil of recent events.

Freya was alive; the book they'd pinned their hopes on had gone.

But there was copious forensic material, which when assembled, might give them an insight into what had happened up to this point.

Traces of the suspect's DNA had now been identified at all three crime scenes. In the first, it had already been established that he'd had sex with the victim, and that the cingulum had had contact with his skin.

The evidence at the other two sites was less conclusive. A swab taken of Shannon's mouth had traces of Mark's DNA on it. But there was something else as well. A microscopic fibre of the same type to that found in Leila's throat. The cloth may well have carried DNA from one scene to another, by accident or on purpose.

Other things didn't add up.

The hand that had pushed Shannon's head underwater, nicking her skin and leaving DNA in the cut, didn't belong to Mark. The shape and dimensions of the fingerprint bruising didn't match him either. Like the original crime scene, he may have been present, but in Rhona's considered opinion, Mark hadn't done the deed.

The third scene was the most puzzling of all and posed for Rhona the maximum number of questions. Mark could not have inflicted those wounds, unless he had done so with his least-used hand.

Once your brain decided whether it was left- or right-handed, humans used the chosen hand. Some were lucky enough to be able to use both, but as far as she was aware, Mark Howitt was not ambidextrous. To exert a force like throwing a ball, a punch, stabbing, you used your strongest arm.

The arm that had forced the knife into Barry Fraser's eyes was not the arm that Mark led with. On that alone, Rhona found it difficult to believe that he'd inflicted the fatal wounds. Yet his DNA was on the face and neck of the victim.

If the cloth that suffocated Leila had been used again . . .

She updated the R2S software with her findings.

At the end of the day, should it ever come to court, the jury would decide.

But who could be brought to court to face the charges? Not Mark Howitt.

Writing reports eased the mind. Rhona always made them as detailed and explicit as possible. That often meant she wasn't required to appear in court to support them. Science was clean, but couldn't stand aside from the inevitable.

Why did people do what they did?

She realized she longed to talk to Freya about what had happened that fatal night in the tower room. She wanted to examine the residue and establish what had caused the fire. But most of all, she needed to know what had happened to the Book of Shadows. Without realizing it, the book had become uppermost in her mind.

It wasn't scientific. It had, for Rhona, no basis in reality, yet it held, she suspected, a window on the truth.

And all forensic scientists wanted to look through that window.

She was surprised by McNab's arrival in the lab, but not exactly put out by it. She was in truth glad to see him out of hospital, despite the bandaged arm and shoulder.

'Coffee?' she offered, to break the tension between them.

He nodded enthusiastically and she set about filling the machine, usually Chrissy's job, and spooning in the coffee.

'Make it strong,' he urged.

As she did so he told her about a letter to Bill from a deceased Mark Howitt Senior, explaining how he had become involved with Leila Hardy. Rhona dropped the scoop and the final spoonful of coffee sprayed along the surface.

'He chose to die with his wife,' McNab went on. 'He left the sealed letter for the boss at the scene.'

'So Mark's father was the owner of the denied DNA?' Rhona said.

'Yes, although not one of the Nine.'

'And the theory that Mark died to protect him . . .'

'Probably true,' McNab said.

Rhona set the coffee machine on. Listening to it humming seemed the only normal thing about this moment. They remained silent until she handed the coffee to McNab.

'We're not going to find them, are we?' she said.

'The boss won't give up, and neither, I suspect, will we.'

69

There are three ways to traditionally kill a Witch. Hang her, drown her or burn her.

The fire in the tower had raged all night. He recalled another fire that had happened before he'd come here, in the 100-year-old Bower Building just off University Avenue. The building had been completely destroyed, including a great deal of research material.

Maybe that had been his inspiration?

But like then, as apparently now, there had been no fatalities reported, so the chances were the Witch hadn't died.

His anger rose to burn in his throat.

He was in the section on the occult and had asked not to be disturbed. In truth, he was amending the catalogue to take account of the missing items, including the book on runic alphabets he'd taken to the old library on Saturday evening.

He couldn't imagine it had survived.

He had his story straight for whoever came to speak to him. And someone would come. He had nothing to hide. He had helped a colleague out by supplying a book she required. A little against the rules as the book in question should never have left this building, but then the main building was still on campus as he'd said jokingly in his conversation with Freya.

There was the small concern regarding the signet ring and the likelihood that he would be questioned about Dr Charles. He could only answer in good faith. The man had presented himself as a benefactor of the Special Collection and asked to speak to their current PhD student whose thesis was on Witchcraft, a strong interest of his.

That much was true. The fact that he and Dr Charles also shared a worldwide interest in the trade in ancient tomes and pamphlets on the occult need not be revealed.

At this point in the thought process, a small niggling doubt arose. Should he land in trouble over this, he doubted whether he would have the back-up of Dr Charles or anyone else in the group. As such, he had material hidden away that he knew they would be interested in, to trade with. It was all a matter of planning and organization.

He withdrew a book to gaze again on the illustrations which featured the many and varied methods used to torture and dispose of Witches. The colours were still as bright as when they'd been painted. The terror and cruelty as vivid on the page as in the minds of those who had devised them.

People imagined that Witchcraft was no more and that the enlightened mind had taken its place. He knew differently. Witchcraft was as powerful and established as it had always been. Its ancient artefacts and writings were eagerly sought by those in power, throughout the world. Like fine wine, it only rose in value.

He would have preferred to have retained Leila's Book of Shadows as a reminder of all that had happened, but because of what it was suspected to contain, it had needed to be destroyed.

He was a little sorry about that.

Hearing the sound of the door opening, he returned the

book to its allotted place and went to see who had disturbed him.

As he passed the main gates, McNab registered that the smoke and the acrid smell of the fire had gone, yet he could still taste it on his lips and feel its effect in his lungs. He stopped before attempting the hill to the main library and tried to take a deep breath, which only resulted in a fit of coughing. He checked his mobile for any message from Danny. When there wasn't one, he decided to assume all was well with him and Freya.

There were questions he required answering and Grant Buchanan, he believed, was the only man who could do so.

When he asked for Mr Buchanan at the front desk, he was informed that he was working and had asked not to be disturbed. McNab showed them his badge and insisted.

The man behind the desk made a call which wasn't answered.

'I'm sorry, he's not picking up.'

'Then someone can deliver me to him.'

'We're a bit short-staffed at the moment.'

'Tell me where to go and I'll find him myself.'

Grant waited for his visitor to appear, ready with an admonishment for disturbing him after strict instructions not to.

At that moment something strange happened. He thought he saw Leila's auburn head pass by on the other side of the bookshelves. It was both familiar, yet disquieting. Then the face appeared, her face and yet not her face. He stared, slightly unnerved, as his brain finally reminded him that this was Leila's younger brother who stood looking at him.

His first instinct was to be angry, both for having been

frightened by the similarity and by his sudden appearance, but instinct warned him that this was not the reaction required. He must remain solicitous, just as he had been before when he'd found Danny and Freya here with the Book of Shadows.

'Danny. I'm so pleased you're here. I've been calling the hospital and the police trying to find out if Freya was still in the building when the fire—'

'Freya's in hospital. She's fine. The Book of Shadows was destroyed in the fire.'

Grant adopted a suitably sad expression. 'That's unfortunate.'

'But then, as you reminded me, a Witch's Book of Shadows should be burned on their passing.'

'That was a throwaway remark. I apologize for it. As long as Freya's all right.'

How like his sister, he looks, Grant thought. Those green eyes, the hair, even the shape of the face and the flashing anger when challenged.

'How did you know the suspect had confessed to my sister's murder?'

A cloud appeared on his horizon, a dark cloud that suggested a storm was brewing.

'I didn't,' was all he could muster.

'Are you calling Freya a liar?'

Leila's male equivalent had moved towards him with, he thought, the stealth and quietness of a cat about to spring.

He took a step backwards and met the desk where he'd been viewing the images of tortured Witches.

'Do you know what Leila's instructions were about her book?' Danny spat at him.

He shook his head, no longer trusting his voice.

'That by burning it, her death would be avenged.'

He composed himself. Things were not as acute as they had at first seemed. The brother knew nothing. He was merely angry and upset. Before he could find a suitable retort however . . .

'I don't believe that Wiccan stuff. I prefer my own version of revenge.'

The *yag-dirk* now in Danny's hand was undoubtedly Leila's, taken like the Book of Shadows from her altar. He accepted in the seconds that followed that he should have cleared her temple when he'd had the chance. The night he'd met with the suspect in that building, he had chosen not to, because it would have aroused suspicion.

He was paying the price now for that error of judgement.

He contemplated shouting, but the basement was sound-proof, as was most of the library, the idea being that you shouldn't be disturbed. He might wrestle with the young man but he would surely lose. Then again, if the young man harmed him, he became the criminal.

He therefore chose to say what he really thought about Leila Hardy. 'Your sister overstepped the mark. She thought herself more important than she was. She actually believed the stuff she peddled, but she wasn't selling magick, she was selling sex.'

The remark hit home as he knew it would. Danny made a lunge at him, which he'd prepared himself for. What he hadn't anticipated was an addition to the fray. The policeman appeared from nowhere, like an avenging angel, grabbing the blade in his bandaged hand.

There was a brief struggle as the two men fought for supremacy, but there was no doubt in his mind who would win. Eventually order was restored.

'As you saw, this mad man attacked me—' he began.

The look the detective threw him stopped him mid-sentence.

'I'd like you to come with me to the station, Mr Buchanan. We have some questions to put to you regarding the deaths of Leila Hardy, Shannon Jones and Barry Fraser.'

70

It was a strange group that gathered one week after the fire, in so much as two of those present weren't police officers or forensics or those normally associated with the investigation of a crime or crimes.

Danny and Freya looked out of place, and definitely not of this world, Rhona thought.

Danny was clean shaven, his hair now cut as short as his sister's. Freya, tall and striking in a quieter way, looked both resolute and a little apprehensive.

And who could blame her?

Addressing a room full of detectives was a daunting prospect.

Magnus too was there, standing at the back, his part in the investigation acknowledged.

Bill asked Freya to begin by telling her story as she recalled it. All of it from the beginning. Rhona felt McNab's tension, and his affection, as Freya mustered herself to speak to the assembled officers.

Once begun, she spoke well and with authority. It was obvious that she'd chosen to ignore any preconceived ideas the company might have against Wicca and Witches in general. In a short space of time her honesty and forthrightness had won most of them over, not as believers, but at least as willing to try and understand.

She spoke of the importance of the Ferguson collection, and its value worldwide.

'Think of the tablets from Mount Sinai,' she explained, 'or the original writings of Jesus or Mohammed. Witchcraft is practised everywhere in the world in many various forms, like Christianity or Islam. Whatever has been written about it is precious and very valuable to both believers and unbelievers.'

She spoke of Leila and Shannon and what she'd discovered in the Book of Shadows. Her recall was explicit, not of all the details of the Nine entries, but of Leila's translated wish that the book should be burned, because by doing that, her death would be avenged.

Finishing on that particular statement, Freya took her seat.

Rhona took to the floor immediately afterwards, silencing the ripple of discussion that had followed Freya's pronouncement. Scientific findings rather than Wiccan predictions proved a more comfortable place for the team.

Leaving aside how the fire had been started, Rhona concentrated on the debris they'd sifted from the back room.

'There was no key anywhere in the inner room. The only way the door could have been locked was from the main room, and that's where we found the key. Which means that Freya had been locked in and, according to the fire department, the fire started deliberately.'

Even if they couldn't get Grant Buchanan on the other killings, they could certainly charge him with the attempted murder of Freya Devine.

In the excited babble that followed, McNab took centre stage and introduced Danny, who then spoke about his concern for his sister and the video clips he'd taken. The clips were shown and the link between Freya's story of the signet ring highlighted. The mock-up of the man who'd called himself Dr Peter Charles now appeared on the screen.

'We believe this man may already have left the country. Freya recalled some data she translated on him including, importantly, his date of birth. The name Peter, which was recorded in the Book of Shadows, she believes was his chosen magick name. His real first name she suggests will have the same name number. The letters will add up and subsequently reduce to 1, as does his date of birth.'

Bill indicated the image now on the screen:

1	2	3	4	5	6	7	8	9
A	B	C	D	E	F	G	H	I
J	K	L	M	N	O	P	Q	R
S	T	U	V	W	X	Y	Z	

$$P+E+T+E+R = 7+5+2+5+9 = 28 = 10 = 1$$

'We'll maybe get the Tech team to deal with all the possibilities conjured up by that,' Bill said as a ripple of amused consternation went through the group.

The atmosphere in the room is upbeat, Rhona thought. *We have Buchanan and we have the possibility of his accomplice. It wasn't everything, but it might prove enough.*

Freya asked to speak to Rhona when the meeting was over and Bill offered them his office. McNab didn't accompany them, although Rhona could tell by his body language that he really wanted to.

Rhona was aware he was still concerned about Freya, but he hadn't revealed why, even though she and McNab were on better terms now, the *Stonewarrior* secret they shared diminished by more recent events.

Once they were alone, Freya said, 'I wanted to thank you for your help. You were right to let me visit Leila's flat. I shouldn't have left there without speaking to you first. If I had, things may have turned out differently.' She paused. 'But what I really wanted to ask was this: Do you have the forensic evidence to prove Grant killed Leila and Shannon?'

Her full report was taking form, but despite the extent and depth of the forensic analysis, Rhona doubted whether it would be enough to guarantee a conviction. In particular, the hand on the video had not been a match for Grant Buchanan and his DNA had not been included in the dolls. She saw little point in raising Freya's hopes.

'We have evidence, but it isn't conclusive. What I can say with conviction is that Mark Howitt wasn't responsible for their deaths, or the death of Barry Fraser. We *are* clear that Grant Buchanan attempted to murder you.'

Freya nodded. 'Then their deaths may go unavenged?'

'The law isn't about revenge, Freya,' Rhona said.

Freya gave her a small smile. 'No, you're right. It isn't.'

Rhona thought back to Freya's words later as she stood at the kitchen window, watching the sun set over the convent garden.

She'd wanted to add that the law was about seeking justice for the victims of crime, but had stumbled at that point for two reasons. One was the look on Freya's face, the other, Rhona's own sense that she had somehow failed the victims.

A pair of arms surrounded her.

'What are you thinking about?'

'A cat,' Rhona said.

'Tom? He's in the sitting room on the sofa.'

'No, Leila's cat. I called the SSPCA. Apparently they re-homed it, but it didn't stay at the new owner's for very long. I think it may be hanging around Leila's, hoping she'll come back.'

'Are you planning to rescue it?' Sean said.

In truth, Rhona hadn't considered it, but now that Sean had mentioned it, maybe she should?

'A Witch's cat should really live with a Witch,' Sean said. 'What about Freya?'

Rhona smiled, imagining McNab's reaction to the big black cat making Freya's flat its home.

'I'm not sure the cat would stay, even if Freya agreed to take it.'

'Some cats are better left alone,' Sean stated.

He turned her round and kissed her.

'You ready to eat now?'

'Yes,' Rhona said, 'I am.'

71

When McNab woke in the early hours of the morning Freya was no longer beside him, the place she'd lain cold to the touch. He rose and went looking for her, knowing where she would be.

The door to her temple was closed, but he detected the scent of incense and saw the flickering candlelight below the door.

McNab knew he couldn't disturb whatever ritual was being played out beyond that door. Her trust in Wicca was important to Freya. She'd told him she'd looked on death that night in the old library, and hadn't been afraid, because of her beliefs.

But the time Freya spent in there seemed to be getting longer.

When he'd questioned her about it, she'd mentioned something about scrying, which apparently enabled a Witch to see into the past or the future. She'd shown him a mirror, one whose face had been painted with black enamel, its gilt frame painted with symbols.

'Wiccans believe if we focus our thoughts on the black mirror, we can look into the past and sometimes the future.'

McNab could tell by her expression that Freya was trying to be honest with him, and reminded himself that his mother had been a firm believer that Jesus had died on the cross for his sins, of which there were many. He'd loved his mother, but hadn't believed a word of it. The same went for Freya.

'Okay,' he'd said. 'What does the black mirror tell you?'

'What happened the night Leila died.'

What had surprised McNab most was that Freya's interpretation of events matched his own so closely, to the extent that the team were already working that line of enquiry.

Grant Buchanan, he believed, *had* been watching Leila and *had* been in The Pot Still or its environs that night. He'd followed Leila and Mark home to the flat and contacted the man they knew as Peter. The plan had been to dispose of Leila and pin the blame on the man she'd picked up. The hand in the video seen stuffing the cloth into Leila's mouth had not been Grant's, however. And they had no way of proving it belonged to Peter Charles, unless they found him, although they were fairly certain he was the signet ring wearer on Danny's clip. The other two men in the clips hadn't been identified.

Both Buchanan and the elusive Peter had been involved in stealing artefacts from the Ferguson collection. Shannon had suggested to Freya that she'd found something out about the collection via the old library. That in itself probably put Shannon in danger.

As for Barry Fraser, he'd been set the task of keeping an eye on Leila by Danny and he'd been involved in making the videos, but McNab also thought there was a chance Barry had spotted Buchanan at The Pot Still that night, but hadn't known who he was until later. A good enough reason for his death.

Danny had done the right thing in lying low. It was probably the only reason he was still alive. Buchanan had been vociferous in his claims that Danny Hardy had attacked him with a knife in the university basement and that only McNab's intervention had saved his life, something McNab had flatly contradicted. He'd given a different version of the story, omitting the knife, which fortunately the boss had believed. Leila's knife now lay on Freya's altar alongside her own.

Freya had watched him carefully as she'd told her black mirror story, noting the moments of recognition on his face.

'That's what *you* think happened, isn't it?' she'd said.

'Close to it,' had been all McNab was prepared to admit.

Jeff Barclay hadn't figured anywhere in Freya's deliberations, which fitted as well. Jeff's DNA hadn't found a match with the samples taken from Leila's flat. How and when he'd left the pub was still uncertain, but he had been charged with obstructing police enquiries.

All in all, Freya's contemplation of the black mirror had produced as good an understanding of the crime as he and his team had. As for the Nine, as they'd called them, Barry's DNA hadn't been a match for his namesake in the doll, and although Mark Howitt Senior had been identified as one of Leila's nine, he'd claimed not to know such a group existed. If so, then maybe Leila had placed him with the others because he'd bought sex magick from her as they had, or simply because of the significance of the number nine in Wicca. The Book of Shadows was gone with all its fine detail of the men she'd encountered, but, McNab reminded himself, they still had the DNA samples, Leila's simple drawings and what might be their first names. Not enough to go on at the moment, but maybe in the future?

The chanting from within had stopped.

McNab, keen that Freya wouldn't find him lurking there, went back through to bed.

When she climbed in beside him minutes later, he drew her into his arms.

'You okay?' he asked.

'I am now,' she said with a satisfied smile.

72

The book on the varieties of runic scripts used in Witchcraft would have brought an excellent price. He was sorry that it had gone, but its destruction had served a greater purpose.

The man whose name had been given as Dr Peter Charles congratulated himself on the outcome. The old library had been destroyed and with it the Witch's Book of Shadows. Anything the Witch had written about the group of men she'd serviced was gone.

He was aware of the confession and the subsequent suicide of the suspect, Mark Howitt. Had they known that night that the man Leila would take home was the son of a judge who had connections to the Witch, the plan would have been changed. However, the connection had proved to be beneficial in the long run.

Had the brother not interfered, it would have gone no further than the first Witch. On his head lay the blame for the subsequent deaths. Still, sufficient forensic evidence had been planted on the other two to give credence to Mark Howitt's confession.

True, one Witch remained alive, although her connection had been more with the Book of Shadows and, according to the report he'd received, she hadn't shown it to the police before it had been destroyed.

She might recall their meeting, of course, but he had

departed the country by the time of the fire and there was little chance of tracing him. There was one other loose end, his contact in the Ferguson collection, who had since been apprehended with regard to the fire, but he was confident that nothing the man might say could lead directly to him.

The group were now dispersed and would no longer be in contact with one another, at least for a while. Should they wish to reconvene, another European city would be chosen. Lucerne would be his choice.

The Ferguson collection had drawn them to Glasgow and he'd succeeded in making some of the rarer items available to the members of the group. Some of them were copies, but still valuable in the worldwide trade of precious and significant writings on the occult.

The man fingered his ring, as he was wont to do when thinking. His instinct told him that all would be well, and he trusted his instinct. His flight would be boarding soon, but there was still time for another drink. He waved the waiter over and ordered a double gin and tonic.

Ten minutes later he noted from the departure board that it was time to make his way to the gate, and decided to visit the Gents first. Toilets on aircraft were narrow and cramped, and the first-class lounge offered a better alternative.

The lounge had been quiet, the toilet was empty.

He chose a cubicle and entered, securing the door behind him.

As he unzipped his fly a strange thing happened. He heard what sounded like a cat hissing and was immediately reminded of the Witch's cat. The night he'd visited her in the altar room, it had been sitting there, its green eyes focused on them as she had brought him to climax. She had pushed him backwards at that point to lie on the sofa, her knees gripping his waist. Then to his surprise she'd shouted an order and the cat had sprung up to settle on his face, its claws kneading his shoulder, the suffocating feel of it on his face heightening the intensity of his pleasure.

As he allowed the memory to wash over him, his prick hardened, preventing him from urinating.

He gripped himself, encouraging the memory now, playing it live here in the cubicle. He felt the cat on his face, his open mouth full of its fur. He heard the loud purring, the chants of the spell she'd chosen. He experienced the tightening of the cingulum, the desperate need for air, all driving him towards ecstasy.

Then suddenly the imagined grip of the cingulum became like a metal band constricting and compressing his chest. He let go of his penis as the pain grew in intensity, spreading over his shoulder to descend his left arm like a red-hot poker.

I need to breathe.

He tried madly to push the imagined cat from his face, knowing all the time he wasn't choking on its fur, but having a heart attack.

As he dropped into unconsciousness, he was back in the Witch's temple, the suffocating body of the cat on his face, its claws tearing at his shoulder. As he felt the Witch move against him, there was no mounting ecstasy, only pain, each of her thrusts, he knew, propelling his heart swiftly towards its final beat.

73

When he opened his eyes, the doll was there on the pillow, green eyes staring into his, red hair wild. Of course he'd been dreaming, because when he woke up properly, the doll had gone.

Some nights later when they'd put out the lights, he heard the sound of their hard plastic bodies clicking and clacking together. The noise had invaded his cell, keeping him awake.

He knew a great deal about magick, although he didn't believe in it. Therefore he ascribed his symptoms to stress at the upcoming trial. He asked to see a doctor, but chose not to describe what kept him awake at night, saying only that he couldn't sleep.

Shortly after that, the visitations became more frequent and were now a combination of vision and sound. They consisted of a curtain of swaying dolls, their colliding limbs like the cackle of Witch laughter as they swung from the ceiling on their red cords, their shiny bead eyes fastened on him.

It was at this point that he considered his options.

Death being one, the other, confession.

Time and his state of mind would tell which one he chose.

74

The cat dropped from the roof onto the ledge and eased its way in through the open window, springing silently to the floor.

No longer sleek and well-fed, its green eyes wore a hungry look.

Hearing a sound in the hallway, it headed in that direction.

A snap of the letter box saw three circulars thrust through. The cat stood for a moment, anticipating something else, its tail upright, the tip swishing.

A draught from the open window heralded a series of clicks and clacks from the room it had entered by.

The cat made a beeline back there to stand and stare up at the swaying dolls. It turned, sensing a presence, and sprang towards it, rubbing its body against the slim legs, weaving between them, its purr as loud as the clicking curtain of colliding limbs.

Notes and Acknowledgements

My lecturer in astronomy at Glasgow University was Professor Archie Roy. He really was ambidextrous and could draw two circles and fill them in with diagrams at the same time.

I met him again many years later when he had become the foremost authority on the paranormal in Scotland, while also Emeritus Professor of Astronomy, with an asteroid named after him: (5806) Archieroy. I called him up one day to discuss a speculative piece for television that I was writing and we met in the university common room where he told me many tales about his work with the Scottish Society for Psychical Research.

Later I attended a series of lectures run by the SSPR at the university in which he told the story of the old library and what it contained and how this had sparked his interest in investigating the paranormal. So that much is true. I merely substituted Freya at Newcastle University for my own experience at Glasgow.

The Ferguson collection does exist and details about it can be found on the university library's website, some of which I used. As far as I am aware, it is still intact, and is still as valuable in terms of its contribution to our understanding of such matters. When I tried to locate the exact position of the old library as described by Professor Roy, I was unsuccessful, so I chose my own location in the tower,

435

mainly because I used to have lectures in moral philosophy in one of the tower lecture theatres. I particularly remember the cooing sound of the pigeons directly above us as we tackled Plato's *Republic*.

As to Wicca, I found during my research much to commend it as a way of worship, including the Wiccan Rede, oft quoted in the text. Witchcraft is not merely legendary; it was, and is, still real. Some would say its doctrine is far more relevant to the times than the majority of established church texts, insofar as it acknowledges a holistic universe, equal rights, feminism, ecology, attunement, brotherly and sisterly love, planetary care – all part and parcel of Witchcraft, the old, yet new, religion.

However, misconceptions still abound and my knowledge is not great enough to prove them all wrong. Suffice to say that every religion has its dark and bright side. And every force for good can be changed into one for evil. You only have to recall the Inquisition to know that.

Torturing and killing women by naming them as Witches was a job perfectly designed for those who delighted in the sexual torture of the female of the species. As Magnus says in the book, there were psychopaths back then too.

I couldn't help but think as I did my research that Rhona's knowledge of forensics and the science of DNA would have been seen as a type of Witchcraft not so long ago. In fact in some parts of the world, Rhona, the forensic scientist, would be regarded as a Witch at this very moment.

Lin Anderson